the Concealed

the Concealed

SARAH KLECK

Translated by Michael Osmann and Audrey Deyman

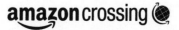

Text copyright © Sarah Kleck

Previously published as *Die Verborgene: Roman* by dotbooks Verlag in 2014 in Germany. Translated from German by Michael Osmann and Audrey Deyman. First published in English by AmazonCrossing in 2015.

Translation copyright © Michael Osmann and Audrey Deyman (AAD Abies)

Published by AmazonCrossing, Seattle

www.apub.com

Amazon, the Amazon logo, and AmazonCrossing are trademarks of Amazon.com, Inc., or its affiliates.

ISBN-13: 9781503947801
ISBN-10: 1503947807

Cover design by Laura Klynstra

Printed in the United States of America

To my parents, who gave me life,
and to my husband, with whom I may be who I am.

Love's not Time's fool, though rosy lips and cheeks
Within his bending sickle's compass come;
Love alters not with his brief hours and weeks,
But bears it out even to the edge of doom.

—William Shakespeare, Sonnet 116

PROLOGUE

They say time heals all wounds. I am still waiting . . .

For as long as I have lived, I cannot remember a winter as cold and harsh as this. An ice-cold wind blew around my ears the day I climbed the snowy hill with difficulty and closed the jagged wrought iron gate behind me with a metallic clank. The sound startled a crow, which, after a few excited flaps of its wings, settled cawing on a snow-covered treetop, eyeing me malevolently. Snow had fallen so heavily these last few days that even the mighty linden trees lining the area came close to collapsing beneath their white burdens. Now it was only snowing lightly. Small, weightless flakes floated from the steel-gray sky, caught in my hair, and melted on my face. I wandered among the rows and let the silence sink in. Apart from the crow, not another living soul was around.

I finally stopped in front of a rounded, white stone, breathed in deeply, wrapped my arms around myself, and closed my eyes. This usually helped me tune out the chaos in my head and the pain in my heart—giving me a temporary reprieve for a clear thought—but it didn't work this time. I felt an overwhelming despair rise inside me, pour down over my cheeks in a flood of tears, and burn inside my throat. Sadness and anger nearly set me trembling. I wrapped my arms ever tighter around my body so I would not shatter.

Why did you leave me behind all by myself? Don't you see I can't do all this alone? Tell me what to do!

Please tell me what I'm supposed to do without you! Please! I miss you so much!

CHAPTER 1

An endless stream of mourners followed the brown wooden coffin borne by six men in dark uniforms to the top of the hill. I trudged along through thick fall leaves behind the coffin. It was unseasonably cold for late October, and my frozen hands fiercely clutched the white lilacs she loved so much. It hadn't been easy to get the lilacs at this time of year, but it was a small comfort for me to be able to offer her favorite flowers to her one last time.

I continued on, despite not feeling my legs beneath me as they carried me forward. When the six men abruptly halted, I stumbled. A deep, black hole gaped at my feet. As I looked down into it, I began to shake, not because of the biting cold but because of the feeling of helplessness that overwhelmed me. I no longer felt my body, and almost had the sensation of floating over myself, watching from above as they lowered the coffin into the black earth. Despair gripped me, took possession of every fiber of my being, and forced me back into my tormented body. A searing pain shot through my chest, making me cough. A bloodcurdling cry rang out in the distance and made every one of my hairs stand on end.

That's her voice!

Where is she? I must go to her!

Turning, I looked for help but realized from the looks on the pitying faces of those in attendance that *I* was the one who had screamed.

A terrible, dull emptiness engulfed me and would not release me.

I bowed down with my last ounce of strength and placed the white lilacs on the coffin in which my sister would sleep forever.

***

Almost three months later. I opened my eyes and read the inscription on the rounded white tombstone:

ZARA LAKEWOOD

BELOVED SISTER

WONDERFUL HUMAN BEING

I wiped the tears and snowflakes from my face and concentrated on why I had returned here. I had not come back since the funeral—I probably wouldn't have survived if I'd come any sooner. But now the weight in the inside pocket of my black coat reminded me I wanted to tell my sister that something had happened. I pulled the heavy letter out and looked it over. It was addressed to Evelyn Francis Kathrin Lakewood.

Careful not to trample the flowers still decorating the grave under a thin crust of ice, I placed the envelope on the stone and took a step back.

"I was accepted by Oxford—what do you say to that?"

After completing my A levels, we had started searching for a good university for me, and, at Zara's urging, I had applied for psychology at Christ Church in Oxford—though I did not give myself much of a chance and I had no idea how I'd pay for it. As it happened, I'd just been offered admission to the Hilary, or winter, term in January because some fool had dropped out after the first trimester, and my name was apparently at the top of the waiting list. I wanted Zara to be proud of me. I owed everything to her . . .

When our parents died in a car accident when I was little, Zara fought like a lioness to gain custody of me—and she won.

She saw to it that we stayed together and I wouldn't have to go to a foster family. Since our parents left us almost nothing, Zara got a job in addition to her police training duties. It was my responsibility to focus on school and do the chores. She usually came home after midnight from her shift at the restaurant, leaving again for her classroom at the police academy a few hours later. Zara had barely turned eighteen, only to be burdened with a household and a seven-year-old schoolgirl. She had looked after me for the past twelve years as if I were her own child, not just her little sister. She had seen to it that the bills were paid, there was food on the table, and I always had clean clothes. She never let it show when we were broke again, and whenever I needed money for a school trip or something, she only said, "I'll figure it out, don't worry." Somehow she always found a way.

When I cried at night, she took me in her arms and comforted me until I fell asleep again. She was my mother, father, friend, and sister all in one, depending on what I needed at the time.

She was the best person I'd ever known. I still loved her above all else. I missed her so much it almost killed me.

CHAPTER 2

"Congratulations!" Mrs. Prescott said, pressing me so tightly against her chest I was almost breathless. I had come this afternoon, as I did every Tuesday and Thursday, to the Prescotts' to look after little Timmy. Apart from my job at Beamen's, the local liquor store, where I worked as a clerk during the week, I also babysat five-year-old Timmy. I'd just told Mrs. Prescott I would begin studying psychology at Oxford in a few days, and after separating myself from her and gasping for air, I saw she had tears in her eyes.

"After what happened to your sister . . . ," she said and swallowed, "a change of scenery should do you some good." Thick tears rolled over her powdered cheeks.

"Yes," I said, my voice trembling. "I think so, too."

"Do you know how you'll pay for it?" asked Mrs. Prescott, concerned.

"Well, last week I was granted a partial scholarship. That should at least cover my tuition and housing. Together with Zara's life insurance, I should be able to get by for now."

Mrs. Prescott nodded. "We'll miss you very much," she said, tears coming to her eyes again. "Especially Timmy."

"I'll miss you all, too," I admitted, bending down to lift up Timmy, who had clasped my leg. When I picked him up, he slipped his slender arms around my neck with a firm grip—a sight that set his mother's lips quivering again.

"I'd better leave now," she finally said, wiping the tears from her eyes and smudging her carefully applied eye makeup in the process.

Dana Prescott worked at the reception desk of a luxury hotel. I watched Timmy until her husband, Jim, a successful attorney, who usually worked late meeting clients or attending business dinners, came home. The Prescotts became parents late in life—both were over forty—and both dearly wanted a child but were unable to conceive for a long time. When they had finally given up hope, Mrs. Prescott became pregnant with Timmy, whom she lovingly called her "little miracle."

"What do we want to play today, Timmy?" I loosened his iron grip from around my neck.

"I can see something you can't see," he answered, full of excitement, and squirmed when I set him down again.

I smiled. There may have been nothing to hold me in this place, but I would truly miss him.

A few days later I was nearly finished packing when my gaze caught the framed photo on my nightstand. A smile crossed my face when I grabbed it to take a closer look. Zara and I had been to the fair that day and rode the huge roller coaster three times in a row, until we'd nearly gotten sick. Happy and lighthearted, we'd laughed into the camera. A shiny object was hanging around my neck in the photograph and caught my attention, so I looked a little closer. On its own, my free hand wandered to my neck and felt for the amulet under my sweater. I pulled it free and looked at it for the umpteenth time: an equilateral, downward-pointing triangle made of a blue-green mineral, dangling from a fine-linked silver chain, two superimposed waves engraved into it.

My mother found it one day at a flea market when she was almost due with me. The vendor demanded a steep price for it. Though she'd liked the amulet, she was about to put it down when I began to kick inside her—she'd told me the story at least a hundred times. It was as if I was destined to have this ornament. So she bought it. For me.

On the evening of my sixth birthday, she had come into my room and sat down beside me on my bed. She had carefully taken the blue-green amulet from her neck and put it around mine.

"It will protect you," she had whispered as she lovingly ran her fingers through my hair and kissed my forehead. "Never take it off."

I felt a lump rise in my throat and swallowed hard. *Pull yourself together!* There wasn't time now to melt from self-pity. If I didn't hurry, the train would leave without me. I carefully wrapped the picture frame in a towel and set it in my suitcase.

When I looked up again, I started with a fright. For a moment, I thought someone had appeared out of thin air and was standing across from me. But a second later, I saw I was standing in front of the long mirror on my cabinet, looking at my own frightened face. *Dear God!* My heart was pounding. I'd become terribly fearful lately, probably because of that creepy guy I'd first noticed at Zara's funeral. He had stood somewhat off to the side and watched me the whole time. At first, I thought nothing of it because lots of unfamiliar people had attended. But I had come across him again and again over the following weeks. The first time was a few days after the funeral. He stood as if petrified on the other side of the street and openly stared at me. Soon after, he got in line at the same register at the grocery store but only bought a pack of gum. One evening, after I had babysat Timmy, I even thought he had followed me home. As if to confirm it, he rode in the same bus I took daily to Beamen's. There, he skulked around the parking lot for hours and looked through the windows of the store. I was tempted to call the police, but when I headed for the bus stop after closing, he was gone, and I hadn't seen him since. However, I still half expected him to be standing there every time I turned a corner, his hands in the pockets of his gray wool coat, his sparse hair combed back, and the same frozen expression on his face, as if he were a spy from the thirties. It made sense that I would find this guy creepy—but it was strange that my own reflection frightened me.

I took a step closer. Was that really me? When had I last looked into a mirror? I barely recognized myself. I looked haggard and my cheeks were sunken. When had I last eaten a proper meal? I couldn't remember. I'd completely lost my appetite in the last few weeks. I'd noticed from my loose-fitting clothes that I'd lost weight, but I didn't want to waste time thinking about food, so I'd simply tightened my belt and left it at that. I'd always been slender, but now I seemed downright fragile.

My long, medium-blonde hair, which reached halfway down my back, was uncombed and loosely knotted together. It used to have a golden sheen but now looked dull, colorless, and unhealthy. I stepped up to the mirror to look more closely at my face. I was so pale my skin almost appeared transparent. Heavy shadows showed under my eyes. Zara had marvelous, beaming green eyes. Mine were a few shades darker green with a hint of blue. They'd lost their shine and now appeared empty and lackluster. My eyelashes, too, were not as dense and long as they used to be. My once-full lips had almost taken on the color of my skin. I could have passed for a corpse, and the black clothes that I'd taken to wearing enhanced that impression. I gladly looked away from the frightening apparition in the mirror and turned my attention back to packing. Then I took one last look around the small apartment to make sure I hadn't forgotten anything. I was glad that the next tenant was willing to take the furniture, especially the heavy leather couch; otherwise, I'd have had to deal with it myself. I locked the door one last time and dropped the key, as arranged with the new tenant, into the mailbox. Then I took my bags and walked away without looking back. My entire life, or rather what was left of it, fit into two suitcases.

The Prescotts' silver minivan waited in the street. "Here, Evelyn, here," Timmy excitedly called at me as he waved. As I expected, they'd all come to say good-bye. *My substitute family*, I thought with a touch of sorrow. After all, these three people were the closest thing to a family that I had. And if I was really honest with myself, they had a piece of my heart. They were the only ones I liked being around. The only ones I spent time with. I had no friends. I'd never mixed well with people my age. That's why I was always a loner at school, always a bit more grown-up than my peers. I was never able to get excited about childish pranks, so I mostly kept to myself and watched others play, goof around, and go through puberty. My childhood had suddenly come to an end with my parents' death. If Zara had not taken care of me, I would have . . . oh, I don't know. I probably would have gone through an orphan's usual life: being passed around from one foster family to another, finishing school with mediocre grades just to do some job I'd hate for the rest of my life. But thanks to Zara, I was on my way to Oxford, one of the best universities in the country, maybe the world.

Gentleman that he was, Jim Prescott stepped out of the car to take my suitcases and stow them in the back of the van. I helped him by pulling open the van's sliding door to sit in the backseat with Timmy, who tried with all his might to free himself from his booster seat so he could climb on my lap.

"Did you really think this out?" asked Mr. Prescott as he settled back into the driver's seat. "Our offer still stands. The house is large enough and—"

I interrupted him to assure him for the hundredth time that I was certain. I wanted to get away from this place that reminded me every second of what I had lost.

Mrs. Prescott apologetically smiled at me from the passenger seat.

"I called Ruth last night, my cousin in Oxford—do you remember her?"

"Yes, she's a taxi driver there, isn't she?" I said.

"Exactly. She's promised to pick you up from the train station tonight," Mrs. Prescott said. "Don't worry, I only told her that you're Timmy's babysitter and starting school at Oxford. After all, you're going there to begin a new life, and you should decide on your own who, what, and how much you tell."

"Thank you," I said. I would have assumed one did not tell a stranger one's entire life story.

For the rest of the twenty-minute drive from Fleetwood to the Blackpool train station, everyone except for Timmy, who was still wiggling in his booster seat, seemed lost in thought. When we arrived, I released him from his seat. He thanked me by leaping onto my lap. Now came the moment that I'd dreaded since I told the Prescotts that I was moving away: parting. Dana, always very emotional, bordered on a nervous breakdown. Sobbing, she buried her face in her hands and blew into a tissue until it almost tore apart.

Oh boy! I'd always found these situations awkward. I never learned to handle them well and was more than relieved when it seemed to be over and everyone had calmed down.

"We have a little something for you," said Jim with a firm voice and pressed an envelope into my hand. "This should get you by for a while."

"No, I can't accept this. You mustn't . . . ," I protested, surprised.

"No buts," he said and closed my hand around the full envelope.

"But I . . . ," I started again only to be rewarded with an unrelenting stare from Jim, who still had a comforting arm around his wife. "Thank you," I finally said and put the envelope in my pocket.

"Let me know you made it safely," Dana said, detaching herself from her husband and pressing me against her for a third time.

I said, "Of course," shook Mr. Prescott's hand, and gave Timmy a big kiss on the cheek. Then I walked with my suitcases into the station, where the monitor informed me that my train would leave from platform 4 in exactly three minutes.

With my big purse around my neck and a heavy suitcase in each hand, I ran through an underground passage and reached the train just as the doors were closing. *That was close—damned good-byes!*

Still out of breath, I entered the next car, looking for an empty seat. I stored my things in the baggage compartment, dropped exhausted into the seat, and pulled my MP3 player from my bag by its headphones. A small dark-blue booklet was entangled in the cords and fell out. My bank account book. I opened it and stared at the amount, shaking my head. I still couldn't believe it.

The image of the bank, the broad wooden desk, and the wide chair in which I sat a few weeks ago appeared before my eyes.

"Ten thousand," I said in disbelief.

The notary calmly repeated, "Ten thousand. Your sister made a few preparations. You were to be secure in case something happened to her." He had just read her will, which simply stated that I was to have all of Zara's possessions and was registered as the beneficiary of her life insurance, which she had purchased without my knowledge. Though she never said it, I knew how angry Zara was at our parents because they had left us nothing but a few chairs and a worn couch.

"And a personal note from your sister." The notary continued reading the will and cleared his throat. "Do something sensible with it. I love you," he had quoted. I had burst into tears. *I love you, too!*

Before sadness could overcome me again, I angrily pushed the earbuds into my ears and scrolled up and down the MP3 player's display until I found what I was looking for—the rough sounds of "I'm Shipping Up to Boston" by the Dropkick Murphys seemed to be just the right thing for the occasion—and cranked up the volume until I couldn't hear myself think anymore.

The four-hour ride was uneventful—I even fell asleep a few times—and when the train finally entered Oxford, darkness shrouded the historic town. Outside the train station, after I had heaved my suitcases from the train, a middle-aged woman called me to her cab. *That must be Ruth, Mrs. Prescott's cousin.*

"Hi, I'm Evelyn Lakewood," I said as I stood before her. "You're Ruth?"

"Yes," she answered with a beaming smile. "Hello, Evelyn, welcome to Oxford."

With our combined strength we stashed the suitcases in the trunk before I got in and gave her the address of my future home, which I had scribbled on a sticky note.

"One of the university dorms," she said with a nod and drove off. When she saw that I was rubbing my cold hands, she turned the heat up as high as possible, and an intense scent cloud hit me. Taxis have a very special odor, one that cannot be compared to other cars. An overwhelming mixture of leather and mint was powerfully enhanced now that the hot air was blasting. While I held my hands to the vent, I looked out the window and saw that the beauty of the old buildings in this distinguished town could even be admired in the dark. The architecture of the "city of dreaming spires" had always fascinated me.

"What are you taking, dear? Dana didn't tell me much about you," Ruth said after we'd driven a few miles.

"Psychology at Christ Church," I said, returning her smile. She almost appeared motherly, with her soft facial features and light-brown curls rippling out from underneath a red beret.

"First year?"

"Yes, it starts tomorrow. I was accepted off the waiting list," I said and sighed. "The others are a full trimester ahead."

"That must make you nervous," she said.

"A little."

"My daughter graduated from here last summer. She studied medicine. She's working at St. Mary's Hospital in London now."

"You must be proud," I said, stating the obvious.

"Oh, I am," she eagerly agreed. "Your family must be proud of you, studying at a famous college like this."

I swallowed hard; Mrs. Prescott had indeed spilled nothing.

"I hope so," I pronounced with a hoarse voice, which caused Ruth to throw me a questioning glance. "My parents died when I was very young," I explained after a short pause, without knowing why I would tell a stranger something so private. "My big sister Zara looked after me then . . ." I let the sentence hang.

"Looked after you?" Ruth asked, as if she were unsure whether she should ask the question or not.

"Zara died three months ago while on duty. She was a police officer." My voice trembled.

"I'm sorry to hear that, dear," she said with sincerity. I just nodded since I was afraid the lump in my throat would overpower me if I kept talking, and for a while neither of us said anything.

"Here we are," Ruth finally announced and pointed out a splendid building in a typical early seventeenth-century style. The taxi stopped at the entrance.

"Thank you." *For simply being a nice person!*

She scribbled something on a piece of paper and got out to help me pull my suitcases from the trunk. Afterward, I tried to pay her for the ride, but she vehemently declined.

"Here's my telephone number." She held out the paper. "Call me if you need to talk." This sudden familiarity surprised me. She placed the paper in my hand and closed my fingers around it. I wanted to say something but was unable to speak. Though I was embarrassed, I let her hug me.

"When the pain fades away, love remains in its purest form," she whispered into my ear. At these words, the dams burst. As much as I wanted to hold my tears back, I could not. All the sorrow, rage, and despair, all those feelings that I hadn't admitted to for such a long time came crashing on me with full force. There was no point in resisting so I cried on the shoulder of a stranger.

"Better go inside, Evelyn, or you'll catch a cold," she said as soon as I had my tears under control.

"Thank you, Ruth. For everything." She stroked my cheek with the back of her hand, got into her cab, and drove off. I breathed a sigh of relief, took my suitcase, and looked around. I was standing in front of the snow-covered entrance to the dorm. Though I had never been here before, I knew the building from pictures I'd seen on the Internet. It was one of those imposing old buildings for which I admired this town so much. A heavy, dark wooden door and tall windows decorated with spires and ornaments gave the building a dignity normally reserved for people. There was something mysterious, almost mystical, about this winter scene.

A resident assistant was waiting for me in the spacious entrance area. He was a pedantic-looking pimply type with glasses, and he looked somewhat like a youngish professor and behaved that way, too. He led me up a broad, varnished staircase with a wobbly railing that led to my room on the second floor. The RA rattled off the house rules in a surly voice. While I only half listened to his explanations about rules and consequences, I looked around my room.

It was bright, larger than I expected, and had a small bathroom. I sighed with relief. I had pictured a shared bathroom where I'd have to line up in the morning to wait my turn to brush my teeth. There was also a large, curtained bay window that would let in light during the day. The bed and nightstand were large enough, the mattress was good as new, and the antique-looking dresser and wardrobe had enough room for my paltry possessions. A narrow desk with a wooden chair completed the furnishings.

Simple but beautiful. When the RA finally left, I started unpacking. First, I stashed my clothes in the closet, then I put my sheets and blanket on the mattress and put my toiletries in the medicine cabinet in the small bathroom, which was equipped with a sink, a toilet, and a narrow shower. I didn't expect a bathtub, but I was a little disappointed that there wasn't one. I loved water and liked to disappear in it. At home in Fleetwood I could be at the water in minutes, but here I would have to do with this tight shower stall. At least I didn't have to share. I wrote a brief text to Mrs. Prescott to let her know I'd arrived okay. I wanted to spare myself a phone call that could last for hours.

Finally, I set two framed photos on the small nightstand. One was of my parents when they were about thirty, looking lovingly into each other's eyes. The other was the snapshot of Zara and me, which her former boyfriend took at the fair. Again I felt the lump in my throat and tears welled up. What was the matter with me today? What was with all the crying? Oh, whatever. Since I had started to cry, I might as well do it properly. Then it'd be done with for a while. I carefully pulled the little black box out of my subconscious and hesitantly opened it. Only one or two memories; I didn't want to look at more. Only a few images. Images that I normally didn't allow myself because they were too painful. Because I feared they would wreck me. Now I very deliberately allowed it. I saw Mom and Dad before me. They held hands and smiled at me. Zara. She was with them. Looking happy.

Sobbing, I buried my face in a pillow. I was all alone in this world.

CHAPTER 3

Light shone through the curtain and gently woke me.

Where am I? Suddenly I remembered—I was in my dorm room in Oxford. *What time is it?* I reached for the alarm clock on the nightstand. It wasn't there. *Damn!* It was probably in my suitcase. I sat up and realized I was still wearing my clothes from the day before. A glance at my phone told me it was a little after 7:30. My first lecture started at 8:00, and I didn't have a clue where I was supposed to be.

Great, that's a nice start!

There was no time to shower, so I just brushed my teeth and splashed a little water on my face to wake up. Since I couldn't find my hairbrush, I ran my fingers through my hair and put it in a ponytail.

I slipped my black boots on, threw on my coat, grabbed my bag, and rushed out the door.

It was 7:50 a.m. as I charged across the frozen cobblestones of downtown Oxford. I turned a corner and stopped in my tracks. I thought I'd just seen a man out of the corner of my eye—a man with black leather gloves and a blank expression. I spun around, eyes wide, but I saw only an ordinary streetlight. I was starting to worry that I was losing my mind. What would this guy want in Oxford, two hundred miles from where I last saw him? That was completely absurd. I banished the thought and continued walking. I had a blue folder with all the papers I needed for the first day, and I pulled it out of my bag to see where my first lecture was.

While I ran through the mighty gate of Tom Tower, the main entrance of Christ Church College, and across the courtyard, I scanned the documents in the folder and finally found my schedule.

Monday, 8:00 a.m., lecture: Narcissism and Destructiveness, Professor Carl Bronsen, hall 7.

Where the heck is hall 7?

"Can I help you? You look lost." A young woman with a Burberry scarf and shoulder-length red hair smiled at me.

"Yes," I said. "I have to be in hall seven in five minutes—do you know where that is?"

"Narcissism and Destructiveness with Bronsen?"

"Yes, exactly," I said, relieved. Obviously, she knew her way around.

"Then you'd best turn here," she said and pointed in the direction. "Turn right again after about a hundred yards or when you reach the small fountain, then go all the way to the top of the stairs and you'll be at the door."

I tried to memorize the route, thanked her, and ran off.

"No problem," she called after me, sounding as if she couldn't suppress her laughter.

I almost thought I'd run too far when I finally arrived at the small fountain. Then I turned right, ran up the stairs, and stopped abruptly as I found myself outside the dining hall. I frowned and looked around for hall 7. No, this was definitely the dining hall. There were no lecture halls here.

I took my phone out of my bag—it was 8:00.

Did I turn too early? Did the redhead make a mistake? I was definitely in the wrong place. I remembered that I had a map of the campus and went through my folder until I found it.

Okay, let's see . . . This is the dining hall, there's the small fountain that I came by, and that should be hall 7.

I traced my recent route on the map with my finger, and then it hit me. That redhead bitch deliberately sent me in the wrong direction when I had already been standing in front of the entrance to hall 7!

I ran back all the way, slipping on the ice and nearly falling. I arrived to the lecture hall out of breath. I was almost ten minutes late.

Damn! I breathed deeply and slipped through the door as quietly as possible. I tiptoed in, trying not to attract attention. Then I saw an empty seat in the last row. Perfect. So far almost no one had noticed. I pushed down the wooden seat and sat on it, relieved, until the seat collapsed under me and I crashed to the floor with a dull thud. A word I never used in public escaped my lips.

At once I felt heat spread across my face and color my cheeks bright red.

This can't be happening, I thought and carefully pulled myself up. When I looked around, I saw to my horror that almost every head in the lecture hall—and there were at least fifty—was turned my way; I wanted to disappear. Suddenly the ceiling light flickered. Something was probably wrong with it, and fortunately that drew the attention away from me. I looked around embarrassed. The contents of my bag were scattered on the floor. I started collecting my things and attempted to ignore the malicious giggling and a sarcastic "Everything all right, Blondie?" It was the redhead, who now looked down on me from her seat—with no intention of hiding her malice.

Oh God, this can't be happening!

Suddenly a slim hand with short, brightly colored nails held out my copy of Erich Fromm's *Anatomy of Human Destructiveness*. Gentle gray-green eyes met my glance.

"Did you hurt yourself?" the girl sincerely asked, smiling broadly, the stud in her right nostril gleaming. She had a heart-shaped face framed by hair dyed dark red and violet.

"No, I'm all right," I said and hastily added, "Thank you."

"There's an empty seat next to me," she whispered after we had collected my things. And now that we were standing opposite each other, I noticed how petite she was—at most five foot three, because I was taller by at least four inches. She had noticeable breasts, considering her delicate figure. I nodded and followed her. The professor had reluctantly stopped his lecture and was shaking his head, clearly angered by the disturbance I'd caused.

"Eyes to the front, show's over," he said, admonishing his students to concentrate.

After thoroughly checking the stability of the seat, I sat down beside my helper and, although I was sure the worst was over, I couldn't shake the feeling that I was being watched. Searching for the cause of my discomfort, I raised my head—and saw . . . *him*. His glowing dark-blue eyes were still fixed on me while all the others were looking forward. I felt hypnotized.

"I'm Sally," the girl whispered and tore me away from those unbelievable blue eyes.

"I'm Evelyn. Thank you for helping me," I added after a short pause. I was truly grateful. Especially because she gave me the feeling of not being completely surrounded by nasty, self-indulgent people who send you in the wrong direction out of pure spite.

"Are you sure you didn't hurt yourself? That looked pretty bad," she said with concern, but she also looked a little amused.

"Nah, everything's all right." The thought of my fall made me giggle a little.

"Man, everybody looked your way. Even that arrogant Calmburry. And he's normally only interested in himself," Sally said, visibly making an effort to suppress a chuckle.

"Calmburry?" I had heard the name before. The ceiling lights flickered again. What was going on with that light?

"You're not from here, are you?"

"No, I'm from Fleetwood." That sounded as if I should be ashamed of it.

"Jared *Lord* Calmburry. The one up front there with the short brown hair," she said, pointing toward the stranger with the indigo eyes who had been staring at me. Now she had my undivided attention.

"And . . . who's he?" I asked, trying not to sound overly curious.

Sally looked at me as if I were from Mars. "He's the only survivor of the Calmburry clan. His family is one of the oldest in England. Or rather, *was*. They all died in a plane crash twelve years ago—both parents, his sister, and his uncle. He was the only survivor. It was all over the news." She looked at me, baffled. "Didn't you hear about it?"

"No." *Perhaps because I was distracted by my own parents' death twelve years ago!*

"I really feel sorry for him," she continued, "but I still can't stand him."

"Hmm," was all I could say. A ringing started in my ears. Jared Calmburry was the last of his family . . . like me. He had lost everything . . . like me.

I looked as discreetly as possible at the stranger sitting four rows in front of me. His gray sweater looked expensive, and his short brown hair, which changed into a dark shade of gold at the tips, was perfect— at least as far as I could tell. I tried to remember what his face was like when we looked each other in the eye.

As if he had read my thoughts, Calmburry leaned a little to the side and turned his head to answer a question from his neighbor, or so it seemed. His profile was so handsome. A small straight nose, dense and dark eyelashes that framed his exceptional eyes, and perfectly smooth, pure skin. His soft, masculine face was breathtaking. Jared was neither slim nor too muscly. He had an athlete's figure, and I wondered what kind of sports a body of such perfection might play.

"I know he looks good, but trust me: he's not worth the trouble!" Sally whispered in my ear. I was so focused on his appearance that I almost fell from the chair when she spoke to me.

"And he only hangs out with his own kind. If you don't have at least a million in your account, forget about it."

Feeling ashamed for gawking at Jared Calmburry so blatantly, I turned away and concentrated on the lecture. With only modest success. My gaze kept returning to him.

When the professor finally announced the end of the lecture, Sally departed with a short "See you, bye," and hurried out the door. I had no time to ask where she was off to in such a hurry, and a moment later my eyes were again on Jared, who was pushing through the other students to the center aisle of the lecture hall. Suddenly, someone blocked my view.

"You really stole good old Professor Bronsen's show," said a kind male voice.

"It would seem that way," I admitted.

"He's not very pleased to have his hour-long monolog on *libido* and *destrudo* interrupted." A grin spread across his face. "Let's hope he doesn't know you by name, or he'll deduct a point from your exam for that little stunt." The boy's grin broadened even more. I nodded and shot a glance over his shoulder, looking for Jared. He had disappeared in the crowd pressing toward the exit.

"By the way, I'm Felix," he said and, when I didn't react, he added, "Don't worry, your name is safe with me. I won't say a peep to old Bronsen." He raised his hand as if to swear an oath and put on a playfully serious expression. "Promise!"

"Oh, sorry," I said, shaking my head and holding out my hand. "I'm Evelyn."

"Now, *Evelyn*," he said tenderly, "what's your next lecture?"

Still somewhat surprised by this unexpected conversation, I went through my bag, pulled out my by-now-crumpled schedule and took a look at it.

"Introduction to Psychology with Professor Harrison in hall four."

"May I walk you there? I know every decrepit chair in this college. One crash landing should be enough for the day, shouldn't it?" Again, a smile spread across his face and, now that I took a real look at him, I noticed how pleasant Felix appeared. Tousled black curls framed his oval face and perfectly matched his dark eyes around which laughter lines were beginning to appear. His grin was so broad that dimples formed in his cheeks and showed off his white teeth. I noticed that his left incisor was slightly crooked and extended a bit over its right neighbor. Still, Felix was handsome. I couldn't help but return his smile.

"Okay," I said, "after you."

We made a path through the other students leaving the lecture hall.

"I haven't seen you here before. Did you switch colleges? Subjects?" he asked as we stepped outside. It had started to snow again, and thick, wet flakes landed on my face. Since I didn't have a scarf, or a hat or gloves, I settled for wrapping my coat tighter around me and drawing my head in to stay warm. Felix did the same.

"No, today's my first day," I called out against the ice-cold wind. "I was accepted off the waiting list."

"Well, then this was a successful start," he said, alluding to my fall with a smile.

"You can say that again. I just arrived last night, slept in this morning and . . . well, you know the rest." I kept silent about the redhead sending me in the wrong direction. "What year are you?" I asked when we had trudged a few steps across the snow-covered lawn away from the footpath crowded by the student herd.

"Also my first year, but I started in October."

"How do you like it so far?"

"The lectures and seminars are pretty good," he said, "but the people here? Let's just say it'll take some time to get used to them."

"What do you mean?"

"Look around." He seemed agitated. "All brats of rich parents. All members of an elite society, with bottomless bank accounts they show off at every opportunity."

That reminded me of what Sally had just said.

"Are you talking about anyone in particular?" I asked because I couldn't make sense of Felix's sudden shift in mood.

"Most students here are that way," he said, "but I think the worst is that *Calmburry*." I listened closely. "Always surrounded by his groupies. It's best to avoid those society types from the start."

"Has he done anything to you?" I asked, eager to find out more about Jared.

Felix smiled. "You know, someone like me has to work hard for everything—I'm here on a scholarship and worked my ass off for it. Someone like him just buys what he wants. I'm sure his grades come with a generous donation from his filthy rich inheritance." Felix's unexpected hostility made me shrink back, and we walked in silence beside each other until he asked, "What's with you? Do you have money?"

I was startled for a moment by his direct and indiscreet question, but a glance at his face told me he was not entirely serious.

"Am I supposed to answer that?" I asked with raised eyebrows.

"No, you don't," he said. "I could tell right away that you're different from the others."

What was that about? Was he flirting with me? We'd only known each other a few minutes.

"Err . . . thank you," I said, embarrassed and amused. Felix broke out laughing.

"Here we are," Felix said as soon as he stopped laughing. "Lecture hall four."

"Thank you," I said and slipped by him toward the entrance.

"Evelyn," he called after me, "do you know where the dining hall is?" That was one thing I knew only too well.

"Yes, why?"

"Would you like to have lunch with me?"

"Yeah, sure," I answered without thinking and regretted my quick acceptance a second later.

He smiled. "Okay, then let's meet outside the dining hall during the lunch break. Later."

Before I could respond, he turned and went back in the direction from which we'd just come.

I really needed to get it together. The day had gotten off to a terrible start—I slept in, fell for that redhead's rotten trick, and then a complete stranger dazed me with a single look. And now Felix had ambushed me twice. If I didn't watch myself, Heaven knows what might happen.

I closed my eyes for a moment, shaking my head, breathed in deeply, and stepped through the mighty carved door. I shook the snow from my coat and dried my hair with a handkerchief before looking for a seat. My classmates sat down and Professor Harrison started his Introduction to Psychology at ten o'clock on the dot.

Leonard Harrison was a textbook example of an Oxford professor. He wore the obligatory tweed jacket over a dark-blue sweater-vest from which a white shirt collar popped out. His outfit was completed by worn black leather slip-on shoes and pants that rode too high. To hide his bald dome, he had combed his sparse gray hair across his head. The gold-rimmed half-moon glasses sat on the tip of his nose, and when he smiled to greet the class, he revealed a row of crooked and yellowed teeth.

Most of what he discussed in his lecture I already knew from my psychology prep course, but I still took thorough notes. After all, I was missing several months of material compared to most of the others here.

When Harrison finished his lecture, I looked at my schedule and noted with satisfaction that both Statistics and History of Psychoanalysis were also held in hall 4. So I could simply stay seated and lean back.

Stats with Professor Sigmund Gallert made me nervous. I never was big on math and Gallert's speech impediment—a kind of mumbling lisp—didn't make following the complex calculations any easier since I continuously had to suppress a giggle. It didn't seem to affect my classmates. Although I had understood reasonably well what Gallert was relaying, I needed to quickly catch up on the material I'd missed. Maybe I could join a study group. I decided to look around for one.

Happy to hear Gallert's liberating "Enough for today," I leaned back and attempted to relax.

Then, like after Introduction to Psychology, I observed how most students quickly left the hall while new ones poured in. There was one difference, though: this time it seemed more hectic. Several students pressed by those flowing out shortly after the lecture to secure themselves a seat. It proved to be really crowded a few minutes later and even the otherwise unpopular seats in the front row were soon taken. Even when all the seats had been filled, more people came in and, annoyed at not being able to get a seat, sat down on the center aisle stairs. My expectations for this lecture grew by the second. *History of Psychoanalysis, Professor Karen Mayflower*, I read one more time from my crumpled schedule and looked up full of anticipation when the don's door loudly opened at the front of the hall and someone entered.

Professor Mayflower was a well-dressed and very attractive woman in her midfifties who seemed highly intelligent. She impressed me at first sight and had me hanging on her every word. An hour later, I'd almost filled half my pad with notes. I'd written so much I was straining to look at the paper. Was I imagining this, or was it really bright in here?

I was wondering if extra-bright fluorescent lights were being used when I felt a penetrating stare from behind me. I slowly turned and stopped midmotion. Jared Calmburry was sitting about five rows back, distinctly elevated by the slope in the hall, and he was staring at me. I turned to the front again with lightning speed. The lights began to flicker at that very moment.

What does this mean?

I still felt his stare on the back of my neck and fought with all my might against the urge to turn around. Had his eyes borne down on me all this time and I didn't notice because I was so focused on Professor Mayflower? Or was I just imagining it all, and Calmburry wasn't watching me? Why would he? After all that Sally and Felix had told me, he wouldn't bother with someone like me. But then why did I always feel his gaze resting on me? I carefully turned my head and looked at him again. He looked directly into my eyes—and my heart skipped. So I was not mistaken: Calmburry was looking at me. Even from this distance I could almost see his deep blue eyes shining. His jaw muscles were clearly tensed and the expression on his face was curious and skeptical. But there was something else . . . *Fascination* maybe? I couldn't put my finger on it.

"Would you kindly pay attention to the class, my dear?"

I froze. Did she mean me? I turned around and saw Professor Mayflower's admonishing look. But then her expression changed. Her eyes widened, and she opened her mouth in disbelief, her look alternating between me and Calmburry.

"Nimue," she said, confused. *"That's impossible!"* For a brief moment, the professor appeared to be suffering a stroke. Then she shook her head as if to dispel a thought, muttered something that sounded like "Excuse me," and bolted out of the hall before the lecture was over.

"What did she say?" the girl beside me asked. Everyone watched Professor Mayflower disappear, then stared at me as if I was some animal that had escaped from the zoo. For the second time this morning, all eyes were on me. Once again, this unpleasant feeling made me want to disappear.

What the hell does this mean?

Looking for an explanation, I turned to Jared Calmburry, but his seat was empty. He must have escaped out the door. How had he managed to leave so fast?

Completely dazed, I slipped my coat on and left the building with the other students, who still eyed me quizzically. It was snowing heavily outside, so I pulled my coat's collar over my head and squinted to see in the dense white haze. The ice-cold flakes landed on my face.

"With this weather, I thought I'd better pick you up. So you won't get lost." Felix said, walking beside me with a smile. He had pulled his jacket half over his head, too. How did he know where I was?

"Hi, that's kind of you," I said into the storm. I was actually relieved to see him. He offered me his arm and I accepted, grateful for his support.

"So, does everybody stare at you like that?" Felix said when he noticed the fellow students who couldn't keep from gawking even in the snowstorm.

"No idea," I lied and picked up the pace through the relentless snow in an effort to escape their dreadful looks.

"You didn't fall again, did you?" He stopped and looked at me with concern.

"No. Come on, let's go," I urged him, which he seemed to like because he was grinning and let me pull him along.

"It would appear," Felix noted with a mocking undertone, "that Calmburry is sliming his way into Mayflower's favor!" Alarmed, I turned and saw Professor Mayflower, who, somewhat protected from the wind and snow, was standing in a narrow passage between two buildings talking to Jared Calmburry while gesturing wildly. By contrast, his posture was relaxed, and he appeared to be appeasing her. As if he sensed my presence, Jared looked up and stared at me with those indigo-blue eyes. First, he appeared curious, but when his gaze caught Felix, he seemed perturbed. Professor Mayflower turned when she noticed Jared's changed behavior and cast a look that was both infuriated and desperate.

"What's her problem?" Felix asked and guided me toward the dining hall. I reluctantly detached myself from Jared's look and moved on. I was starting to believe I was going crazy.

When we entered the dining hall, I wiped the thick, cottony flakes from my coat. Felix shook his black curls so vigorously that he reminded me of a wet dog, scattering droplets of water throughout the entire entrance area. It looked so funny I had to giggle.

When we'd climbed the stairs, Felix explained the dining hall process while I was completely occupied with the many impressions this historical hall offered. Since I wasn't hungry but was still confused about Professor Mayflower's strange behavior and especially about Jared Calmburry, I took the first thing I could identify—spaghetti with tomato sauce—and sat down across from Felix at one of the huge tables that extended across the entire room. Numerous paintings of famous graduates of Christ Church, some of them life-size, hung on the dark wall paneling.

"MacMillan, you're not already hitting on the new girl, are you?" Sally stood behind Felix with a full tray in her hands and smiled at me.

"A word to the wise, Evelyn: you have to be careful with this guy." She winked at me and sat down beside Felix, who looked less than thrilled.

"Wouldn't you rather sit somewhere else, Sally?" he asked annoyed.

"I only want to see how my new friend's doing," she said, "and I find *you*, the worst of them all, with her!"

I couldn't tell how serious she was, but I figured a small warning probably resided in her playful comment.

"I see you two know each other," I said with a smile.

"We're in the same study group," Felix explained, whereupon Sally aggressively added, "But usually of different opinions."

"No, you're usually just opposed, no matter what it's about. That's why we're the only two left—all the others have had it with you!" Felix said, visibly angered.

"Is that so?" Sally asked.

I couldn't help but giggle at the thought of how these two scared off the entire study group with endless arguments and fighting.

"If Evelyn joins, there'll be three again. What do you think?" she asked me.

"Oh that would be great. I wanted to join a study group, anyway." Both of them smiled, but then I had a thought and bit my lower lip. "How well . . . do you know statistics?" I asked. Hopefully, the answer wouldn't force me to look for another study group.

"Stats are my specialty," Felix proudly said. "In fact, anything with numbers is no problem for me!"

I sighed with relief.

"Don't be such a braggart." Sally rolled her eyes.

"What? I happen to be good in math," he said and shrugged.

"Well, you have a healthy self-image," I said, smiling. "Still nice to hear, though. I didn't get that much out of today's class."

"Not to worry," Sally said. "Einstein here will set you on the right track."

"Shut up, Sally," he said.

When we'd finished lunch—that is, when I was finished poking around in my noodles—we placed our dishes on a cart and went into the courtyard. It was still snowing but not nearly as intensely as before. However, it was bitterly cold when I went to the next seminar with Sally. We discovered over lunch that we had the same classes in the afternoon.

Behavioral Psychology with Professor Marvin Fisher was really interesting. Apart from classical conditioning according to Pavlov, Fisher also discussed operant conditioning according to Skinner, something I was deeply interested in. I considered influencing human behavior by means of rewards and punishment an exciting, though dangerous, issue. Sally, on the other hand, seemed less enthusiastic and lolled distractedly in her seat. "Aren't you going to take notes?" I asked. "This could be on the exam."

"I have all the notes from a second-year student," she answered, sounding bored. She groaned a few minutes later when Fisher wrapped up his lecture. The next seminar was also today's last. I'd made it.

As we entered the room, Sally suddenly seemed nervous. She continuously smoothed her hair and repeatedly checked her makeup in her small pocket mirror. I couldn't fathom the change in her behavior and, as I looked around, I noticed that most other girls were also behaving somewhat strangely, like Sally. They were all concerned with their appearance. Looking for an explanation, I peeked at my thoroughly abused schedule—I would have to rewrite it tonight.

Communication Psychology with Professor Irvin Martin, I noted without finding anything special. But when the professor entered the room, I understood why all the girls had turned into tormented groupies. Professor Martin was a stunning man in his midforties who seemed to have stepped out of an advertisement for men's clothing, and the girls openly adored him. Was he married? I looked over his hand, searching for a wedding ring. He was wearing a seal ring that looked like a family heirloom on his right hand. It was made of gold and on the level, oval surface was a smooth dark-blue gem where it looked like a crest was engraved. That was the type of ring you got when you were a member of an elite society, but it was definitely not a wedding ring. It would appear that Professor Martin wasn't married, which also explained the girls' behavior—they seemed to believe they had a real chance with him. I merely considered him likable, perhaps even a bit fatherly.

That was it—the first day done, I thought after the lecture and said goodbye to Sally, who still wasn't able to take her eyes off Professor Martin.

Tired and cold, I made my way to the dorm, took my phone out, and called Mrs. Prescott to give her a report on my first day at Oxford.

Only when I told her that my battery wouldn't hold out much longer was I able to interrupt her flood of words and hang up. After arriving at the dorm, I freed myself from my coat and heavy boots and went to the bathroom. There I stripped and stood under the shower. For a long time I just stood there, enjoyed the pleasant warmth of the water, and reflected on the day. That hadn't exactly been a successful start. First there was sleeping in, then that redhead, and, who could forget, the picture-perfect crash landing in the first lecture. Everyone had stared at me. Every one of them. But only one interested me: Jared Calmburry!

What was it with him? So far, I'd never been that interested in boys but now I was astonished at myself. Why did he fascinate me so much? I felt a real urge to see him again. I tried recalling his perfect face, visualize his perfect traits—his indescribable blue eyes. How it would feel if he . . .

What the hell is wrong with me? I shouldn't think this way about Jared—after all, I didn't even know him. I vigorously shook my head to drive out these ridiculous thoughts. What was far more important: I had found friends. Sally and Felix even wanted to include me in their study group. At least something good had come from this strange day. The tension in my neck and shoulders relaxed as I rubbed my favorite, apple blossom–scented shampoo into my hair. When the water went cold, I turned it off, wrapped myself in a large towel and spun another around my dripping hair. Then I picked up my clothes, which I'd carelessly scattered around the room, turned up the heat and, after carefully brushing my long hair, which really was necessary, slipped a soft fleece blanket around my shoulders and sat down at the desk. I wanted to be better prepared for tomorrow.

First, I took the unusable schedule out of my bag and transferred it to another piece of paper. Then I pulled the campus map out and tried to memorize it—especially the paths to the buildings in which my lectures and seminars were held. When I'd had enough of that, I sorted the papers in my folder, which were still in disarray in my bag. When I'd finished with that, I pulled out my laptop and opened the university's homepage to inform myself a little about my professors. I started with Professor Irvin Martin, whose adventuresome life deeply impressed me, moved on to boring Professor Gallert, and then arrived at Karen Mayflower. My hands became clammy at the thought of her strange behavior. I clicked on the link to her CV. It chronologically described her impressive scientific training and career. It also listed several of her publications, works with titles such as *From the Knights of the Round Table to Modern Democracy: An Anthropological Perspective*; *Avalon: A Psychological Approach*; and *Excalibur: Symbols of Power* stood out among the litany of terribly dry-sounding book and article titles. I frowned. Apparently Professor Mayflower had a soft spot for early British mythology. I wouldn't have thought that about her.

Suddenly, there was an image in my mind. I saw her talking and gesturing at Jared. Jared Calmburry . . . There he was again, taking up all my thoughts. I inadvertently typed something on my keyboard and when my eyes returned to the screen, Google showed tens of thousands of hits for his name. I scanned the first few. Apart from the ubiquitous *Jared Calmburry is on Facebook* notices, I found the image of an ancient-looking family crest. But there was something else that drew my attention. Several newspaper reports with pictures of a burning plane wreck—judging from its size, it must have been a private jet—flitted across the screen. A horrible sight. How did Jared survive? It seemed impossible, judging from the pictures. But he did survive . . . and lost everything at the same time. A feeling I was all too familiar with. I was so terribly conscious of his loss that it felt like mine. I shared his fate. I felt his pain.

Something was opening that should have stayed closed. Images flooded in. A crushed car. The chalk outlines of two people on the road. Zara, who held my hand as we stood before two black coffins, who forced me to look into her eyes when I could no longer breathe—no longer find air. Me . . . alone in front of another coffin. Dark brown. White lilacs in my hand. *No!* I hit my right hand hard against my forehead. One, two, three times. I attempted to drive out the images. Four, five. I forced myself to breathe deeply, fill my lungs, and attempt to calm down. Breathe in. Breathe out. Breathe in. Breathe out.

I slipped these memories back into my little black box, carefully locked it and buried it deep inside. Deep. So deep that no one could find it. Least of all myself.

CHAPTER 4

The alarm clock went off at 6:00 a.m. Though I had fallen asleep early, I felt exhausted. I blamed it on the unfamiliar surroundings together with the events of the past months, which I still had a hard time dealing with. Still, I got up without pressing the snooze button, which was what I would normally do. Today I wanted to be safe and arrive too early for my first lecture rather than too late. I quickly went to the bathroom to get ready for the day. I brushed my teeth, washed my face, combed the tangles out of my long hair, and put it in a ponytail. Although I was much too early, I decided to go outside and look around the campus.

A wonderful morning. The sun was rising with a strong red-orange glow on the horizon and revealed a clear, cloudless sky still carrying a few final stars from the previous night.

The frost-covered branches of the many ancient trees, between which narrow footpaths wound, provided a sublime backdrop for the snow-covered buildings of the legendary university. A small, frozen duck pond on the banks of the Thames was behind the main building and completed the image. A winter landscape that could have come from a Grimms' fairy tale.

No one was out this early in the morning, and I enjoyed the quiet. *Zara would have liked it here.* The thought brought tears to my eyes. She wanted me to come here. Without her urging I would never have applied. She was convinced this was the right path for me.

At that moment, I missed her so much it hurt.

Suddenly, I heard rapidly approaching footsteps in the snow. A jogger. I turned around to see the dark-clothed runner coming in my direction along the footpath through the trees. He was only a few feet away and trotting in long, smooth strides. My breath stopped when I recognized his face. His eyes widened, as well. As if out of nowhere and without having felt a gust of wind or even a breeze, the snow whirled up a dozen feet all around me and robbed me of my sight. A second later, the white wall passed and the stirred-up snow gently settled back on the ground. Had I just imagined this? The runner slowed his pace until he stood in front of me. A moment later, as we stood opposite each other and looked into each other's eyes, Jared said, "Why are you crying?" He asked this with such empathy my legs almost gave way.

I answered as if in a trance. "I . . . I miss my sister." It was the truth. Plain and simple. But why was I so honest with a complete stranger? How did he have this effect on me?

At the sound of approaching steps in the background, I came to again. I blinked—the first time since we had been standing opposite each other—and saw four more runners coming toward us. They wore the same running clothes as Jared. He must be the fastest of them and had gotten ahead.

"I'm Jared," he said when he noticed the other runners. I felt paralyzed. "What's your name?" he asked, looking back and forth between me and the other joggers.

"E—Evelyn," I said.

He smiled tenderly, baring a row of perfect white teeth. Then he turned and joined the other runners as they caught up with us. One of the four—the one with the darkest hair—gave me a disapproving look as he passed. Two frowned and the fourth, a large guy with green eyes, smiled. I stood there like a complete idiot and stared after them. What the heck had just happened? Why didn't I have it together when Jared was around?

Motivational Psychology with Professor Warden started at eight. I had almost an hour till then. I decided to get a coffee at a small café near the main entrance. It was one of these old-fashioned breakfast cafés with dark wood paneling, not some generic chain. Luckily it was open. A few students and professors yawned in lined at the register. I ordered a coffee to go. When I was about to snap the white plastic lid on the rim of the thick paper cup, somebody patted me on the shoulder.

"Good morning," Felix said with a smile.

"Oh, good morning," I replied. I was happy to see him. Seeing him made me feel normal again and helped me sort my thoughts.

"You didn't sleep in today by the looks of it."

"No," I said, smiling, "not today."

Felix ordered a coffee. "Let's sit down." He pointed to a small round table at the back of the café. I nodded—after all, I still had forty minutes until my first lecture.

Felix did most of the talking, which was fine with me. He talked about his residence, about how it was impossible to get a wink of sleep there because of the constant parties. That's why he did most of his studying in the library. Then he talked about his family. He told me he grew up in one of the most disadvantaged sections of London and his mother took a second job just to send him and his younger brother to an expensive school. The two were supposed to make something more of themselves than their alcoholic dad. Next, he started talking about his brother, and as I noticed the direction the conversation was taking— one I was eager to avoid right now—I looked at my watch and told him it was time to get going. Felix, who was also taking Motivational Psychology, accompanied me to the lecture hall, talking the entire way.

It was pleasant just listening to him. Since I didn't want to stop his flow, I only contributed an occasional "ah" or "hmm" to the conversation.

He continued to chat undeterred after we arrived at the lecture hall, even when Professor Warden started to show the first slides. As much as I liked talking with Felix, I found it difficult to follow the lecture and concentrate on the slides the professor was projecting on the wall. Was it impolite to ask him to be quiet during the lecture? I was about to ask him whether it would be better to leave our conversation until later when from the row in front of us a redhead turned and hissed at him to shut his stupid mouth. I recognized that face right away. It was my special friend who had amused herself by sending me in the wrong direction.

Suddenly, I wasn't at all interested in following the class anymore but took a lively part in the conversation with Felix. I told him about my residence, described my room in detail, and explained what I liked about the building. Felix almost glowed with delight over the turn in conversation. Unlike the redhead, who repeatedly sent us angry glances.

"How long have you been friends with Sally?" I asked after enumerating the peculiarities and delights of Gothic architecture.

"Friends? I'm not sure I'd call us that. More like *frenemies*—half friend, half enemy. She always tries to outdo me. It turned into a regular competition during our first trimester over who gets better grades," he said and added with a smug grin, "usually I win."

When the lecture was over—I had to admit with embarrassment that I heard next to nothing and my notebook was empty—the redhead swung her horrendously expensive bag over her shoulder and would have hit my face if Felix hadn't blocked it at the last second.

"I told you at the start," he said a little louder than necessary, "they need getting used to." Again, we were rewarded with an angry look. I thanked him for intervening. She surely would have given me a black eye with her dumb bag.

The remainder of the morning was pretty quiet. Felix accompanied me to most of my classes and, when we went together to the dining hall, I discovered just as we were about to sit down that Sally was sitting with some people farther up front at the huge table. She waved at me with a laugh.

"Look, there's Sally. Let's sit with her," I said and lifted my tray. Felix showed little enthusiasm for sitting with the others but followed me, anyway. The three girls and two boys with whom Sally sat at the table were involved in an animated discussion about the British government's integration policy and only nodded a greeting at Felix and me as they continued their heated debate.

"Are you following Evelyn's every step now, or what?" Tact was really not Sally's strong suit.

"Oh, shut up," Felix said. I had to suppress a giggle.

"Should we meet on Thursday?" Sally asked me.

"Thursday?" I asked and tried to remember if I'd forgotten something.

"We always meet on Thursday to study. And since you're part of our study group now . . ." She shrugged.

"Of course. Where?"

"We meet alternatively at one of our places. It would work at my place. My mom has a late shift at the hospital, so we'll have a few hours of peace and quiet."

"Aren't you living in the dorms?" I asked.

"No, I grew up in Oxford and still live with my mom."

"Oh. Good, then we'll go to your place on Thursday. Do I need to bring anything other than my papers?"

"I would say lots of patience if you want to follow Felix's endless digressions," Sally said, nodding in his direction. She really didn't miss an opportunity when it came to provoking him.

"You mean *your* incessant digressions," he said, annoyed. Sally rolled her eyes and turned to me again. "Are you going to be in Personality Disorders later?"

"No, I'm taking Psychology of Emotions with Professor Ginsburgh. I've got Personality Disorders on Friday," I answered after checking my schedule.

"Well, Felix, then you'll have to make do with me during the next hour," she said. He raised his eyebrows and shot Sally a warning look.

"What?" she asked, being coy. "You're in the right place with Personality Disorders, my friend."

After exchanging phone numbers, I left and was rather happy to be able to fully concentrate on my course. I arrived at the building on schedule—thanks to my time spent studying the campus map the evening before—and climbed the stairs to the entrance. I was about to enter when I was suddenly left breathless. Right under the stone arch stood . . . Jared Calmburry, holding the heavy wooden door open for me. My mouth dropped open, and he had a breathtaking smile on his immaculate face.

"Move along!" an impatient voice grumbled behind me, and I was pushed by the cluster of people who had been lining up behind me. I hadn't noticed that I was blocking the entrance. I hurried past the amused Jared to get in, sat down in the first place available, and immediately looked around for him.

"Is this seat free?" My heart stopped. Suddenly, he stood next to me, pointing at the chair to my right, which I was using to rest my things.

"Oh . . . sure," I said and grabbed my coat and bag so he could sit down.

Pull yourself together and don't stutter like an idiot. He had caught me so off guard at the door that my hands were still trembling. I prayed he didn't notice.

"Please excuse me for running off so fast this morning," he said with a satiny voice and looked me in the eye. The indescribable deep blue beyond comparison.

"Are you a runner? I mean, do you run competitively?" *Oh man, couldn't you have thought up a better question?*

"Half-marathon and marathon," he said without turning his gaze from my eyes.

"Wow," I said, impressed. I admired anyone who could complete a half-marathon, let alone a full one.

"I run a little over six miles every morning with my teammates," he said.

"And you're the fastest one."

"Usually," he said without sounding like he was bragging. "What's with you?" he asked. "Do you run, too?"

I frowned. Me and running? That had always been torture for me in gym class. "No, running's never been my thing," I said, causing him to smile. "I'm more of a swimmer." I was forced to smile as I remembered how startled my dad was when I simply stripped off my water wings as a two-year-old and swam free. Those things were more of a hindrance than a help to me. I felt better in the water than on solid ground. The carefree feeling of lightness and the loving caress of the water on bare skin was . . . simply wonderful.

"Water is my element," I said and smiled at Jared. His eyes widened and he looked at me as if I had just slapped him.

"Did I . . . say something wrong?" I asked, confused.

As if he needed to concentrate, Jared shut his eyes and rubbed his forehead. Then he looked at me again. "No," he said and averted his eyes. At that very moment, Professor Ginsburgh entered the hall and started the lecture.

Jared made no attempt to converse and attentively followed the lecture. I glanced at him every few minutes and was completely unsettled by his sudden change of mood and had no idea how to behave. A few times I nearly talked to him but couldn't muster the courage. It's like he wasn't aware of me.

When Professor Ginsburgh finally ended the lecture after a torturous eternity, Jared suddenly rose and hurried out the door after a formal "Good-bye, Evelyn."

Good-bye, Evelyn? What was that?

I thought. We spoke of running. I said that I didn't like running but preferred to swim . . . Did he have some kind of problem with swimming? That was absurd. But something had bothered or even shocked him. It made no sense. What confused me most was that a small part of me—notwithstanding the many questions in my head—had enjoyed how it felt when he pronounced my name. Even if it was coupled with *good-bye*.

I was one of the last in the lecture hall to get up, and I walked lost in thought to the door. Just as I reached the bottom of the stairs and was about to go outside, I suddenly hit something hard with my foot. I stumbled and only caught my balance at the last moment.

"Hey, Blondie, are you trying to get with Jared?" a malicious voice asked behind me. Unbelievable—the redhead had actually tripped me. I was happy that I didn't give her the satisfaction of falling flat on my face. Then I became enraged.

"Did you just trip me?" I asked, drilling my eyes into her. Flanked by a friend, she was standing before me and looked at me with narrowed eyes. I wished I could hit her.

"Nobility shouldn't mingle with the plebs, don't you think?" Her voice dripped with superiority.

"What's your problem?" I said.

"You know . . . Christ Church used to be a good school, but since they started to let just anybody study here"—she made a dismissive hand motion—"the standards are declining quickly!"

"Evelyn, that's where you're hiding!" Sally said, preventing me from slapping the redhead. With Felix in tow, she hurried up to me.

"Madison, my dear, how are you today?" Sally asked with an overly sweet voice. "Aren't you supposed to be drowning kittens in the river?"

Felix stepped up beside me as if he had to protect me from Madison and her friend. Madison recognized that she had better move along, pulled her friend by the arm, and stomped off with a beet-red face.

"Hide and hair, shade in shade," said Sally as if reciting a poem, and Felix burst out laughing.

"What did that stupid cow want?" he asked when he'd settled down.

"She tripped me when I was going out the door."

"She did *what*?" Sally asked.

"Yes," I said, outraged. "Can you believe it?"

"Did you fall?" Felix asked, worried.

I rolled my eyes. Did he think I always fell? "No," I said, irritated.

"Did she say something to you?" Sally asked, ignoring Felix.

"Yes, along the lines of 'Nobility shouldn't mingle with the plebs.'"

"Nobility? Whom did she mean?"

"I'm not really sure," I said. "Probably Jared Calmburry."

"What do you have to do with Calmburry?" Felix asked. What gave him the right to speak to me in that tone?

"He sat down beside me during the lecture," I said.

"Why? Was there no other seat?" Sally asked.

I raised an eyebrow and looked at her.

"No, no, not what you think," she quickly explained and attempted to appease me. "I just mean . . . normally he only sits with his buddies. As I've already told you: they prefer to be among themselves. And as far as Madison's concerned—everybody knows she's had a crush on Calmburry forever and would do anything to get together with him. She's a real bitch to any girl who crosses her."

"What did Calmburry want from you?" Felix asked, a hint of reproach in the question.

"Nothing. What would he want?"

"What did you talk about?"

I felt like I was in a police interrogation. It was really none of Felix's business. I didn't answer and was grateful when Sally shut him up with "What's it to you, stalker?"

Since we all had Social Psychology as the last lecture of the day, Felix, Sally, and I went to the lecture hall together. I had no interest in chatting with the two of them—or rather, subjecting myself to a cross-examination—so I focused on the professor and took more notes than required.

When the lecture ended, I quickly left. I longed for a warm shower.

Back in my room, I stripped on the way into the bathroom, leaving a trail of clothing. As always, warm water immediately helped. I could finally think more clearly and relax my muscles. It was as if water supplied my cells with energy and vitality. I closed my eyes, opened my mouth, and let the water run over my face. I only turned it off when the temperature noticeably dropped, and then I got out and dried myself off. I pulled on some jogging pants and a T-shirt before gathering up the clothing I had carelessly dropped and putting it into an improvised laundry basket—one of my suitcases. Fortunately, there was a laundry room in the basement of the dorm so I didn't have to wander into town to look for a laundromat.

Since there was nothing better to do, I grabbed the laundry suitcase and headed for the basement. On my way, I passed two girls who were arguing loudly in the middle of the hallway. Going down the stairs, I almost bumped into the RA, who had shown me my room and explained the house rules. Obviously, the noise from the arguing girls had attracted him and he seemed determined to quiet them down. He reminded me of one of those whistle-blowing cops in old black-and-white movies.

There were three washing machines (one was being used) and a dryer. Detergent and fabric softener sat on a wobbly shelf that was poorly screwed into the wall above the machines. There was also a small cash box for laundry fees. I stuffed my clothes into one of the empty machines, added detergent and fabric softener, and started the load. Then I fished a few coins from my pocket and dropped them into the cash box.

After standing around for a while watching the washer spin, I noticed it was only a little after six o'clock—too early to go to bed. How was I going to spend the evening? I hadn't been to the library yet. And as far as I knew, it was open until ten. So I went upstairs where the pimply RA was still trying to keep the two girls from scratching each other's eyes out, carefully dried my hair so I wouldn't catch a cold, put on a good pair of pants, and was on my way.

It had become dark, and I was a little afraid despite the streetlights. I've been terribly fearful of the dark since my parents died. For a while after, Zara kept the light on at night because I wasn't able to fall asleep without it. It got better over time and at some point I no longer needed the night-light. But now, with Zara no longer there, it was almost as bad as back then—especially after seeing that strange guy. Could he really have followed me to Oxford?

I hurried along the snow-covered footpaths, looking around every few steps, and reached the Bodleian Library after a few minutes.

It was impressive. So huge and imposing that I didn't know where to start.

Countless ornaments decorated the vaulted, stucco ceiling. Several giant shelving units extended along the central aisle. They were filled with books that smelled of worn leather, faded parchment, and ink. I closed my eyes and inhaled the scent. Books always had such a wonderful smell. Everywhere in the world. There was always something familiar about that. Something constant. I took a moment to enjoy it.

"Good evening," an older, colorfully dressed woman with short gray hair greeted me at the information desk.

"Good evening," I said, somewhat surprised. I hadn't noticed her when I entered. "Would you please tell me where I can find the psychology section?"

She explained the route to me with the help of a laminated building plan glued to the dark wooden counter. Then she gave me a friendly smile and turned back to her magazine. I thanked her and, passing the wide, dark-brown reading tables at which a few students were seated, I headed in the direction she had indicated.

I passed giant shelves with scientific literature. Some books were rather new and others had heavy, worn bindings that showed they'd passed through many hands. I've always had a weakness for older books like these. Their smell, their feel, everything about them was somehow magical.

While I walked through these aisles, one section in particular caught my eye. It was marked with a large *FE* and held only ancient, leather-bound books. Each seemed to have its own story. I couldn't resist running my finger over their worn spines as if trying to become part of their history.

Ow!

I shrank back from the book I had just touched as though I'd received an electrical shock. I hesitated. What was that? Astonished and curious, I pulled the book from the shelf and took a closer look. It was very old and seemed to have been restored several times. A barely visible embossed pattern had nearly been worn flat on the front cover. I ran my fingertips over it and traced the delicate lines. I recognized a sword crossing a staff at the center. Above it, a stylized sun, moon, and stars were shown in a circle. This symbol seemed familiar. I was almost certain I'd seen it somewhere. Now my curiosity was really piqued.

I carefully opened the book and started deciphering the faded writing. It took considerable effort to decode the medieval letters. After a few pages, I had decided to put the book back on the shelf when a word in the middle of a sentence caught my eye—*Calmburry.*

I felt hot. I shut the book and looked at the embossed design on the leather cover. *Of course!* Why didn't I think of this right away? It was a crest. The family crest of the Calmburrys. I'd come across it on the Internet when I googled Jared's name.

My hands were moist. Suddenly, it felt as if I were doing something forbidden. I didn't want to be caught with this book in my hands so I warily looked over my shoulder to make sure I wasn't being watched. No one was in sight. I could hear the librarian at the information desk turning a page in her magazine. I cautiously reopened the book, took a deep breath, and started reading again.

The Calmburry family tree extended far back into the Middle Ages. As far as I could tell, there was talk of a Kenneth Calmburry, who lived around AD 500 and had lands in the northwest of Wales that extended all the way from modern Liverpool deep into Snowdonia National Park.

He and his wife Eowyn had eleven children, but only eight made it through their first year of life. Two more children died during a major famine that hit the entire region hard. The four remaining sons, Mael, Byron, Kelby, and Myrddin, as well as the firstborn, Imogen, and the youngest, Moyra, during whose birth Eowyn died, were to divide the lands of their father after his death. But an intense dispute broke out between them over their inheritance. Envy, greed, and distrust drove a wedge between the siblings, and two factions formed. The three older ones, Imogen, Mael, and Byron, fought hard over the inheritance while the younger ones, Kelby, Myrddin, and young Moyra, refused their share for the sake of peace. Many years of arguing passed, during which the land was not cultivated and it became unusable.

When the siblings finally came together in their father's house to definitively divide up his possessions, a terrible accident happened. At night, Imogen's youngest son snuck into the stables to look after the horses. By accident, he set the animals' hay on fire. Mael, Byron, and Imogen all died with their families in the fire.

After a period of mourning for the lost siblings, the younger ones divided their beloved father's land evenly among themselves and cultivated it. Soon more people settled there and built small villages, where they raised crops and bred animals for the market. The three siblings were pleased with their work and were proud to have preserved their father's memory. Kelby, who owned the northern part of the lands, married a stunningly beautiful woman whom he dearly loved and was always faithful to, though she gave him no heirs. Moyra dedicated herself to faith and went into a nunnery in Ireland after Irish monks spread Christianity throughout Wales.

But Myrddin felt the call of the wider world. During his travels throughout Europe, he apprenticed with many healers and masters. In every country he visited, he took a wife and each bore him a healthy heir. Some years later he finally returned to England and . . . ding-dang-dong echoed through the library halls. I was so startled that the heavy book fell from my hands, hitting the floor with a loud thud.

"The library will close in a few minutes," the voice of the woman at the information desk sounded over the loudspeakers. Impossible! That couldn't be right. I pulled my phone from my bag.

Indeed, it was almost ten. How long had I been reading? It must have been more than three hours. I quickly collected my belongings and picked up the book. I was torn. Should I put it back on the shelf and return the next day or should I check it out and, as a consequence, reveal my interest in the family history of the Calmburrys—if that's what this was? For a moment, I hesitated and bit my lower lip.

I couldn't help myself—I grabbed the book and calmly walked to the information desk, though I would rather have run.

"Hello," I said to the librarian behind the counter. "I would like to check this one out." I shyly pushed the book over to her.

She raised her eyebrows, took her red, sparkly glasses that were dangling from her neck by a cord, and put them on. She was probably suffering from severe age-related farsightedness because she had to hold the book as far away as her arms would allow. How did she manage to read her magazine?

"Oh," she said, surprised, and looked at me. "I'm sorry, but this book is noncirculating. To be precise, it's not even supposed to be removed from the FE section. I must ask you to return it." She pushed the book back across the counter.

"Oh . . . okay," I said and reached for the book.

The old woman probed me with her eyes. "You know what? I'll return it for you," she said after a short pause and grabbed the book so suddenly I had no time to react. She was probably afraid I would steal it.

"Have a pleasant evening."

"Yes . . . you, too," I said and looked one more time into her eyes before turning and heading for the exit. There was nothing to do about the book but come back tomorrow.

While walking the streets back to my dorm, I was angry at having revealed my interest in the book and not having been able to check it out despite that. Madness! The hours I had spent in the library seemed like minutes. The history of the Calmburrys had enraptured me so much I had become completely immersed. As soon as classes were over tomorrow, I would return to the library to continue reading. I could hardly wait.

That night I dreamt of Eowyn. Her long black hair gently flowed in the breeze, and the gleaming white dress in which she was wrapped rippled in smooth waves around her perfect body. A wonderful glow enveloped her entire figure in light. She stood there, otherworldly and beautiful, looking at her youngest son, Myrddin. He kneeled at her feet and looked up to his angelic mother, full of awe and love. With a hint of a smile, Eowyn leaned forward and tenderly kissed him on the forehead. As her lips touched his skin, part of her golden radiance passed to him.

CHAPTER 5

I awoke the next morning thinking of the book. I could hardly wait to find out more of Myrddin's story. But first I had to get through the day. I quickly brushed my teeth, washed my face, and dressed. As I made my way to the lecture hall for Psychology of Memory, I saw Felix waving in the distance. Though I still resented the tone he'd used with me yesterday, I didn't let it show.

"Hey, there you are," he said. "You were gone so quickly yesterday I didn't get a chance to say good-bye."

"Well, I was really tired," I lied. Maybe I should forgive his behavior—after all, he'd only wanted to help.

"Hmm, when I started school here, I was pretty beat for a while. But that passes," he said, smiling.

"I would hope so." I smiled back.

"Do you have plans for the afternoon?" Felix asked.

"Well, I'm planning to go to the library, so . . ."

"Oh good, I'll come with you. I can show you around a little." I wasn't expecting that. Nothing against Felix, but I wanted to go there by myself to read in peace.

"That's nice of you, but you don't need to come with me. Surely, you have better things to do than spend the afternoon in the library."

"No problem, it's my pleasure." Apparently, not even a sledgehammer-like hint could discourage him. I sighed.

"Shall we?" he asked and held the door open for me. I forced myself to smile and entered the lecture hall. Felix sat beside me as soon as I was seated, and just like the day before, he appeared more interested in me than in the professor. But today I wanted to pay attention. And since Madison wasn't nearby and I had no reason to talk to Felix during the lecture, I asked him to save our talk till lunch. I'd barely closed my mouth when I heard giggling behind me. Someone seemed amused that I had silenced Felix. Curious, I turned around and saw an amused-looking young man with moss-green eyes. He gave me a friendly wink, which earned him a forceful kick under the seat from his ill-tempered neighbor. They both looked familiar.

But why?

Suddenly I remembered them. I'd seen them running. With Jared. I remembered that the one with the green eyes smiled while passing. And the other, the dark-haired one, looked at me as if I'd just run over his dog.

"Do you know those two?" Felix asked.

"No," I said and concentrated on the professor before Felix was tempted to continue. I spent the next hour silent out of necessity, eyes directed to the front. My thoughts wandered, although I was determined to concentrate. The book wouldn't let me go. Was this really Jared Calmburry's family chronicle? I just couldn't get *him* out of my head.

At noon, I found Felix beaming as he waited for me outside the dining hall.

"You really are turning into a stalker," Sally said after we joined her in the cafeteria line.

"Very funny," Felix said.

"How can you stand having this nuisance clinging to you like a burr all day?" she asked me with feigned horror. Sally really didn't miss a chance to annoy Felix.

I shrugged. "I'm tough," I joked. Both Sally and Felix laughed. Since I was not particularly hungry, I just took a bowl of fruit salad and poked at it while listening to Sally's report on her morning misadventure involving tripping over her cat, a flying bowl of muesli, and a flokati rug, which she would probably have to throw out.

Before we separated, Felix proposed meeting at the library after the next lecture. If I was going to have a few minutes to myself with the Calmburry book, I needed to use this opportunity: I'd skip my class and go then. Although I had terrible pangs of guilt—after all, I was at the very beginning of the trimester, and I didn't want to make skipping classes a habit—curiosity won. A few moments later, I was in the library, where a middle-aged, stout brunette greeted me at the information desk. I returned her greeting and made a beeline for the FE section. I stepped up to the shelf where I had found the Calmburry chronicle the night before and reached up to pull out the book when I noticed it wasn't there. I looked at the other books on the shelf. It wasn't among them. Where could it be? Then I remembered: the gray-haired librarian had wanted to return it.

She may have forgotten. I returned to the counter.

"Hi," I said, suppressing my agitation. "I'm looking for a book. It's not in its place. Maybe you can help."

The woman smiled. "Which book are you looking for?"

"It's from the FE section," I said. "I wanted to borrow it yesterday— I didn't know that books in the FE section are noncirculating—so your colleague said she'd return it. But it's not there, so I thought perhaps she forgot to return it." *Great, you sound like a nut!*

"I'll take a look," the woman said and disappeared into her little office. I tapped my fingers on the counter while I waited. She returned shortly without the book.

"Sorry, there's nothing there. Maybe you can show me where you found the book."

The librarian accompanied me to the FE section, and I showed her the gap where the Calmburry book used to be.

"Oh," she said, "I'll have to report that. The books in the FE section are very old and very rare first editions and are incredibly valuable!" Then she went back to make a phone call.

I feverishly began searching the neighboring shelves and even the floor. Someone may have put the book on the wrong shelf—at least I was hoping for that. I searched one shelf after another as if possessed, almost completely forgetting my surroundings. Suddenly, I bumped so forcefully into something that I fell and landed on my hands and knees. I got up as fast as possible and rubbed my arm, which had absorbed most of the impact.

"Easy, little one!" Beaming green eyes looked at me with concern. "Everything all right?"

Oh no! I had bumped into Jared's teammate who was sitting behind me this morning.

"I'm Colin," he said with a smile and extended his hand. I hadn't noticed in the lecture hall how tall and muscular he was. No wonder I felt as though I'd run into a tree.

"Evelyn," I said, shaking his hand.

"I know." His roguish smile broadened.

"And how would you know that?" I asked.

Colin cocked his head to the side. "When a girl who looks like you comes to this university"—he made a hand motion that took me in with a sweep—"the news spreads fast. Especially, if she causes so much . . . excitement on the first day." He could only mean my crash landing in the lecture hall. Had everyone heard about it?

"Oh," was all I was able to say. Colin, who apparently thought my reaction was hilarious, laughed out loud and earned himself an admonishing look from the librarian. She emphatically pointed to a sign that said "Absolute Silence."

"Oh," he said and giggled. "I'd rather not get into trouble with her. We should be quieter."

"You mean you should be quieter," I replied, smiling. Colin seemed to be a really nice guy.

"Were you looking for something?" he asked. "You looked so helpless."

"Yes, I saw a book yesterday that . . . well . . . I really liked it and now it's gone."

"Maybe someone borrowed it," he said.

"I doubt it. When I tried to check it out yesterday, I was told it's noncirculating and shouldn't be removed from the FE section."

"It was a book from the FE section?" he asked with sudden interest. "Which one?" He looked at me very seriously. All of a sudden, I was not so sure whether I should tell him.

"One . . . with a pattern on the binding," I said.

"A pattern? What did it look like?" he followed up excitedly and ran his hand through his short blond hair.

"Why are you so interested?" I asked.

Colin smiled. "I'm on your side, little one. You can trust me."

"On my side? I didn't know I had a side. What are you talking about?" He looked deep into my eyes. This guy meant what he said—whatever it was.

"So what does the pattern look like?" he asked again. But with a softer voice.

"It was a kind of . . . crest. With a sword in the middle crossed by a staff . . ."

"And above it the sphere of the firmament." He completed my sentence in a calm voice.

"Y—Yes." I looked at him in disbelief.

"You know," he said, looking into my eyes, "maybe you should pay Professor Mayflower a visit." Then he turned and left.

"Wait, what do you mean?" I said a moment later, but Colin had already turned the corner.

"Oh, that's where you are! I thought we were going to meet outside," Felix said. It took me a moment to make him out between the ceiling-high bookshelves. He walked toward me with a somewhat frustrated look.

"Oh hi. Sorry, it was so cold outside I came in," I lied.

"So, would you like a guided tour?"

"Yes, please."

While Felix escorted me through the huge library, Colin's words went through my head. *I am on your side.* What did he mean by that? And why should I *pay Professor Mayflower a visit?*

"That's it, I think," Felix said, ending the tour about a half hour later.

"Thank you, that was really nice of you," I said, and Felix smiled in return. He looked at me seriously for a moment.

"Do you feel like getting a drink with me tonight? It's always pretty nice at Berry's on Wednesdays. They have happy hour until nine."

Was he asking me out on a date?

"Sure. Why not?" I said. After all, I hadn't made any plans and I'd done my laundry the night before. And Felix was such a nice guy, too. But right off the bat a real date? Thinking about it, maybe it wasn't such a good idea . . .

"Should we ask Sally, as well? It'll probably be more fun with more people, don't you think?"

"Yes," he said, somewhat discouraged. "Sure, we can ask her." Felix's words did not match his expression.

"Cool, I'll give her a call."

Berry's was a rather old pub with wooden floors and dark siding. It smelled of sweat and beer the moment the door swung open. There were several pool tables and dartboards in the back around which young people—presumably all students—had clustered. The room was so full that people even settled in on the hard stools by the bar and put their heads together to be heard over the loud music. Sally spied a table that was opening up. She frantically grabbed my hand and pulled me behind her while pushing through the crowd.

"Perfect," she said as we sat down. "We've got the best view of the pool tables from here." She gave me a wink.

"What do you want to drink, girls?" Felix asked.

"Guinness," Sally said cheerfully.

"I'll have a ginger ale, please."

"Coming up," Felix said, then he turned and made his way to the bar.

Sally leaned forward. "The hot guys always meet here on Wednesdays to play pool." She laughed. Then she turned back to the pool tables, set her elbows on the table, and rested her chin on her hands.

"That guy at the front." She extended her chin to show me where to look. "The big, dark-blond one with the green eyes—can you see him? I'd let him do a few things to me . . ." Her tone was so unmistakable that she might as well have drawn a diagram. I asked myself how much experience she had with guys. Judging from her *if you know what I mean* look, she had more experience than me. But that wouldn't take much. I had almost no experience in this department. Suddenly, I spotted the guy Sally was talking about.

"Colin," I blurted out, surprised.

She turned to me in a flash. "You know him?" She looked stunned.

"Yes. I met him in the library."

"You've got to introduce me to him," she said and clawed my blouse in feigned desperation, pulling me so close that our noses almost touched. "Pu-lease!"

"One Guinness and one ginger ale." Felix placed the drinks on the table. "Everything okay with you two?" he asked.

Sally let go of my blouse. "Yes," she said and rolled her eyes. "Sit down and keep still!" Then she looked at me again. "Come on, aren't you going to introduce me?"

"I don't really know him. I only know his name and that's about it."

"Who are you talking about?" Felix asked.

"Colin, shhh!" Sally said. Then she turned to me again. "Do you know his last name?"

"No, sorry," I said and suppressed a laugh.

"Sullivan," Felix said as he recognized Colin.

Sally repeated the name *Colin Sullivan* in a dreamy way. "Do you know him?" she asked Felix.

"I've seen him around." It was clear he wasn't enthusiastic about the direction our conversation was going.

"What about Professor Martin?" I asked Sally. "Won't he be jealous?" I couldn't suppress a grin anymore, and Felix obviously liked the way I was teasing her about her obsession with the good-looking professor.

"Oh be quiet, you two," Sally said. The twitch at the corner of her mouth gave away that she was trying hard not to laugh. Still grinning, I tried again to find Colin among the pool players. What harm could it do to introduce them? Even if I didn't know more than his name. But! I *did* know something about him: he was a friend of Jared's. They ran together every morning. At least, that's what he told me.

Then I saw Colin. His back was turned to us while he sipped his beer. It looked as if he was giving advice to another player, whom he half blocked from sight, on how to sink the last two striped balls in opposite corners to win the game. The friend told Colin to be quiet, then shot with lightning speed and sank the first ball in the front right corner and the second ball in the back left. Colin cheered and high-fived his partner. A wad of cash changed hands. Colin smiled and pocketed the cash as his buddy stepped into the light to receive his half. Could it be . . . ? *Jared!* As if I had said his name out loud, he immediately turned in my direction and stared intensely at me. The light flickered and shone noticeably brighter than before. Then, just like that, it was pitch-black in the pub and the music stopped. Girls screamed and a few guys complained. Someone shouted, "Lights! Did you pay the electricity bill?" Then the lights came back on again.

"Just a fuse, no need to panic," the bartender said from behind the bar.

It took me a moment to collect myself and search the room for Jared. He was nowhere to be seen. Only Colin was standing where I expected Jared to be. Had Jared actually been here? It had all happened so quickly. No! I was sure I saw him. That wasn't just my imagination—or was it?

"Hello, Earth to Evelyn . . ." Sally leaned halfway over the table, waving her hand in front of my face.

"Sorry, what did you say?" I asked, shaking my head.

For a second, she looked as if she doubted my sanity. "Well? Are you going to introduce me to him or not?" She nodded in Colin's direction. "Come on, he's looking at us."

I lifted my head, and my eyes met Colin's. The expression on his face was . . . friendly. Just friendly. After what had just happened, I would have expected something else.

Colin's words echoed in my head: *I'm on your side, little one. You can trust me.* Trust him? Even though I didn't know what was behind that, I sensed it was true.

"All right." I got up and pulled Sally by the arm. "I'll introduce you."

"How do I look?" she asked as we walked toward the pool tables, and she quickly ran her fingers through her hair.

"Ravishing. As always," I said, rolling my eyes.

Colin sipped his beer without taking his eyes off us.

"How's your arm?" he asked when Sally and I came within earshot. I rubbed my right shoulder, which had suffered the brunt of the impact.

"Still hurts a little," I said, "but it'll get better."

Sally threw me a questioning glance, and Colin took a step toward her and held out his hand. "Hi, I'm Colin," he said.

"Oh yes." I remembered my mission. "Colin, this is my friend Sally. Sally, this is Colin."

"Hi," she said a few moments later.

"Hi," he said with a broad grin.

"Do you want anything else to drink?" Felix was suddenly standing next to me and held my ginger ale under my nose. "Happy hour is over soon."

"No, thank you." I took the glass from his hand and sipped from it. Colin and Sally didn't look as if they needed company. So I took Felix by the arm and pulled him back to our table.

"I think it's better if we give those two some space," I said and cast a glance at Colin and Sally, who seemed to be getting along really well.

"Hmm. Then again, I don't mind having a break from Sally," he said, rolling his eyes. "She can really get on my nerves." I couldn't resist laughing. The way Sally treated Felix, provoking him every chance she got, I could understand why he felt that way.

"So, tell me a little about yourself. We've only talked about me the last few days. I know almost nothing about you." He looked at me full of expectation.

Oh no! Did we have to go there? What should I tell him? *My whole family is dead, and I'm here at Oxford because I want to make my sister in Heaven proud of me?*

I decided to start with something harmless. "I'm from Fleetwood, north of Liverpool." *Lame!* Sounded like a geography lesson. I had to add something personal. "I grew up and went to school there." *Still lame!*

"Fleetwood, hmm?" he said. "And . . . is there someone you left behind there? Someone . . . *special?*"

I almost had an attack of hysterical laughter. Did I leave someone behind? I was the one left behind!

"I mean, is someone waiting for you there?"

"No." I couldn't suppress the bitterness in my voice. "No one is waiting for me in Fleetwood." *Absolutely no one!*

Felix seemed relieved by my answer. He looked at me with a big smile. Had he not heard the sadness in my voice? Or had I become that good at hiding my feelings?

Felix, in any case, seemed to be gaining speed. "Tell me something about your family. Do you have any siblings?"

No, not that question! Not that damned question!

"I . . ." I felt the sadness rise in me but suppressed it. "My . . ." I swallowed hard. I squeezed out: "My parents died when I was little." I held my breath.

Felix looked at me with empathy. "I'm so sorry to hear that, I didn't know." *How would he know?*

He tenderly put his hand on mine. "You don't have to talk about it if you don't want to." I felt his eyes on me while I stared at his hand, which had closed around mine.

"What graveyard mood do we have here?" Sally! "I barely leave you alone with Felix and you get all depressed." She cocked her head and gave me an encouraging smile. "Would you like to play a round of pool?" My eyes flitted to Colin, who was leaning against the pool table. I had played two or three times a few years ago and found it fun. Anyway, just about anything would be better right now than Felix's pity or my crying in front of all these people.

I shrugged. "Why not?"

Sally clapped for joy and pulled me to the pool table.

"What's the matter? Aren't you coming?" she called over her shoulder. I hadn't noticed that Felix was still sitting at our table. He casually rose and followed us. I had the impression that he wasn't happy with the idea of playing a round of pool with us. Colin put his hand out to Felix and introduced himself. Felix mumbled his name and reluctantly shook hands.

"Guys against gals or mixed?" Colin asked.

"Mixed," Sally said. "How about the two of us?" she asked, batting her eyes at Colin.

"Sounds good," he said. "Evelyn and Felix can start."

Since I wanted to watch first, I let Felix break. He sank two of the striped balls into the corners.

"Evelyn and Felix get stripes, we get solids," Colin said. Since we were alternating, Sally was next. She awkwardly set up the cue, shot, and almost slashed the green cloth with her clumsy attempt and didn't even come close to hitting a ball. She looked apologetically at Colin, who winked at her and said, "It happens." She had completely succumbed to his charm.

My turn was next. I carefully aligned my cue, struck the white ball, and managed to hit one of the striped balls into the front right corner. But my second shot was a failure.

"Not bad," said Colin, which earned him an angry look from Felix. I didn't think those two would become friends anytime soon. Now Colin skillfully worked the cue on the table and struck as fast as an attacking cobra. Two balls disappeared into corner pockets.

"Wow, that's fabulous!" Sally said.

"You think?" he replied. "Then you should see Jared. I've never beaten him." He shook his head with wounded pride.

"Jared *Calmburry*?" Sally followed up. "Is he a friend of yours?"

"Yes and yes," he said and looked at me. "The best I've ever had."

"You're friends with that arrogant bastard?" Felix said, only to receive a glare from Colin, who looked like he wanted to rip Felix's head off.

"Oh, you know him?" Colin asked in a challenging tone.

"I know enough guys like him," Felix said with narrowed eyes. "Throws around cash as if he's damned Bill Gates." He snorted with contempt.

"You know *no one* like him." Colin took a step toward Felix. "And you'd better watch your mouth, my friend!"

"I'm not your damned friend!" Now Felix took a step toward Colin, firmly gripping the cue. I was sure he'd use it as a weapon if he felt forced to do so.

"You don't say!" Colin took another step.

"Okay, that's enough," I said with a firm voice and stepped between the two snarling dogs. "Maybe we'll have the game some other time." I turned to Sally. "Come on, let's go home, it's been a long day. Felix, will you walk with us?" Colin and Felix glared at each other, then Colin calmly turned his head and held his hand out to Sally.

"It's been a pleasure meeting you, Sally." He flashed his breathtaking smile. "I hope we see each other again soon." She turned red. Then he turned to me and also gave me his hand. "I'm delighted to have run into you again, Evelyn." He leaned in close to me. Felix stiffened. "Please don't let anyone try to convince you of anything. Form your own opinions of people." He leaned even closer and whispered, "You won't regret it." He winked at me, glared again at Felix, then turned and left.

Won't regret it? The line echoed in my head as Felix and I went through the dimly lit streets back to my dorm after we had dropped Sally at her door. I had felt as if I was in a guessing game since arriving at Oxford. It was obvious Colin was saying I should form my own opinion of Jared. But it was a mystery why I would *not regret it*. For that I would have to get to know him first, but after my last encounter in the lecture hall and him vanishing without a trace from the pub—provided that really was him, because I was not 100 percent sure—it appeared as if he didn't want to know me. So it wasn't my decision. It was really up to Jared whether I could form an opinion of him.

Felix hugged me outside the heavy door to my dorm, kissed my cheek, and gently brushed my hair, which was a little too touchy-feely for my taste.

"I'm sorry about what happened to your parents. Don't worry too much, or it'll pull you down," he quietly said and headed for home.

CHAPTER 6

When my alarm rang, I fumbled for it on the nightstand without opening my eyes. As soon as I was able to lay a hand on that nerve-killing thing, I pressed the snooze button and pulled the covers over my head. Five minutes later, my tormentor rang again, and I got up grumbling and trotted into the bathroom to get ready for the day.

I'd adjusted well to Oxford over the past few weeks. I got into such a good routine that one would believe I'd been here for years—but it hadn't even been two months. It was only six weeks, to be precise. Six weeks that, when I thought about them, had mostly brought good things.

The great friendship that had developed between Sally, Felix, and me was particularly delightful. We had lunch together most days and usually sat together when we had the same classes. And then there was our weekly study group. So far, we'd mostly met at Sally's because she had the most space in her place, and her mother, Pamela, usually worked at the hospital on Thursdays.

It was also good that I was able to keep up well with my course work despite missing the first trimester, and I had no real difficulties understanding the subject matter in any of my classes—except for statistics, of course.

The negative . . . Well, you probably couldn't call being ignored by someone you don't actually know negative. But the really bad part was that being ignored by a stranger meant so much to me. I couldn't stop thinking about him even though he didn't seem to notice me anymore. Worse yet, the less attention he paid me, the more my interest in Jared Calmburry grew.

After his sudden disappearance from Berry's, I intended to confront him about why he'd reacted so strangely in the lecture hall and avoided me ever since. But that turned out to be more difficult than I anticipated. Felix had prepared me for Jared always being surrounded by his group, but that was an understatement—they were outright shields for him. It almost appeared as if the guys he surrounded himself with were not his friends but his bodyguards. Whenever I attempted to talk to him, someone just happened to block my way and Jared was gone. I realized pretty soon that there was just no getting to him. To top it all off, Jared never even dignified me with a single look when we met by accident—whether in town, in a lecture, or in the dining hall. In the end, I lost heart and gave up on him. I was forced to accept the fact that I was invisible to Jared. Although I didn't appear to exist to him, it didn't stop me from casting furtive glances at him at every opportunity.

I couldn't help it. I even went so far as to sit a few rows behind him just so I could watch him unobserved. I attentively followed each of his hand movements and tirelessly attempted to read his thoughts from his facial expressions. I'd become really good at tuning out ambient noise when Jared spoke so I could hear his voice. One among hundreds.

The force of attraction he exercised over me, despite his apparent disinterest, was almost magical. And that was definitely not good for me.

"Study group—six o'clock at my place," Felix said as I made my way to Somatic Psychology that Thursday after lunch. I hoped Sally would hold back with her needling so we could really use the time for studying. When she picked me up at my dorm, as agreed, we walked through streets slippery from the gradually melting snow. Dusk settled. Since my already-crappy sense of direction abandoned me completely in the dark, it took my full concentration to memorize the way. We heard music at the end of the street, which appeared to come from a large building ahead of us. Sally groaned. Hadn't Felix talked about the constant parties at his place?

Sally shut her eyes. "This can't be happening! Felix said there wouldn't be a party tonight!"

We entered the lighted entrance area, where Felix met us with a conciliatory gesture.

"No party tonight, right?" Sally said.

"Sorry," Felix said, visibly embarrassed. "But come in."

Head slumped, he led us up the stairs to his room.

"I knew that nothing was going to happen on my floor today, but I never thought about the ground floor." He raised his hands. "Sorry!"

"I think we'll manage," I said. Sally gave me an angry look. "It's not *that* loud." And it really wasn't. You could hear the bass but the guests were pretty quiet. At least so far.

"Let's get started before they start in on the piñata!" Sally said sarcastically and started to dig her papers out of her bag. Felix gave a guilty nod.

As I looked around, I noticed his room was slightly larger than mine. Apart from a bed and nightstand, he had a cabinet and a dresser, just as I did. But Felix also had a set of chairs he had placed by a large bay window. The room appeared tidy except for a dried-out plant beside his bed, which had obviously seen better days. But there was something missing.

"Don't you have a bathroom?" I asked.

"Shared bathrooms," Felix said. In that case, *my* room was clearly preferable.

Sally urged, "Let's get started," and sat down on one of the two chairs at the table. "What should we do first?" she asked and motioned for me to take the chair next to her.

"Stats, if you two don't mind," I said as Felix pulled over his desk chair with a scraping noise and sat down with us. "I want to go over probability calculations again."

"No sweat," Felix said and looked over my folder with interest. "So . . . probability calculation attributes to each event a probability of its occurrence . . ." He spent the next two hours turning me into a stats ace.

"That's enough," Sally said shortly after eight and shut her folder. "I feel like my head is about to explode," she added and rubbed her temples. I had to agree with her. Grateful and exhausted, I collected my things and stashed them in my bag.

"What do you think, girls?" Felix asked while dragging the chair back to the desk. "Since there's a party here, we might as well join in, right?" He shrugged. "Do you feel like it?"

"I'm pretty tired," I said, yawning and stretching my arms.

Sally appeared determined not to miss the fun. "Come on." She pulled me up by my arm. "One drink."

I was pretty beat, but I didn't want to be a stick-in-the-mud, either. "Oh fine," I said, giving in. "But just one."

"You can leave your things here," Felix said and started toward the door. I followed them downstairs.

At the bottom of the staircase, a couple was busy kissing and had settled on a step, blocking our path. Since the lovebirds made no effort to allow us any room to walk past, Sally, Felix, and I were forced to step over them. On the ground floor, the party was in full swing. In the hallway and the rooms, whose doors were wide open, several people milled around drinking from plastic cups and beer bottles. Somebody had dimmed the lights with colorful scarves and silk cloths to create a great ambience. In one of the rooms, an oversized sound system had been set up. It was responsible for the bass reverberating throughout the building. Felix led Sally and me into a room in the middle of the hallway. A wobbly camping table held a beer keg and several bottles of cheap whiskey and Coke. As if it were the most natural thing, he flipped the tap and handed us plastic cups overflowing with foam.

"Cheers," he said, grinning as he raised his cup.

"Cheers," Sally and I said in sync and raised our cups. Sally appeared to be in her element and began swaying to the music.

"I'm going to make the rounds," she said a moment later and headed out the door.

"MacMillan, how are you? Long time no see!" a deep voice loudly called out behind me. A big strawberry-blond guy roughly pushed me aside and headed toward Felix. He shook Felix's hand while talking loudly. Then he pulled Felix close, hugged him, and patted him force-fully on the back.

"O'Malley, you Irish bog rat!" Felix said, grinning. "About time you showed yourself around here again."

I felt a bit uncomfortable between the two guys. So I decided to take off and look for Sally. "I'll have a look around," I shouted to Felix, who was so deeply involved in conversation with the strawberry-blond hulk that he didn't appear to hear me. In the hallway, I pushed through the laughing and dancing crowd to look for Sally. After a few minutes, I spotted her purple hair at the end of the long hallway. I laughed and shook my head when I saw her. How did she manage to find Colin among all these people in such a short time? Did she know he would be here? I took a step closer to see better. She was standing on her tiptoes to make up for their difference in height.

Although he had bent down toward Sally, he was still at least a head taller. While she was talking to him, animated and wildly gesticulating, beer spilled out of her cup onto her hand and then the floor. Colin seemed to be paying close attention to her and smiling all the time. Sally and I had talked several times about Colin, so I knew all too well how serious a crush she had on him. It was lovely that they had finally found each other.

Suddenly, a thought came to me while I was standing there watching the two of them: if Colin was at this party . . . was *he* here, too? It certainly wasn't improbable since I usually saw Jared and Colin together. An unfamiliar heat suddenly spread from my stomach. My hands were moist. If Jared really was here, should I try to talk to him? After all, we were at a party and everyone was a bit more relaxed than usual. Maybe he wouldn't avoid me this time. I started turning around, frantically looking for him. Why was just the thought of Jared making me so agitated? In the hope of calming down, I took two large sips of beer. It helped—but not much. *Calm down. He's probably not here and you're driving yourself crazy for nothing.*

A second later, I felt someone staring at me. I quickly turned around and looked straight into Madison's angry red face. Her hate-filled eyes were narrowed to slits. *What's her problem now?* She looked at me, then to the side. When I followed her glance, it was as if I'd been struck by lightning. *Jared!* He was coming through the crowd toward me. My heart skipped and sank to the bottom of my stomach.

Suddenly, I realized why Madison was so enraged. Only a few steps separated Jared and me. I just stood there with wide eyes as if rooted to the ground, my heart pounding in my throat, and my hands were so clammy that I could barely hold my cup. Then, he was in front of me and looked at me with his deep blue eyes. Hadn't I wanted to ask him something? I couldn't remember how to speak. If I were to open my mouth, I'd probably only babble.

"Hi," said Jared in a gentle voice. He looked deeply into my eyes.

"Hi . . . ," I said.

Instead of saying something else, he just stared at me. It felt as if he was looking into my soul. As if he knew all my secrets from a single glance. Everything I had ever done, thought, or felt. It was thrilling and frightening at the same time. I wished he would say something.

Anything to relax the situation a little. But Jared looked at me unperturbed. And despite the uncomfortable feeling he caused inside me, I could not turn away.

His intense, captivating look made me believe I would be lost in the depths of those blue eyes. Only my last ounce of reason kept me from throwing my arms around his neck and begging him to be with me forever.

"Are you happy, Evelyn?" The melodic sound of his voice caught me completely unprepared. I needed a moment to regain my balance. Couldn't he just say something *normal*? Something that didn't pull the rug out from underneath me? Something banal like everyone else says?

Was I happy? Why did he ask me that? Could I ever be happy after all that had happened in my life? Had I ever been happy?

"Are *you* happy?" It burst out of me before I'd even completed the thought.

"No," he said without looking away. "Can you be happy when what you desire most will bring you to your doom?" Unspeakable sadness resonated in his voice and caused me to shiver all over. Although I didn't have the slightest idea what Jared was talking about, I somehow felt . . . struck. As if his question had something to do with me.

"Probably not," I said. Jared narrowed his eyes in concentration. It was apparent that he was suffering. I didn't know why, but I suddenly had the urge to comfort him. Without thinking or even being aware of what I was doing, I extended my hand and took hold of his. It was firm and warm. An intense tingle pervaded my entire body from the tips of my toes to the ends of my hair and only allowed me to breathe in bursts. My heart lost its rhythm and hammered wildly in my chest. He stared at me with wide eyes. Jared obviously needed a moment to collect himself, just as I did. Then his look became clear. He narrowed his eyes again and furrowed his brow.

"I'm sorry," he said, withdrew his hand from mine, turned, and disappeared through the crowd.

A strange pain flashed through me as I looked after him. I would rather have run after him but I remained rooted to the ground. It had felt so incredible to hold his hand. Had he not felt it, too? Maybe it had been unpleasant for him?

"Don't make anything of it," Madison said. "You know he's only making a fool of you, don't you?" I heard her malicious comment as if through a thick pane of glass.

"Keep it to yourself, Madison. Just admit you're never going to be with Jared," Colin interjected.

"Yeah, why don't you beat it?" Sally said. She and Colin had positioned themselves beside me and stared at Madison until she stomped off. But not without turning back and casting me a last, derisive look.

"Evelyn, I have to apologize for Jared's behavior," Colin said. "He's under a very rotten influence, you know."

I looked at him with uncertainty.

"You shouldn't give up," he said and winked. "I've never seen him react to a touch like that, and I've known him almost my whole life."

"You were watching us?" I asked, horrified.

"Well, not exactly watching," said Sally, a little embarrassed. "Besides, almost everybody was looking."

What? Almost everybody in here saw how I took Jared's hand and how he rejected me?

"Because of the light," she explained apologetically. "At first, I thought a fire had broken out."

"Light?" I asked. I hadn't noticed any light.

"Yeah, a strange light where you were standing with Jared." She shook her head and shrugged. "No idea what it was. Probably just a faulty lightbulb or something. Didn't you see it?" she asked with disbelief.

"No, I didn't." I ran through the situation again in my mind. All I could remember were Jared's indigo-blue eyes and his unbelievably handsome face. But then I remembered what Colin just said.

"What do you mean, 'He's under a very rotten influence'?"

Colin bit his lip. "I really shouldn't talk about it." He looked at me and added, "I'm sorry."

"What did you talk with Calmburry about?" Sally asked.

I thought for a moment. "He asked if was happy," I said, knowing how stupid it must sound.

Sally looked at me with raised eyebrows. "What?" She had a confused look on her face.

"What did you answer?" Colin asked.

"Nothing," I said. "I asked him if *he* was happy."

Colin looked at me with interest. "And?"

"He says he isn't happy because what he desires most will bring him to his doom," I quoted Jared and felt incredibly silly for doing it. Sally confirmed my feeling by looking at me as if I had hit my head. But Colin only nodded. "What did he mean by that?" I asked.

"I can't tell you," Colin said. "But that's the rotten influence I was talking about. Someone has persuaded him that what he most desires will kill him."

"Kill?" I asked horrified. *Death* sounded rather different from doom.

"Sorry. I've already told you too much!" Colin said. But I was not yet willing to give up. There was something between Jared and me. I had felt it when I took his hand. He must have felt it, too. But why had he been avoiding me? Why had he disappeared each time?

"Has he . . . been *promised* to someone or something?" I was a little embarrassed because it sounded so cliché.

Colin laughed. "If only," he said. "No. He hasn't been promised to anyone."

Suddenly, I was roughly grabbed by the arm and pulled away from Colin and Sally.

"There you are," Felix said and squeezed my elbow tighter.

"Ow!" I blurted out and pulled my arm from his painful grip.

"Sorry, I didn't mean to hurt you," Felix said and looked at Colin. He didn't sound as if he was truly sorry. But I wanted to avoid the two of them starting up where they had left off at Berry's and asked Felix to show me around his residence. He hesitantly turned away from Colin to introduce me to some of his friends.

"I'm really tired, Felix," I told him a half hour later. "I think I better go home."

"Just stay a little bit longer," he said, but I was already looking for Sally to ask her if she'd go with me. When I found her, she was deep in conversation with Colin. They looked so happy that I didn't want to ruin their moment. So, as soon as I got rid of Felix, I ran up to his room, got my things, and headed home alone.

The farther I was from the residence, the sparser the street lighting became. I regretted my decision to go home alone after only a few steps. Although I told myself the darkness shouldn't bother me, I couldn't quite control my fear. On the contrary—it increased with every step I took deeper into the night. Even when I was little, I had always had the feeling that something was lying in wait for me in the dark. Watching me. Biding its time. Ready to pounce. *Damn!* What was I thinking? I could have slapped myself. What if that strange guy with the leather gloves were to appear out of nowhere?

Suddenly, I heard snapping twigs. I held my breath and felt a burst of adrenaline. On alert, I opened my eyes wide and picked up the pace. *What a stupid idea to walk through town alone at night.* I listened attentively to the darkness. Again I heard snapping. Was somebody there? Was somebody behind me? Beside me? More snapping. Now I was sure: there was somebody right behind me. I could sense it, almost feel their breath on the back of my neck. I had to get away. Right then. Whoever was following me, I knew deep inside me they had bad intentions. Someone roughly grabbed my shoulder and pulled me back. Panicked, I screamed. Pure adrenaline shot through my body again and burned in my blood vessels. I knew it was too late to run. Only one thing left to do: fight! I quickly turned around, ready to attack.

"I didn't frighten you, did I?" Madison said in her fake sweet tone. "I'm so sorry!" Her voice was drenched in scorn.

Okay. I breathed in and out a couple of times. *Calm down, it's only Madison, trying to scare you! Just Madison. Nothing more than a girl! Just Madison.*

"I'm warning you one last time," she said, her voice suddenly very serious. "Keep away from Jared or you'll regret it!" I stared at Madison with wide eyes. Her facial expression hardened.

"Can you see this?" she asked, pushing up her glittering gold bracelets to reveal a tattoo on the inside of her wrist. "Can you see this?" she repeated even angrier and held her wrist in front of my face. I shrank back after looking at it more closely. Even in the pale-blue moonlight, I could see the pattern made by the dark-blue lines on Madison's skin: a sword and a staff crossing in the center, below a blue circle with three symbols. *Damn!* It was the Calmburry crest. It looked exactly as I remembered it but without the curved and intricate edging that usually surrounds a crest. Without it, it looked more like a symbol or a seal but it was unmistakably tattooed into Madison's skin.

"What the—"

"Do you know what this is?" Madison asked, switching to her sweet voice. "That is the symbol of the bond Jared and I share," she said with conviction and angrily stared at me while waving her tattoo in front of my face. But now that I'd overcome the first shock, my heart wasn't pounding in my chest and I could think clearly again, and I started to feel enraged. What was this redheaded bitch thinking, ambushing me in the middle of the night and frightening me like this? She wasn't going to get away with it as easily as she did when she tripped me outside the lecture hall.

"Jared and I belong together! Is that clear?" Madison's voice now sounded strangely high-pitched as she recognized that I was no longer afraid of her. Instead I was on the verge of wringing her neck.

"Don't you think I should have a say in this, too?" *Jared?* Was that Jared? I turned around and there he was.

"J—Jared, I . . ." Madison stuttered. She hadn't counted on *him* being here.

"I've told you before," he calmly started. "Nothing will become of us—we will *never* belong together!" he continued, deliberately echoing Madison's words. "Leave Evelyn alone!"

"But I . . . ," Madison mumbled. "She has . . ." She looked helplessly back and forth between Jared and me.

"Go home!" Jared finished the argument and turned to me. His look was incredibly gentle. "May I accompany you to your dorm?" he asked. "Just to make sure no other crazy person attacks you," he added and cast a last angry look at Madison, who was about to leave. A silly nod was all I managed for an answer. Even in the darkness, the perfection of his gentle and distinguished facial features was captivating. All of a sudden, I remembered what it felt like to hold his hand. The tingling throughout my entire body. The warmth. The goose bumps. The eerie magnetism that emanated from him . . .

At that moment, I noticed that my hand, as if on its own, had risen to his, and I pulled it back at the very last second. My face grew hot, and I knew I had turned beet-red. I sincerely hoped the pale moonlight would mask the color. I only dared to look at him when my pulse was normal again. I was astonished to see that Jared was gasping for breath in the same way I was, and he looked at me with wide eyes. Then he blinked several times.

"Let's go," he said.

"Okay," I answered, eager to control my breathing and keep up with his long strides.

While we hurried through the dark streets, Jared and I didn't say a word to each other. Though I had to concentrate on keeping up with his pace while not slipping on the slushy street, all my thoughts circled around him and our previous encounters. Suddenly, Jared stopped. I looked up and saw we were standing right in front of the entrance to my dorm. How did he know where I lived? He hadn't asked me, and I hadn't told him.

"Good night, Evelyn," he said and turned.

"Jared!" I said a little too loud for fear that he might disappear without a trace again.

He stopped but didn't turn around.

"Jared, I . . ." *Damn, what did I want to say?* "Thank you." It was all I could think of at that moment. Not that I wouldn't have been able to deal with Madison on my own but I was still grateful to him.

"No problem," he said and walked away into the darkness.

CHAPTER 7

"BEEP, BEEP, BEEP, BEEP," my alarm cried to end my short, almost sleepless night. I pressed the snooze button and rubbed my swollen eyes so I could open them at least a little to see how late it was. Just how many nights was I going to cry through?

After Jared simply left me at the door, a sheer unbearable desperation had overcome me. A strange, cruel longing—one I could not put a name to—possessed me, rendering me unable to think clearly. All I knew was that it had something to do with Jared—that I felt this longing for him. Again, tears welled up in my eyes. *Pull yourself together, you damned crybaby!* I felt bitter and got out of bed.

After showering and dressing, I tried to reduce the swelling of my cried-out eyes with cold water, with only moderate success. I gave up a few minutes later and left the building with swollen eyes. Just as I was out the door, the phone vibrated in my pocket. I pulled it out and looked at the display.

"Hi, Sally," I said in a hoarse voice.

"Evelyn!" she said angrily. "Where the hell did you disappear to yesterday? All of a sudden you were gone, and Felix said you wanted to go home with me. I was worried!" That was a lot of accusations all at once for a Friday morning.

"I was tired and went home," I explained.

"Alone? Why didn't you ask me? I would have walked with you."

"You were getting along so well with Colin. I didn't want to interrupt," I said and took a few steps toward the lecture hall.

"Yes, I . . . ," Sally stuttered, embarrassed. "I mean, we . . ." I wasn't used to Sally being speechless. I was pretty surprised.

"What, you . . . ?" I asked, amused.

"We . . ." Sally took a deep breath. "Colin and I kissed," she suddenly burst out. "Oh man, Evelyn, I am just so struck by him!"

I couldn't hold back my loud laugh. "You don't say." I was happy for the two of them—they seemed made for each other. They could hardly take their eyes off one another at the party. I began to think about the past evening and suddenly remembered how I'd held Jared's hand and he'd simply left me standing there without turning back. The yearning and desolation overcame me again. I breathed heavily into the phone.

Sally recognized my sudden change in mood. "What's the matter?" she asked. "Did something happen last night?"

"No, no. Everything's okay," I lied in a very unconvincing way. I could almost feel Sally raising her eyebrows on the other end. "Tell me," I said, trying to distract her, "what's with you and Colin?" Sally hesitated. She knew I was keeping a secret. "Come on. I want all the filthy little details," I egged her on with feigned cheerfulness. When I arrived ten minutes later at the lecture hall, I had heard all about Colin and Sally making out at the party.

"I have to get off now, my lecture's starting," I said. "What's with you? Don't you have lectures?" I asked after noticing that Sally, unlike me, did not appear to be under pressure.

"I'm taking the day off," she said. "Colin and I want to meet later for coffee, and I don't know what to wear." I shook my head, grinning. That girl was simply incorrigible.

"Have fun," I said.

"Thanks. I'll call later. Bye."

When I'd hung up, there was a message on the screen. There were seventeen calls since yesterday evening. Four were from Sally. The other thirteen were from Felix. In ten-minute intervals. To avoid being interrupted by an overconcerned call from Mrs. Prescott, I had turned my phone off while studying and hadn't felt it vibrate because I had been crying so much. Felix had called me thirteen times. Wasn't that a bit over the top? Or was he worried about me? It wouldn't have been without cause, considering what happened on the way home.

"Evelyn!" *Speak of the devil.* Felix sprinted toward me, almost slipping on the muddy path. "Where the heck were you last night? I thought you wanted to go home with Sally, but I found her making out in some corner with that idiot Sullivan—and no trace of you!"

"I went home alone."

"And I called at least ten times. Why didn't you answer?" Felix was talking so loudly and excitedly that some of our classmates turned to look at us.

"I didn't hear anything, sorry." *It was thirteen times to be precise,* I wanted to add. Still agitated, he shifted from one leg to the other but then abruptly stopped.

"What's the matter? Have you been . . . *crying?*" he asked after interpreting my swollen eyes correctly. But I didn't feel like getting into that conversation or justifying myself for something that was none of his business.

"Calm down, Felix. Everything's okay. I didn't want to bother Sally and Colin, so I went home alone. Nothing bad happened."

"I was worried," he said. His tone reminded me of a father telling his child that he was disappointed and did not approve of whatever the child had done. What was all this about? Was he trying to guilt me?

Anyway, it was time for class, so I went in, sat in the last row and tried to be as inconspicuous as possible. I didn't want to attract more attention with my swollen eyes than I already had as I'd stood with Felix yelling at me. As expected, Felix sat right beside me and dropped clumsily into the chair after folding down the seat in an elegant motion. I tried to get into the lecture a bit, ignoring Felix. Personality Disorders was one of my favorites. I had been looking forward to it all week . . . Suddenly I was confused because Felix had never sat beside me in this lecture before.

"Don't you have Personality Disorders on Tuesdays?" I asked, which immediately rattled him.

"No . . . I . . . Yes, but I wasn't able to follow it too well, so I thought I'd better listen to it again," he stuttered. It was obvious he was lying.

"Ah," I said and left it at that.

Felix did not leave my side over the next three lectures, which were fortunately the only ones that day. Although I was not happy with the tone he took with me in the morning, I still tried to be natural around him. He was probably just worried about me because I hadn't picked up the phone. After all, we were friends and that meant we cared about each other—didn't it? In any case, I decided not to read anything into it.

When we left the lecture hall after the seminar on psychotropic substances, my anticipation for the coming weekend rose, so I was in a good mood when Felix and I went downtown for lunch.

"What do you feel like?" he asked with a smile when we arrived in the old town.

"No idea. Pick something," I said, not that hungry.

"Then let's go to Nam Ho, they have the best egg rolls in town."

"Okay," I said and let Felix guide me to a small restaurant decorated with Chinese characters. We were greeted by a broadly smiling, almost toothless Chinese man at the counter. Felix ordered two egg rolls and a large bowl of fried noodles with vegetables. Then he guided me to one of the small tables in the angled room, which was hardly larger than my dorm room.

"The best egg rolls in town," he repeated, full of anticipation. "You'll see."

Although the prospect of Chinese food didn't excite me just then, I tried to let Felix's good mood infect me a little.

A few minutes later, the toothless Chinese man placed egg rolls and a mountain of fried noodles at the center of the table so we could help ourselves.

"Bon appétit," Felix said and bit into a steaming hot egg roll, burning his mouth in the process.

"Ow, dey're hod," he mumbled with a full mouth and attempted to swallow. I couldn't help but giggle.

Suddenly, the tinkling of the chimes above the door announced the arrival of new customers. A group of young men about our age entered the small restaurant laughing and joking loudly. Looking more closely, I noticed they were all wearing the same jackets. Probably some student society thing, I figured.

"Shit. Frat boys," Felix said when he noticed the new arrivals and confirmed my assumption. His previously elated mood was gone. Now Felix appeared downright hostile. It was as if he'd been replaced by an angry double.

A tall dark-haired guy at the center of the group drew my attention. Although I didn't know his name, I knew immediately that I'd seen him before. He was the one who'd given Colin the kick under the seat in the lecture hall when he giggled because of me. He was one of the guys who ran with Jared and always cast me a poisonous glare when we met. I looked him over, and he spotted Felix and me at the small table in the corner. He immediately stopped laughing and cast a penetrating glare in our direction.

I really lost my appetite then.

"Say, is that dumb fucker staring like an idiot at you or me?" Felix asked and raised his voice so everyone in the restaurant could hear him loud and clear.

"Pardon me?" said the dark-haired guy, who left the group and took a step toward us.

"Was I talking to you?" Felix said while slowly rising.

"You've got a really big mouth, MacMillan!" said the dark-haired guy as he came closer to our table.

"Better watch your own mouth, Mayflower."

I was surprised by Felix's words and shrank back, then looked at him, feeling suddenly distant. Except for the noise of the bubbling deep fryer in the kitchen, the restaurant was dead silent. Even the old Chinese man had taken off. Just then, the chimes at the entrance tinkled again. I looked to the door and opened my eyes wide with fright. Jared!

Seeing him immediately quickened my heartbeat. My breathing became faster, too, and my knees went soft as . . . Stop! I didn't have time right then to stare at him foolishly. After all, hell was about to break loose here, and I couldn't afford to be distracted.

Jared only needed a second to see what was going on.

"Aiden, leave the little shit alone," he said in a calm voice and put his hand authoritatively on the shoulder of his dark-haired companion. "He isn't worth the trouble," he said to drive his point home.

"Oh, how nice!" Felix mocked. "The mama's boy convention has assembled. What's on today's agenda? How to buy a university degree?"

"Felix, what's this about?" I asked, taken aback. I couldn't understand why he was so angry, even hateful, and would not stop provoking these guys. After all, he was alone, and now there were six of them. Or was I supposed to be on his team? I saw from the corner of my eye that Jared was clenching his teeth as if trying to keep himself from teaching Felix a lesson. At that instant, the light in the restaurant started to flicker, which made the entire situation seem even more threatening. Did the whole town have issues with its power lines? The power company needed to look into this. But . . . hold it! Didn't the lights flicker every time Jared was nearby? Or were those the only times I noticed? Strange . . . Somehow, I was overcome with the impression that this flickering really had something to do with him or, rather, his presence—as if a kind of high voltage emanated from him.

I still didn't dare look at Jared. I was sure that the unique blue of his eyes would immediately daze me, as it did every time. The tension in the air was tangible. If I wasn't alert and lost myself in Jared's eyes, I'd wind up in the middle of a fight. If that wasn't where I already was.

"We'll leave," Jared said after a deep breath, and then he turned.

Something about his tone told me the others in his group would follow. Aiden stared at Felix for a moment before he joined the others.

Felix snorted with contempt. "Don't be afraid, Evelyn. I'm looking after you," he said as soon as we were alone.

Excuse me? He was looking after me? He had been the one who had provoked those guys to the point of explosion. He had started all this shit!

If I owed anyone gratitude, it was Jared. He even overlooked Felix's offensiveness to prevent the situation from escalating. And this much was clear: Felix would have had the worst of it had the situation escalated. Absolutely. Six against one—you didn't need to be a psychic to know how that would have gone.

Another thought occurred to me: Did Jared just . . . protect me? Or was I only imagining it? Was this even about me? Had he only wanted to prevent his friends from getting into trouble? On the other hand, he had stood between Madison and me. He had even walked me home so another crazy person wouldn't ambush me. He had wanted to protect me from all that.

But did he also want to defend me?

"Let's eat before it gets cold," Felix said, interrupting my thoughts and grinning. "They won't come back." His smile broadened. Was he for real?

"I feel sick. I'm going home," I said, grabbed my coat, and headed out the door before Felix could comprehend what was going on.

I disappeared into the first alley before he could follow me. Strange. This wasn't the first time Felix's behavior went from one extreme to another in a matter of moments. Sometimes he became riled up so easily I found it a bit eerie. He was unpredictable. And that made me think.

Without knowing where I was going, I turned from one alley into the next until the paths became more and more narrow and I was surrounded by tall brick walls. Those must have been the unappealing backsides of the buildings near Corn Market Street. *Whatever.* I'd wanted to explore Oxford one day on my own, anyway. As long as there was daylight, I'd find my way back. The main thing was I'd be left alone by Felix for the day.

"What are you thinking? You know that's impossible!"

I stopped on the spot when I recognized the voice—beyond a doubt, that was the dark-haired guy: Aiden. He was standing around the corner in a small alley only a few feet from me. I tiptoed closer, tried to breathe as quietly as possible, and strained to hear him.

"She will kill you, and then everything will have been for nothing!" he angrily said through gritted teeth.

"I know you and your mother are convinced of that, but have you considered that Colin may be right?" Jared! I gasped and held my hand over my mouth so I wouldn't betray my presence.

"Colin's wrong!" Aiden said.

"And what if he's not?" Jared asked, still calm and collected.

"Are you even listening to me, man? She. Will. Kill. You." There was no doubt that Aiden believed what he said. "We can't allow that to happen, you know that!"

We? Was there somebody else in the alley?

"Tell Karen I won't let it come to that!" Jared said and no longer sounded as calm. On the contrary: it was the same commanding tone he'd used just a moment ago in the restaurant.

"Then you'd better do something soon. You know she doesn't have a sense of humor when it comes to your safety," said Aiden, somewhat less agitated and with a trace of . . . submissiveness.

"I know," Jared said coolly. Then it was quiet for a moment. Only their regular breathing told me they were still there.

"Come on, the others are probably waiting," Jared said conciliatorily, and I heard him pat Aiden on the shoulder. "Surely you haven't eaten yet," he teased him with a laugh.

"That asshole MacMillan . . . ," Aiden said as their steps became more distant. "Next time I won't hold back—not even for your sake. Somebody needs to shut his mouth," I heard him say before they turned the corner and I couldn't make anything else out.

I stood frozen in the alley for a while and tried to process what I'd just heard.

"She will kill you," Aiden had said.

Who was *she*? Why would she want to kill Jared? Did he have enemies? Was he really in danger? One thing was certain: Aiden was convinced of it. Aiden Mayflower . . . Jared spoke about his mother and Felix, too, had made a barbed comment about Aiden's *mama*. No. That couldn't be a coincidence. He must be Professor Mayflower's son. Their ages also matched up. She was in her midfifties; he was in his early twenties. Without a doubt, Professor Karen Mayflower was Aiden's mother. Aiden said she didn't have a sense of humor when it came to Jared's safety. His *safety*. Somehow that sounded completely exaggerated. As if one were speaking of the queen or the prime minister, whose bodyguards were ready at all times to throw themselves into the line of fire.

Suddenly, an image shot through my head. I saw Professor Mayflower before me as she spoke to Jared—on my first day after she had looked at me so strangely and then stormed out of the lecture hall—and just then I knew it was true. Mayflower wanted to protect Jared from someone. But who? Who was trying to take Jared's life? Was it about money? Perhaps. After all, Jared was the sole heir to a fortune according to Sally and Felix. But Aiden clearly spoke of a woman. "She will kill you," he had said.

An insight struck me like lightning. Jared's words echoed loud and clear in my head: "Can you be happy when what you desire most will bring you to your doom?" He'd said it himself. What he desired would lead him to his doom. Would kill him. She would kill him. And she was . . . the woman he desired, the woman he loved. I became dizzy. Why were Aiden and Jared talking about this immediately after our encounter in the restaurant? Why had Jared told me at the party he was unhappy? And why had Colin been encouraging me not to give up on Jared? Had Jared also felt what I'd felt when our hands touched? I barely dared to even consider the thought: Was I the one he desired? Was *she* . . . me? No.

That could not be right. What reason did I have to harm Jared? It didn't make sense.

My thoughts collapsed upon themselves like a house of cards, and I no longer knew anything. I wasn't even sure if I'd really heard everything or just imagined it. My powers of reasoning were abandoning me, leaving my mind in chaos. I was becoming seriously worried that the events of the last few weeks and months were causing me to lose my sanity. Was I really starting to see things that weren't there? Were these conversations I believed I'd overheard real or not?

I was trotting numbly through the narrow cobblestone streets of the old town when I noticed a movement on one of the side streets. Was that . . . ? I hurried with determined steps toward an entrance where I thought I had seen a man. A man with black leather gloves and a dark-gray wool coat. A second later, I turned the corner and there he was with the same ice-cold expression on his face. I gasped. He had followed me here! Every cell of my body urged me to run. But . . . no! I would not let this guy scare me anymore! It was now or never!

"Who are you? What do you want from me? Why are you following me?" I yelled.

He approached me in a calm manner. I was incapable of moving.

"Get away from here!" he said. "Get away or I will no longer be able to do anything for you." He turned without another word and disappeared into the maze of alleys and narrow streets.

CHAPTER 8

Get away or I will no longer be able to do anything for you. The man's words echoed through my head when I woke up in the morning. Why should I get away from here? And what was that supposed to mean, he would no longer be able to do anything for me? I sluggishly sat up and rubbed my temples. What was it all supposed to mean? I shook my head with my eyes shut. I was going to go stir-crazy if I didn't find a distraction. Since there were no lectures on weekends, I'd have to find some other way to get through the day. Sally hadn't called in the evening, so I assumed she was planning to do something today with Colin.

I'd had enough of Felix for now. Especially since he had called at least five times last night and sent several texts. Apparently, he wasn't able to understand my sudden disappearance and didn't have a clue what was going on with me. So be it. I decided to spend the day on my female narcissism assignment for Bronsen, which was due soon, after I'd taken a refreshing shower. My phone rang just as I was getting dressed. I cast a disdainful look at the display, assuming it was another one of Felix's calls. However, when I saw Sally's name, I was surprised and pressed "Accept."

"Hi, Sally," I said.

"Good morning, Evelyn. Sorry I didn't call yesterday. Colin and I hung out all day."

"That's okay. I understand you want to spend time with him. What are you doing today?"

"Listen, something strange happened yesterday," she said and abruptly stopped. "I want to talk to you about it." Her concerned tone startled me.

"Sure," I replied, perplexed.

"Shall we meet at the library in half an hour?"

"Okay. See you there," I said and hung up.

I repeated Sally's words. "Something strange happened." Had Colin done something to her?

***

"Evelyn," Sally called from afar. She stood at the entrance of the Bodleian and waved at me.

"Hi," I said when I was only steps away. "Everything okay, Sally? What happened?"

"Let's go inside. I'm freezing my butt off out here," she said and hurried toward the entrance. I followed her to a reading desk.

"What's the matter?" I said as soon as we had sat down. I was seriously starting to worry.

"I was hanging out with Colin all day yesterday," she started with a lowered voice and looked me straight in the eye. "It was really wonderful. He was so attentive and nice and . . . it was really perfect."

I returned her smile. "That's lovely, Sally. I'm really happy for you. You wanted to meet just to tell me that?"

Sally took a deep breath. "Later in the evening, Colin got a call. From Aiden Mayflower—Professor Mayflower's son. I don't know if you know him. In any case, Colin left the room to talk to Aiden. So I didn't hear everything they talked about." Sally breathed deeply again. "After a few minutes, they were arguing. Colin yelled at Aiden and called him an idiot. He got really angry. Then he hung up."

I gave Sally a questioning look. I still didn't know what she was driving at.

"In the conversation there was talk of a High Council and some decision it would have to make." She leaned forward. "The whole time, the names Jared, Karen, and . . . *Evelyn* were dropped again and again," she quietly continued.

I looked at her completely dumbfounded. I had not expected that. "What? Do you think they were talking about me?"

She sized me up. "After Colin hung up, he came back in and told me he had to meet Jared, that it was urgent. And he insisted I spend the day with you—in public."

"Why with me?" I asked her, desperately trying to understand. "And why in public?"

She leaned even farther over the table and looked deep into my eyes. "Colin says you need to be looked after for a while."

"What?"

"Shhh." Sally put a finger to her lips.

"What the hell does he mean by that? Why would I need looking after?" I asked in a quiet, though no less defensive, voice.

"I don't know any more than I've already told you. But believe me—Colin was dead serious! It looks like someone has it in for you. And it has something to do with Jared Calmburry and someone named Karen."

A dark thought made me shudder. "Karen Mayflower," I said while I attempted to sort through my thoughts.

"Professor Mayflower?" she asked and thought for a moment. "Well, it makes sense. She's Aiden's mother. But what does she have to do with all this?" The question was meant more for herself than for me.

As much as I pondered, I could not make the pieces fit. Someone had it in for me, as Sally put it. And Jared, Colin, Aiden, Karen Mayflower, and, most likely, the man with the leather gloves all had something to do with it. But what? Sally also spoke of a High Council . . . "And how long is all this supposed to take? I mean staying in public and all that," I asked, frustrated.

"Colin said he'd tell me when it's over." I knew she would have liked to tell me more but apparently it didn't make sense to her, either. But she was taking Colin's warning seriously—that much was clear.

I would have preferred to be alone for a few minutes just to think in peace and quiet. Instead, I let my eyes wander across the overflowing bookshelves until they stopped on a tall, slender figure heading straight for us.

"Felix," I burst out when I recognized him. "What's he doing here?"

"I called him and asked him to meet us."

I looked at Sally surprised and annoyed.

"I thought one more couldn't do any harm. Don't you want to see him?" she asked.

"Actually, I saw enough of him yesterday!"

"Hello, Evelyn," he said when he arrived at our table. "I see you're still alive!" He was about to leave when Sally grabbed him by the arm.

"What's going on between the two of you?" she asked, confused.

He closed his eyes and took a deep breath. "Evelyn seems to enjoy driving me crazy with worry," he said and gave me a look that was both sad and angry. "Where were you?" he asked desperately, and I could see in his eyes that he was really worried. I immediately felt guilty.

"I'm sorry, Felix," I said. "But you really upset me in the restaurant yesterday. Why did you get so angry? I almost didn't recognize you."

Regret was all over his face. "I didn't want to frighten you. I'm sorry." As a peace offering, he extended his hand to me. His expression brightened when I accepted and shook his hand.

"So," he said to Sally. "What's up? Why did you call me?"

"Well, I . . ." Sally stopped midsentence when she saw my look.

She realized immediately that I didn't think much of inviting Felix. After all, we were talking about the same people who had infuriated him so much the day before.

"It's Saturday—I thought the three of us could do something nice," Sally said, just barely making the save.

"Don't you have a date with Sullivan today?" Felix asked with a negative tone. "I thought you two were inseparable now."

She rolled her eyes and shook her head. "Shut up, Felix!" Finally, the old Sally was back.

"Do you feel like a guided tour of town?" she asked me, ignoring Felix.

"Sure, why not?" I said and we got on our way.

"Finally!" Sally said, relieved when her phone rang in the late afternoon. After touring the town exhaustively and—at my request—viewing all the imposing old buildings of almost every department, Sally, Felix, and I had retreated into a cozy little café in the downtown area.

"Is it Colin?" I asked and rubbed my sore feet.

Sally nodded and held the phone to her ear. She almost dropped it in her excitement. "Hi, Colin, what's up? What's happening?" She spoke so fast her words almost blurred together. I held my breath.

"You guys are almost acting as if you were waiting for Sullivan's call," Felix said in a wary tone. Sally and I had not enlightened him about the real reason for the sightseeing tour. Although I wanted to avoid making him suspicious, I didn't react to his assumption. Instead, I listened closely to the phone call, which confirmed Felix's observation. I could hardly wait to ask what Colin was telling her and searched Sally's face for hints of good or bad news. Suddenly her expression lightened a little and she nodded.

"Okay, I'll tell her it's all clear." She nodded again. "Will I still see you today?" Sally asked hopefully and a second later a smile spread across her face.

"Okay, till later. I'm looking forward to seeing you!" She hung up still smiling.

"Oh God, how sickening," Felix said and rolled his eyes. *I'm looking forward to seeing you,"* he repeated in a squeaky voice and batted his eyelashes. If that was an attempt to imitate Sally's voice, it had failed miserably.

"So, what's going on?" I asked.

"Debriefing," Sally answered curtly so as not to give away too much to Felix. Although I would have liked to find out all the details, it was clear that I just had to be content with "debriefing" for now.

"What debriefing?" Felix asked. "What the hell are you two talking about?" A question mark virtually hovered over his head.

"Mind your own shit," Sally snapped back, causing Felix to turn red with anger. Without taking further notice of him, she said that she'd go home to get ready for her date with Colin. "I'll see you tomorrow, Evelyn. Tell you all about it," she said and winked at me. I guessed I'd have to be patient. Although it was hard for me to let her go, I wished her an enjoyable evening and watched her almost dance out the door. Sally had such a crush on Colin that you might have found her picture in the dictionary next to the entry for *lovestruck*.

"And what shall we two good-looking kids do now?" Felix asked and put on his puppy-dog face. It made me grin. I liked Felix though he sometimes overreacted in strange and rather impulsive ways. He had walked his feet sore today only because I wanted to see beautiful buildings. And, totally unlike Sally, he hadn't complained once. He just seemed to take delight in me enjoying myself.

"Not a clue," I said and laughed. "Any suggestions?"

"We're young—we can do anything we feel like. Be a little creative!" he said and waved his arms.

I thought for a moment. "Okay, then let's go . . . swimming." It was the first thing I could think of. But thinking a little more about it, it really was what I most felt like doing. I hadn't been in the water for a long time and was truly yearning for it.

"Swimming?" Felix said with little enthusiasm and frowned. "Then again . . ." He looked down my body and stopped at my crossed legs. "Why not?"

I raised my right eyebrow and gave him a warning look.

"What? I'm a guy, after all," he said and smiled. "Let's go swimming," he said and put his jacket on.

After we had hurried to our rooms and picked up our swimming gear, we met at the indoor pool of the athletic building. My arms and legs began to tingle with anticipation. I quickly changed and had already swum a lap when Felix emerged from the changing room in his oversized, brightly colored Bermuda shorts.

"Come on, I'll race you," I said when he was in the pool and gave him a big grin. The feeling of finally being back in the water almost made me euphoric. I enjoyed every movement as I dove, turned underwater, and surfaced only when I ran out of air.

"Oh man! I was starting to think you'd never come back up again," Felix said while trying to keep up with my pace. "Are you training for the Olympics or what?" he asked, amazed.

"Nah," I said smiling, "I just like being in the water."

"You don't say! Are you sure you aren't a mermaid or something?" he joked.

"Pretty sure, yeah," I said with a laugh. "So, what about it? Are you going to accept my challenge?"

"Of course, my little water sprite!" he said and started swimming as fast as he could. I already knew after the first few strokes that he didn't stand a chance and slowed the pace somewhat so I wouldn't bruise his ego too much. But only six laps later Felix pulled himself up on the edge of the pool using the last of his strength. He panted, completely out of breath, "I can't anymore! No idea how you do it . . . You win! I give up!" I felt a little sorry for him, but I hadn't had nearly enough. I didn't feel tired and had the feeling I could swim forever.

"I'll swim a few more laps, okay?" He lifted his arm and waved weakly. Since I was swimming alone and didn't have to consider Felix, I really let go. I swam and dove as fast as I could. I loved water. Always had. It was almost as if it charged every cell in my body with pure energy.

Felix had caught his breath again and was watching me from the edge of the pool. I began to feel uncomfortable under his gaze and dove a last time to the bottom of the pool, nestled against the gentle waves that my movements had stirred up in the water, then surfaced again and swam over to Felix.

He was looking at me with disbelief, eyes wide open.

"What?" I asked.

"I . . . I've never seen anything like that!" he said and shook his head. "You should be in the Olympics—seriously!"

"Don't exaggerate," I said. "I just like being in the water—that's all."

"I've noticed!" he said. "And what now? Do you want to swim a bit more or should we go for a drink at Berry's?"

I considered briefly if this might be a date and decided we could have a drink as friends. After all, we'd already spent the entire day together. Why shouldn't it be okay to do something together with just Felix?

"Okay, why not?" I said and smiled.

After I'd showered and dressed, I went out into the hall and dried my hair under the blow-dryer. I was about to put it in a ponytail as usual, when Felix took the hair band out of my hand.

"Why don't you leave your hair down today for a change," he suggested and smiled. "It looks nice."

"Oh all right," I said, a little embarrassed, took my bag, and went with Felix to Berry's. We managed to grab the last bar stools.

"Two ginger ales," Felix ordered, without asking me what I wanted. He remembered what I'd ordered the last few times.

"Cheers," he toasted me with a smile and raised his glass.

"Cheers," I returned his toast, clinked my glass against his and took a sip.

"So, confess," Felix said. "Who in your family is descended from a fish?"

"Ha, very funny!" I said. I was still enjoying the euphoric feeling of swimming. My whole body felt good. It was like . . . the opposite of pain.

Felix and I chatted and joked for a while, and as I slowly became sleepy after another ginger ale, I gratefully accepted his offer to walk me home.

"Here we are," he said when we arrived at my dorm. "I tried to get a room here once—having your own bathroom, you know—but it didn't work. Instead I wound up at party central," he said, annoyed.

"At least you don't have to go elsewhere if you feel like a bit of company," I said.

"Hello?" he said with wide eyes. "Own bathroom!" It was the only argument that counted as far as he was concerned.

"Point to you," I agreed. I would not have traded my bathroom for anything in the world. *Except for Jared,* I thought and smiled a little at my silly thought.

"Well, how about it?" Felix asked in a casual tone. "Will you show me your bathroom? Just so I know what I'm missing, of course," he said.

Of course, I repeated the idiotic justification in my thoughts and mulled over how I could make it clear to Felix in a firm but friendly way that I was going upstairs alone.

"Another time, Felix. I'm tired and going right to bed." For a second, it appeared as if the word *bed* would be Felix's cue for another comment. But he gave me a friendly nod and departed, saying, "Then

I wish you a good night, Evelyn. Sleep well!" I wished him the same and climbed up the stairs.

That night I slept like a baby and when I woke up on Sunday morning, I was as relaxed and well rested as I'd ever been. I knew that water—especially swimming—was good for me, but I'd never before felt the effect so clearly. I was completely immersed in this pleasant, warm feeling—and I wanted more. Even before I opened my eyes, I resolved that I must get to the swimming pool as fast as possible.

This time I already had the tingling sensation of anticipation when I left the dorm for the athletic building. I could hardly wait to be back in the water. When I arrived at the pool, I changed so quickly into my bikini, which was still wet from the night before, that I almost fell. I tripped over my feet and banged into the walls of the narrow changing room. When I finally stepped to the edge of the short course pool, I was irritated to find I was not the only one here this early on a Sunday morning. A small group of competitive female swimmers had already arrived for training.

Since they didn't appear to notice me, I jumped from the edge—prohibited—into the water. My movements were soft and flowing despite their speed. I was fully immersed in the experience and swam lap after lap, lost in thought without any awareness of time passing. When I finally looked at the face of the huge, plastic-wrapped wall clock, I found to my astonishment that I'd swum for more than an hour. Suddenly, I remembered that Sally wanted to meet me, and I was more than anxious to find out what she had to say. I promised myself to return soon and swam to the edge of the pool with a heavy heart.

"Hey, Blondie, you swim pretty fast with your skinny legs!" No! It couldn't be . . . but it was! I recognized her deprecating tone at once. Madison stood at the top of the metal ladder on which I was just climbing out of the pool. She was wearing a tightly cut, black Speedo bathing suit with matching cap and goggles. The three girls next to her were wearing the same outfits, which suggested they were together on one of the university's swim teams.

"What do you want, Madison?" I asked.

"Nothing. I just wanted to say hello," she said with a mocking grin, while her three companions broke out giggling.

"Hello," I said and pressed past them toward the changing rooms.

"You wouldn't . . ." she started in her overly sweet tone but stopped midsentence. She stared with wide eyes at the blue-green crystal amulet I wore around my neck. I'd never taken it off since Mother gave it to me all those years ago. It had become so much a part of me that I was hardly aware of it. But now Madison was looking at it with such a shocked expression that my hand involuntarily moved to my neck and clasped the triangular ornament.

Madison swallowed hard. "Where did you get that?" she asked, emphasizing every word. She looked as if she was about to bite off her tongue.

"What makes you think that's any of your business?" I said, outraged.

With that, I left for the changing room, grabbed my towel and apple blossom shampoo, which I had packed the night before, and went to the shower. While I soaped myself, I hoped Madison would finally leave me alone. I didn't know what her problem with me was. She had a big crush on Jared, I knew that, but I wasn't with Jared, nor was there any sign that I ever would be. So, what was this all about? I closed my eyes and let the water roll over my face when I suddenly sensed movement behind me—somebody was there. I started to turn around but my head was suddenly slammed with full force against the wall. The blow hit me so unexpectedly I didn't have the slightest chance to react. Completely disoriented, I fell in the narrow shower stall and tried to see something—anything—with my suddenly blurry vision. As if this wasn't enough, the shampoo burned my eyes, robbing me of even more of my sight. Then I felt fingernails claw into my throat and rip the amulet from my neck with a forceful pull. Still numb from the blow to my head, I flailed and tried to strike my attacker. But my hands connected with nothing. My clouded vision cleared up seconds later and I barged out of the stall. Enraged, I pushed all the shower stalls open, ran along the aisles of the changing rooms and then back to the pool, and searched every corner of the whole damned building, but the assailant—most likely female—was nowhere to be found. *Madison,* I thought and felt a burning rage rise inside me. She had stolen my amulet and tried to seriously hurt me.

I felt my throbbing forehead. It was swollen and sticky. I needed to clean the wound right away. Back in the shower, I looked down and saw that the water running down my body was tinged with red. Although I was almost boiling over with rage, I took a moment to carefully wash out the wound until the bleeding stopped. Then I turned the water off and headed into the changing room. A small mirror was installed there and I was able to take a closer look. My forehead was swollen, but I could tell this was just a surface wound. The bleeding had completely stopped. It almost looked as if my forehead had not bled at all. It was as if the water had closed the wound. I'd noticed this phenomenon a few times before—which is why I made a habit of thoroughly washing any injury with water. I knew this had always worked better for me and Zara than anyone else we knew, but none of my injuries had ever healed this fast before. Nevertheless, I'd have a bruise for the next few days. The deep claw marks on my throat had already turned into nothing more than light-red scratches. When I'd finished looking over my injuries, I had an eerie feeling and reached for my neck. *My amulet,* I thought and found it difficult to hold back my tears. It was a gift from my mother. She had said it would always protect me and I should never take it off. And I never did—I'd worn it all these years, day after day.

You'll pay for this, Madison!

"Heavens, what happened to your head?" Sally said when we met up. As we had agreed, I was waiting for her in the small café in town where we had warmed up after yesterday's sightseeing tour. I took a quick glance into my little pocket mirror. The bruise on my forehead was already sporting all the colors of the rainbow. I sighed deeply and after she had sat down at the table, I told her as calmly as possible what had happened.

"What the hell does that stupid cow want your necklace for?" Sally asked, horrified.

"You'll have to ask her that," I said.

"Do you want to report her to the police? I'll come along if you want."

"No. I can't even prove it was her."

"Screw proof! We know it was her! You can't let these snobs walk all over you!" Sally was really angry.

"I have no intention of letting that happen. But there isn't much the police can do without proof—even if they wanted to. I'd have a lot of paperwork to fill out and that'd be all!"

"Fine, but what do you intend on doing?"

"Very simple: I'm getting my amulet back!" That was the only logical answer as far as I was concerned.

An unholy grin spread across Sally's face, which reminded me of the evil smile of the Grinch. "Do you already have a plan?" She left no doubt that she would stand by my side no matter what.

"Not yet. I think I'll decide that in the spur of the moment."

"Well, okay," she said. "We'll have the element of surprise on our side." *We? Our?* Sally was really ready to take up my cause. I could see that she was in the process of hatching a plan to get back at Madison and retrieve my amulet. She would not hesitate to take her on—for my sake. Although we hadn't known each other very long, everything felt familiar with her. At that moment, I was grateful for having found Sally. I gave way to my inner impulse, leaned across the table, and gave her a firm hug.

"What was that for?" she asked, confused, after I'd let her go.

"Thank you for being there for me," I said.

"Well, we're friends, aren't we?" She looked just as moved as I was, averted her eyes, and traced the pattern on the wooden table. "We're there for each other." For a moment neither of us said anything.

"So . . ." I wanted to change topics to prevent any more blushing. "Tell me what Colin said. Why does he think I need watching over? And what is this debriefing?"

"Colin didn't say as much as I hoped. So I can't reveal any details."

"Okay. What exactly did he tell you?"

"Colin feels he shouldn't talk about it at all."

Where had I heard that before? "He already said that at the party." I urged her on, eager to find out more.

"Anyway, he told me there are people who don't like seeing you near Jared."

"Madison," I said.

"Hmm . . . I think it goes a bit deeper than that. From what I can read between the lines, Madison is only a dim light. What did he call her?" Sally thought for a moment. "Oh yes, *pain in the butt*! He said Madison was a little pain in the butt." Her eyes flitted to my bruised forehead. "A pain in the butt that has clearly gone too far!"

"What do you mean 'a bit deeper'?" I asked.

"I can't tell you in detail, but I believe somebody is planning to do something to get you to stay away from Jared."

I thought about my encounter with the man in the dark wool coat. *Get away or I'll no longer be able to do anything for you.* I swallowed.

"And who's behind it all?" I asked.

"He didn't say. But in Colin's phone call there was talk of Jared, Aiden, and Karen Mayflower. It must have something to do with these people."

"Did Colin say why I'm supposed to keep away from Jared? After all, he's the one keeping away from me. So, what's this all about?"

"He only repeated what he already told you at the party . . ."

". . . that Jared is under a rotten influence," I finished the sentence for Sally.

"Yes, exactly. Whatever that means."

Thoughts bounced around in my head and theories sprang up. I tried to make a sensible whole from the snippets of conversations and comments I'd gleaned. Someone had persuaded Jared that what he desired would kill him, but what was it he desired? Why did someone want to keep me away from him? That was insane! What he desired would kill him. It echoed in my head. Did he desire me? Would someone want to harm me because I represented a danger to Jared? That was completely absurd!

"What exactly is going on there? Between Calmburry and you, I mean," Sally said, interrupting my chaotic thoughts. Her forehead became deeply furrowed.

I snorted. "I wish I knew!"

"Do you like him?" she asked.

"Yes," I answered and looked at my hands. Sally didn't ask anything else.

Strange. That someone would seriously try to harm me—in whatever way—left me completely unmoved. After all that had happened to me, I was not even afraid of death. On the contrary: there had been days when I would have welcomed it with open arms. I was not particularly attached to my life. What bothered me about the whole thing—what almost drove me crazy—was this tormenting uncertainty. The unsolvable riddle. Then I suddenly thought of something I had forgotten to ask Sally.

"So, who did the debriefing come from?"

"Colin says that some High Council has decided not to do anything for the time being. About you, I mean. He says you're safe for now and don't need to worry."

"High Council?" I repeated in disbelief. "That sounds like something out of a movie about the Middle Ages." I was frustrated even though this ought to be good news. I had had much higher hopes for this conversation, but instead everything had become even more complicated. Sally couldn't help it because she had already told me everything she knew. I really had to be careful not to dump my frustration on her. Better to say nothing than say something I'd regret later. So we sat silently across from each other for a few minutes, shifting our eyes back and forth between our hands and the ceiling. I only got a hold of myself when the waiter approached and asked if we wanted to order something.

"I'd like another cup of tea," Sally said.

"Nothing for me, thank you," I said without looking up. "How do you think Jared and Colin fit into all this?" I asked Sally in a calm voice after the waiter had gone.

"I've been trying to figure this out the whole time," she said, puzzled.

"Do you think it's a cult?"

"A cult? No, I don't think so," said Sally after reflecting for a moment. "That doesn't fit Colin." She shook her head. "He told me his parents died when he was quite young . . ."

Another one, I thought and immediately felt connected to Colin in a peculiar way.

". . . and that he grew up with Jared in a foster family. Perhaps it has something to do with that," she said. "Maybe some Mafia thing?" Judging from her puzzled expression, it was clear Sally didn't believe this.

"I doubt it. And I didn't know Colin and Jared grew up together."

"They're like brothers," Sally said with a smile. Colin seemed to have told her something about his childhood, in which Jared had played a critical part.

"So, you don't think Jared is—what did you call him—arrogant?" I asked, quoting her.

"Colin would go to hell and back for him, he said so himself. So, Jared can't be all that bad. I think he's one of those people you have to get to know before you can really judge him," she said.

Oh, how I would love to get to know him. I lacked the courage to say this out loud.

The rest of the day drifted along. In the afternoon, after Sally had gone to her date with Colin, I met up with Felix. He noticed my injury right away even though my forehead already looked much better than in the morning. He was beside himself after I told him a toned-down version of what had happened at the pool.

"I'll kill her," he shouted, ready to go after Madison. I held him back.

"Let it be, Felix," I pleaded. "I'll deal with it."

I was able to dissuade him with great difficulty. He never quite got over his rage, so I left him early in the afternoon. Let him settle down a little. I was not in the mood for his company when he was in that state.

At home, I thoroughly washed my bruise under the shower and slipped into my soft flannel pajamas. I felt a little stupid going to bed while it was still light outside, so I decided to work on my narcissism assignment. Four hours and three meager pages later, I decided it was okay to go to sleep. Especially because my eyes kept closing while I was sitting at the desk.

CHAPTER 9

The following morning I didn't feel as rested as on the previous day, but the feeling of wellness that I always enjoyed after swimming was not entirely lost. I needed a few seconds to properly awaken, and then I remembered what had happened at the pool.

My amulet. I brushed my fingers over my neck.

I felt my forehead and carefully checked my injury. The swelling had gone down even more. My head still felt a little spongy just below the hairline but no one would notice if I put on a little makeup. At least not from a distance.

A look in the bathroom mirror confirmed my impression. The swelling was barely noticeable, and the bruise was fading. I smeared a layer of my rarely used foundation on my forehead. The tube had probably passed its best-before date long ago and was so dried up that, using all my strength, I managed to squeeze out only a drop of the skin-colored cream.

When I looked at my schedule, my heart skipped a beat. Narcissism and Destructiveness, I read and was forcefully reminded of my first day at school. I had met Jared after that terrible fall—the thought alone still made me blush with embarrassment. How he had looked at me . . . I would have given anything to know what he thought at that moment.

The mere thought of seeing him again in a few minutes made me tremendously nervous. What should I wear? Should I put on more makeup? Perfume? Or just go natural?

After a bit of back and forth I slipped into a pair of very tight black jeans and combined them with a thin, dark-green turtleneck sweater. Since I had a little time, I dug out my makeup and with a shaky hand tried to apply the eyeliner. I also did my best to apply a little mascara and light-brown lipstick. The result was . . . well . . . unconvincing. So I gathered a handful of suds and washed the entire masquerade off my face. That meant I had to start over again with disguising my head injury, but it beat walking around all day looking like a sad clown. I limited myself to putting on a bit of foundation and left the building without further experimenting.

The closer I got to campus, the more nervous I became. When I was almost there, I feverishly looked for Jared and Madison. I could barely wait to lay my hands on that bitch.

"Hey, your forehead already looks a lot better," said Sally, who suddenly appeared next to me.

"Oh hi, Sally. Yes, I covered it with some makeup. How was your date with Colin yesterday?"

Sally grinned from ear to ear. "We're officially together as of yesterday," she said, outshining the morning sun.

"Oh how lovely!" I said, delighted.

"By the way, I told Colin what Madison did at the pool, and he immediately called Jared," she said in a muffled voice.

"And?" I asked.

"He must have totally lost it. Colin only said Madison would regret it."

"How so? For my sake?"

"Who else's? Since the two of you held hands at the party in Felix's residence, it's clear Jared is into you!"

"What?"

"Anyone who saw you two in that moment knew for sure." She frowned. "You seem to be the only one who didn't notice."

"But . . . he always avoids me!"

"No idea why he does that," Sally said. "Lack of interest in you is definitely not the reason."

I searched Sally's face for the slightest hint of doubt—but there was none. She was completely convinced of what she had said.

"Is everything okay with you?" Her worried tone caused me to snap back. "You look as if you just peed yourself."

"I . . . I'm all right," I answered, shaking my head and trying to form a clear thought.

"Have you seen him since?" she asked, getting on her tiptoes to look over the heads of our fellow students.

"No," I replied, and I also got on my tiptoes and searched the cluster of people that had formed at the entrance of the lecture hall.

"Hey—I'm here." Felix waved his hand in front of my face.

"Who says we're looking for you?" Sally said and stretched a little more.

"Oh, I see!" Felix said. "When you see her, let me know. I'll get her!"

"Who?" I asked.

"Madison, of course! Who else?"

"Oh." I'd completely forgotten Madison for a moment in my feverish search for Jared.

"Let me see." Felix carefully brushed my hair out of my face to inspect my bruise. "Looks much better than yesterday," he said, surprised.

"I covered it a little," I said and draped my hair at an angle across my forehead.

Except for Felix, Sally, and me, almost everyone had disappeared into the lecture hall.

"What are you waiting for?" Felix asked and gently pushed me toward the entrance. "Madison isn't out here. Let's go in."

When I entered the lecture hall behind them, I scanned the rows of seats for Jared. So I would have the best view, I sat at the back and searched row after row for him. Again and again. But I couldn't find him or Madison anywhere. And finally I had to admit it—Jared wasn't there. Downcast, I exchanged a look with Sally, who signaled with a shrug that she hadn't seen him either. Why hadn't he come? Was he sick? Why was Madison not here? Was there a connection?

Lost in thought, I tuned out Professor Bronsen's lecture. Only after an eternity of torment did he end the lecture and dismiss us. I trotted off to my next class after reassuring Felix that he didn't need to accompany me. Although I attempted to keep myself from doing it, I searched the crowd for Jared. In vain. It was clear I was badly looking forward to seeing him and not seeing him made me so unhappy . . . I hadn't counted on that.

After surviving Introduction to Psychology with Harrison, and Stats with the lisping Professor Gallert, hope sprang forth again. Next on my schedule was History of Psychoanalysis with Professor Mayflower, and I knew for sure Jared attended that lecture. Well, he usually did. After all, I'd seen him there quite a few times. To keep my disappointment down, I dampened my hopes and attempted to resign myself to not seeing Jared that day. But there was something I was not going to miss: Karen Mayflower. I had thought a lot about her in the last few days and intended to watch her very closely. Any shimmer that shed a bit of light into the dark would be welcome.

As always, seats were taken within minutes. When Professor Mayflower entered the lecture hall through the don's door at the front, I looked over the crowd one last time. Jared had not shown up and, despite being prepared for his absence, the disappointment hit me full force. I tried to suppress the rising depression and focused on the professor. She appeared to be . . . angry. Even before greeting the students, she pulled a note out of her pocket, unfolded it, and started to read. "Due to overregistration in the course that by far exceeds the capacity of this lecture hall, the following students can no longer participate in History of Psychoanalysis." Professor Mayflower looked at her note and examined the crowd. We looked at each other, and I thought I saw her eyes widen before she again looked at the paper and started reading the names.

"Grant Fullman, Linda Harroldson, Kevin Jasper, George Kline, Sandra Oldman, Rebecca Orphans, Holden Kley, and . . . Evelyn Lakewood." What? Could this be true? She was actually kicking me out of her class! While the other students vocally protested, I got up and left the hall without saying a thing. Dozens of curious looks followed me. Was I imagining it or did Professor Mayflower emphasize my name? Considering how upset she was in her first lecture and after all that I'd heard from Colin, I knew that my name was not listed by accident and that there was no point in insisting I be allowed to continue attending the course. But what was her problem with me?

Lost in thought, I trudged across the campus courtyard and reviewed all my encounters with Karen Mayflower. Suddenly, I remembered Colin's remark. When I met him in the library—or, rather, ran into him there—he advised me to visit Professor Mayflower. Although I didn't know what that was supposed to lead to now, I decided to follow Colin's advice. At least I could ask her why she kicked me out of her class. So I went straight to her office, sat on the floor across from her door, leaned against the wall, and waited.

Thirty minutes later, I heard her voice. She was walking along the corridor with Professor Bronsen. The two were talking in a very animated way about a joint publication and were so caught up in their conversation they didn't notice me. Without even looking in my direction, they went into Mayflower's office and she slammed the door.

I spent another fifteen minutes sitting on the floor, chewing my fingernails until Bronsen finally left. I hastily scrambled up and knocked on the door.

"Come in," Professor Mayflower called with an impatient voice. I hesitated for a moment and even toyed with the idea of just leaving. But I decided not to give up and entered.

"Good day, Professor Mayflower," I said with a firm voice.

"Yes?" she answered without even looking up from her desk.

"My name is Evelyn Lakewood. I . . ."

She raised her head and fixed her eyes on me.

Focus! "I am—or rather was—in your History of Psychoanalysis class."

"Really?" she said in a tone that left no doubt she knew what I was talking about.

"Yes, and I want to know why I was kicked out."

"Several students were selected at random," she said while sitting up in her office chair and taking off her reading glasses. "Everyone had the same chance."

"Is there another way to participate in the course?" I asked.

"Sorry, but that's not possible." She looked at me unyieldingly. But I was not yet willing to give up.

"That's too bad," I said. "I'm . . . enthusiastic about your lectures." It was the truth. Embarrassed, I let my eyes wander around the room. Then, as if struck by lightning, my eyes stopped on the overflowing bookshelf on the right side of the room. I saw a book lying flat on the books standing upright. Could that be . . . ? I forced myself to blink.

Indeed! I recognized that worn, dark-brown leather binding at once . . . *The Calmburry book!*

When Professor Mayflower realized what I'd discovered, she was on her feet in a flash, standing right in front of me and attempting to block my view of the bookshelf.

"As I've said, I can do nothing for you in this regard, Miss Lakewood," she said, trying to brush me off. I stood there rooted to the floor and looked into her eyes. That seemed to unsettle her a little because she started shifting from one foot to the other. "And now please excuse me," she continued. "I have assignments to grade."

She was kicking me out—again. Since I had no idea how to counter, I was left with no choice but to leave the office. What could I have said to her? *I know the Calmburry family history is over there and you are hiding it from me.* I didn't think so.

I tried to organize my thoughts as I stepped outside. What was the Calmburry book doing in Mayflower's office? Was she hiding it there? What was it I wasn't supposed to discover? I couldn't figure it out. No matter how I looked at it, it didn't make sense. The only thing I was completely sure of was this: Karen Mayflower was the one who wanted to keep me away from Jared.

"What's with you?" Sally asked at lunch, shaking my shoulder. I was so lost in thought I hardly noticed her trying to talk to me. The lunch break was almost over, and I could hardly remember anything that had happened since I'd left Mayflower's office. I must have been sitting there silently, staring into space. My usual spaghetti with tomato sauce sat nearly untouched. When I looked up, I saw Sally's concerned face.

"Hello, are you in there?" she asked, wide-eyed, and shook me again.

"Yes, everything's all right," I said and pulled my arm away.

"Um, you were totally gone!" Sally said.

"I was thinking."

"Thinking? More like you were on another planet!"

"Where's Felix?" I asked to change the subject. I wondered why he wasn't sitting at our table like usual. I seemed to remember him in line with us at the counter.

"He said he had to take care of something. Didn't you hear him? It was like two minutes ago." She squinted and put her hand on my forehead to check my temperature. "Is everything really okay?"

"Yes, of course," I said and pushed her hand aside. Still, I had to admit that it bothered me how far gone I'd been the last few minutes.

"Let's go. It's time," I said to Sally and rose. Sally lifted her tray and followed me after giving me one last probing glance.

Behavioral Psychology was fascinating as always and distracted me somewhat from the chaos of my thoughts. I immediately sensed how good it was for me not to think about Jared Calmburry, Karen Mayflower, or that dumb book at least for the duration of the lecture.

Unlike me, Sally had little interest in the lecture and spent the whole time texting with Colin under the desk. She still found time to size me up at regular intervals. Apparently, she was worried I was sick or might have gone bonkers.

"Stop looking at me," I said after she'd looked over for the hundredth time.

"Okay," she said and raised her hands. "I'll never look at you again!"

"Sally, please don't be offended. But you don't have to worry. There's nothing wrong with me." But to be honest, things weren't okay at all, and I couldn't hold it against Sally that she'd noticed.

"Is it because Jared hasn't shown up today?" she asked me as we made our way to Communication Psychology. She wasn't going to let this go.

"I don't know," I answered with a sigh that confirmed Sally's assumption that I wasn't okay.

"Don't worry," she said and rubbed my arm. "We're going to find out what's going on."

At that moment, Professor Martin stepped into the room and started his lecture. I had to grin at the thought of how Sally normally behaved in his presence. I was eager to see how she'd act now that she was together with Colin.

A few moments later I determined she was not worshipping *Irvin* nearly as much as she had a few weeks ago. Still, you could see she still thought he was attractive and wanted to please him. I couldn't suppress a giggle and was immediately admonished with a look from Professor Martin to be quiet. Now it was Sally who giggled. Embarrassed, I directed my eyes forward and followed the class. It appeared Martin had prepared some interactive communication exercises we were supposed to work on with role-playing games in groups of two. While he went through the rows and passed out the worksheets, I again noticed his distinctive seal ring. It was exceedingly beautiful and gleamed an unusually strong, dark blue. A deep indigo blue that shone in the same unmistakable way as . . . Jared's eyes. *Damn!* Was there anywhere I could be safe from him?

When Professor Martin came over to give us the instructions, I had my first opportunity to see his ring up close. I was so fascinated by the jewel that I would have preferred to hold his hand and take a longer look. I resisted the impulse with difficulty and satisfied myself with casting a short look at the ring while the professor placed the worksheets on the table. As I'd suspected, there was an engraved symbol worked into the flat, dark-blue oval crystal. I recognized a sword and a sort of staff that crossed in the . . . It was as if lightning struck me! *"The Calmburry crest!"* I almost screamed. It was exactly the same symbol that decorated Madison's wrist. I looked at Professor Martin, who held his ring hand behind his back when he noticed my stare. He looked at me equally shocked for a moment, then inhaled deeply, put on a nonchalant expression, and continued to distribute the worksheets as if nothing had happened. All this happened so fast Sally didn't notice anything.

For the rest of the lecture, Professor Martin played it cool. At first, it was too much for me, and I didn't know how to handle the situation. After all, Professor Martin knew as well as I did that he was trying to hide something from me. Nevertheless, I decided to play along for the time being and conscientiously worked on the assignment. Especially since I didn't want to draw any more attention from my classmates than I already had. Still, I couldn't keep my mind from desperately trying to put the pieces of the puzzle together to form a harmonious and logical whole. Jared, Karen Mayflower, Professor Martin, Aiden, Madison, Colin, the crest, the debriefing, the strange guy who had followed me here from Fleetwood . . . I feverishly tried to connect everything but soon reached my limits. What surprised me despite the rising frustration was that the feeling inside me was of wild determination. I would solve this riddle—no matter the cost.

Shortly after the start of the lecture, I dared to look at Professor Martin one more time and was surprised at what an outstanding actor he was. He didn't show any sign of discomfort. Even when I looked directly at him and couldn't help casting a challenging look his way, he only responded with a friendly smile and continued his lecture, not the slightest bit unsettled. If it weren't for the fact that he hid the ring, I might have doubted myself because of his splendid performance. No. I was certain: whatever was happening, Irvin Martin was involved.

As Sally and I walked part of the way home together, I toyed with the idea of telling her about the ring. However, I decided against it since it still made little sense to me. She was about to meet Colin, and, after she had assured me that she'd keep me up to date as soon as she found out something new about Jared, I left it at that.

When I'd pulled the door shut behind me and put my bag in the corner, I opened the top drawer of my dresser and pulled out my laptop. I placed it on my narrow desk, which it almost completely covered. Impatiently I tapped my fingertips on it until it booted up. I'd already decided during Martin's lecture to start searching this way. After all, I'd found the crest for the first time on the Internet.

I typed Jared's name into the search engine and found, as expected, the pictures and newspaper articles about the horrible plane crash that had killed his entire family. I swallowed hard and banished the approaching thoughts of his dead family members. I had no time for another meltdown. I scanned the other search results on the first page. As with the last time I googled Jared's name, a Facebook notification and a link to the University of Oxford appeared. But what I was looking for was nowhere to be found. I ran through the second, third, and fourth pages and followed a few links only to abandon them a few minutes later. No sign of the Calmburry crest. Strange . . . I could remember that I had seen the engraved symbol pretty much right away when I searched last time. I hadn't paid very close attention then, but I was pretty sure it had been there. About ten Google pages later I decided to try another search engine. It also produced no results. It was as if someone had deleted the Calmburry crest from the entire Internet.

How was this possible? I remembered a TV report I had watched about a year ago with Zara. It was about the traces information left behind on the Internet and how difficult it was to remove them. I remembered this so well because afterward we had talked about a case Zara had worked on. A girl who had been bullied by her peers had reported this to the police because some of her classmates had put some embarrassing pictures of her on the Internet and added nasty comments. Zara told me what a huge effort it had been to delete the pictures. And even when she and her colleagues had succeeded, the pictures reappeared on the Net over the following weeks and months. How, then, could the crest disappear so thoroughly if even the police could barely erase something? Did someone like Karen Mayflower have the means to do this? My head was starting to hurt. Instead of finding the desired answers, more questions had arisen, and it was maddening. After hours of fruitless searching, I finally fell on my bed, exhausted.

When the screaming of my alarm tore me from sleep the next morning, a tormenting feeling of frustration overcame me. I had to do something about this. I jumped out of bed and pulled my schedule out of my bag. Felix, as always, would accompany me to my four morning lectures. I hoped to see Jared in the afternoon in Psychology of Emotions—how fitting.

As expected, Felix saw me outside the lecture hall and greeted me from afar. When I approached him, I remembered him disappearing during lunch the previous day. He had to *take care of something*, Sally had said.

"Good morning, Felix," I said when he was within earshot.

"Morning, Evelyn."

"Hey, where did you disappear to yesterday during lunch?"

He shrugged. "You looked totally exhausted at lunch, absent-minded, and not yourself. So I decided to get her," he proudly stated.

"Get who?"

"Madison, of course! As you said, the business at the pool really got to you. Are you still having trouble concentrating today? You should have gone to the hospital right away on Sunday. You've probably got a concussion—I figured that's what was wrong at lunch yesterday."

"A concussion?" I said in a lowered voice as I finally grasped what Felix was driving at. He was blaming my absentmindedness on Madison's attack in the shower and the head injury I sustained. But I had been racking my brain the whole time over Jared, the book, and Karen Mayflower. I couldn't resist laughing. Felix didn't have a clue how wrong his assumptions were. But since I didn't feel like telling him why I had been so absentminded, I gratefully accepted the opening.

"You decided to get her?" I asked, anxious to find out what happened.

"Yeah," he said, now almost looking downcast.

"And?"

"And nothing. I couldn't find the bitch. And I looked everywhere for her. In the library, the lecture halls . . ." He breathed deeply. "I searched the whole damned college. But nothing." He sounded frustrated.

I frowned. Madison was nowhere to be found? Strange. Now I was even more anxious to see Jared and wished he would show up for the afternoon lecture. But I didn't want to get my hopes up.

"What would you have done to Madison if you'd found her?" I asked and tried to imagine how an encounter between the two of them might have gone. He shrugged. "No idea, I never thought it out. I just wanted to get her. Maybe I would have grabbed her by her shoulders and shaken her," he said and smiled at the thought.

"Trust me, I would have liked to see that," I confessed, laughing.

"Come on, let's go in," Felix said. "Let's not make old Professor Warden wait too long. Any lecture could be his last!" he joked.

"You're right. How old is he, really?"

"As far as I know," Felix said, "he served in World War I. And he's not getting any younger."

The first three lectures passed quickly, thanks to Felix's pleasant company. I let his good mood infect me, which helped me forget the damned puzzle that had kept me so preoccupied all this time. After the lunch break, for which Sally did not show up because she now preferred to eat in town with Colin, I made my way to Psychology of Emotions with Professor Ginsburgh. I had pretty much resigned myself to not seeing Jared and trotted to the entrance. It was pointless to look for Jared among the other students, but since I couldn't be sure I'd resist the temptation to look for him, I stared at the ground.

"Hi, Evelyn."

I gasped and looked up. Jared was standing in front of me, looking into my eyes. The explosion I felt in my stomach at seeing him released a million butterflies. I was incapable of speaking.

"I heard you got hurt. How are you? Are you okay?" he asked with concern, and his voice had a slightly angry undertone.

"I . . . I'm just fine," I managed to say.

"I heard you hurt your head," he said and eyed my forehead. When he discovered the yellow-green shadows of the healing bruise, he clenched his teeth so hard his jaw muscles protruded. My hand wandered to the spot on my head where it had banged into the tiled wall of the shower.

"Not nearly as bad as it looks," I assured him. "Almost healed." He closed his eyes and breathed in—to try to control himself, it seemed. This gave me an opportunity to look at him closely. He was wearing sneakers and jeans with a broad, dark-brown belt that perfectly matched his leather jacket. He wore the jacket over a light-gray hoodie and looked breathtaking. It probably didn't matter whether he was wearing a tailored suit or old, worn sweatpants—Jared *always* looked breathtaking. When he opened his eyes again, he caught me looking him over. I immediately turned away.

"Shall we go in?" I asked when I noticed that all the others had already disappeared into the lecture hall.

"No, I have to get going," he said reluctantly.

I frowned. "But then why did you come here if you're not going to the lecture?"

He shut his eyes and breathed deeply again as if he needed a moment to decide whether to tell me the truth or not. "To see you," he finally said but quickly turned and left.

CHAPTER 10

The library!

I almost shouted it out loud when it dawned on me to look there one more time for clues. Even if the Calmburry book was in Mayflower's office—unless she'd already hidden it somewhere else—I might find another book that would help me.

Since I'd arrived at Ginsburgh's lecture—a few minutes late because I'd had to gather myself after my encounter with Jared—I'd been puzzling things over incessantly.

He had come just to see me and pulled the ground out from underneath me. If Sally was right and Jared was into me, why was he always running away when he saw me? Who could have such a strong influence over him that he would keep away from me against his will? I knew the answer: Professor Mayflower. But why?

Carefully trying to avoid Felix and Sally, with whom I was about to have Social Psychology, I took a detour to the library. I set aside my feelings of guilt by reminding myself I wouldn't make a habit of skipping classes, but my curiosity was simply getting the better of me. When I arrived at the library, I stopped to consider where to begin my search. I decided it would be best to start where I'd come upon the Calmburry book and headed straight for the FE section. I inspected every weighty volume that resembled the chronicle. Most of these works, like the Calmburry book, stemmed from the deepest Middle Ages.

At the start of my search I came upon a number of horrible manifestos by the Catholic Church—cold-blooded, bestial instructions set down by the Inquisition for torturing and killing supposed heretics. Another book consisted exclusively of detailed, stomach-turning descriptions of the cruel witch hunts that occurred between 1450 and 1750. It included disgusting things, such as instructions for building a pyre large enough to burn a dozen supposed witches at once. Finally, I even laid hands on a copy of Heinrich Kramer's *Malleus Maleficarum*, commonly known as *The Hammer of Witches*. The discussion in the first few pages on the nature of women was despicable and made me want to throw up. This cleric called for the godless, inhumane murder of thousands and thousands of women and girls. But what was even worse, congealing in my gut as a mass of black anger and hatred, was that the death of these innocents was to be preceded by a humiliating and barbarous torture to extract a so-called confession from them. I forced myself to put *The Hammer of Witches* back onto the shelf before I lost focus out of sheer rage. The next book described the curative powers of various native herbs and their uses in medicine and healing. I would pull a book from a shelf, start reading, shut it in disappointment, and return it to its place, only to pull out another and then another. Although they were interesting and informative, none of the dusty folios contained even the slightest trace of the Calmburry family.

Two unsuccessful hours later, feeling morose, I brushed my fingers listlessly over the wooden shelves, which mostly held worn, leather-bound books that were carefully categorized, row by row. Suddenly I noticed something. Because I had been so fully occupied with the books, I hadn't noticed at first that the bookcases in the FE section were not ordinary bookcases. I felt irregularities in the varnished wood under my fingertips and took a closer look. It appeared that not only were the books particularly old—the librarian had spoken of rare and extremely valuable manuscripts and first editions—but the shelves holding the numerous volumes also appeared to be priceless antiques. Fine, delicate carvings had been worked into the wood by a true master. Looking closer, I recognized symbols among the numerous engraved ornaments and intricate decorations, especially the sides of the broad bookcases facing the center aisle. I gently brushed several feet of one shelf's side with my fingers.

Then I took a step back to appreciate the artwork as a whole. At first, I was slightly irritated that the artist let his masterpiece end so abruptly at the right wall without having his carvings run out as delicately as he had begun them and as I had expected them to. But then I realized the flourishes, lines, and ornaments continued on the side of the next case to the right. Although it was set up several feet from its neighbor, it was impossible to miss that the two bookcases somehow belonged together. I took another step back and recognized that the carvings on the sides of the third and fourth cases would also fit together into a single, seamless work of art.

Because this part of the FE section consisted of at least ten shelving units set up at regular distances and all appeared to be covered by the same carving, I took several steps back to get a better picture.

Unexpectedly, I bumped into the next row of shelves on the opposite side of the center aisle. *Damn!* From here I couldn't see how the whole picture of the carved woodwork on the individual six-foot-wide, twelve-foot-tall sides fit together.

I had to get farther back. But how? I suddenly noticed a rolling ladder leaning against one of the shelves; it extended so far up that even books on the top shelf could be reached easily. The ladder could be pushed on its wheels to the end of the shelf on the side opposite the center aisle and parallel to the shelves in the FE section. That should do. I moved it over, climbed all the way up and, full of anticipation, looked over the center aisle to the shelf sides in the FE section.

I almost fell off the ladder, looking down from so high. I could see about seven of the ten shelves in total and, even though a quarter of the overall work was hidden from sight, I was certain the carving on the shelf sides could only be *one thing*: the woodworker had carved the Calmburry crest in painstaking detail into the wooden surface, and it was nearly the size of a movie screen. Unbelievable! I was astonished and held firmly to the ladder. I blinked and looked at the huge carving again. Yes, beyond any doubt, this truly was the Calmburry family crest. What the heck was it doing there? Was this the *Calmburry wing* of the library?

I knew from Sally that Jared's family was one of the oldest in England. And I knew they'd accumulated a huge fortune over the course of time. But could it be that the Calmburrys donated an entire library section to Christ Church? All those rare works must be worth a fortune. Not merely a few thousand pounds. No. A *real* fortune! Was this family really so rich it could simply give a treasure like that to the College? Was the explanation that simple? Just a donation from a filthy rich family?

Suddenly, I thought of the creepy nighttime encounter with Madison. She had shown me her tattoo. Her very *special* tattoo. She was wearing the crest on her wrist. Was she related to Jared? That would seem pretty improbable. After all, she had a crush on him. Unless . . . No, I didn't even want to think it! So, assuming they were not related, why was Madison wearing the crest of the Calmburry family on her skin? Was it the *symbol of the bond* between Jared and her, as she claimed? Full of conviction. Full of pride.

Bond—what a strange word to use. And then there was Professor Martin. The crest stood out on his blue seal ring. And he had definitely wanted to hide it from me. Just like Professor Mayflower had wanted to hide the book from me. Deep inside, I felt all this—the carvings on the shelves, Madison's tattoo, Professor Martin's seal ring, and Karen Mayflower's more-than-strange behavior regarding the book—was only the beginning. There was more. Much more.

I pulled my cell phone out of my bag as I left the library. I had felt it vibrate during my feverish search, but I hadn't paid any attention since it could only have been Mrs. Prescott, Sally or, even more likely, Felix—and I didn't want to be disturbed.

I had two missed calls from Sally, four from Felix, and several texts from Felix.

```
Where are you?
What's going on? Everything okay?
Damn it, Evelyn, where the hell are you?!
```

With a deep sigh, I typed an answer.

```
Felix, everything's okay. I had a headache
and went to lie down.
```

Since he was making more of my injury than he needed to, I thought this was as good an excuse as any, and even though it was a lie, I didn't feel guilty. After all, Felix wasn't my dad or my boyfriend. I was a free person and could decide on my own what to do. I was slowly getting the feeling he wanted me to ask his permission to come and go. Felix's answer arrived only two minutes after I had pressed "Send."

```
Sally and I were worried about you. Where
are you now?
```

Before I got a chance to write, the cell phone vibrated again. Sally was calling.

"Hi, Evelyn, Felix says you've got a headache and that's why you didn't come to Social Psych?" The strange tone of her voice told me she hadn't believed my excuse and was curious what I'd really been up to.

"Is Felix with you?" I asked.

"No, I'm in the restroom. He's waiting outside," Sally said in a quiet voice.

"I was in the library trying to find out something about Jared."

"And?"

"I had moderate success. But I'm pretty sure of one thing: the whole business that he and Colin are involved in is much bigger than I thought."

"Hmm," Sally said. "I've found out nothing new from Colin. He says he'll get into big trouble if he talks about it. What did you find out?"

"Do we really have to talk about this on the phone while you're in the restroom?"

"You're right. Should we meet tomorrow during the lunch break? We'll get rid of Felix."

"If only it were so simple," I said with a sigh. "Very well, till tomorrow," I said and hung up.

I was more than eager to hear Sally's thoughts on my discoveries. But just as I had feared, it wasn't easy to give Felix the slip during lunch the following day. He was still very concerned about my health and bombarded me with questions all morning: Do you have a headache? Are you feeling dizzy? Are you tired?

In the meantime, I really regretted taking advantage of his opening to use my injury as an excuse. It appeared he didn't intend on letting me out of his sight for even a second.

Sally rolled her eyes behind Felix's back when the hundredth attempt to distract him failed.

I could barely keep him from skipping his own afternoon lecture to accompany me. I loudly said, "Felix, please! I'm fine—I don't need a babysitter following me around!"

"As you wish," he said, miffed, only to apologize ten minutes later in a text. I took a deep breath of relief when the last lecture was over and I would be able to hide in my room—peace and quiet for a few hours. Since Sally wouldn't have time this evening because she had promised her mother to help her paint the apartment, we agreed she would pick me up at the dorm the following day for the study group at Felix's place. But this time a little earlier than usual so we could talk beforehand undisturbed.

During lunch in the dining hall on Thursday, Felix was particularly attentive and helpful. Even toward Sally, which puzzled me.

"Just stay seated, you two," he said. "I'll get us some coffee." Sally and I looked at each other with surprise.

"What's with him?" she asked when he'd walked away. "Does he feel guilty about something?"

"No idea," I said and shrugged.

"Doesn't matter . . . So, what did you find out at the library?" Sally whispered and leaned over the table.

"I didn't find out anything specific . . . But I did discover *something*."

"What is it?"

"Did you know that the Calmburrys have their own family crest?" She shook her head.

"Well, they do. I found it on the Internet when I googled Jared's name. And I discovered this crest on a book in the library a few weeks ago. It was very old and had the crest embossed right into the leather binding."

"And what was the book about?"

"It was a sort of chronicle of the family history of the Calmburrys— at least, that's what I suspect. It goes back to the early Middle Ages."

"And?" She didn't seem to get what I was driving at. I hesitated for a moment before continuing.

"The crest keeps popping up in other places, too—"

"Shhh. Talk later," Sally said and nodded in the direction Felix was coming from with three cups of coffee in his hands.

"You're welcome," he said and laughed as he distributed the cups.

Sally looked at Felix suspiciously. "Thank you."

"Thank you, Felix," I said and sipped from my cup.

"Yuck, it's so bitter!" Sally said as soon as she'd taken the first sip, contorting her face in disgust. I sipped my coffee again. It tasted normal.

"Then you'll have to have a chocolate milk next time if you think coffee tastes too bitter," Felix said and held out two sugar packets. "Here's some sugar for you!"

"What's with you?" Sally asked and gave Felix a skeptical look while pouring the sugar into her coffee and stirring.

"Still tastes weird," she said after taking another sip.

"Whatever," Felix said. "Should we meet at six at my place? We can go to the party afterward. There's one on my floor this time. But don't worry, they don't start until eight. We'll have enough time to study in peace," he said in my direction.

"Okay, sure," I said and looked at Sally. "You'll pick me up again, won't you?"

"As agreed." She winked at me.

"Great, then we'll see each other later," I said as Sally got up and sipped from her cup one more time, causing her to shake her head.

"Till then, you two," she said, and then I was off to my lecture.

Once at home I immediately jumped into the shower and got ready for the party. When I stepped out and wondered about what to put on, a thought sprang into my head: What if Jared was there, too? My hands went moist. Would he talk to me? Ignore me? Or just leave as he'd done so many times before? Whichever it would be, I wanted to be prepared. So, after a long back and forth, I decided to put on my favorite outfit, a pair of stonewashed jeans and my black blouse.

When I was done, I put the papers I needed for studying in my bag and looked at the time. It was already shortly after five. Sally and I had agreed she'd pick me up at five on the dot. I began to worry at twenty past five and called her. After several rings, she finally picked up and moaned into the receiver.

"Evelyn, I can't make it. I'm sick." She sounded awful.

"What's wrong?"

"No idea. But I've been miserable since lunch today. I'm sure it was that damned coffee! I knew something was wrong with it. Are you feeling sick, too?"

"No, I'm fine," I said. "Can I do anything for you? Should I come over?"

"No, no. Go study. My mom will look after me. She's making chicken broth for me."

"Isn't there anything I can do for you?"

"That's really nice of you, but I'll sleep a bit and hopefully we'll see each other tomorrow."

"Okay. Get well and have a good night!"

"Till then," she said, clearly feeling terrible.

I hoped it was nothing serious and she got on her feet soon. Since I was already late, I grabbed my bag and headed to Felix's.

"Hi," he said as I was about to climb the stairs at the entrance of his dorm.

"Hi, Felix," I said and squeezed by two guys who were lugging the speaker of a huge sound system into the building.

"Did Sally call?" I asked and followed Felix up the stairs to his room. It was odd that he didn't ask about her.

"No," he said. "Where is she? Isn't she coming?"

"No, she's sick. Something really must have been wrong with her coffee at lunch."

"Maybe some detergent residue was left behind when they cleaned the machine," he said without showing genuine interest in Sally being sick.

"But then why was everything okay with our coffees?" I couldn't figure it out. I was also a bit confused by Felix's strange behavior.

"Oh, she'll come around. Sally's tougher than she looks," he said. "Let's get started before they crank up the music." He nodded toward the two boys, who had just climbed the last step and, breathing heavily, were now setting the speaker down.

"Okay," I said, still feeling a bit skeptical.

"Stats?" Felix asked as we sat down at the small table in his room.

"Stats!" I said with determination and dropped my folder on the table.

"Anything in particular?"

"Maybe you can explain the difference between descriptive and inferential statistics one more time?"

"Hmm, hang on for a moment. I have to read up on that myself." He frowned and moved his chair closer to mine so he could leaf through my folder. "Oh yes. Right." Apparently, he had found what he was looking for. "So, descriptive means telling it as it is." I nodded. "In descriptive statistics, data is presented in an orderly form using key figures, tables, and graphs and making them comparable with each other. The data collected—for whatever purpose—is structured and described." He looked at me. His face was really close to mine. "Clear so far?"

"Yes . . ." I said hesitantly since I found his physical closeness a little disturbing. Especially since Sally wasn't around and Felix and I were alone.

He continued, smiling. "By contrast, inferential statistics deals with the question of whether the collected data is also valid and meaningful beyond this point." Again he moved his chair closer. "If, for example, it's found during data collection"—he took the pen out of my hand, brushing my fingers more than necessary—"that a pen—" BOOM, BOOM,

BOOM. I was startled as the giant sound system in the hallway, right in front of Felix's door, began to pound away at a deafening volume. The bass caused the furniture to vibrate. I looked at the wall clock. It was just before 6:30. The party, Felix had assured me, would not start before eight. I looked at him, concerned.

"Sound check," he said with his eyes closed. "Just ignore it!"

"Ignore it?" He couldn't be serious. It would probably have been easier to ignore a jet engine than that pounding, nearly eardrum-busting bass.

Then the music broke off as abruptly as it had started and Felix continued as if nothing had happened. "That a pen, when I let go, drops to the grou—" BOOM, BOOM, BOOM. My pulse, which hadn't quite recovered from the first time, must have shot up to two hundred. Suddenly, there was silence on the floor. "When I let go of the pen, it drops to the ground. It's the purpose of inferential statistics to determine whether this is also true for other objects. Whether this statement can be generalized." Felix's calmness suggested to me that sound checks of this kind were part of his daily routine. But I had serious problems focusing. In addition, more and more people were gathering outside the room, distracting me even further. Girls clicked up the stairs in high heels and traipsed along the hallway. Guys followed them, stomping and making the wooden floor creak under their steps. People talked, laughed, and clowned around. A few minutes later, the monster sound system was cranked up again—and this time it stayed on, clearly no longer a sound check. A look at the clock showed me it was only a little after seven. The party was in full swing an hour earlier than scheduled. The attempt to cram stats had become pointless. I raised my eyebrows and looked at Felix with reproach. But instead of apologizing for the noise or saying anything, he just looked deep into my eyes. He must have been watching me for a while without me noticing. Then, with a flash of determination in his eyes, he leaned forward, took stray strands of my hair, and wrapped them around his index finger as he looked at them.

"You're really special." He looked into my eyes again. "Do you know that?" He gently brushed my hair and stroked my cheek with the back of his finger. I held my breath. What was this?

"You're marvelous," he whispered into my ear. Suddenly, I had the urge to shrink back. I liked Felix. I really did like him, but I knew I didn't like him that way. Would never like him that way. I had to make it clear to him I only wanted to be friends. Just friends. Nothing more. I pulled back a little. Felix froze and looked at me earnestly.

"Felix . . . I . . . I like you . . . ," I said.

"And I like you," he said. "A lot." A smile spread across his face and he leaned forward.

"Felix, please let me finish."

"I felt it the first time I saw you," he said in a gentle voice and ran his fingers through my hair. "You and I, we're made for each other."

"Felix, please listen to me. You must have misunderstood something."

"What is there to misunderstand?" he said, again with a gentle voice, and leaned forward with closed eyes, one hand still on my cheek.

I pulled back again just before our lips touched. If I didn't make myself very clear right now, I didn't know what this situation might lead to.

"Felix, I am not in love with you," I finally said with a firm voice. "I like you—but only as a friend."

"What is that supposed to mean?" he asked, irritated.

"That means we are friends, and I feel the same way about you as I do about Sally. I'm not in love. Sorry if it looked that way to you."

Something in Felix's look changed, became hard. "What do you mean by that? Am I not good enough for you? Do I not have enough cash in my bank account? Is that it?"

Deep inside, I shuddered. I moved my chair back and created more space between us. "Felix, please—"

The expression on his face frightened me tremendously. "No *please*," he said. "You've been waving your ass in front of me for months, and now you want to tell me you're not into me?" He snorted with contempt. "You don't even believe that yourself!"

I got up and slowly moved toward the door. The booming bass from a hip-hop song roared from the hallway.

"Damn it, Evelyn, don't fight it!" Now he was on his feet. "We belong together! I felt it from the first moment. And you did, too—so let your heart decide. You know you want me!"

I began to tremble. How could he believe I was in love with him? Had I been giving out such confusing signals without knowing it? I needed to take control of the situation. "Felix, listen to me—"

"It's because of that asshole Calmburry, isn't it?" he shouted, full of rage. "Don't you think I haven't noticed how you look at him?" He grabbed me roughly by the shoulders.

"Let go of me, Felix. You're hurting me," I said, frightened, and attempted to free myself from his grip. But instead of releasing me, he took my face roughly in his hands and kissed me forcefully. He pried apart my lips and shoved his tongue into my mouth. "Let me go now!" I screamed hysterically. The penetrating bass in the hallway drowned out my voice. With all my strength I tried to push him, but he grabbed me by the arms.

Panic rose inside me. "What's come over you?" I shouted. "You're hurting me, damn it! Let go of me!" I screamed again. But as I screamed, he tried to kiss me again, so I attempted to pull away again. Then he stared into my eyes. Something in his look told me he wouldn't let me go. He grabbed me harshly and pushed me down on the bed. A second later, he was over me, pressing his mouth against my lips, which were now throbbing with pain. His hands slid over my blouse and, a moment later, he was working on the buttons, then he gave up and ripped the fabric.

I kicked at him with all my strength and dug my fingernails as deeply as I could into his skin. He grabbed my wrists, gripping them so hard the circulation was cut off and, at the same time, he used his full weight to push my body onto the mattress. Then he let my right hand go, so he could grab both my wrists with his left hand. The other brutally slid down my body, ripped open the buttons of my jeans, and pulled them down to my knees with a firm tug. I was twisting underneath him and screamed with all my might for help. As if to mock me, the music boomed even louder than before. Again, his mouth hit against mine mercilessly. Tears of desperation rolled down my cheeks.

No, please no!

He hastily started to work on his own jeans, impatiently tore open his fly, and pulled them a bit lower. Then he pulled on my panties.

Oh God, please don't! It was going to happen. He would take what he wanted and no one would help me.

Dear God, please help me!

As firmly as I could, I pulled up my knees and rammed them into his stomach, causing him to let go of my hands and cough painfully. This was my chance! I grabbed the lamp on the nightstand and hit him over the head. He let go of me with a scream while the lamp splintered into a thousand pieces. I got up as fast as I could, but Felix recovered, grabbed what remained of my blouse, and pulled me back onto the bed.

"Stop this bullshit!" he hissed through clenched teeth, pinned me to the mattress with all his weight, and spread my legs with his knees. I felt his erection against my thigh. I was paralyzed with fear and horror. I couldn't even send a last prayer to Heaven. The anguished cry inside me did not pass my lips as I began to see Felix's eyes glow. He brought himself into position. I closed my eyes and attempted to separate my mind from my body, but I'd never seemed as closely connected to it as I was right now.

Dear God, please help me!
Let me die!
Just let me die!

Suddenly, someone was rattling the door. Nothing happened. It was locked. Of course.

Then the walls began to shake and blur before my eyes. An earthquake? Before I could consider and answer, the door flew open with a deafening crash. The room shook. The light flickered intensely. An invisible force grabbed Felix, pulled him from me, and flung him into the far corner of the room. I was suddenly hurled off the bed in the opposite direction and hit my head on the floor. I glanced around for an explanation as to what had just happened.

Then I saw *him*.

Jared was standing in the middle of the room walking toward Felix as if in slow motion. Step by step. What was that unusual golden glow surrounding him? A reflection of the light in the hallway? And what was that expression on his face? Focus? Control? He looked as if he was trying to . . . restrain himself? Felix had pulled himself up and was now standing opposite Jared, who sized him up for a moment, then brutally punched him in the face. Felix stumbled and reached out to hit back. But Jared effortlessly evaded him, grabbed Felix's head, and headbutted him with such force that I heard an awful cracking sound; he had broken Felix's nose.

Felix went down and then kicked at Jared who, completely unimpressed by his wild flailing, slowly pulled him up by the hair before punching him in the face with a right and ramming a left into Felix's stomach, making Felix double over coughing. Dignified and yet threatening, Jared kneeled over Felix, who was spitting blood. The ceiling light was flickering wildly. Bright, dark, bright, dark, bright . . .

Jared spoke slowly and clearly, emphasizing every single word. "Should you ever even as much as look at Evelyn again, you will be eating through a straw for the rest of your life. Do you understand?"

Felix avoided the murderous stare, but Jared roughly grabbed him by his hair and forced him to look into his eyes.

"Have. We. Understood. Each. Other?" he said through clenched teeth.

"Yes," Felix said with difficulty.

"Good!" Jared let Felix's hair go, slowly stood up, and turned around. When his eyes flitted across my torn blouse and my jeans at my knees, hatred flared up in his face again, but when he looked into my eyes his look softened. Hastily, I pulled up my jeans and wrapped the remains of my favorite blouse around my bare torso.

He extended his hand and I took it without hesitating. He carefully helped me up. "Are you okay?" he asked, deeply concerned.

I automatically reached for the back of my head. My hair was wet and warm at the spot where I had hit it against the floor.

"Just a flesh wound," I said, "nothing more."

"I'll take you to the hospital, that'll have to be stitched." His tone made clear that objecting was futile.

He quickly took off his sweater and gave it to me, nodding. I was ashamed of how I probably looked and gratefully accepted the large dark-gray sweater and pulled it on. It was warm and smelled of . . . *him*. Jared put his arm around my shoulder to support me.

"Come," he said tenderly, "I'll take you away from here."

I leaned against him and let him lead me. I was safe.

CHAPTER 11

Outside Felix's room, Colin was busy keeping at bay the partyers who, attracted by the ruckus, wanted to sneak a peek into the room. When I finally stepped into the hallway supported by Jared, Colin turned toward us, looked me over, and clenched his hands into fists. Then he looked up from me to Jared.

"If you hadn't already seen to that scumbag, I'd give him a little company about now," Colin said and turned back to the gawkers, who stepped back. I must have been a miserable sight.

Jared led me past the curious onlookers, down the stairs, and out the door. I shrank back from the cold night air and leaned even closer against him. Although he was only wearing a T-shirt, he didn't look the least bit cold.

"Evelyn, do you have any idea where Sally is?" Colin must have been right behind us. He seemed genuinely concerned.

"At home," I said, and all of a sudden it made sense—the bitter coffee, Felix's strange behavior when Sally didn't show up. "She's sick. I think Felix put something in her coffee so she wouldn't come to our study group tonight."

"What?" Colin burst out, enraged, about to turn around to give Felix a little *company* after all. Jared grabbed his arm and held him back.

"Better drive to Sally's place and check how she's doing!" His voice was firm. "Take the Ducati," Jared called over his shoulder. "I'll drive Evelyn in your Mustang."

"Right," Colin agreed, swinging himself onto the black motorcycle parked outside the entrance. Colin and Jared pulled their keys out from their jeans at the same time and tossed them to each other. Jared caught Colin's car keys effortlessly in passing, led me to a dark-blue Mustang in the parking lot, opened the passenger door, and helped me get in. He carefully put the seatbelt on me and almost soundlessly closed the door. Then he raced around the car to get in on the driver's side. The eight-cylinder engine started up with a penetrating roar, and we drove off.

"Are you sure you're okay? Apart from that head wound, I mean," Jared said as we turned onto a busier street.

"Yes," I said, which caused him to examine me with a sideways glance.

"Honest," I said, "I'm fine." Judging by his look, he'd only believe me when he'd heard it from the doctor's mouth.

Suddenly, the expression on Jared's face darkened. "I can't believe what that . . . ," he said and inhaled deeply. "If I'd come even a second later . . ."

"But you didn't," I said as soon as I realized what he was getting at. I couldn't drive out the thought either. If he'd indeed come a second later . . . Suddenly, I tasted bile in my mouth.

Before I knew what was going on, Jared had stopped the Mustang. He got out, ran around the car, and held the door open for me.

Oh yes. I realized what was about to happen. I got out as fast as I could, scrambled a few feet from the car, and threw up in some nearby bushes while Jared carefully brushed the hair out of my face and ran his other hand down my back.

This can't be happening. I'm puking my guts out and he's stroking my back!

When it was finally over and I'd emptied my stomach, Jared held a bottle of water out to me. Where on earth did he get that? I gratefully accepted it, thoroughly rinsed out my mouth, and washed my face while Jared went back to the car to give me some privacy.

"Shall we continue on?" he asked when I returned to the car.

"Yes," I said, lowering my eyes. "Thank you."

"That was the shock," he explained. "Please don't feel embarrassed about it."

"I'll do my best," I said, now feeling even more embarrassed.

I stared out the window for the rest of the drive because I could no longer look Jared in the eye. When we finally arrived at the hospital, I got out before he could open the door for me. He registered me at the reception desk and described my injury. Then he led me up a staircase to the emergency room, where my name was called a few moments later.

"I'll wait for you here," he said as I got up from my chair. "Do you need anything?"

I shook my head and went to the treatment room, where a cheery, rotund nurse—probably in her midforties—received me.

"What's wrong, girl?" she asked.

"I have a wound on the back of my head."

"Let's have a look." I tilted my head forward to let her examine me.

"Hmm, I'm afraid it'll have to be stitched," she said. "Do you have any other injuries?"

"No, but . . . I just threw up and . . ." Could I really ask her for this? "Would you perhaps . . . have . . . a toothbrush for me?"

The nurse laughed. "Typical girl," she said. "Loses a ton of blood, but the important thing is having fresh breath!"

Now I had to smile.

"Just wait a little. I'll see what I can do."

"Thank you," I said and a few minutes later she returned with a bright red children's toothbrush and a sample-size tube of strawberry-flavored toothpaste.

"If that's your boyfriend out there, I can understand wanting the toothbrush," she teased while handing over the toothbrush and toothpaste.

"No. He's not . . . my *boyfriend*."

"But he brought you here, didn't he?"

"Yes, he did. But . . ."

"Well, maybe he wants to be?" she said with a smile and winked at me. While she left the room to get a sterile suture kit, I walked over to the sink in the corner and thoroughly brushed my teeth. Twice. Then I washed my face again and was about to sit on the gurney when the nurse came back into the room with a silver-haired doctor.

"So, Miss . . . Lakewood," the doctor read my name from the clipboard in his hands. "Let's patch you up," he said and went to work.

After disinfecting my wound and suturing it with six stitches, he hid it under a thick muslin bandage. When he was done, I energetically jumped from the gurney and almost fell. *Oops!* My legs were wobblier than I'd thought. As soon as I'd recovered my balance, I shot a quick glance in the mirror over the sink and decided I looked like a . . . total ninny. No. I looked like a total ninny who'd attempted to disguise herself as a sultan! The bandage had to go. That much was for sure. Especially considering *who* was waiting for me. With the excuse of wanting to wash my hands one more time I waited until the doctor and the nice nurse were out the door, tore the ridiculous bandage from my head, and threw it in a trash can before I stepped into the hallway. As soon as Jared saw me, he jumped up from his chair and came toward me.

"So, how are you?" he asked, still highly concerned. "Did they have to stitch it?"

"Six stitches," I said while he walked around me to inspect my treated injury.

"Didn't they put a bandage on you?" he asked.

"You don't need a bandage for something as little as this," I said with feigned casualness.

Jared looked at me with raised eyebrows. "Ah," was all he said but the suspicious twitch at the corner of his mouth told me he knew what had happened to my bandage.

"Well, come on, I'll drive you home," he said and led me, with an amused smirk, to the parking lot, where he held open the passenger door of the Mustang for me. I got in and watched him walk around the car. Although I felt awkward staring at him so obviously, I couldn't take my eyes off him. He'd saved me. Had he not been there, something terrible would have happened. No idea if I'd ever been able to get over it. Probably not. How could I have misjudged Felix so badly? If Jared hadn't been there . . .

But he *was* there! He'd saved me, he'd . . . protected me!

I followed every one of his movements, breathed in his scent, noted every breath, every blink, every tensing and relaxing of his facial muscles. He was just so gorgeous. The more I observed him, the stronger my desire became to find out more about him. I wanted to know what music he listened to, what he liked to eat, which season he liked most, whether he had a happy childhood when his parents were still alive. I simply wanted to know everything about him.

Suddenly, it became clear to me that this was the time—me alone with him in the car—the opportunity to find out more about Jared. A one-time opportunity to finally ask all those questions that kept me awake at night. This time he couldn't just take off as he always did. Unless, of course, he'd rather jump out of a moving vehicle than talk. But what should I ask him? What should I start with? A bit of small talk first? Or just go all in right away?

"Is there anything I can do for you?" Jared asked with a smile.

"I . . ." *Damn!* Of course he'd noticed I'd been staring at him the whole time. I breathed deeply and cleared my throat. I needed a firm voice for what I was about to say.

"Jared, really, thank you for everything you've done for me," I said. At least, I didn't sound as if I were about to burst into tears any moment. That was something.

"Not for that," Jared said.

What? I felt stumped. "I shouldn't . . . thank you for what you did?" Now I did sound as if I were about to cry.

He looked at me again. "I'm the one who's grateful," he said.

"You? But why?"

"Arriving there in time for you," he said with a firm voice. He was grateful for having arrived there in time for me? The butterflies were let loose in my stomach.

Suddenly, I noticed Jared was turning onto the street where my residence was. *Damn!* I'd waited too long. I needed to stall.

"Why weren't you at school much this week?" I said. It was the only thing I could think of.

"I had to settle a few things at home."

"Oh." I had hoped for a better answer. Or, at least, one I could follow up on. But instead, Jared took the wind out of my sails, and valuable seconds passed. I needed more time. Since my brain was obviously in standby mode, I couldn't think of even one somewhat sensible question. Anything I thought of would have left me looking like a complete idiot. I was so busy pushing words back and forth in my mind, I only realized we had already arrived when Jared was holding the door open for me. *Double damn.* He'd be gone in a minute.

"May I walk you to the door?" he asked. "Just to be on the safe side." Was that concern or anger in his voice?

"Sure," I said.

That should buy me a little time. I had to think of something. Ask him a question. Any question.

"Will you be at school tomorrow?" I asked as we walked side by side.

"I don't know yet," he said and breathed in deeply. "It depends."

"On what?" I asked, but instead of giving me an answer, he simply stopped, turned to me, and looked deeply into my eyes. His face was so close to mine. The intensity of his gaze caused me to fall silent. While he looked at me, a parade of emotions flitted across his face. Then his expression became sad.

"Sleep well, Evelyn," he said and exhaled lightly. Then he stroked my cheek so lightly with the back of his hand that I hardly felt it. I gasped. Although he had barely touched me, his fingers left a hot tingling on my skin. I shut my eyes, but he let his hand fall away. A second later, Jared turned and walked toward his car.

No! I couldn't let him walk away this time. I had to know what it all meant and why he behaved so strangely toward me. He definitely owed me a few answers!

"Wait!" I desperately cried out and ran after him. I caught up with him after a few steps, and he stopped and turned toward me. All of a sudden, I forgot what I wanted to ask him—I didn't even know anymore why I'd run after him. His stunning appearance left me in awe. He looked at me, and as before, I could see he was infinitely sad.

At that moment, I longed for nothing more than to see him happy. To *make* him happy.

I didn't know what it was about. Maybe because we were alone and darkness hid us like a protective cloak from curious onlookers. Maybe it was because this feeling was even more intense than before. But I finally lost my last shred of self-control. I didn't know why and I really didn't care, but at that moment I gave in to my inner longing, threw my arms around Jared's neck, and kissed him. For a second, he stood there motionless, then he wrapped his arms around me. One hand on my hip, the other on my back, he pulled me in and pressed my body so tightly against his I could feel his heart hammering wildly in his chest.

He returned my kiss with a heartfelt sigh—long and intense. Then he withdrew and moved his lips along my neck while moaning with each breath, moving his hand along my back and pulling me even closer. Almost trembling I threw my head back and wrapped my arms even tighter around his neck. Every muscle in my body appeared to vibrate.

"Oh God, Evelyn," he whispered into my ear. A second later I again felt his lips on mine and his tongue in my mouth. I had pictured countless times what it would be like to be so close to Jared . . . but reality made fantasy pale in comparison. It was so much better than I had ever dreamed. I attempted to pull him closer to me and prayed the moment would never end. But in the next second, he detached himself, pushed me gently away, and looked into my eyes. I wanted to melt into his arms, but he held me back with gentle pressure.

"I'm sorry," he whispered, full of pain, stroked my cheek one last time, got into his car, and drove off into the darkness.

CHAPTER 12

I stared at my alarm clock until its penetrating beeping finally released me from my almost-sleepless night. Although I fell asleep long after midnight, I'd lain awake a full two hours, staring alternately at the ceiling and the alarm, waiting for the damned thing to finally go off. Sighing deeply, I rose and went to the bathroom.

Last night's feelings once again overwhelmed me. A mixture of longing, sadness, pain, and desperation—a debilitating cocktail of emotions. I had no idea what to do about it. Or even what would help me feel a little better. All I knew was that Jared had created this turmoil of emotions inside me. The memory of that unbelievable kiss flared up in my thoughts. That was probably the best sensation I'd ever felt—followed immediately by one of the worst: rejection. Why had Jared left me there and disappeared? As much as I tried, I couldn't understand it. How could something that felt so right be so wrong? Why, for Heaven's sake, would he not explain it? I'd racked my brain all night over this. Did Jared not feel what I felt? Why didn't he stay with me? I didn't get it. Only one thing became painfully clear to me last night: I was totally hooked on loving Jared Calmburry and didn't want to spend another day of my life without him.

I toyed with the thought of calling Sally to ask her how she felt but decided against it. If she was still sick from Felix's treacherous attack, she would surely still be asleep now. So I decided to call her after my first lecture if she hadn't shown up at school. Hopefully, she'd be a bit more rested by then.

When it was finally time to get going, I grabbed my bag and went out the door, but a sudden thought cut off my breath as if I were caught in a stranglehold. *Felix!* I tried to overcome my panic. What should I do if I saw him? How should I behave? What would he do? Attack me? Ignore me? Or would he try to talk to me? I trembled.

Twenty minutes had passed before I'd calmed myself down enough to enter the lecture hall, long after the lecture had already begun. I snuck in as inconspicuously as possible, sat at the very back and began to search row after row for Felix. Three times. He wasn't there. I sighed with relief.

Either he was so seriously injured he had to be treated at the hospital or he had heeded Jared's warning to keep away from me. I truly hoped the latter was the case and I would never again have to look at that pig.

As soon as my lecture was over, I took my cell phone out of my bag and called Sally. "Hi, Evelyn," she moaned into the receiver.

"Sally, how are you?" I asked, concerned.

"Awful—I puked all night," she answered, repulsed. "But how are *you*?" Her voice sounded incredibly strained. "Colin was here last night. He told me what happened. Are you okay?"

"Yes," I said. "Nothing . . . happened to me. Don't worry about me."

"And Felix? Are you going to the police?"

"I haven't thought about that yet, to be honest."

"But you should. That psychopath should be locked up!"

"You know he put something in your coffee, don't you?"

"Yes." Sally's voice sounded bitter. "The doctor thought the symptoms suggested a poisonous herb. Probably digitalis."

"A poisonous herb?"

"Hmm."

"What?" I erupted. So far I had assumed Felix had given her a simple emetic—a few hours of nausea and that would be it. But I shuddered at the thought of him outright poisoning Sally. And digitalis, to boot—even a few grams could be lethal, or at least, that's what I thought I remembered from biology class.

"And what happens next? Are you being treated? You'll be healthy again soon, right?"

"I have to take pills with activated charcoal and the doctor says I'll need lots of rest."

"Yes, please rest. Can I visit you tomorrow?"

"I'd think so."

"Sally, I told you to stay off the phone. You need to get some rest." Sally's mother was scolding her in the background.

"Okay, till tomorrow," I said. It was best if she listened to her mother and got some rest.

"Yup, till then."

"Get well . . ." I wanted to wish her well but Sally had already hung up.

I endured the next two lectures without really participating. Fortunately, I didn't run into Felix. So I decided to banish this horrible memory I would always associate with him into that little locked box of my subconscious where I carefully kept all the other dark moments of my life so they would not rob me of my senses. When the time came, I would open that box and survey its contents. One after the other. And try to process everything. Somehow.

My thoughts should have been put at ease—if that other matter weren't there. As much as I tried not to, I watched for Jared the entire morning. There was nothing I longed for more than to see him. To talk to him. To . . . feel him. I returned again and again to the previous night. His intoxicating scent—leather, sweet cedar wood, and something that reminded me of suntan lotion. How he had wrapped his arms around me and pulled me close, pressed me against his chest—so close I had felt his heartbeat. And then that kiss—that kiss . . .

My breathing turned heavy when the longing threatened to overwhelm me. If I hadn't held on to the stair railing, my knees would have probably given way.

Since I didn't have lectures on Friday afternoon and I was only going to visit Sally the following day, I wondered how I'd spend the rest of the day—without going crazy with longing. Since I didn't know where, how, or when to reach Jared, the best thing would be to concentrate on something else. I somehow needed to find a distraction. Now. Fast. But what would I do? I didn't feel like going for a stroll in town. And if I went to the library to pass the time, I would only think about Jared and possibly look for more information on the Calmburry crest. Precisely what I wanted to avoid. And working on my assignments—I lacked the patience for that. So what would I do?

I already knew the answer: Water! I needed water. Even when nothing else worked, water always helped revitalize my strength and made me feel better. I didn't want the experience in the shower to keep me from that.

No—nobody would take the joy of swimming from me. Especially not Madison. In any case, I hadn't seen her since then. Maybe I was lucky and she had moved or was studying at another college that would fit more appropriately with her social status.

I went home on a whim, packed my swimming gear, and walked to the sports facility. Since most people were probably eating lunch at that time or had already started their weekend, I was the only one in the pool, which I was happy about. Without losing much time, I jumped into the water and swam lap after lap. I had no idea how long I swam, and I only got out after my arms and legs had gradually become heavy from exertion. I had achieved exactly what I wanted. I felt well and, more importantly, I'd fully released my energy. After showering—not without looking around several times—I slipped into my clothes and started home. It was dusk, and the cold drizzle was turning the remains of the snow into slush and chilled me a little. So I hurried home and went to bed without even looking at the time.

I awoke late the next morning and stretched my limbs in all directions because they were stiff from not moving all night. Madness! I must have slept for more than twelve hours. I couldn't remember when I'd last been so tired. I rose yawning and went to brush my teeth and comb the knots out of my hair. Fortunately, all that water had caused the injury on my forehead to heal and the wound at the back of my head to narrow to a small scabby scratch. The absorbable sutures would see to the rest.

When I was done with my hair, I took my wallet, cell phone, and key, put them into my small purse, and left for Sally's. I stopped at a small florist's on my way to buy a get-well bouquet. It was pouring out.

"Hello, Evelyn, nice to see you," Sally's mother greeted me at the door after I'd climbed the six steps to the narrow town house and pressed the bell with the label "Pamela & Sally Flynt."

"Come on in. She's upstairs in her room." Although I'd never had much opportunity to talk with Pamela because she was mostly running off to work when I visited, I really liked her and thought their relationship was wonderful. It was so loving.

"Hello, Pamela, how is she?"

"Much better than yesterday," she said and you could really see how relieved she was.

"You brought flowers?" she asked, touched, when she noticed the bouquet wrapped in colorful paper. "She'll be delighted. Go upstairs. I just have to get a little shopping done. You're staying a while, aren't you?"

I nodded.

"Okay, then we'll see each other later," Pamela said while putting on her raincoat. "Till then."

"Yes, see ya."

After she'd shut the door behind her, I took my boots off, hung my coat on the overfilled coatrack, and went upstairs. I gently knocked on the door.

"Yes?" Sally said, straining.

"Hi, it's me." I spoke with a lowered voice even though she was awake. It seemed more appropriate. "How are y—?" Sally's appearance stopped me. Propped up by two pillows, she lay in bed half seated and was holding an oversized teacup in her hands. She had two dark, almost black shadows beneath her eyes while the remainder of her drawn face appeared as pale and translucent as her bed sheet. Her normally intricately styled hair stood out in all directions, and the outlines of her body under the cover suggested she'd lost weight. I also noticed that even her gums were colorless. She looked dreadful. It was difficult to imagine what she'd been through the last few days!

"Hi, Evelyn—you look as if you've seen a ghost," she joked.

"Well," I answered, trying to smile, "I couldn't be much paler than you."

I sat down on the bed beside her, next to the dozing black-and-white cat curled up at the foot of her bed.

"I brought you some flowers," I said because I didn't know what to say in light of the disturbing sight of Sally looking like death warmed over.

"Thank you, that's so nice of you."

I held the bouquet out to her, but she didn't seem strong enough to hold it. So I put the flowers on the nightstand. I'd ask Pamela for a vase when she got back from shopping.

"Did you go to classes yesterday?" Sally asked.

"Yeah, why?"

"Did you see Felix?"

"No," I answered coldly. "And I hope I never see him again!" What he'd done to me was one thing but that he'd almost killed Sally just to be with me . . . That shithead would have walked over bodies—literally.

"Maybe you're in luck," she said. "I could imagine Colin doing away with him. Or Jared." Sally smiled about her comment, but I couldn't entirely get rid of the feeling that it could be true. And to be honest, there was a small part of me that wished it was.

"Has Colin been with you?" I asked to distract myself.

Sally nodded. "He didn't leave my side." A hint of a smile showed around her colorless lips. "Until Mom sent him away."

"I can imagine that," I said and smiled.

"And do you know who else was here?" she asked after a pause.

"Who?"

Sally smiled. "Jared."

"*Jared* was here?" I said.

"Yes, last night. Colin had already been here most of the day. I fell asleep some because I was so exhausted, but when I woke up, Jared was sitting next to Colin." She closed her eyes and hesitated as if she were searching for the right words. "While I was waking up," she started, "if I'm not altogether mistaken . . . I saw something remarkable." She frowned, focusing. "There was a sort of . . . light. A golden light." She shook her head. "I know this sounds crazy but when I saw this light and felt its warmth, I felt better, just like that. Much better. I haven't thrown up since, and my blurry vision was suddenly gone, and my heart started beating more regularly."

"And you think Jared had something to do with it?" I asked.

"Well, this light . . . did somehow . . . come from him." She searched my face. "I talked with Colin about it later. He said Jared had a kind of . . . gift."

"A gift as a *healer*? Are you serious?"

She shrugged. "All I know is that I've felt better since he was here. I wasn't saying anything else."

"Don't you think that's because of the medicine the doctor gave you?" The thought that Jared was responsible for Sally's recovery seemed a little far-fetched to me.

"The doctor said the symptoms would probably last for days and only gradually recede. But I felt better all of a sudden after Jared's visit." She shrugged again. "No idea what's behind it—I'm just telling it like it is."

I looked at Sally, perplexed. How was that possible? Did Jared really have a *gift*?

I heard the house door shut.

"I'm back," Pamela called up the stairs.

"I'll go ask your mom for a vase," I said and nodded toward the bouquet. Still confused, I walked down the stairs.

When I caught up with Pamela in the kitchen, she was putting the groceries away.

"May I help you?" I offered.

"Yes, please put the apples in the fruit bowl, will you?" She laughed. "By the way, you've got a nice boyfriend." She winked and disappeared into the small pantry next to the kitchen to put away some pasta and a few cans.

"What boyfriend?" I said while reaching into her shopping bag and taking out the apples.

"Well, this Jason," she said with a strained voice. She sounded as if she was trying to reach the uppermost shelf on her tiptoes.

"Jared?" I asked.

"Oh yes, Jared, I think."

"What makes you think he's my boyfriend?" I asked as I put the apples in the fruit bowl.

"He isn't?"

"No." My answer sounded like a question.

"Does he know that? He seems to be pretty crazy about you." Back in the kitchen, she put fresh vegetables away in the fridge. "When Sally was asleep, Jared and Colin talked about you outside the door."

"About me?" I hesitated. "What did he say?"

"That he can't stop thinking about you, that it's almost driving him crazy, and so on. The usual stuff when you've got a total crush on someone."

I clung to the table because my knees were giving out. *He* couldn't stop thinking about *me*? Was this a dream? "What else did he say?" I asked, trying to sound as calm as possible.

"When they noticed I was in the next room, the conversation stopped pretty quickly. But if you ask me, what I heard was pretty unmistakable." Pamela winked again. That longing flared up inside me, and suddenly I felt the urge to be alone and think in peace and quiet about everything.

"Do you have a vase for the flowers I brought Sally?"

"Of course." She took a slim vase from one of the kitchen cupboards, filled it halfway with water, and handed it to me.

"Thank you," I said and went upstairs again.

My thoughts were racing. Jared couldn't stop thinking of *me*? Now I really couldn't understand why he always avoided me. What was that about? Didn't he want to be with me? Didn't he have feelings for me? Or had I misunderstood something? Was there possibly another reason he couldn't stop thinking of me?

"Is Colin still coming today?" I asked Sally while taking the flowers from their wrapping and putting them in the vase.

"He said he'd try," she said, somewhat downcast. "Things are crazy at his place." She sighed.

"Did he say why?"

"No," she said. "But I think it has something to do with Jared."

"What makes you think that?"

"He indicated that Jared's in a little trouble and that he has to support him."

"Trouble?"

"That's what Colin said. I didn't get what he meant by that, either."

The unbridled longing arose once more. I could think of nothing but seeing Jared, talking to him, asking him all the questions that ached inside me, questions only he had the answers to.

Sally's mother was suddenly standing at the door. "How are you, my little angel?" she asked, sat down on the other side of the bed, and placed her hand on Sally's forehead to check her temperature.

"Good," Sally said. "I'm even a little hungry."

"That's a good sign," Pamela said and laughed. "What would you like?"

"Pancakes," Sally said after a brief moment of reflection, which caused Pamela and me to laugh.

"Well, if that's what you want, I'll head downstairs again and make the best pancakes you've ever had." Pamela tenderly brushed the hair out of Sally's face. "Are you staying for lunch, Evelyn?" she asked me, smiling.

"No. Unfortunately, I have to go." Apart from the fact that I wasn't hungry, I couldn't stand just hanging around. I had to do something. I had to . . . find Jared. "Get well," I said to Sally and hugged her goodbye. "Bye, Pamela, till next time," I said and hugged her before going down the stairs, slipping my shoes on, throwing on my jacket, and hurrying outside.

Fortunately, the rain had stopped—at least for the moment. My plan was as good as futile even with the best conditions. Especially since Colin, whose number I'd gotten from Sally, couldn't be reached and I was left to my own devices. There was only one thing left to do: start searching!

I intended to seek out all the places I'd seen Jared. Since Sally's place wasn't far from the old city, I decided to start my search there.

And so I stood outside the little Asian restaurant a few minutes later, when I was suddenly overcome by the thought of Felix. It sent a shiver down my spine. I had only been with him here a few days ago. I shook my head and attempted to chase the thought away. A look inside the restaurant made me sigh. Jared wasn't there. I roamed through the narrow streets in which I had encountered him and Aiden by chance, hoping to spot Jared, but I was unsuccessful. When I tried to reach Colin again after an hour, a friendly female voice answered and said the person I was calling was unavailable at the moment and that I should try again later. Colin had probably turned off his phone.

Finally, I had to admit it: it was useless. I'd never find Jared this way. Also, it had started to rain again, so I decided to stop my search for the time being. I went home to dry my things and reward myself with a warm shower.

I got into bed with wet hair and tried to sleep a little. But when not even that succeeded, all that was left for me was to dully stare at the ceiling and dwell on my dreary thoughts. I felt incredibly lonely.

Jared was—in every way—unreachable, Sally was out of action, and Felix . . . Felix was definitely not an option anymore.

Suddenly, my eyes wandered over my scattered papers and abruptly stopped on a crumpled piece of paper. I got out of bed, picked it up, and smoothed it out. Then I called the number from the paper. After the third ring, I heard a woman's voice that seemed familiar in an odd way.

"Hayman, good evening."

"Good evening . . ." I started hesitantly. "Am I speaking to Ruth?"

"Yes, who's this?"

"This is Evelyn Lakewood . . . You picked me up at the train station several weeks ago."

"Oh, hello, Evelyn, I'd hoped you'd call me. How are you? Do you like the college?" she asked cheerfully. She remembered me—I felt relieved.

"Oh yes, it's very . . . beautiful here."

"Have you had supper?" she asked and saved me from spelling out how lonely I felt.

"No, not yet," I answered hopefully.

"You know, since my Hanna is no longer here, I have to eat alone all the time. I'd enjoy a little company. Would you like to drop by?"

"I don't want to cause you any trouble," I said but was secretly really grateful for Ruth's invitation.

"I'd be delighted if you could visit me, Evelyn," she said. "Can you be here at seven?"

"Yes, I'd be delighted to come."

She described the way to her place. It wasn't far at all from my dorm. I could get there comfortably on foot.

"Till later. I'm looking forward to it," Ruth said.

"Yes, till later. And . . . thanks," I said and hung up.

About twenty to seven, it was already dark outside and the sparse light of a few streetlights lit the street at irregular intervals. I felt a strange constriction in my chest and picked up my pace. The strange feeling of being followed overcame me once more and I felt a nervous fear rise yet again. The thought of that man went through my head. *"Get away or I will no longer be able to do anything for you."* I would have run if the cobblestone pavement hadn't been so slippery from the slush and the risk of falling so great. I looked around every few steps, but except for a cat that almost frightened me to death, I couldn't see anything.

A few minutes later, I stood in front of Ruth's building, relieved. I quickly looked for her name among the labels and pressed the bell. Suddenly, I realized I was standing there empty-handed. *Damn!* I should have brought something. Flowers or a bottle of wine. But it was too late for that.

"Hello?" Ruth said through the intercom. Her voice calmed me.

"Hi, Ruth—it's Evelyn."

"Hi, Evelyn, come on in. Second floor, apartment on the right." A buzzing sound told me she'd opened the door. I quickly went in and closed it carefully after looking around one last time. I thoroughly wiped my wet boots on the doormat in the entrance area of the building so I wouldn't spread the slush through the entire stairwell. Then I walked up to the second floor, where Ruth received me at her doorstep with a smile.

"So nice of you to have come, dear," she said and greeted me with a warm hug. "I hope you're hungry. I made lasagna."

"Oh, wonderful," I said and entered the flat with Ruth. Her home was small but furnished with loving care. I felt comfortable right away. Apart from countless books distributed across a number of shelves without any recognizable system, several colorful accessories and photos of smiling faces radiated comfort.

"Is that your daughter?" I asked and pointed at a particularly pretty picture that showed Ruth with a startlingly beautiful young woman.

"Yes, that's Hanna," she said proudly while taking my coat, putting it on a hanger, and hanging it in the maple closet in the hallway. "The photo was taken this summer, shortly before she moved to London."

"She's beautiful," I said.

"Isn't she, though?" she said, touched.

When I looked around the flat, I noticed there was no evidence on the shoe rack or in the closet that Ruth was living with a man.

"Do you live here by yourself?" I asked.

"Yes."

"What about Hanna's father?" I asked, digging further. I hoped I wasn't overstepping my bounds.

"Oh, I never married." She smiled. "Come, let's go into the kitchen. Supper should be just about ready."

My stomach growled at the delicious smell that greeted me in the kitchen, which had been put together with a colorful assortment of furniture. I hadn't sensed a true feeling of hunger for weeks, but this aroma got my mouth watering.

"It smells delightful," I said, and Ruth rewarded me with a charming smile. She asked me to sit down at a small square table she'd already set with multicolored dishes and candles of varying sizes. She filled our glasses and then took the pan out of the stove with crocheted potholders and set it on the table. My stomach growled again, causing us to share a laugh.

She took my plate and placed a large piece of steaming lasagna on it with a wooden spatula, then served herself.

"Bon appétit."

"Bon appétit, Ruth," I replied and impatiently cut a piece with the fork and pushed the still too-hot lasagna into my mouth. The taste of savory tomatoes, soft pasta, fine herbs, and melted cheese caused me to moan. "I think this is the best I've ever had," I said after I'd swallowed the first bite and was already guiding the second to my mouth.

Ruth laughed.

"Well, tell me," she said a few minutes later. "How do you like Oxford?"

"It's beautiful here," I said, carefully considering what to tell her and what to keep to myself. "Especially the buildings. The architecture is fantastic."

"How's the dorm?"

"Great. My room is fairly small but completely sufficient. I even have my own bathroom."

"And the college? You're at Christ Church, aren't you?"

I nodded. "The courses I'm taking are really interesting," I said while taking another bite of lasagna, "but because I'm several months behind, I really have to work hard to catch up. That's why I joined a study group right away. We meet once a week." That should have been, we *used to meet* once a week.

"Excellent," she said. "Hanna was in several study groups. That's got to be better than working alone in the library."

I tried to force a smile and placed the last piece of lasagna in my mouth. "That was delicious. Thank you so much."

"Did you have enough?" she asked.

I rubbed my full belly. "More than enough," I said, smiling.

We cleared the table, and while she started washing dishes, Ruth told me of her work as a taxi driver. I offered to help her with the dishes, but when I reached for a wet plate, it suddenly slid out of my hand and broke on the rack. I cut my thumb trying to catch it. It wasn't a deep cut, but it bled immediately.

Ruth took my hand and inspected it. "Fortunately, it's not deep," she said. "Let's get you a bandage." She took me to the bathroom, where she sought out disinfectant, a bandage, and scissors. "Can you manage by yourself?"

"I think I can manage," I joked. "Sorry about the plate." Ruth made a dismissive hand motion to tell me I needn't apologize and went back to the kitchen to pick up the shards.

I let plenty of water run over the wound—as usual—until it stopped bleeding, then I disinfected the cut and put a bandage over it. When I was done, I went past the overflowing bookshelves to the kitchen, scanning the titles as I went. As if hit by lightning, I stopped at the title of one book.

Nimue, I read on the thick green binding. Where did I know that from? I had heard that word somewhere before. I pulled the book from the shelf.

"Everything all right?" Ruth called from the kitchen.

"Yes," I said, lost in thought, and looked at the book in my hands.

"I hope you left some room for dessert." She was drying her hands on a checkered towel when I entered the kitchen.

"What do you have there?" she asked and pointed at the book.

"What does Nimue mean?"

"Nimue was the Lady of the Lake. The Guardian of Avalon. Don't you know the old legends? The legend of Arthur?"

I reflected. "Yes, I know the legend of Arthur. King Arthur, the Knights of the Round Table, Sir Lancelot, Merlin . . . But this is the first time I've heard of Nimue." *Well, not the very first time,* but I couldn't think of why the name seemed familiar.

"Then it's high time," said Ruth with a smile and turned to the counter to prepare the dessert. "Nimue is a key element in the Arthur legend. She was the one who gave Merlin Excalibur—you know, the sword Arthur would later pull out of the stone. Unfortunately, she doesn't have the best reputation, but in my opinion she's not been given due credit."

"What do you mean?"

"Nimue was Merlin's lover. However, in many narratives, it's said she didn't love him but only seduced him to steal his magical powers. It's even said that she killed him, that she buried him alive in a cave." Ruth snorted. "Utter garbage, if you ask me."

"So you think she loved him?"

Ruth turned and set two bowls of vanilla ice cream and hot raspberries on the table. Then, with a meaningful look, she took the book from my hand, turned pages until she'd found the passage she was looking for, and began to read:

> Thus I turn my back on immortality,
> preferring your love to eternal life.
> For all the time in the world is meaningless,
> compared with just one day by your side.

She pressed the open book against her chest and looked at me. "I believe Merlin and Nimue loved each other with all their hearts," she said after a short pause. "A love that was stronger than death." Ruth was visibly touched.

I was startled. "Was Nimue immortal?"

"She was the Guardian of Avalon, the legendary, mist-enshrouded island that's said to contain the source of eternal life," Ruth said almost in a whisper. "Eternal youth and beauty," she added, lost in thought, but I suddenly had the strange image of a young woman in the arms of a doting old man.

"What did Nimue see in an old man like Merlin?" I asked with a frown. I found the thought a little off-putting.

Ruth laughed. "In the fifth century, the average life expectancy of a person was barely thirty-four years—anyone in their late thirties was considered geriatric back then. That's why Merlin is shown as a frail old man with a white beard, because this is our idea of a man in the last years of his life. But he was probably only a few years older than you." She smiled. "And to Nimue, age played no role. She was a wise spirit in the body of a beautiful young woman," she added thoughtfully.

Neither of us said anything. I was lost in thought, so I barely touched my dessert.

"And what does the lake mean? You called her . . ."

"The Lady of the Lake, yes. Nimue was a magical creature—water was her element."

Water was her element. I was startled. That was precisely the phrase I'd told Jared before he stared at me in shock. Back then in the lecture hall when he sat beside me. He had stared at me just as upset as . . . *But of course!* Suddenly I remembered where I'd heard that name before. Professor Mayflower had used it on my first day, before she fled from the lecture hall. I stared into empty space, shocked. What did it all mean?

"What's the matter?" Ruth asked, concerned, tearing me from my thoughts.

"Nothing," I said. "I just . . . I just thought of something," I said and started to eat my melting ice cream.

"Why are you so interested in Nimue?" she asked and turned to her dessert.

I didn't know what to say. Surely I was just imagining things and would look ridiculous if I talked about it. And that was the best case. It was more likely Ruth would consider me crazy. I had to think of something.

"Well, I read on the Christ Church homepage that one of my professors is interested in British mythology, and I'd like to get some brownie points with her by having a little bit of background knowledge." This excuse came easier than expected.

"You mean Professor Mayflower?" Ruth asked.

I gasped. "Yes, that's the one. Do you know her?"

"No, not personally. But I've been interested in the Arthurian legend since my childhood. I got that from my mother—it was as if she were possessed by it. And in some circles the name Mayflower is well known."

"In some circles?" I repeated and leaned forward with anticipation. Ruth also leaned forward a little and suddenly spoke in a lowered voice.

"In this area there is talk of a secret society that calls itself Legatum Merlini."

"Merlin's Legacy," I translated. I'd never been an ace in Latin, but my knowledge of the language was good enough.

Ruth nodded. "A centuries-old order that has taken on the duty of protecting and preserving Merlin's legacy."

"And what is that legacy?" I asked.

"My mother sought the answer to that question all her life." Ruth looked off into the distance and became pensive. I gave her a moment to return to the present from her memories.

"What do you know about it?" I asked as soon as Ruth's look had cleared up again and she smiled at me apologetically.

"Well," she answered, reflecting. "Supposedly, the Order has a kind of secret identifying sign. Shortly before her death, my mother spoke of nothing else."

"What does this sign look like?" I asked and couldn't shake the suspicion that I'd known the answer for some time. "Do you have a picture of it?"

Ruth got up and hurried to her book collection. I couldn't tolerate staying seated with all this anticipation and shot up from my chair and followed her into the hallway.

"Let's see," Ruth said and stroked her finger along the spines of the books. "Ah, here it is." She pulled a dark-blue volume from the shelf, licked her index finger, and began leafing through the book. I shifted back and forth from one leg to the other.

"Here," Ruth said an endless ten seconds later and pointed at a tiny symbol at the very bottom of the last page. The tension was difficult to bear—I impatiently looked at it and—

"I knew it!" I burst out when I recognized the symbol.

Ruth looked at me, surprised. "You know what that is?" she asked excitedly.

"Yes," I said and all of a sudden was pervaded by a remarkable inner calm. It all finally seemed to make sense. "That's the Calmburry family crest."

Incredible! They all really did belong to a secret society. Jared, Colin, Madison, Aiden, Karen Mayflower, and Professor Martin. That's why they all behaved so strangely. They were trying to keep something secret. Something that had to do with *Merlin*. I laughed inside. Sally hadn't been that far off the mark when she suggested the Mafia.

"Where have you seen this before?" Ruth asked and suddenly seemed really excited. It looked as if she had not only helped me move ahead but that I was also in possession of a piece of the puzzle she was missing. For a second I weighed whether I could trust Ruth and then concluded that if I couldn't trust *her*, I couldn't try anybody.

I took a moment to collect myself, then breathed in deeply and told Ruth my entire story. Starting with my first day at the college with the crash in the lecture hall. Jared. Professor Mayflower, who stared at us in shock and then stormed out. I described how I'd come across the book in the library and what I'd read in it. I talked about Madison, her tattoo, the attack in the shower, my amulet, and Professor Martin's seal ring. Finally, I told her about Felix and how Jared had saved me and about Sally, who believed she'd been healed by him.

When I was done, I exhaled loudly. It had felt so good to finally talk to someone about all these things. It felt as if a huge weight had been lifted from me. I felt so liberated and relieved I almost burst into tears. Only when I was sure nothing would happen did I look Ruth in the eyes.

"Incredible!" she said and shook her head in disbelief. She appeared to be in turmoil. "My mother spent nearly her entire life trying to solve this puzzle, and now . . ."

"What now?" I asked. I had not expected this reaction.

"Now she's no longer here to see how it was solved," Ruth said and her voice was suddenly filled with a deep sadness.

"*I* solved it? What do you mean?"

She was silent for a short while, then furrowed her brow. "You read about Myrddin in the Calmburry family chronicle, didn't you? Eowyn's youngest son," she reminded me.

"Yes. What about him?"

Ruth looked at the ceiling in thought. "I know much about Myrddin from my mother. But I'd never associated him with the Calmburrys. Though it seems so obvious . . ." For a moment Ruth appeared completely lost in thought, and when she continued to speak, it seemed more like she was talking to herself. "Was that what Mom had found out? The discovery she spoke about? She wanted to tell me . . . but the accident . . . She never got around to it . . ." Ruth shook her head. "Why did I never figure it out myself? It's almost as if this family is somehow . . . shielded." She shut her eyes, focusing. "And yet everything unmistakably points in that direction. The plane crash . . . Karen Mayflower takes in little Jared as her foster child . . ."

Wait a minute. "Jared grew up with Karen Mayflower?" Had I heard that right? "Ruth, what do you mean by that?" I could not make any sense of her words.

She needed a moment to sort her thoughts, and her eyes began to glow when she continued to speak. "Do you have any idea *who* Myrddin Calmburry was?" She breathed in very deeply, and her voice had a grave ring to it when she said, "The medieval name Myrddin eventually became Myrdin, later Merdin, and finally . . . *Merlin.*"

It was as if I'd been robbed of my speech when I understood what she meant. "Does this mean . . . ?"

"If what's written in the book Mayflower is trying to hide in her office is true and if it's also true that the symbol I showed you is the family crest of the Calmburrys, then . . . Jared must be a descendant of Merlin—the greatest magician who ever lived. The last one, too, if I'm not mistaken. As far as I know, his entire family died in the plane crash." She leaned forward over the table. "Do you understand what this means?" she asked, almost trembling with anticipation.

I stared at her, my mouth open. Incapable of making a sound.

As if she feared being overheard, Ruth lowered her voice to a whisper. The new insight resonated in her every word. "*He* is the one the Order wants to protect. He *is* Legatum Merlini—Merlin's Legacy!"

I had to let that sink in for a moment.

Jared was not only supposed to be the member of some secret society but also the reason for its existence?

"Evelyn, dear—are you feeling all right?" Ruth asked, concerned. "You look awfully pale."

"It's okay," I said, clinging to the table and struggling against the feeling of dizziness. Ruth looked me over and busied herself with one of the cabinets in the kitchen. When she turned around, she was holding a bottle with a handwritten label and had two small glasses in her other hand. She placed the bottle and glasses on the table in front of me and poured us each a little of the clear liquid.

"Drink this, then you'll feel better."

I smelled the astringent liquid and scrunched my nose. "What is this?" Did I really want to know?

"Spirit of Melissa. According to my grandmother's secret recipe. It's good for the circulation." Ruth smiled. "My grandmother swore by it, and she lived to ninety-eight! Cheers," she toasted and held up her little glass so I could clink mine against it.

"Cheers." I closed my eyes, held my breath, and drank. My throat burned, my voice failed, and I fought for air but . . . Ruth was right. As soon as the spirit's warmth spread in my stomach, my circulation stabilized, and I felt how my organs were again supplied with sufficient blood.

"Better?" she asked.

"Better!" I said and tried to concentrate. "So, you believe Jared is a descendant of . . . Merlin? Merlin the Magician?" I asked when I'd overcome the first shock.

"Yes," Ruth said, full of conviction.

I swallowed. "And you also think . . . I mean . . . You believe in . . . *magic*?" I somehow felt like a little girl asking her mother about the Easter bunny.

Ruth smiled. "Think about what your friend Sally told you today."

"She spoke of a . . . golden light and feeling immediately better after Jared had been with her," I said while my thoughts raced.

"And did Jared's friend not speak of a gift?"

I nodded numbly. Could this be true? Was there really such a thing as . . . *sorcery*? Was Jared a—I barely dared to even think the word—*magician*? Did he have abilities that went beyond those of a normal human? Sally, in any case, seemed to be convinced of it. She was certain of having seen this golden light and having felt its warmth. A golden light emanating from *him*. Didn't Sally see a light when I held Jared's hand at the party? Didn't she even say everybody looked at us because of this strange light? I'd been so captivated by Jared's look that I never noticed, but . . . what had happened in Berry's? On that evening when I'd played pool with Colin, Sally, and Felix. At the very moment when our eyes met, the lights started to flicker before they suddenly went off and Jared disappeared again. The flickering . . . Didn't the light in the little Asian restaurant also flicker? When Felix had provoked Jared? And what about my first day, at the exact moment when I saw Jared the very first time? I remembered how I'd wondered about the lighting in the lecture hall. And when he saved me from Felix—the entire room had shaken and the light flickered wildly . . .

Could that have been . . . *magic*?

Sally's healing, the flickering, the quake . . . ?

"Do you believe in magic?" I asked Ruth again.

"Without a single doubt," she said with a firm voice.

CHAPTER 13

Warm water flows, comforting my bare skin.

Although I do not yet need to breathe, I swim to the surface and slowly emerge. I'm in the midst of a blue-green lake in a forest clearing overgrown with wildflowers. The water's surface fractures the sunlight into a thousand tiny diamonds. I close my eyes, breathe in deeply, and absorb the sun's warmth. Pure joy floods through me.

"Nimue," someone whispers in the distance. I open my eyes and see Jared standing on the pebble shore of the forest lake, surrounded by glowing golden rays. So bright they almost blind me. He looks at me with a tender gaze.

I beckon him to me, letting him know he should come into the water. But he only smiles at me, shakes his head, turns, and disappears among the trees.

"Don't go!" I heard someone call, woke up, and noticed to my surprise that it was my own voice yelling out. I sat upright in my bed and attempted to hold a clear thought. The dream was still in my head, and I had difficulties getting rid of the confused images that seemed so real to me. I spent several minutes sorting my memories. What had really happened? Had I only dreamed it?

I'd been at Ruth's—that much was real. I remembered the delicious lasagna. But I especially remembered our conversation. We had talked about Jared—that had also happened. Suddenly, I heard Ruth's voice in my head: *He is the one the Order is trying to protect. He is Legatum Merlini—Merlin's Legacy!*

Was that possible? I swung my legs over the edge of the bed. Was Jared really a descendant of Merlin the Magician? I closed my eyes and rubbed my temples in a circular motion. The thought had made so much sense when I had talked about it deep into the night with Ruth. In fact, it seemed the only logical explanation for what I had recently experienced and observed. But now that I sat at home on my bed—in my favorite checkered pajamas—everything suddenly appeared in a different light.

I looked around the room. There were several open books on top of a half-finished assignment on my desk, and a pile of stuffy clothes had accumulated in my laundry suitcase. Everything around me appeared so . . . normal, so routine. To be honest, I'd expected something else after last night. Some change. But everything appeared as it had always been.

I hesitantly got up and went into the bathroom, where I hung my pajamas on the towel rack and stepped into the narrow shower. I just stood there for several minutes, let the warm water splash on me, and attempted to relax. As always, the flowing water helped. While my head gradually cleared, a suspicion increasingly arose in me that all of this was rather ridiculous, and I'd just gotten sucked into the whole business. *Sorcery.* I shook my head. Wasn't it totally childish to believe in something like magic? Now that I was back to reality, it caused me obvious difficulties. In the meantime, I felt outright embarrassed to have considered something so absurd.

And yet, there was something deep inside me that could not simply let go of the thought. It would explain so much—even if in a completely crazy way. No matter how I looked at it, there was only one way of finding out the truth.

I made my decision while drying off. I had to talk to Jared. Right now. The digital alarm clock on my nightstand showed 6:40. I hastily dried my hair, dressed, and left.

The first weak rays of the sun began to brighten a gradually sprouting spring landscape as I followed the narrow footpath at the back of the main building on the Christ Church campus. When I arrived at the small duck pond, I stopped by the mighty oak and looked for a darkly dressed runner.

Jared didn't make me wait long. Only a few minutes later I heard quick footsteps coming toward me. I waited for the right moment, stepped out onto the small path, and blocked his way.

"Evelyn," he called out startled and stopped only inches away from me.

"I have to talk to you, Jared," I said, trying to sound as resolute as possible. I didn't want to show under any circumstance that the mere sight of him unsettled me.

He looked at me with his deep blue eyes. "I wouldn't know what about," he said with studied casualness.

I immediately felt a stinging in my chest—I was unprepared for Jared's rejecting tone. He strained to narrow his eyes and swallowed with difficulty.

"I have to get going." His voice had an unbearably final tone. He ran past me without another word and was already a dozen feet away before I'd overcome my rejection, let alone been able to react to it. No! If he didn't talk to me now, he never would. I had to stop him. At any cost.

"I know about Legatum Merlini!" I shouted after him. He stopped immediately—virtually frozen on the spot. "And I know what your family has to do with it," I added in desperation, fearing my first revelation wouldn't suffice to make Jared stay. It worked. He slowly turned and came back to me.

Then I heard steps—the other runners couldn't be far away. I didn't have much time. Jared, too, hadn't missed that we'd have company any moment. He clenched his teeth with a snort.

"We'll meet here—in exactly an hour," he said and sounded almost angry.

I nodded eagerly. "Okay." My relief was obvious. Jared had consented to meet me. He would talk with me. I would finally get answers! I could have leaped in the air for joy. But since I thought it better not to let Jared's friends see me I disappeared behind the huge oak to wait until they had passed.

"Right here. In an hour," he repeated and ran off. A few seconds later the other runners passed by.

That was close.

The next hour was probably the longest of my life. I impatiently walked up and down the footpath, cast a glance at my watch, stood still for a moment, and then started the whole routine over again. Finally, after a torturous eternity, I saw him. Jared came from the same direction as he had an hour ago. Instead of running clothes, he was wearing sneakers, loosely fitting, dark-blue jeans and a black, hooded soft-shell jacket that suited him incredibly well. He looked so good that I briefly forgot what I wanted to talk to him about. My hands became clammy. What should I start with? Should I ask him something? Or wait for what he had to say? Would he even say anything?

"Hi," I said when he finally stood before me.

"Hi," he said and narrowed his eyes. I felt stumped. Why did Jared appear so hostile? But then he breathed in deeper, and his expression became softer. "You're really stubborn," he said after a short pause and betrayed a hint of a smile. When I saw the friendlier look on his face, I regained courage.

"Why are you avoiding me?" I asked, surprising myself with my demanding tone.

"Because . . ." Suddenly a sad expression appeared on his face. "I must," he said, tormented.

"Because you *must*?" I repeated. "Who says that?" Instead of giving me an answer, Jared averted his eyes. I felt a lump in my throat. "Karen Mayflower?" I guessed, almost certain I'd hit the mark. "I thought so . . . She kicked me out of her lecture," I said angrily. Then I cautiously took a step toward him. He looked at me, questioning and pained. I halted, breathed deeply, and went another step toward him.

"Evelyn, please," Jared said. "We shouldn't talk to each other."

"We don't just need to talk to each other," I said, surprised by my words, and took another step forward so we were right next to each other. My entire body began to tingle when I lifted my hand and firmly closed it around his. A veritable firework went off in my stomach. The memory of our kiss ignited inside me, almost making me float on air. It felt unbelievable to be so close to Jared. I moved even closer to him and deeply inhaled his intoxicating scent. I would have preferred to close my eyes then and give myself fully to him. However, something else was more important at that moment. I was here to get answers, and for that, I had to be in full possession of my wits. I reluctantly let go of his hand and took a step back. He stood there and looked at me as if under a spell.

He was hardly breathing.

"Please, Jared," I said, "I have to talk to you."

He nodded, first hesitantly, then more assertively. "Okay," he finally said and sighed. "Let's take a walk," he suggested and indicated a small wood that adjoined the campus. I joined him, and while we were walking side by side, I feverishly thought about how to begin. Should I tell him about my talk with Ruth? About the book? Or about . . . my feelings for him?

"How do you know about the Order?" Jared asked, suddenly breaking our silence.

"From a friend." As long as I didn't know what this Legatum Merlini Order was about, I had to be careful. The last thing I wanted was to get Ruth into trouble.

"A friend?" he repeated skeptically, raising his eyebrows. In the meantime, we'd arrived at the edge of the small wood and entered under the protective conifer ceiling that shielded us from the growing drizzle. Jared followed a narrow, hardly recognizable path that wound through the thicket. Nothing could be heard. No street noises, no chatting students. Only the sounds of our footsteps on the moist forest floor. As soon as we were submerged in the thicket, a comfortable feeling spread inside me. Here, under the shelter of the trees, I was alone with Jared. Just the two of us—no one else to bother or watch us. The thought was truly uplifting. I gathered my courage again, took Jared by the arm, and forced him to stop and turn toward me.

"Are you a descendant of Merlin the Magician?" I asked.

Jared froze. He had not expected this. His eyes widened, aghast. At first, I would have preferred to take back the question, but then I managed to resist this impulse and looked at Jared insistently. "You can trust me, Jared," I said with a soft voice, took a step closer, and held his hand again. He stared at me helplessly for a few seconds, but then he contorted his face into a pained expression. He looked at our hands. He appeared in turmoil, as if a battle were raging inside him. I would not let go.

Then—after an endless moment—he finally looked at me. His face was gentle and vulnerable.

"Yes," he said.

I gasped. So it was true! What had appeared completely ridiculous, even absurd, this morning in the familiar surroundings of my room, had suddenly become true. Jared was a descendant of the great magician

Merlin, whom I had only thought of as a myth, a figure of legend, until just now. Ruth was right!

"Everything all right?" Jared looked at me, concerned.

"Yes, everything is all right," I said. "It's just different hearing it from you."

He smiled weakly. "I can imagine."

Jared's confession left me shocked. Still, I was tremendously glad for it. He was willing to open up to me, to tell me the truth. I could not risk having him change his mind—I had to keep our conversation moving, ask him more questions. I'd have time later to think over the answers.

"And do you have any . . . special . . . abilities?" I cautiously asked. I deliberately avoided words such as *magic* and *sorcery*. Should my assumption that, like his famous ancestor, Jared himself had magical abilities be wrong, I'd make myself a laughingstock in his eyes. If he didn't have me committed right away. So, it was advisable to carefully steer the conversation in the right direction instead of coming out and asking if he was able to pull rabbits out of a hat.

Jared breathed in deeply. "Yes," he said, appearing almost liberated.

I had no idea how much my face revealed, but for fear that I give too much away, I looked at the ground. Jared gave me a moment.

What had I expected? I was finally getting the answers I had yearned for. And now I was surprised that my assumptions were true? To be sure, I would have preferred a *normal* explanation—but I had to take it as it was. And I was curious.

"How did you find me?" I was now looking into Jared's eyes. "In Felix's room, I mean."

"Well, that has something to do with energy."

"Energy?"

"Yes. I can . . . feel it." He looked as if he feared having revealed too much.

"How do you mean that?"

He looked at me for a long moment, then breathed in deeply as something in his expression changed. His resistance crumbled and then it broke—the decision had been made: Jared had decided to trust me. He looked into my eyes and began to talk.

"Every living creature, whether plant, animal, or human, is surrounded by energy," he explained. "To be precise, every living creature consists of energy. Its own, individual energy pattern." He looked at me as if to size me up. I nodded, urging him to continue. "Perhaps you can imagine it best as colors. Every living creature is surrounded by an aura, an energy field colored with very individual nuances."

I was enraptured by Jared's unexpected burst of words and greedily soaked up each and every one. The more I found out, the better. I simply wanted to know everything about him.

"Can you see this energy? The colors, I mean," I asked.

"I can always feel it. In some people I can also see it but only if I concentrate really hard," Jared said, laughing gently. "Believe me, I know how crazy this sounds." He shook his head.

"No!" I wouldn't have asked him to stop talking for anything in the world. "Then you found me that way? Did you feel my energy?"

"Yours and . . . his," he said coldly.

"How did you know I was in danger?"

He walked slower and turned toward me. "The energy of a creature is variable. The base color is always the same but with different shades. Depending on its emotional state. So if a person is sad, there's a dark shadow in their aura. If they are happy, the energy radiates, bright and shining. The better I know a person, the more I can differentiate these fine shades." Jared closed his eyes. "I was able to clearly detect fear and desperation in your energy. And in Felix's . . . ," he said and snorted. "Let's just say I could feel his intention."

I swallowed. "How does that work?" I asked as soon as I'd recovered my voice. "Is that possible from afar or do you have to be nearby?"

"It's all a matter of concentration. But I'd say I have to be at least in the same building."

"So you were at the party at his place?"

"Yes, but only for a few minutes."

"Do you often go to parties?" Why was I asking such a stupid question?

Jared briefly smiled. "No, not really. But . . . I'd hoped to see you there."

I had to resist throwing my arms around his neck. "I'd imagined it somewhat different," he added as his face hardened.

"I'm so glad you were there," I said and looked at my hands. I hadn't noticed we had stopped walking.

"So am I," he said, placed his finger under my chin, and gently lifted my face so he could see into my eyes. His look was tender.

"Your energy is radiant green-blue," he said. "Like a deep, clear mountain lake. Like . . . your eyes. Simply wonderfully beautiful!"

I swallowed. "You can see my energy?" I asked, confused and embarrassed.

"When I concentrate on it," he said and took his hand from my chin.

"And why . . . can you see mine and not others?" I asked, trying not to blush.

"To be honest, I'm not sure." He shut his eyes. "But I think I can see yours because I feel attracted to you . . . very attracted."

My heart leaped. We walked a few feet and again only the sound of our steps could be heard. The woods gradually cleared and we were in a small glade—almost circular and surrounded by trees. Bits of snow were left in shadowed places under the trees, where the sunlight could not reach. Suddenly, Jared took my hand, pulled me a bit closer, and looked at me seriously.

"Evelyn, I want to show you something," he said. He held my hand, and I only managed a silly nod.

"There's something else," he said and sized me up. "I can feel the energy, but I can also . . . affect it. I can direct it, if you will."

"Okay," I said.

The corner of Jared's mouth twitched. "Best I just show you," he said and led me to a spot at the edge of the clearing where there was some snow.

"Can you see?" he asked.

I bent forward and discovered a thin, pale green stem that extended about an inch above the snow.

"A sprout," I said.

Jared nodded. "Look closely." He let go of my hands and kneeled. I was tempted to take his hand again for a moment, but the curiosity of seeing what Jared wanted to show me was too great. I crouched next to him full of anticipation and waited.

Jared bent forward slightly and, as if praying, closed his hands around the awakening crocus shoot. Then—I barely dared to trust my eyes—a light spread within his almost-folded hands. Just for a heartbeat. Slowly he turned his palms upward again. Startled, I opened my eyes wide. The delicate shoot that had struggled through the slowly melting snow cover blossomed and turned a violet that deepened from one moment to the next. I shut my eyes and then looked again. It was real—where there had just been a thin, pale green stem, there now stood a deep-violet flower. It was incredibly beautiful.

"Jared, that is . . . I would have never thought . . . Thank you," I finally said.

"You're thanking me?" Jared stood up. "Aren't you afraid?" He looked at me, suspicious.

"Why would I be afraid? That is"—I didn't really know how to say it—"a miracle . . . You're a miracle."

Jared breathed in, relieved, beaming at me. For a moment, I just stood there, marveling at the perfect crocus flower, when suddenly a thought went through my head. I frowned as I looked up at Jared.

"Why didn't you . . . ? When Felix was . . ." I was looking for the right word. "When he was forcing himself on me, why didn't you use magic?"

Hatred flared up in Jared's face. He clenched his teeth and rubbed the perfectly shaped bridge of his nose with his thumb and index finger.

"Because, when Felix was forcing himself on you, I didn't know whether I could control myself."

Control? What did he mean by that? "You mean your magic would have really hurt him?" Suddenly, I saw the image of Felix lying on the floor and spitting up blood. "I mean, hurt him even more?"

He opened his eyes with a telling look. "The day I first saw you, my magic changed. Suddenly, it became more difficult to control."

"The flickering . . . ," I said. "*You* made the light flicker. And *you* made Felix's room shake. I didn't just imagine that."

"No, you didn't," he said when he had understood what I was driving at. "But I didn't do it on purpose. I just wasn't in control." He looked into the distance. "And if I hadn't attempted to shut off the magic for a moment with Felix . . . it would have ripped him to shreds." He closed his eyes and clenched his teeth. "I mean that literally."

I believed his every word. Again hatred flared up in his face. His jaw muscles protruded; his hands were clenched into fists. "It was difficult for me not to do it," he added.

A shudder ran down my back at the thought. When he looked at me, I saw regret in his face.

"I'm sorry if I'm frightening you." His voice was almost shaking with concern. "Please excuse me." I tried to conjure up a smile but could only turn and look into the woods.

"What did you mean just now?" I asked after a while. "Your magic has changed."

Unexpectedly, a smile spread across Jared's face, then he hastily looked around. Did he want to make sure no one was watching us?

"Before I met you, *that* was my magic." He pointed to the perfect crocus he'd made bloom. "But now . . ." He closed his eyes, tilted his head forward, turned his palms upward, and spread his arms. First, I thought he wanted to meditate, but then this golden light sprang from his hands. Only, it was a little stronger this time. Brighter. Jared's appearance was the most marvelous thing I'd ever seen. He looked focused and completely relaxed. I could have spent an eternity here just looking at him. Him and his magic. "Now *this* is my magic," he completed his sentence, opened his eyes, and let his hands fall again.

I had to force myself to turn away from him again. My curiosity won out. I blinked and looked around. The view before me caused my mouth to drop open.

In the clearing, which was only half the size of a football field, thousands of crocuses shot from the ground and bloomed in the most splendid colors. A sea of violet, yellow, and white flowers, each one unique. It was indescribably beautiful, and I didn't know whether I was awake or dreaming. I was speechless for minutes. I attempted with all my heart to memorize this image. I wanted to keep this memory forever.

"Do you like it?" Jared finally asked.

"It's marvelous!" I felt a tear sneak from the corner of my eye and start running down my cheek. Slowly I turned back to him. He looked deep into my eyes. Then he hesitantly lifted his hand and caught the stray tear with the tip of his finger. While he looked at the tear, his fingertip began to glow in splendid gold and transformed my tear into something else. Something sparkling.

"Is that a . . . ?"

"A diamond, yes," he answered my question, looking into my eyes again. This blue, this incredibly deep blue. "May I," he looked at me hopefully, "keep it?"

"You want to keep my *tear*?" I asked.

"As a memento," he said. "I never want to forget this moment."

A wild swarm of butterflies was fluttering in my stomach. I turned embarrassed from his gaze and stared at my hands.

"Then you feel . . . like I do," I said, touched.

He carefully took my chin between his thumb and index finger and lifted my face, and our eyes met. He was so close, I could feel his breath on my skin. *Oh God, he smells so good!*

My heart fluttered so intensely I feared it would leap from my chest. Then, as if I weren't already about to explode, Jared leaned forward, tilted his head to the side, and breathed in deeply. With an almost inaudible sigh, he came closer and opened his mouth. My heart was about to burst.

"Jared, damn. Where have you been all morning?" Startled, I opened my eyes and discovered Colin, who was just stumbling into the clearing from among the trees. "I've looked for you everywhere—" He stopped. "Oh, I didn't want to . . . I hope I'm . . . not disturbing," he said, surprised when he noticed that Jared wasn't alone. That I was with him.

"Hi Colin," I said, annoyed and a little embarrassed. Did he have to show up now?

"Hi, Evelyn, how are you?" he asked somewhat impishly, grinning broadly. "I see the two of you have finally become acquainted."

When Colin glanced over the meadow covered in splendid crocuses, I could see from his face that he knew what had happened. And he seemed delighted by the turn of events.

"What's up, Colin?" Jared asked, giving him a warning glance.

"I . . . Well, everybody's looking for you. We were worried," Colin said.

"Karen, too?" Jared asked.

"Yup, she's already on her way."

Jared looked at me with an unfathomable expression. "Then I can tell her the good news," he said with a sarcastic undertone.

"What news?" I wanted to know.

"That I will *no longer* keep away from you," he said in a firm voice. My heart leaped.

"Come on, let's go," he said to me, smiling, and we followed Colin back through the woods toward the college. After we had walked a few feet, Colin turned to me, grinning like the Cheshire cat, and winked, so Jared cuffed him lightly on the arm.

"Ow," Colin said, rubbing his shoulder.

"Have you no decency?" Jared asked, irritated, and motioned Colin with his hand to give us a little privacy. Colin made an offended face but did as Jared said, putting a few paces between himself and us. I couldn't suppress a grin. But then I thought of Karen Mayflower and my smile died as quickly as it had come. How would she react when she saw Jared and me together? So far, she'd done everything within her power not to let us get closer. All of it, if Ruth was right, for the sake of a mysterious Legatum Merlini secret society. What a strange association!

"What is it with this Order?" I asked while walking through the woods beside Jared.

He sighed. "The members of the Order have made it their duty to safeguard Merlin's legacy by protecting my family." He shut his eyes. "Unfortunately, they didn't succeed very well." His voice suddenly sounded like that of an old man.

"Jared, I . . . I'm so sorry." My words were more of a whisper; I empathized deeply because I knew too well what he'd been through.

He smiled. "After the death of my family, the members of the Order took me in and raised me."

"Karen Mayflower?" I asked.

"Yes, as long as I was a minor, she was my guardian."

Colin had reduced the distance between us and was now walking almost in step with us.

"Two years later, that one joined us." Jared nodded with a smile in Colin's direction.

"We grew up like brothers," Colin said and gave Jared a punch in his side as retaliation for Jared's punch a moment ago.

"Why did Mayflower take you in?" I asked.

Colin smiled. "You mean because I'm not special like Jared?"

"No, no. I didn't mean it that way," I said.

They both laughed. "Oh, don't worry about it," Colin said in a good mood. "But you're right. Karen doesn't just take in waifs and strays—she isn't welfare, after all." Colin and Jared exchanged a meaningful glance.

"So . . . why did she pick you?" I asked again, turning to Colin.

"My great-great-great-great-grandmother was a Pendragon," Colin said, looking me straight in the eyes.

I stumbled. *"Pendragon?"* Did I understand that right? "As in . . . *Arthur* Pendragon? *King* Arthur Pendragon?" I was struggling to keep my composure.

"You should see your face!" Colin said, holding his belly and laughing. I stopped abruptly, looking at the two, dumbfounded.

"You're joking!" I said to Colin. "You two are the descendants of Merlin and Arthur?"

"It looks that way," Jared said, letting Colin's laugh infect him. I guess my reaction was hilarious. I had to let it sink in for a moment.

"What happened to your family?" I asked Colin, who suddenly turned serious.

"They were also killed," he said after a short pause.

"Also? I thought your family died in a plane crash, Jared?"

"Yes," he said coldly. "But it wasn't an accident."

"You mean they were murdered?" I asked anxiously.

"There you are, damn it!" I looked up, surprised to see Aiden Mayflower coming toward us on the muddy path.

"Jared, we looked everywh—" When Aiden saw me, his mouth dropped open. He stopped, staring at me with wide eyes. "Jared, what's this all about?" he asked without taking his eyes off me. His words resonated with disapproval. "Do you know what'll happen if my mother finds out?" He made a dismissive head motion toward me. His apparent dislike made me shudder. What was that supposed to mean? I'd never done anything to him.

"We're on our way to see her," Jared answered with a firm voice, clasping my hand. A firework had been lit in my body. Jared held my hand to show Aiden that we—him and me—belonged together.

"Are you nuts?" Aiden said, horrified. "She'll never allow it!"

"It's not for *her* to decide. And not for you, either," Jared said, silencing Aiden. Aiden stopped in the middle of the path as if rooted to it, staring at us in disbelief.

"Calm down," Colin whispered and roughly pushed him aside so we could continue on our way. When I passed Aiden, he cast me an angry look and immediately pulled his phone from his pocket. His fingers whisked at lightning speed across the touch screen, then he held it to his ear.

"We found him," he said, then listened to the response. "Yes, in the woods. Okay. See you in a minute." He nodded, hung up, and put his phone back in his pocket. "They're waiting at the eastern edge of the woods," he said while following us. I felt his stare digging into my back.

While we followed the path to the east, there was ice-cold silence. I didn't feel well in Aiden's presence; sensing he was watching my every step made it worse.

"Would you please go ahead, Aiden?" Jared asked unexpectedly. The sharp tone in his voice surprised me. Without saying a word, Aiden pressed to the front and took the lead.

"Better?" Jared asked in a whisper when Aiden could no longer hear him.

I nodded. Jared must have sensed how ill at ease I was in Aiden's presence.

"There they are," Aiden said a few minutes later, accelerating his pace. I stretched my neck to look past Colin and saw Karen Mayflower rushing toward us across the soggy forest floor.

"Jared, where were y—" She broke off the moment she saw our intertwined hands. She stopped in her tracks. Aiden went to her to take up a position behind his mother—as if he wanted to cover her back.

"What does this mean?" she demanded in an authoritative tone.

"I'm together with Evelyn," Jared said. His relaxed tone turned her red with rage. It appeared as if Karen was used to being treated with deference.

Suddenly, a movement at the forest edge about thirty feet away caught my attention. Three more people had just entered the thicket and were making their way toward us. I could see that it was a man and two women. When they came closer, I froze. An attractive woman was in the lead. She was probably in her early forties, decked out in full riding clothing, as if she were just returning from an outing. Her brunette hair with some gray at the sides was put up into a bun, which lent her appearance a certain strictness despite her feminine face. Another woman followed right behind her. She was only a little older and had tied her long red hair into a braid that hung over her right shoulder. Her clothing was conspicuously elegant. The typical Burberry checker pattern on her scarf, the subtle elegance of her beige trench coat, and the knee-high dress she wore underneath suggested she was very well off. Though I had never seen the redhead before, she somehow seemed familiar, but at that moment, I couldn't place her. Behind those two— this was the reason why I briefly froze—Professor Irvin Martin came toward us, the seal ring on his right ring finger.

"I repeat my question, Jared: What does this mean?" Karen said, enraged as Professor Martin and the two women caught up with her and Aiden.

"This means I will be spending more time with Evelyn from now on," Jared said. It was clear he wouldn't change his mind. Karen Mayflower's face was so red it looked as if her head might explode.

"I cannot allow that!" she shouted while one of the capillaries in her eye burst and discolored part of her iris. She gesticulated wildly with her arms until the uppermost button of her blouse popped open and revealed a shimmering, gold-and-blue jewel. It was the same as the one I had discovered on Professor Martin's seal ring. She wore it on a fine gold chain around her neck.

"That's not for you to decide," Jared said. He looked around, staring at each person. "For none of you," he said resolutely.

So far I'd said nothing, but the fact that Karen Mayflower turned red with rage merely when Jared and I talked with each other forced me to speak.

"Why should Jared keep away from me?" I said, my voice sounding firm, even challenging, despite the tension I felt inside.

Professor Mayflower stared at me in horror, but instead of answering my question, she angrily curled her lips and looked over my head to address Jared. "How much does she know?" she asked.

Jared clenched his free hand into a fist in response to the lack of respect she showed me. Then he closed his eyes, breathed deeply, and answered.

"She knows who I am, and she knows about the Order," he said in the same rough tone she had used on him.

"And she knows who I am," Colin added, suppressing a malicious grin. He didn't seem to take any of this seriously. On the contrary. Apparently he had a riot needling his foster mother to the boiling point. Karen's facial color changed from pink to red and then to deep burgundy.

"Karen," Professor Martin gently said. He took a step forward, laying his hand on her shoulder to calm her.

Her eyes had narrowed to tiny slits, and she looked at each of us, one after the other, then her brow furrowed and her eyes filled with tears. "Everything I do is to protect you," she said desperately and looked into Jared's eyes and then Colin's.

"Protect?" Colin said. "From what?" He seemed angry and pointed at Jared and me. "Look at those two! They're totally in love. What are you afraid of? That they'll kiss each other to death?"

"Don't be silly, Colin," the redhead who had kept in the back said. When I looked at her more closely, I knew who she resembled. Actually, *resembled* didn't quite cover it—it was as if she had sprung from the same mold as Madison. Judging from her age, she could be her aunt or her mother. "You know exactly what this is about!" she added, giving him a warning stare.

"All I know is that you've been indoctrinating Jared forever with this shit!" Colin was really beside himself.

"What? What are you talking about?" I said. "Tell me: Why should Jared keep away from me?" I asked again, this time more forcefully.

The brunette woman in riding gear unexpectedly stepped toward me. "You have no idea who you are, do you?" Her voice was more penetrating and deeper than I'd expected based on her feminine appearance.

I was startled. "Who *I* am?"

"Enid, please," Karen Mayflower pleaded.

"No, Karen. She must know," the rider interrupted her sharply. "That's the only way we can prevent the worst." Enid fixed me with her blue-gray eyes. "Have you never wondered why you are different from other people?" she asked me. I felt Jared stiffen next to me.

"Different?" I asked. "I'm not different." I had taken a defensive posture.

"Oh really?" The rider laughed but without appearing haughty.

"Enid, please!" Karen pleaded again. "She already knows too much—you're endangering all of us! Especially Jared!"

"Can't you see that it's already too late for anything else?" Enid said.

"But the Prophecy!" Karen said.

"What prophecy?" I asked.

"The Prophecy of the Nymphs of Avalon," Jared said with a firm voice. He seemed determined to resist Karen and tell me the truth.

"Nymphs?" I asked.

"Yes, nymphs," Enid said. "Elfin nature spirits that are at home in the forests of Avalon."

Serious dizziness overcame me. Avalon? Nature spirits? For a moment I was unsure if this all was just a dream, and I toyed with the idea of pinching myself so I'd wake up, but then I felt Jared's hand in mine. Its strength and warmth steadied me. He was here in flesh and blood, touching me. No, this was no dream—Jared was definitely standing with me, and my heart was fluttering like the wings of a hummingbird. That meant there were only two possibilities: either these people were playing a really nasty prank on me, or . . . it was the truth.

"Perhaps we should not overtax Evelyn right away. After all, this is all very new for her," Professor Martin said.

Jared looked at me. "You're probably right," he said. "But she still has a right to know who she is."

Before I was able to say anything, Enid came a few steps closer. In an imploring tone, she said, "Did you ever hear or read anything about how Merlin died?"

"Merlin?" Didn't Ruth say something about that? Something about a cave? Yes! She had told me about Nimue and had said that some legends relate that she had killed him to steal his magic. But Ruth didn't believe this version of the story.

"I once heard he supposedly was buried alive by a lover in a cave," I said skeptically. Where was this supposed to lead?

Enid nodded. "Yes, that's the way it's written in some traditions."

Colin snorted contemptuously and opened his mouth to speak, but Enid looked at him with raised eyebrows, silencing him immediately. Apparently, he had far more respect for her than for Karen Mayflower.

"And do you know who his lover was?" Enid asked me.

"Nimue," I said. "The Lady of the Lake, so I was told by Ru—. By a friend."

Enid smiled at me. "Yes, that's right." She took another step toward me. "Some members of the Order"—she looked briefly at Karen and the redhead—"are convinced that these traditions are true, and, if transferred to the Prophecy, would mean that Jared will be killed just as Merlin was: by the hand of his lover."

Jared will be killed, I thought, feeling naked terror. My thoughts took me to the narrow passage where I'd overheard Jared's conversation with Aiden. *She will kill you,* Aiden had said.

"What is that supposed to mean?" I asked.

"Enid," Professor Martin said, "isn't all this a bit much so soon?"

I looked back and forth between the two of them. "What has all this got to do with me?" I wasn't going to leave this place until that question had been answered. "Do you really believe I'd kill Jared?" I was barely able to utter those words. The thought that I'd even harm a single hair on his head was absurd and utterly insane, not to mention the fact that I was physically incapable of it. And what was all that babble about Merlin and Nimue? "Are you trying to say that I'm like Nimue?" I looked at them all with curious eyes.

"Not quite." Now it was Jared who answered my question. He breathed in deeply and squeezed my hand a little tighter. "You are not like Nimue," he said. "You *are* Nimue!"

For a moment, I stood there stunned, unable to make a sound. Again, thoughts raced through my head. I only found my voice a few seconds later.

"What?" I said. My eyes widened with incomprehension as I looked around. *I* was supposed to be Nimue? That couldn't be true!

Enid seemed to have anticipated this reaction. She smiled gently. "Did you ever wonder about how you react to water?"

"How I react to water? That can't be . . . I'm not . . . You must be mistaking me for someone else," I stammered, shaking my head.

Enid paused, looking at me earnestly. "Isn't it true that you feel best in water?" She was now standing right in front of me. "That it even has a healing effect on you?"

I let Enid's words go through my mind. She was right—water did have a stronger effect on me than on most. One might even say a *healing* effect, as Enid had called it. But . . . how did she know? I looked suspiciously between her and Jared.

"Evelyn," Enid said, bringing my attention back to her blue-gray eyes, "how many generations back can you remember in your family?"

"My . . . No idea. Except for my parents and my sister, I never got to know anyone in my family. I only know my grandma from an old black-and-white photo that had been on my mother's nightstand." I frowned.

"Your family is dead, right?" Enid asked carefully. "Your parents and your sister."

I nodded hesitantly, trying to swallow the lump in my throat. "How do you know that?"

She took a deep breath. "The Order has been watching Nimue's descendants for generations," she said, lowering her gaze. For some reason, I couldn't rid myself of the feeling she was keeping something really important from me. "When we heard of your sister's death . . . we thought Nimue's bloodline had died out," she continued, gently shaking her head. "Until you suddenly arrived at Oxford. Do you understand what I'm saying?" She gave me a moment before continuing. "*You* are the last of Nimue's bloodline—the last daughter of the Lady of the Lake, the Guardian of Avalon."

"How do you know?" I asked.

"Believe me, Evelyn, it's the truth," Jared said and Enid nodded.

"But . . . how can you be so sure?"

Enid hesitated a moment, while I watched from the corner of my eye how Aiden was desperately trying to comfort his mother, who was breaking down in tears.

"Because there's an ancient magical link between you and Jared," she said. "Jared's magic immediately reacted to you. And he has . . ." She stopped to look at Jared as if she were asking him for permission.

"I'm deeply in love with you," Jared said, looking intensely into my eyes. "I've been in love with you since the very first time I saw you."

CHAPTER 14

I was lying motionless on my bed, staring at the ceiling. I hadn't closed an eye all night, though I tried. I turned from one side to the other, fluffed my pillow, got up, walked around the room, lay back down, and then started all over. I didn't even shy away from counting sheep. All without success.

In the meantime, morning had come, and the first rays of the sun shone through the rain-wet window and slowly crawled up the covers until they tickled my nose. The night was finally over and, as with so many nights before in recent weeks and months, I hadn't slept at all.

But it was different this time. I hadn't mourned my parents and Zara the whole night, hadn't fallen into self-pity, hadn't cried or grumbled over what I must have done to experience so much suffering in my life. No, last night it was something entirely different that had kept me awake. Instead of sleeping, I'd whiled away the hours racking my brain over what I had just learned. (Though sleep would surely have helped to process the events of recent days in my dreams.) I didn't get very far—admittedly—but I had become ready to accept some things as they were.

First: Jared was the last descendant of Merlin the Magician. Like his legendary ancestor, he had special abilities.

I accepted that.

Second: At least two of my professors were members of a centuries-old secret society whose mission was to protect all descendants of the great Merlin—and, therefore, Jared.

I accepted that, too.

Third: Colin, who was dating my friend Sally, was the descendant of the famous King Arthur—so far, so good.

Although I could only give these matters credence with the full force of my imagination, I had at least decided to accept them.

What caused me considerably more difficulty was that I was a magical being or, at least, descended from one. From Nimue, to be precise—the Lady of the Lake, Guardian of Avalon. The thought caused the hair at the back of my neck to stand up.

No, that couldn't be right. There had to be some confusion.

But . . . what if it were true? What if I really were the last in the bloodline of the Guardian of Avalon? Even if I didn't really dare believe it, I had to admit Enid knew things about me that no one else knew, without ever having met me. She was right on the mark regarding the effect water normally has on me. It's necessary to all human life, but as far as I could remember, it had always somehow been different for me. Water seemed to be the source of all my strength—it made me stronger and more balanced, helped me focus and simply feel better. And, as Enid had said, it accelerated my wound-healing processes. It had always been the same with Zara. So maybe there was something to it. But then I asked myself: If I really were descended from a magical creature, why didn't I have magical abilities?

As much as I thought about it, I couldn't get any further. There was no choice but to let matters take their course. One thing—and this was the real reason for my sleepless night—was far more important to me just then: Jared was . . . *in love with me!*

A hot sensation spread from my stomach with a pleasant tingle through my entire body—from my toes to the tips of my hair.

I've been in love with you since the very first time I saw you. I heard his voice in my thoughts, and for a moment I lost myself in the vision of having been alone with him.

I jumped up from my bed with joyful anticipation. I would see him again in less than an hour. I could hardly wait. I hastened into the bathroom to get ready for the day. I jumped in the shower, brushed my teeth, and combed the knots out of my wet hair. After I had blow-dried it, I decided to leave my hair down in the hopes of pleasing Jared. I quickly got dressed, slipped into my coat, pulled on my boots, and left. I rushed down the stairs to the entrance area of my dorm, flung open the door, raced down the stone stairs outside, and barely managed to slam on the brakes on the edge of a huge, deep puddle that had formed outside the entrance. I stood on the lowest stair with flailing arms, trying to regain my balance, when I heard an amused chuckle.

"Why are you in such a rush?" a soft melodic voice asked. I looked up, surprised, and saw Jared on the other side of the little pond. My heart's rhythm was immediately confounded.

"Please don't tell me you're frightened of getting wet," he said with a broad grin and gave me his hand. "That would be remarkable, wouldn't it?"

"Jared . . . what are you doing here?" I asked and attempted to rein in the butterflies fluttering about my stomach.

"Picking you up, of course," he said with a beaming smile as if it were obvious he'd be waiting outside my residence in the morning. *Damn, he looks so incredibly good!*

"Why?" I asked while he helped me step over the puddle. Although I was looking forward to nothing else in the world, I was confused and felt a bit ambushed. I had actually thought I'd have a little more time to think about what I'd say to him.

He looked at me skeptically. "You've got Narcissism and Destructiveness with Bronsen, don't you?"

"Yes . . . but . . ."

"But?" he said, smiling again. "Would you rather go by yourself?"

"No—of course not. I just find it . . . lovely that you've come to pick me up," I said and was finally capable of giving him a smile.

"Now you know how I felt yesterday when you lay in wait for me when I was running," Jared said happily.

"Oh," was all I could say.

He laughed. "Shall we?" Jared asked after his ringing laughter had shrunk to a warm smile. He nodded in the direction of the lecture halls.

I nodded and walked beside him while taking a moment to process what was happening. Jared had waited for me outside my dorm to go with me to the college. He had come here just to spend time with me. The butterflies in my stomach were going wild. During the night, I'd been very worried Jared might change his mind, but he had really meant it: he'd no longer keep away from me. All of a sudden, I remembered Professor Mayflower's face when she heard those words from his mouth. It cost Jared a lot to resist her will—that much was obvious. He must be really serious about me, or else he would have never taken this on—at least I hoped.

Incredible! I felt my life had turned around 180 degrees within twenty-four hours. Jared had confided his greatest secret to me, he had—for my sake—opposed Karen Mayflower, and he confessed to me he was . . . in love with me. When he accompanied me home last night, I had felt closer to him than ever before, though there had been no more than a quick kiss on the forehead. All the barriers, fears, and secrets that had stood between us had been torn down, just like that. There was only the two of us.

While we walked side by side to the main entrance—I walked as slowly as possible to spend as much time with Jared as I could—an unaccustomed sensation arose in me. I couldn't name it, nor could I tell whether it was good or bad. It felt as if two worlds were colliding inside me. On the one hand, there was the new magical world that I couldn't get enough of, but it also frightened me tremendously. A world revolving around old legends, secret societies, mystical places, legendary figures, prophecies, and magic. Though I'd seen it with my own eyes, much of it was still difficult to grasp. Occasionally, I caught myself questioning if I'd dreamed it all—even though the best proof of the existence of these things was walking right beside me. As inconspicuously as possible, I cast a probing glance at Jared and was again racked by nagging doubt—he was almost too beautiful to be true.

But then on the other hand, juxtaposed to this new, magical one, was the old world—my ordinary life as a college student. This included lectures and seminars, professors, daily lunches at the dining hall, incomplete assignments waiting for me at home, study groups with Sally and Feli—*No!* I clenched my hands into fists. Felix was no longer part of either of my worlds.

"What are you thinking about?" Jared asked. I could see from the look in his eyes that he had felt the change in my mood.

"Hmm . . ." I said, hesitating. "To be honest, I was just thinking of Felix," I said.

Jared took a deep breath. "I don't think he'll dare come near you again."

"What makes you so sure?"

"We're keeping an eye on him."

"We? You mean the Order?"

Jared nodded. "Let's put it this way. Felix is permitted to stay in Oxford under certain . . . conditions. Should he violate them, he'll have to face the consequences."

I opened my mouth to ask what he meant by *consequences* but then thought I might not want to know the answer. "Do you think Sally and I should go to the police?"

"You're free to do so. I just didn't want to pressure you into it."

I nodded.

"And?" Jared asked after I'd been silent for a while. "Are you going to report him?"

"I'm thinking about it," I said, frowning, while trying to chase Felix out of my mind. I was still chilled by the thought of what he wanted to do to me and what he'd done to Sally. Suddenly, the memory of my last visit to see her arose . . . How terribly pale she'd looked.

"Do you know how Sally's doing?" I asked. I felt guilty because she'd completely slipped my mind during the events of the last few days.

"Colin was with her yesterday evening," Jared said in a soft voice. He seemed more at ease with this topic than the previous one. "He said she was like new. Maybe she'll be back tomorrow."

"Thank goodness," I said and breathed a huge sigh of relief. Then, I thought of something I still wanted to ask Jared. I bit my lower lip.

"Well, ask!" Jared said, grinning without looking at me.

"You know that's pretty eerie, don't you?" I said, smiling.

"What?" he asked as if clueless, but his face betrayed him.

"That you know what I'm feeling before I do," I said.

Jared shrugged and played innocent. "So, what did you want to ask me?" he said, now a little more serious.

"Well, I visited Sally two days ago . . ." I looked at Jared out of the corner of my eye to size him up.

"And?"

"She told me you'd been with her."

"Yes, I was with her," he said as if there were nothing to it and looked at me questioningly.

Apparently, it wasn't clear what I was getting at. "Well, Sally said she immediately felt better after you were with her. She spoke of a light emanating from you . . ."

Jared stopped in the middle of the path and looked at me with raised eyebrows, as if I'd missed something really obvious.

"So it's true?" I said. "You healed Sally?"

Jared raised his eyebrows even more. "But I showed you," he said with a touch of embarrassment, "yesterday in the clearing."

"Yes, I know, but healing a human being is on a different level from making a crocus bloom, isn't it?"

Jared shrugged. "It's the same principle."

I shook my head. He had probably rescued Sally but wouldn't brag about it to save his life. In my eyes, his modesty doubled the value of what he'd done for my friend.

"Does Sally know about you and Colin?" I asked. "I mean, who you are?"

"Not directly," he said. "Secrecy is the greatest priority of the Order, but in my opinion it's up to Colin to decide what he does and doesn't tell her." He looked at me apologetically. "I know the two of you are very close, but as long as Colin hasn't made his decision, it's probably better if you don't talk to her about this."

"Yes, of course. She probably wouldn't believe me, anyway," I said, shaking my head. "I'm finding it hard to believe myself!"

Although we'd walked slowly, we'd almost arrived at the lecture hall. I was not ready to walk in yet because there was another matter weighing on me—and that was the question that had kept me awake all night. But while I was burning to have an answer, I was just as afraid to ask the question. Jared must have sensed my inner turmoil, for he stopped and looked at me in anticipation.

"How will this continue? I mean with us," I said, holding my breath.

A gentle smile spread across Jared's face, making his deep blue eyes beam. "I think I've expressed myself pretty clearly as far as that's concerned, haven't I?" he said in his velvety voice. "At least, as I see it."

My ears turned hot and I forgot to blink. When I didn't react right away, the expression on Jared's face changed.

"How do you see it?" Was I hearing uncertainty in his voice? Or just fear? Was he afraid I didn't feel for him what he felt for me? Did he seriously consider that I might not want to be with him? That was ridiculous. When I didn't answer again but just gave him a dumb look, he took my hands and placed them on his chest. His heart was beating almost as fast as mine.

"Evelyn," he started earnestly. "I'm so in love with you that I sometimes believe I'm losing my mind."

My ears started to glow.

"I . . . know that feeling all too well," I confessed a moment later in a weak voice. At that moment, not even a herd of stampeding elephants would have caused me to look away from Jared's indigo-blue eyes. Without being aware of what I was doing, I stood on my tiptoes and stretched up as far as I could. Jared took my face into his hands, bent down to me, and placed his lips on mine. His kiss was so tender and warm I forgot everything around me. *This is what flying must be like!*

He disengaged far too soon. I kept my eyes closed for a moment, inhaling deeply. What was happening inside me was incredible. As if I had just returned home from a long, difficult trip.

When I sensed Jared's eyes resting on me, I opened mine. He looked at me with a content smile that brought the most delicate wrinkles to the corners of his eyes.

"Come," he said tenderly as he put his arm around my shoulder. "Or we'll miss the lecture."

Jared and I entered the lecture hall just as Professor Bronsen stripped off his wristwatch, as usual, and placed it on the table before him so he could keep an eye on the time as he lectured. He'd start any moment. Since everyone was already seated except for us, Jared inconspicuously pulled me to the free seats in the back rows so we'd disappear as fast as possible into the gray mass of students without drawing attention. But we had already been noticed. Students immediately began to whisper among themselves, nudge their neighbors, and openly point at us. Soon the entire lecture hall was filled with a murmur. More and more heads turned our way, and not even strict Bronsen managed to suppress the voices. It was horrible! Again all eyes were directed at me. But . . . no. This time they were not staring at *me*, they were staring at *us*. I felt warm at the thought of calling Jared and myself "we." He led me to the second-to-last row while I tried to ignore my gawking and whispering classmates and follow the lecture. My assignment for Bronsen was due soon, which is why I couldn't afford to miss anything. But as much as I tried to focus, the feeling of having Jared so close to me, of sensing the warmth of his body almost on my skin and inhaling his scent, was simply overwhelming. I hardly dared to look at him as I had during the weeks when he diligently ignored me, but found to my astonishment that he was looking at me, inhaling more heavily each time than before. When our eyes met, I perceived a strange tension between us. The air began to crackle. I reluctantly took my eyes off his breathtaking appearance and attempted to concentrate again on the professor before it became too late to look away from Jared. Then, I felt his fingertips against my hand. I turned toward him. He breathed so heavily, his chest was heaving. He gave me a penetrating look. A tingling heat streamed through me as he firmly took my hand, bent forward, and inhaled the scent of my hair. What was happening in my stomach then had nothing to do with butterflies anymore—high voltage was closer to the mark.

Never before had anyone conjured a similar feeling inside me. This was all so new and unaccustomed to me that I had no idea how to handle these unfamiliar feelings and . . . *needs*. I was terribly afraid of doing something wrong, something that would cause Jared to disappear from my life.

On the other hand, I couldn't get enough. Not enough of *him*. At that very moment, I wished for nothing more than to be alone with Jared.

I managed to withstand his glowing gaze but felt an unaccustomed heat rise inside me. It focused below my trembling stomach and turned my heartbeat into the irregular pounding of a hammer. It was hopeless to attempt to follow the lecture.

When Professor Bronsen finished, after what felt like an eternity, Jared impatiently helped me cram my books into my bag, grabbed my hand, and led me out of the lecture hall, past the gaping students. I didn't care where we were going. The only thing that counted was that he was with me. That we were going somewhere together. But I was unprepared for what came next. With a tug he pulled me into a narrow alley between two buildings, pressed my back against the stone wall, and placed his hands against it on either side of my head. His eyes glowed, while his breathing raced as fast as mine. I couldn't stand it a second longer. I wildly flung my arms around his neck, while he took my face firmly into his hands and pressed his tongue between my willing lips.

Oh God! Finally! Without hesitating, I returned his kiss with a longing sigh, clawed my fingers into his hair, and eagerly pulled him to me. He moved his hands over my body—my hair, my neck, my back, my hips, my behind. I tasted his breath and drew it in while I greedily attempted to pull him even closer. It was simply incredible—like a rush to which I devoted life and soul. The way he had kissed me in the morning outside the lecture hall had been incredible, so tender and so loving. But this kiss . . . This kiss was pure passion.

I noticed much too late that Jared was putting a little distance between us. Gently he kissed me twice on the lips before placing his forehead against mine and looking me in the eyes. His hands rested on my hips.

"I'm sorry," he said quietly. "I should let it start a little slower."

"I've got nothing against fast," I said, panting.

Jared grinned. "You're driving me insane," he said and kissed me so intensely it took my breath away. *Wow!* My knees were trembling long after he'd released my lips again.

"You've got Intro Psych with Harrison now and then Stats with Gallert, right?" Jared asked after I'd caught my breath again.

"You know my schedule?" I asked, surprised. I didn't know if I was supposed to feel upset or flattered by it.

"Yes," Jared said and laughed, looking guilty.

I smiled. Apparently, something inside me found it flattering.

"See you at Karen's lecture?" he asked and kissed me gently on the forehead and on the tip of my nose.

"She kicked me out—have you forgotten already?"

"We'll see about that," Jared mumbled. "Will you please save me a seat?" he asked.

"Yeah . . . sure," I said. "Do you really think it's a good idea if I just show up there? What if she kicks me out again?"

"She only did that to prevent us from getting to know each other."

Never mind getting to know each other, she doesn't even want us to be in the same room together.

"But now that we're together . . ." he said, shrugging, unconcerned.

Together? Incredible what this single word from his mouth did to my body. My heart immediately began to race. *We're together!*

"What are you thinking?" Jared asked, a little amused.

Of course, my inner cries of joy wouldn't be secrets to him. "It felt so good when you said that. That we're . . . together," I said while struggling against my rising embarrassment.

Jared firmly held me in his arms and kissed me passionately for a long time.

"Get used to it. I don't intend to ever give you up," he said, rubbing the tip of his nose against mine.

My legs wobbled as if they were made of Jell-O. "Okay," I said, breathless.

"So, will you save me a seat?" he asked again, smiling while holding me in his arms.

I nodded and looked at him dreamily. I had never before seen such extraordinary blue eyes. Surely, that couldn't even be replicated with tinted contact lenses.

"Till then," Jared whispered in my ear. He wrapped his arms one last time around me and placed his lips on mine before leaving.

"Till then," I said when he'd almost turned his back to me, and he let his fingers glide into his jeans pockets and sauntered away. I watched him till he turned the corner—without even once turning to show his knock-out crooked smile—and disappeared from view. His appearance still took my breath away. Despite his height, Jared never appeared clumsy or awkward, which was probably because he had an athlete's body. For a moment, I lost myself in thoughts of Jared's body, how he'd look naked, how his skin would feel on mine . . . but then I remembered my sense of responsibility, which still existed somewhere deep inside me. I was really here to study. I pushed away from the wall with a sigh and went on my way.

Professor Harrison probably gave the most boring lecture of his entire career. No wonder I couldn't focus on it.

Stats with Gallert was—I wouldn't have thought it possible—even more boring. And so I struggled through the two sessions, counting the minutes until I'd see Jared again. I gave a grateful sigh when Gallert finally packed his things and disappeared through the don's door. I started to look for Jared at once, carefully saving the seat to the right of me, which several incoming students had already tried to claim.

"May I sit with you, Miss Lakewood?"

When I recognized his voice, a comfortable warmth spread through the pit of my stomach. He looked down at me with a broad grin.

"Why certainly, Mr. Calmburry," I said with a voice a little too high, clearing my coat and bag from the chair I'd reserved for him.

The seat sprang up, and he elegantly swung it down and slid into the chair in a single flowing movement.

"Hi," he greeted me, grinning, took my hand, and placed a tender kiss on it.

"Hi," I said with a squeaky voice. My ears began to glow when I noticed the two girls to my left looking back and forth between me and Jared with eyes wide open in disbelief.

"Did you see that?" one whispered to the other. The upset tone of her voice was unmistakable. I would have liked to be annoyed at how shocked the two girls were by Jared's kissing me, but when I looked back into his face I had doubts myself. I was sure no woman in this overfilled lecture hall would have said no to him. Jared probably could have had any girl in this whole damned college. Heck, the whole town! Even the whole country! So why me? Suddenly, I remembered our talk in the woods again, when Enid had revealed to me that I was supposedly the last of Nimue's bloodline. And that there was something between Jared and me, a . . . what did she call it? Yes, an *ancient magical link*. I was stumped. Could that be the real reason? Did Jared only feel attracted to me because I belonged to a particular bloodline? Because I was the daughter of my mother, the granddaughter of my grandmother, the great-granddaughter of my great-grandmother . . . ? Had he only fallen in love with me because it was predestined?

"What's going on?" Jared asked and tore me from my thoughts.

I shook my head. "Oh nothing. I'm a little nervous about how Karen will react to me," I lied unconvincingly while pushing aside the depressing thought that Jared was only interested in me because of a hocus-pocus connection that had come about many generations ago between our ancestors. He frowned in disbelief, but before he was able to say anything, the don's door opened and Professor Mayflower entered.

"Speak of the devil," Jared whispered into my ear and sat upright. I did as he did, nervously trying to focus on what was about to come: Karen's response to seeing me. Especially seeing me seated beside Jared.

As always, Professor Mayflower scanned her audience before starting into her lecture. Jared sat even more upright in his chair. Apparently, he wanted to be seen by her—with me at his side.

Finally, Karen's eyes stopped on Jared's face, which caused a maternal smile to appear. Then she saw me . . . and her smile died. With a mixture of anger and horror, her face changed. Her mouth opened, and for a moment it looked as if she were about to say something, but then she pinched her lips together and continued scanning the lecture hall.

"Good morning," she said in a cold tone into the slim microphone mounted on the lectern.

"Good morning," the majority of students present mumbled back.

"In today's lecture we will deal with defensive mechanisms," Professor Mayflower said as the image of her sobbing in the middle of the forest path with Aiden attempting to console her came to my mind. In my opinion, those two had a strange mother-son relationship. But what did I know about it?

"Defense mechanisms are what?" Karen asked, grabbed a piece of chalk, and let her stern look wander along the rows. The hand of a young woman with long dark hair and a face that seemed to consist of little pits shot up like a bullet. Karen granted her permission to speak with a quick nod.

"Defense mechanisms are defined as psychological mechanisms that process conflicting psychological tendencies or integrate them to protect the mind from these serious conflicts. This mostly happens at the subconscious level," the dark-haired woman said, beaming from ear to ear—apparently very satisfied with herself. I recognized her as one of Madison's friends from the smugness of her smile. She was on the same swimming team and had been with her on the day Madison had ripped the amulet from my neck in the shower. *Strange . . . I hadn't seen Madison since that day. Before that I'd unfortunately come across her several times a week,* I thought, recalling the malicious look she gave me every time we met. Maybe I should be happy she wasn't around to get on my nerves anymore. But I wondered where she'd gone to and what she wanted with my amulet. The way she'd stared at it, I didn't believe she just wanted to be nasty to me. When I thought about it, she really had it in for my amulet. My hand moved to the hollow in my neck that had framed the ornament. I still felt naked and vulnerable without the amulet. Would that ever change?

Jared cast me a fleeting, concerned glance as if he had felt the sorrow in my energy.

"Correct," Professor Mayflower answered, but I wasn't able to connect it to anything for a moment. *What? Oh yes, defense mechanisms!*

"However, it is important to understand that this is by no means an ideal solution to the conflict, as the conflict can return at a later point and in most cases results in the expression of various symptoms," Karen said and waited until the students, including me, had scribbled this into their notepads.

"Now," Karen continued, still visibly tense. "What defense mechanisms are differentiated in psychoanalysis?"

"Repression," a cherub-cheeked girl with glasses called from the first row as Karen wrote the term on the board.

"Compensation," a young girl with light-blonde hair called out, and Karen also wrote that down.

"Continue," Karen demanded, whereupon the terms *displacement, isolation, rationalization, reaction formation, identification, fixation,* and *sublimation* were shouted out from the depths of the room without my being able to associate them with their sources. After she'd scribbled all this on the board, and the students had no more to add, she completed the list with the terms *avoidance, projection, regression,* and *somatization.* She turned to the class again. For a second, her gaze met mine. I did my best not to let her narrowed eyes and angrily curled lips intimidate me. Jared grabbed my hand under the desk and squeezed it for encouragement.

"Good, let's take a look at individual defense mechanisms," the professor continued, unperturbed, and pointed to the term at the top of the board.

"Repression," she read, "is probably the most familiar defense mechanism. Who can tell me what this means?"

The brownnosers in the front row raised their hands quick as lightning. Karen nodded at one of them.

The anointed one cleared his throat loudly. "Repression is the psychological process when imaginations linked to a drive are shifted from the level of the aware to the level of the unaware," he proudly explained. *My goodness, did this guy learn all this BS by heart just for Mayflower's lecture?*

"Yes." Professor Mayflower nodded. "Write it down," she said and asked the brownnoser in the first row to repeat his definition for the record before she read out the second term.

"Compensation." She raised her eyebrows in anticipation and looked into the crowd. Again several hands were raised.

"Hmm . . . Miss Lakewood," Karen Mayflower suddenly called out without taking note of the raised hands in the front rows. I instantly froze. "Would you please explain what the term *compensation* means?" An arrogant grin took over her face. I felt as if I was being throttled, and my heart pounded in my neck. Jared's grip on my hand became firmer. He, too, appeared surprised and did not seem to approve of what was happening.

Okay, let's see. I desperately attempted to focus. *How did that go? I've read something about it somewhere . . . Compensation . . . To compensate for something . . . What was that supposed to mean . . . ? To make up for something one lacked with something else, wasn't it?* I had no choice but to try and hope I'd get it right. Once again all eyes, including Karen Mayflower's, were on me and stared in anticipation.

"Um . . . ," I started, uncertain.

"Yes?" Karen said in an overbearing tone. I blinked. She was trying to embarrass me. In front of all my classmates and, worse yet, in front of Jared. Suddenly, I felt enraged, which seemed to kick-start my brain, and I had the definition as clearly before my eyes as if I were reading it from a piece of paper.

"Compensation is behavior that attempts to make up for psychological deficiencies such as feelings of inferiority. This results in actions that are supposed to demonstrate full worthiness, but the ego somewhat exceeds the goal and overcompensates for the deficiency," I heard myself say.

Jared leaned back, relaxed, and gave me a conspiratorial wink. "Well done," he mouthed. I also got approving looks from the other students. Some had already started scribbling my definition on their notepads.

"Yes," Karen Mayflower said, somewhat confused. "Good . . . Please write that down," she added, suddenly casting me an appraising look, in which I believed I saw something soft. As if she recognized that she'd underestimated me.

Since I felt sure I wouldn't be called on again, I was able to lean back and relax for the remainder of the lecture. But I did sit up straight as a post when it was Jared's turn to define *sublimation*, which he did so sovereignly that I immediately sank back down again.

We didn't get through all the defense mechanisms, which is why Karen promised we'd continue next week where we'd left off. *Still, I did it,* I thought when she packed her things, and I sighed with relief.

"Hungry?" Jared asked me, beaming, and extended his hand to pull me up from the chair.

"Yes," I said, smiling. As if to confirm it, my stomach growled loudly, which made Jared's grin widen even more.

"Do you want to go to the dining hall or somewhere else? A place we can talk undisturbed?"

"Undisturbed sounds good," I said, following him outside. Considering the almost two-hour lunch break we had to ourselves, I felt a happy expectation. Even though Jared and I were officially—there was a tingling inside my stomach when I thought of it—*together* and he had let me in on his greatest secret, there still was much I didn't know about him.

"How old are you actually?" I asked while we were walking to the old town. It seemed a fitting initial question.

"Twenty-one," he said and grinned when he understood what I was up to. "And you?"

"Nineteen," I said without being able to rid myself of the feeling that he already knew.

"Did you start school late?" I followed up when my brain registered that he was two years older but in the same year as me.

"I studied physics after finishing high school and only started psychology last October."

"Didn't you like physics?"

"I did, why?" He seemed confused.

"Because you changed subjects?"

"But I didn't," he said, frowning. "I graduated and then started on psychology."

"You completed a bachelor's in physics in two years?" I asked, impressed.

"Actually, I've got a master's degree," he said, embarrassed. "But it took two and a half years," he added.

I looked at him almost in awe and attempted to push aside the question of what someone like him wanted with me. "Why those subjects?" They didn't entirely fit together in my mind.

"Well, physics examines the phenomena and laws of nature while psychology deals with the experience and behavior of humans. Together with biology they form the pillars of magic," he explained.

I thought for a moment. "So, essentially, you're trying to understand yourself better?"

"Yes, I think you could look at it that way," he said.

"That makes sense, of course." I smiled.

"Where did you grow up?" he asked, and again I had the sneaking suspicion that this was an alibi question.

"In Fleetwood. Do you know where that is?" *A small test.*

"North of Liverpool, isn't it?" he said. Now I was certain he'd already known where I'd grown up. For a flash, the image of a manila folder full of information shot through my mind: my date of birth, CV, report cards, blood type, police report . . . The thought made me grin.

A file on me—that would be taking it too far. But what if it was true? Strangely, I didn't care. On the contrary, I almost felt a little flattered that Jared knew so much about me. After all, this meant he'd been interested in me for a while. You don't inform yourself about someone you don't care about, do you?

Jared suddenly smiled. "Right by the water—how . . . fitting. Did you like it there?"

"Yes, my sister Zara and I had a small apartment . . ." I stopped. I had to swallow when a deep sadness for which I was completely unprepared overcame me. It had been a few weeks since I'd last talked to anyone about my sister. Jared walked more slowly and, when I couldn't speak, he finally stopped and took me into his arms.

"You miss her, don't you?" he whispered in my ear. His words were filled with empathy.

"Every day," I said, trying to swallow the lump in my throat.

"I miss my family, too," he said quietly, moving closer to me. "I had a sister, too. Her name was Laura." We stood there for a moment, in the middle of the path in this wonderfully comforting embrace and shared our pain. It felt so good. Then he bent down and gave me a gentle kiss on my closed lips.

"Do you feel like Indian? Chicken curry?" he asked, suddenly switching the topic but somehow at the right moment.

"Yes," I said, his great timing forcing me to smile before he gently kissed my forehead.

A little later we entered a cozy Indian restaurant from which loud voices escaped as soon as we opened the door. They were speaking in English, Hindi, and a strange mixture of the two. We ordered two portions of chicken curry with rice and two Cokes.

"No, we'll eat here," Jared said, answering a startlingly beautiful Indian waitress when she asked whether it was for here or to go. She shyly smiled at him as her golden-brown skin tone took on a noticeable red shimmer. She looked only about sixteen; otherwise, I might have been jealous.

Jared paid, ignoring my protests. He gave the young beauty a generous tip and a friendly smile, which seemed to completely turn her head.

"I'll . . . bring it to your t-table," she stammered and disappeared, embarrassed, into the kitchen. Oh man, only Jared was capable of confounding someone like that with a single glance—no one knew that better than I did.

We sat down at the last free table. Though the noise forced us to bend toward each other over the table to talk, I was fine with it being loud. No one would be able to listen in on our conversation.

"I think the little lady fell in love with you," I said with a smile and nodded toward the kitchen door.

Jared frowned. "The waitress?"

I nodded.

"I think she just wants to be polite," he said, shrugging, and reached for my hand. I decided not to pursue the topic but to continue our question-and-answer game.

"Who were those two women who joined us yesterday in the woods? They came with Professor Martin."

"The one in riding boots was Enid Speakerman. She's a doctor and number two in the Order after Karen."

When the Indian beauty, still slightly blushing, brought our meal, Jared stopped talking. Only when I had to lean back so she could place the plate on the table did I notice how far we had leaned forward.

"Thank you," Jared and I said in unison, whereupon she smiled back shyly and perhaps even a little apologetically. I returned her smile. I couldn't hold it against her that she liked Jared.

"This means Karen is something like the head of the Order?" I asked.

Jared nodded. "She is the high priestess and Enid is her deputy, basically," he said. "Personally, I'd prefer if it were the other way around."

"And who was the redhead?" I asked, though I suspected I already knew the answer.

"Claire McAdams, Madison's mother."

"I thought so."

"The resemblance is hard to miss," he said with a chuckle.

"And what does she do?" I asked, pushing a forkful of food into my mouth.

"She's also a member of the High Council," Jared said as he started to eat.

"High Council?" That rang a bell. Didn't Colin inform me through Sally that a certain High Council had to decide something, and until then she was supposed to stay with me in public?

Jared nodded while he chewed, then swallowed. "The High Council of the Order consists of seven members. Five of them you already know."

I was startled. "Five?" I asked, starting to count. "Karen Mayflower, Professor Martin, Enid—what was her last name again?"

"Speakerman," Jared said before popping another forkful of curry into his mouth.

"Oh yes, Enid Speakerman and Madison's mother, Claire, right?"

Jared nodded.

"That's only four."

"You forgot me," he said, winking.

"You're part of the High Council?"

"Yes."

"And who are the other two?"

"Judith McHallern and Montgomery Grey," Jared said, eating another forkful.

"Ah. And what does the Council do?"

"Protects Merlin's legacy," Jared said and swallowed. "The High Council decides, in a manner of speaking, what is to be done when danger looms."

"What danger?"

"Any kind of danger to my family and the Order," he said, then quietly added, "or, rather, *myself* and the Order."

Uncertain, I turned away from him. "When I arrived at Oxford, the High Council also made a decision, didn't it?"

"Yes," Jared said, his voice suddenly hardening.

"What was it?"

He hesitated. "That they will not . . . take action against you." This reluctance wasn't at all like him.

"What is that supposed to mean?"

When I noticed Jared's look, I would have preferred to retract the question. *Oh!*

"I understand," I said, subdued and looked at my hands.

After a pause, I asked, "How does this work with these decisions? Do you vote by raising hands, or what?" I couldn't resist laughing at the thought.

"Yes, that's pretty much what we do."

"Seriously?"

He nodded while an amused grin spread across his face.

"And how did the vote about me go?"

His smile disappeared. "It was close," he said.

I suddenly felt a chill. I had a fairly good idea who voted against me. Karen and Claire would certainly not have been on my side. I no longer felt hungry and pushed my half-finished plate aside.

Jared, who had finished eating, looked at me earnestly. "Whatever the High Council would have decided, I would never have allowed any harm to come to you," he said, taking me by the hand. I only managed a nod as my response. We sat across from each other silently while I sipped my Coke.

"Does the Order have other members than those seven? What about Colin and Aiden and the other guys you run with?" I asked to distract myself.

"The Order consists of three levels," Jared said, suddenly appearing much less subdued. "The High Council forms the core and is in turn surrounded by the Circle. That's a kind of inner group that currently consists of twenty people. That includes Colin, Aiden, and the others. Every seven years, the members of the Council are elected from the ranks of the Circle."

I couldn't help a surprised snort.

"What's the matter?" Jared asked, amused by my reaction.

"Well, I didn't expect this club to be something like a democracy."

"Club?" Jared said and then laughed.

Damn, did I just say that out loud? "Sorry, I didn't mean to offend you."

"Don't worry about it," Jared said, laughing, and brushed the hair out of my face.

"And what's the third level?" I asked.

"All those who are not members of the Circle but still belong to the Order. An outer group, in a manner of speaking."

"And how many of them are there?"

"More than five hundred."

"Five hundred? Wow."

Jared nodded. "Yes, but only the Circle is initiated into all secrets. The members of the outer group act in the background. They only know what they need to know to fulfill their duties." He suddenly laughed. "You'd be surprised if you knew how many people in public life belong to Legatum Merlini or did during their lifetime."

"People in public life?"

"Scientists, politicians, musicians, artists, actors, authors, CEOs . . . The list is long." Jared bent a little farther across the table and whispered. "The members are dispersed throughout the world. The Order has a safe house in almost every country."

I was shocked.

"Of course, Oxford is the base and hub. There's no better place to hide a secret as effectively as in this tradition-rich university town." He smiled wide. "For example, we keep most of the Order's literature collection in the college library. A collection like that is hardly noticeable among scholarly works on all conceivable subjects."

I blinked. So I was right: the Calmburry book, the carvings on the shelves, the books on the witch trials, herbal lore . . .

"I know you were there," Jared said as if he had read my thoughts. "Karen even convened the Council because of it." He rolled his eyes in irritation. "Since you showed up, she's called a Council meeting nearly every week. I'm starting to think she's turning paranoid."

I swallowed. Karen really did believe I was a danger to Jared and might even wish to harm him. But that was so ridiculous! For my money, she was definitely paranoid. All this talk about danger and safety . . . Suddenly, something Jared had just said registered.

"How did you mean that?" I asked. "What exactly are you safe from in these *safe houses*?"

"These houses, and especially the headquarters here in Oxford, have protective spells cast on them that prevent anyone from being found as long as they stay there."

Protective spells? "And who would they be hiding from?"

Jared looked down and was silent for a moment. "All those who are not welcome in the house but especially . . . Morgana," he whispered bitterly.

"Morgana?" I repeated just as quietly. "*The* Morgana from Arthurian legend? She's real?" I'd heard it before, but it had never really entered my consciousness.

Only then did I notice I'd leaned so far over the table that my torso was almost completely on top of the table. Jared had also come forward so far our noses almost touched.

"Wait a second," I said, frowning. "Are we talking about Morgana's descendants or *the* Morgana from the fifth century?"

"It's still the same one," Jared said in a muffled voice. *Still the same one? But how . . . ?* I couldn't bring myself to follow the thought to its conclusion because of the painful expression on Jared's face. "She killed my entire family," he said with lowered eyes and suddenly spoke so softly I could barely understand him. "And Colin's. And . . ." He stopped, closed his eyes, then opened them again after a deep breath and looked at me with empathy. "Yours."

I felt my face go as pale as a ghost. "M—mine? Morgana killed *my* family?"

Jared grasped my hand, nodding. A painful expression of empathy—no, pity—in his eyes.

"I'm sorry," he said.

I managed to blink a few seconds later. "But . . . they caught Zara's murderer . . . ," I said numbly. I was totally confused. Did they convict an innocent man for my sister's murder? I remembered when Christopher, Zara's partner in the police department, had appeared unexpectedly at my door. It was soon after Zara's funeral. I could still see the look on his face.

"We got him," he'd said through clenched teeth. "I beat the shit out of him!" Tears were rolling down his cheeks. My eyes stopped at his hands. The knuckles were blood-encrusted and raw in some spots.

Did he ever tell Zara that he loved her?

"How do you know it was Morgana?" I asked Jared. My voice broke.

"From Karen. She told me a few days ago." He hesitated before he continued. "Evelyn, what do you know about how your family died?"

Nothing was more difficult for me than talking about this. I breathed in deeply while trying not to focus on my tightening throat.

"Mom and Dad"—I coughed—"died in a car accident." There it was again—the lump in my throat that told me I was just about to break down in tears. I swallowed with difficulty. "They were squeezed off the road. Their car rolled over four times and hit a tree. They were killed instantly." My voice trembled while my eyes filled with tears.

Jared stroked my cheek. "Was the culprit ever caught?"

"No," I said, wiping the tears from my eyes with the back of my hand. "The police thought he may have been drunk and left the scene."

Jared nodded. "And your sister?" he whispered.

I needed a moment to collect myself and suppress more tears. "She was on duty that night and had been called to a high-rise because of a minor disturbance." I breathed in deeply. "When she took down the personal information of the guy who'd caused the ruckus, he . . . he . . . he shot her in the head and ran off." A flood of images suddenly came to me: Christopher, who rang our doorbell in the late evening, took his hat off and broke down in tears before he was able to tell me what had happened. Me, in the funeral parlor where I had to select a coffin for her. The funeral. Christopher, how he dropped to his knees before her grave and whimpered. A stranger who pulled me away so I wouldn't have to see it. The notary who told me how much my sister had loved me . . .

I buried my face in my hands. Jared stood up, pulled his chair to my side of the table with a scraping sound, sat down beside me, and put his arms around me. It was several minutes before my tears stopped.

"His name is Frank Tempton," I said. "He's doing life in Walton Prison in Liverpool."

"Frank Tempton?" Jared repeated skeptically.

"Why does Karen think Morgana has anything to do with it? Is that supposed to mean Tempton is innocent?"

"Karen only told me Morgana was behind it. This Tempton is probably just one of her minions and killed Zara on her orders."

"But why?"

"So there's nobody to get in her way. That's also the reason she killed my family and Colin's."

"But . . . but my parents and my sister had no magical abilities whatsoever." Desperation caused my voice to tremble. "Just like I don't."

"Well, Colin doesn't have any, either, at least not in the narrow sense." A smile spread across his face. "Which doesn't mean he should be underestimated."

"What are you trying to say?"

Jared chuckled a little. "Colin's a warrior—it's in his blood. Just as there's something in your blood." He turned so he could look into my eyes. "Think of what unusual effect plain, ordinary water has on you. Even after many generations, Nimue's magic is still deeply rooted in you. Even though it's not as apparent in you as in me, you are a magical and very mighty being."

"Oh, Jared, believe me, I'm anything but mighty, and I'm not at all magical."

"Are you sure?" he asked with a tender smile that made his dark-blue eyes shine like stars in a clear night sky. "You enchanted me the very first moment I saw you." Jared tilted his head to the side and kissed me. He gently placed one hand on my waist and stroked my cheek with the other. A sigh escaped me as my arms closed around his neck and my hands tousled his thick, disheveled hair. In the golden light of the Indian restaurant it seemed like liquid caramel, and the way it contrasted with his indigo-blue eyes made Jared appear more angel than man. Another sigh escaped me. Never before had I seen a more beautiful face.

"So Colin is a warrior?" I asked, smiling.

An amused look appeared on Jared's face. "Yes," he said, his smile broadening. "That's why he's the Order's chief defender."

"Chief defender?" I said, frowning. "Is that a kind of function?"

Jared nodded. "That's the title of the office he holds within the Circle. Defense and protection are the top priorities of Legatum Merlini, and Colin's the born fighter. Who better to train the members of the Circle in defense?" Jared shrugged.

I frowned. "Does that mean every member of the Circle is trained to be a fighting machine?"

Jared laughed. "No, but some basic skills are a requirement."

I remembered the day in the pool shower when Madison had snuck up on me, as silent as a cat. And disappeared just as silently. I never stood a chance. I never even saw that it was her.

Jared seemed to sense the change in my mood. All of a sudden he looked concerned.

"What are you thinking of?" he asked.

"Madison and her *basic skills*," I said angrily.

Jared breathed in deeply. "Madison is very ambitious in everything she does. She practices till she drops and has mastered far more than the basics."

"Oh man, her mother must be really proud of her," I said, still bitter.

He snorted. "Yes, she is," he said and averted his eyes. "Colin is castigating himself because he taught Madison the skills she used against you. He trained her, after all." He looked at his hands.

We sat there silently for a little while, but then Jared looked up, beaming at me. "Hey, did you find out all by yourself who I am?" he asked with apparent admiration. I didn't mind the sudden change in topic.

"No, not all by myself."

"Who helped?"

I hesitated. "Please don't be upset, but you said secrecy is top priority for the Order, and I don't want to alert Karen to this person's existence," I said, looking at him apologetically.

"Yes, of course," he said, understanding, though a little hurt.

After lunch, Jared accompanied me to Behavioral Psychology and left me with a tender kiss outside the lecture hall, causing mouths to gape among the women around us. I made an effort to ignore those looks while I searched for an empty seat inside and rummaged through my bag for my notebook and pen. I felt a little uncomfortable without

Sally, who normally sat with me, especially since I felt several sets of eyes on me.

The lecture seemed to drag on for hours. Only when Professor Fisher let us go and I made my way to the next seminar did I feel some anticipation, though it was tempered with a feeling of unease. After all, this seminar would be my first encounter with Professor Martin since we'd met in the woods.

I grimaced at the idea of how Karen Mayflower had taken Jared in as a nine-year-old. Even though she had a son, I saw nothing motherly about her. I remembered Aiden comforting his tearful mother. When I thought about it, her posture almost seemed to reject him as he desperately tried to hug her. Aiden surely couldn't have an easy life with her as his mother.

I watched apprehensively as Professor Martin entered the room under the usual longing looks of the female students. I figured he'd show nothing and offer an Oscar-worthy performance, like he did on the day I recognized the symbol on his seal ring. But to my surprise and the annoyance of the other female students, he gave me a well-meaning look and even bestowed one of his ravishing smiles on me. I was delighted with this and returned it, though hesitantly, since I feared my classmates might lynch me for all the attention I was receiving these days. Therefore, I thought it best to avoid eye contact with Professor Martin for the time being. When this last lecture was finally over, I went outside where Jared, *my boyfriend*, was waiting for me with his breathtaking smile. I went over to him and pressed my lips to his, which caused me to smile even while kissing him. As expected, all the girls nearby either looked at me with wide eyes or glared in anger, but I tried to ignore it. *He's mine! Get over it!*

"May I walk you home?" Jared asked.

"Don't you feel like doing something?" I didn't even try to hide my disappointment.

"The next Council meeting is in an hour, and I have to be there."

"Oh," I said.

Jared looked at me apologetically. "I hope you know that I'd rather be doing something completely different tonight."

"Really? Like what?"

Jared stopped, held my hip, pulled me to him, and let his hands wander over my back to my behind.

"I'm sure I could think of something," he whispered into my ear and kissed me intensely. My blood almost began to boil as I buried my fingers in his dense hair.

"Damned Council meeting," I said quietly when he pulled away. Jared laughed.

CHAPTER 15

I closed my room door and leaned against it, sighing. Suddenly, my phone rang. Had Jared forgotten something? I frantically dug it out of my bag and looked at the screen. Sally!

"Hi, Sally, how are you? I was just going to call you. Colin said you're feeling much better than before and you'd be back tomorrow."

"Hi, Evelyn," she said when I finally let her have a word. "Yes, I'll be back tomorrow. Will we see each other?"

"Of course. Now tell me, how are you?"

"As good as new," Sally said cheerfully and giggled. "Talking about *new* . . . Is there something new with you?"

I had to grin. "Maybe."

"Pfft, don't make me pull teeth. Colin told me, anyway."

"Then why are you asking?" I teased, knowing she was about to burst with curiosity.

"Evelyn!"

"Oh all right," I said, still grinning. "Jared and I are . . . Well, we're . . . together."

"That's wonderful—the four of us have to go out together!"

"We're only getting to know each other, Sally," I said, trying to slow her down a bit.

A few hours later, after I'd showered thoroughly, I crawled under my covers, turned off the lights and peacefully slept with the wholesome feeling of anticipating the coming day. I could hardly wait to see Jared again.

In the morning, I opened my eyes, sat up enthusiastically, leapt to my feet, and headed for the bathroom. I went over to check my phone while brushing my teeth and noticed two messages. The first was from just after eleven the evening before, when I had long been asleep:

```
Sleep well and sweet dreams . . .
```

The second was from just a few minutes ago:

```
Good morning. I'm waiting outside the
door for you.
```

He's here? I brushed my teeth quickly, took jeans and a sweater from the closet without caring if they matched, and brushed my hair. I was ready for the day in record time, and since rushing and anticipation made it look like I'd applied blush, I was moderately satisfied with the result. I charged down the stairs and threw open the door. Jared stood on the stairs outside and smiled at me.

"Good morning," I said with a broad grin when he saw me.

"Good morning," Jared said, put his arm around my waist, and kissed me with his warm, soft lips. I had to keep it together not to throw myself at him.

"Are you ready?" he asked, brushing my cheek.

I nodded, still enthralled by his greeting, and reached for his extended hand.

Our fingers entwined, and we started for the College, where I'd have to attend my morning lectures alone, sadly. I already missed him just thinking about it.

"Did you hear Social Psych is cancelled this afternoon?" Sally asked me during lunch when I sat with her, Colin, and Jared. She looked splendid, and if I hadn't seen her lying pale as a ghost in her bed a few days ago, I wouldn't have believed she'd been seriously ill. But she was back to her old self again.

"Professor Monrose has the flu," Sally said, beaming. By contrast, I felt a wave of empathy. Poor Professor Monrose was so thin and frail, I was seriously worried she might not survive the flu.

"We've got the afternoon off," Sally said and threw her arms in the air.

"I've still got Emotions," I said.

"Well, *almost* a free afternoon," she said.

"I'm off at the same time," Jared said, smiling at me. "We could do something if you want."

Now I couldn't help smiling. The prospect of spending the afternoon with Jared put me in the best mood.

"What do you think of a small excursion?" he proposed.

"What were you thinking?"

"That's a surprise," he said with a wink. He probably didn't want to go into detail in Sally's presence.

After we got through Psychology of Emotions—holding hands under the desk most of the time—Jared and I stepped into the fresh air outside.

"Can we go by my dorm real quick? I don't want to carry this thing around the whole time," I said, pointing to the strap on my shoulder.

"Sure," Jared said, taking my bag off to carry it for me. "That'll give me a chance to look at your room," he said suggestively. I hoped there wasn't any dirty laundry scattered on the floor.

"Are you going to tell me where we're going now?" I asked as we walked to my dorm.

"I'd like to show you something," he said, smiling.

I wrinkled my forehead. "So, you're not going to tell me?"

Jared shook his head, continuing to torture me.

When we finally stood at my door, I turned the key in the lock and stuck my head in quickly to scan the room before letting Jared in. Fortunately, it was reasonably tidy. Although my bed was made up rather poorly because of the morning rush.

"Here we are," I said, spreading my arms. "This is where I live."

"Pretty," Jared said, looking around. "And . . . this is your bed," he said a moment later, stretching out the comment so much I couldn't miss the point. My hands turned moist, and my heart started beating twice as fast. Whether from excitement, joy, or anxiety I couldn't tell. Most likely, it was a mixture of all three.

He took another step toward my bed and examined the framed pictures on my nightstand.

"Your parents?" he asked gently, pointing at the first.

"Uh huh," I said, the excitement suddenly gone.

"And that's your sister?" Jared smiled when he picked up the picture of Zara and me to look at it more closely.

"Yes," I answered proudly. "She's beautiful, isn't she?" I missed her so much at that moment it caused me physical pain.

"Yes, she is," Jared said. "But not nearly as beautiful as her little sis," he said with a warm smile while gently brushing my hair out of my face. When I felt my ears turning hot, I averted my eyes. Jared smiled at my reaction and turned to the picture again. Suddenly he froze. The smile disappeared from his face. His eyes widened.

"Is *that* the amulet Madison stole from you?" he asked, obviously upset. "That she tore from your neck at the pool?"

I was startled by the sudden change in his mood. "Yes," I said. Jared seemed to be in real turmoil. Still holding the picture frame in his hands, he lay on my bed and stared at me.

"What's the matter?" I asked, sitting down beside him. While I was looking for an answer in his face, I took Jared's hand and stroked it to calm him. All of a sudden, he looked in my eyes.

"You don't know what that is, do you?"

I frowned.

"That isn't just some pretty necklace," he said, taking my hand.

"What do you mean?"

Jared hesitated. "That's a magical jewel," he said, holding my hand even more firmly. "According to legend, Merlin made it for Nimue. It's said that he cast a strong protective spell on it."

"A protective spell?" Suddenly, I heard my mother's words in my head. *It will protect you! Never take it off.* So that hadn't just been some line? Had she known the amulet's true meaning?

"Do you understand, Evelyn? As long as you wore it, the amulet protected you."

"Protected me? From what?"

"I have no idea how the spell works," Jared said, visibly frustrated, his expression pensive. "We thought it had been lost long ago, but it had been in your family's possession all this time . . ." He shook his head.

"But it hadn't been in my family's possession," I said.

Jared raised his head, looking puzzled.

"My mother bought it at a flea market in London when she was pregnant with me. I've worn it every day since I was six—until Madison stole it from me." It would have been impossible to miss the anger in my voice. We looked at the picture for a moment. Then I suddenly had a thought. "Do you think it has something to do with her disappearance? Madison's, I mean."

He thought for a moment. "I don't know. But, thinking about it . . . the day she attacked you in the pool was the day she went missing."

"What does she want with my amulet?"

"No idea." Jared sighed. "She definitely knows what it is—every member of the Circle knows that. And she also knows it's very powerful."

He bit his lower lip. "I don't want to know what damage it can do if it gets into the wrong hands," he said, shaking his head.

"Where could she have gone?" I was asking myself more than him.

"I'd love to know," Jared said, carefully removing the picture from its frame and slipping it into his pocket.

"We have to talk to Karen about this," he said, got up from my bed, and held his hand out to me. I reluctantly let him pull me up.

I sighed. "If it has to be. But you're aware I'm not her favorite person, aren't you?"

"She's only concerned for my safety," Jared said to appease me, but he also smiled apologetically, which confirmed my suspicion.

Yes—she couldn't stand me!

A few minutes later, we were back at the College to knock on Professor Mayflower's office door.

"Come in," she said from inside. Jared entered with me in tow. She sat at her desk correcting a stack of assignments.

"Jared," she greeted him, beaming with delight, and then favored me with a forced smile. "What's up?"

"Evelyn and I have to tell you something. You remember that Madison attacked Evelyn in the pool and ripped a necklace from her, right?"

Karen nodded with an earnest expression.

"And you know Madison has been gone since that day," Jared continued. Professor Mayflower frowned, took off her reading glasses, and rose from her cushioned chair.

"What are you getting at?" she asked. Jared carefully pulled the picture out of his pocket and handed it to Karen, who immediately put on her reading glasses and gave it a look. It felt strange to see her with the picture in her hands. The picture meant so much to me. If it had been up to me, she would never have seen it. It had been taken in a very intimate moment between Zara and me. It was nobody else's business—least of all Karen Mayflower's.

"That's the necklace Madison stole from her," Jared said, pointing at the picture.

"Nimue's amulet!" Karen was shocked when she saw the jewel with the blue-green sheen. "What? I thought . . . Has your family owned it all this time?" she asked in disbelief. She stared at me with wide eyes.

"No, my mother bought it at a flea market and gave it to me when I turned six." I was repulsed by the thought of telling this woman about my family. Karen and Jared exchanged glances.

"It returned to them," he said, subdued and pensive.

Karen nodded and shook her head as if this gesture would help her think more clearly. "We must call a Council meeting," she said. "This afternoon. It's best if you come along right away, Jared," she said, then cast a hasty glance in my direction. "Thank you very much, Evelyn." Her words sounded a little forced. "May I make a copy? That way you can have your photo back."

"Yeah, sure," I said, and she disappeared, picture in hand, through the door.

"Sorry," Jared said, frowning. "I really imagined this day differently."

"So did I," I said.

Karen returned and pressed the picture into my hand. "Thank you very much." Again the forced smile, though it appeared gentler this time. Nevertheless, I felt out of place here and not at all well.

"Okay, I won't bother you any longer. I'll leave," I said, trying to appear as cool as possible. Surely those two couldn't have missed the sadness and hurt in my voice. Especially not Jared, who must have felt what was going on inside me. I slipped out the door as fast as possible.

"Evelyn." Jared had caught up to me in a flash. "Sorry things went this way today," he said, scratching the back of his head, a clear sign he was feeling very uncomfortable. "But Karen's right—the sooner we find out what Madison is up to, the better."

I nodded. "It's okay," I said with a dismissive hand motion. *No! Nothing's okay! I feel excluded every time this damned Order comes into play. None of them trust me! But I've done nothing to even remotely deserve this. Damned Order! Damned Karen Mayflower!*

Jared frowned when he sensed my internal rage. "Really?" he asked skeptically.

"Really," I said as relaxed as possible.

He pulled me closer, enclosing me in his arms. "I know you feel excluded," he said in a gentle voice. *Damn!* "I'd feel the same way. But don't worry about it. It's not about you. The High Council is mostly a bunch of straitlaced secretmongers who've all got sticks up their asses."

I couldn't hold back a smile.

"I'm going there because I want to know what that redheaded bitch is up to with your amulet. I want nothing more than to return it to you," he said, kissing me on the forehead. "Enjoy your afternoon. I'll call you later, okay?"

"Okay," I said, still grumbling inside but not nearly as angry as before.

While walking back to my dorm, I thought about how to get this boring afternoon over with. Sally wanted to go to the movies with Colin, which I would have liked, too. But I didn't want to force myself on them. It was always strange being the third wheel.

I got an idea, pulled my phone from my purse, made a call, and grinned from ear to ear.

"Hayman," said a familiar voice.

"Hi, Ruth, it's Evelyn," I said in a friendly tone.

"Oh, Evelyn," Ruth said exuberantly. "Nice to hear from you."

"Do you feel like meeting this afternoon?" I asked. I didn't want to invite myself.

"I'd love to." She really seemed delighted. "I'm driving the night-shift, which means I'm free till eight. Would you like to come to my place in an hour?"

"That'd be great. I've got a few pieces of news."

"Sounds exciting. I'm looking forward to it. See you soon."

"Me, too," I said and hung up in a good mood. I was so happy to see Ruth again, I was almost glad to have a free afternoon because of Jared's superimportant Council meeting.

"Lovely of you to have come." Ruth hugged me tightly when I arrived.

"I'm happy to be here," I said, hugging her back.

"I baked a few scones," she said as we entered her flat. "Would you like some?"

"I'd love some." I slipped out of my coat, which would soon be too warm for the arriving spring, pulled off my boots, and followed Ruth into the kitchen.

"Tea?" she asked, lifting a steaming kettle. When I nodded, she filled our cups with hot Earl Grey. I added a little milk, as always.

"Help yourself," Ruth said, pointing to the still-warm scones, whose aroma reminded me of happy Sunday mornings from my childhood. I took one from the basket in the center of the table, spread a spoonful of clotted cream on it, and reached for the jar of raspberry jam.

"Also homemade," Ruth said, which inspired me to spread two spoonfuls on the scone.

"Mmm," I said after taking a bite.

Ruth grinned while taking a big sip from her cup. "So, tell, what's new?" she asked apprehensively and bit into her own thickly covered scone.

I swallowed the last bite of my scone and took another from the basket. "Oh man, I don't even know where to start." I shook my head. "You were right about everything!"

"Really?" Ruth was astonished. "That Jared Calmburry really is Merlin's last living descendant?" She almost choked on her tea.

I nodded.

"And what about Mayflower?" she asked with wide eyes.

"It's exactly as you said. She's even the high priestess of Legatum Merlini," I nearly whispered and took a sip of tea.

Ruth dropped against the arm of the chair. "My mother was right—she knew it the whole time!" She shook her brown curls in disbelief.

"Ruth, what do you know about Nimue?"

"About Nimue?" she asked. She still did not appear to have grasped it all.

"Yes, it's said she buried Merlin alive in a cave—but you said you didn't believe that's how it was, didn't you?"

"No, I don't believe it was that way," she said emphatically.

"How then?" I badly wanted to know.

Ruth frowned as she concentrated. "Nimue, as I've already told you, left Avalon to be with Merlin." She breathed deeply. "She gave up her immortality and magic for him."

"Why didn't Merlin go to Avalon with her, instead?" I asked and leaned over the table.

"Because he was needed. He was Arthur's right hand."

"But couldn't he have gone with her when he was no longer needed?"

Ruth looked at the ceiling in thought. "I think that's what they were planning," she said, then continued, bitterness resonating in her words. "Nimue couldn't bear being separated from Merlin, so she decided to live for a while as an ordinary woman far away from the enchanted isle. I'm sure she wanted to return to Avalon with him as soon as Merlin had fulfilled his duty. The two of them could have lived there for all eternity."

I looked at her skeptically. "That sounds like a fairy tale." With a grave voice I said, "And . . . they lived happily ever after."

Ruth smiled. "Yes. As kitschy as it may sound—it's the truth. Avalon harbors the source of eternal life, and as long as one drinks its holy water . . ." She shrugged.

"Okay, so, Merlin and Nimue wanted to go to Avalon together as soon as he'd fulfilled his duty, but . . . what went wrong? What happened?" I frowned.

Ruth's look suddenly darkened. "*Morgana* happened," she said in a harsh voice. The name sounded like a four-letter word coming from her mouth.

"Morgana?" I asked, puzzled, wincing at the thought of the evil witch.

Ruth nodded. "Morgana killed Merlin through his love for Nimue. She was after his magic, so she used Nimue to blackmail him," she said, her dark words sending an icy shiver down my spine. "He gave his life to save her."

I looked at my hands, saddened, while countless images shot through my mind. A dark cave, the cruel witch's cold laughter, a young woman collapsing because she couldn't prevent her lover's death . . . Was she really responsible for my family's death?

"What became of Nimue?" I asked.

"After Merlin's death, Morgana stole into Avalon and conjured up a demonic mist no one but she and her minions could overcome. Nimue never made it back." Ruth exhaled heavily. "Nothing was left for her but to bear a human existence. The only thing that kept her alive was the hope of being reunited with Merlin after death."

"What? That makes no sense!"

"I know it sounds paradoxical, but had Nimue killed herself, she would have been eternally damned and would never have seen her lover again."

"That's horrible," I whispered.

Ruth nodded. "A few years later, she got to know a man, married him, and had a daughter—Viviane."

I looked over Ruth's lovingly furnished kitchen. What a sad tale, I thought as I tried to visualize Nimue's hopeless conundrum. The lover murdered, the return home denied, and not even death promising release . . . She must have felt all alone in the world—a feeling I knew too well.

"There's one thing I don't understand. If Nimue was such a magical and mighty creature, why did she want to live as a *normal* human with Merlin? What happened to her magic?"

Ruth leaned over the table and lowered her voice. "Nimue's magic is inseparably linked to Avalon. If she hadn't left her magic there, Avalon would have died."

"What do you mean? *Left it there?*"

Ruth thought for a moment. "She must have removed her magic with a mighty spell from her body to bind it to something else. Maybe to a tree or rock or something."

"Does that mean her magic is still in Avalon?"

Ruth nodded. "I would think so, as long as Morgana didn't find it and bind it to herself."

I froze. "Do you think that's possible?"

"It's possible, though I'd imagine Nimue would have taken all imaginable precautions to prevent that."

I looked at my hands, lost in thought. "And . . ." I hesitated because I didn't know how much I should tell Ruth. "Do you know what became of Nimue's daughter?" My voice trembled.

Ruth lowered her eyes. "No," she said a moment later. "Her trail is lost pretty quickly in the literature. At least, I haven't been able to find anything in the books I've read, and I've read a lot of books."

I restlessly chewed on my thumbnail. "Do you think it's possible that today . . . I mean, could it be that . . . Nimue's bloodline has not yet died out? That there still may be living descendants?"

Ruth gave me a skeptical look. "Yes, of course, that's possible."

"And how . . . probable do you consider it?"

Again she appeared skeptical. "Well, Merlin's descendants survived, after all." Ruth frowned. "What are you getting at?"

"I . . ." Although I would have loved to tell Ruth who the Order thought I was—and risk her thinking me crazy, of course—I feared getting her in trouble. What I had told her about Jared and Karen, she already knew or at least suspected. Since secrecy, according to Jared, was the top priority for the Order, I decided to handle new information cautiously. The last thing I wanted to do was hand Ruth over to Karen.

"I don't really know myself. It was just a thought."

"Just a thought . . . uh huh." She didn't believe me and looked deep into my eyes before smiling. "How's it going between you and Jared?" she asked unexpectedly.

I didn't know why she changed the topic so suddenly since she knew I was holding something back. Nevertheless, I was relieved and turned to telling Ruth for the remainder of the afternoon how hopelessly in love with Jared I was.

Two more cups of tea and another scone later, I stood up and thanked Ruth for the pleasant time with her and for the remaining scones, which she had packed into tinfoil so I could take them home.

"It would be lovely if you dropped by to visit again soon," Ruth said as she hugged me good-bye. "But till then, I'd like to lend this to you." She pulled a dark-green book from the shelf. I recognized it instantly. The name *Nimue* was written in big letters on the spine. I was so uncertain I shifted my weight from one leg to the other as I took the book from her. How much did Ruth know? What did she suspect? Should I just tell her?

"Ruth . . . ," I started without knowing what I actually wanted to say.

"If you want, we can talk about it next time," she said, placing her hand on my shoulder with a loving smile.

"Okay," I said, also smiling. "Thank you."

* * *

"Hi, Jared!" As soon as I saw his name on my phone, that warm feeling spread inside me again. I had just arrived home and was closing the door.

"Hi, babe, how are you?" he asked with a velvety voice.

A silly grin spread across my face. "Good. I'm just back from visiting a friend. Is the Council meeting over?"

"Unfortunately, not yet," he said, which caused my mood to darken. "This business is a bit more difficult than I thought it'd be. Claire totally freaked out when Karen started to talk about Madison. Enid's leveled a conflict-of-interest vote against her, so she's excluded for an indefinite period from the Council."

"Oh," was all I could say.

"I've been trying to reach Colin for some time. Do you know where he might be?"

"He was supposed to go to the movies with Sally." I cast a glance at my watch. "But the movie should be well over by now."

Jared snorted. "I won't get away from here until I've reached him."

"What do you need him for?"

"He's the first one on the substitute list, so he needs to take Claire's spot on the Council." He exhaled. "We don't have a full group without him."

"Hmm." I was so disappointed over possibly not being able to see Jared again today that I could think of nothing better to say.

"Listen, honey," he said, seeming more hopeful. "I'll try reaching Colin again. Will you try Sally and tell her Colin should call me as soon as possible because I can't stand it here any longer without my girlfriend and may go crazy."

I giggled. "Okay, will do."

"I'll call back as soon as I know more."

"Sure—I'll call Sally right now."

"Okay, till later, my little treasure. Sorry it's taking so long."

"Till later," I said and was about to hang up when Jared said my name, causing me to place the phone against my ear again.

"Yes?"

"I love it when you giggle," he said and hung up.

And I love you!

Without wasting any time, I dialed Sally's number. I got her voice mail and hung up without leaving a message. Then I tried again. Seven calls in five-minute intervals later she finally picked up.

"Evelyn, for Heaven's sake, what's happening?"

"Oh, hi, Sally. Glad you picked up. I was starting to worry."

"Sorry, I was at the movies with Colin and forgot to turn on my ringer afterward. What's going on?"

"Jared urgently needs to talk to Colin but can't reach him."

"Jared's looking for you, you're supposed to call," I heard Sally say. So Colin was still with her.

"Oh, damn," he said in the background. He had probably just discovered the innumerable missed calls on his phone. "Jared, what's up?" I heard his voice on the other end of the line before he moved away.

"Do you know what this is about?" Sally asked me.

Since I didn't know to what extent Colin had initiated her into the mysteries of the High Council, I decided to keep it under wraps. "No. Where are you now?" I asked to change the topic.

"At home." Sally sounded strangely embarrassed. "Just a second," she said, and I heard through the muffled receiver how Colin and Sally very passionately parted from each other. I heard Sally's voice only a few seconds later, completely breathless from the wild kissing. If the line hadn't been so old, I'd probably have told them to get a room.

"Everything's great on your end from what I can hear," I said instead because I just couldn't help getting a comment in.

"We slept together," Sally blurted out. "It was totally fantastic!"

At first, I didn't know how to handle her frankness, but I was also happy for Sally. So I spent the next half hour listening to her describe her date with Colin—all the explicit details. When she had finally ended and revealed to me she was about to take a hot bath to relax her sore muscles from the afternoon, we said our good-byes.

I dropped, exhausted, on the bed and pulled my heavy black boots off. I hadn't taken them off because I'd been distracted by all the talking, even though I'd been home for about an hour. I lay completely dressed on my bed and stared at the ceiling, lost in thought, when I suddenly remembered the book Ruth had given me. I leapt to my feet, ran to my bag, which I'd put down beside the door, and held the thick, green volume in my hands. Without taking my eyes off it, I grabbed the thick fleece cover from the back of my chair, wrapped it around my shoulders, sat cross-legged on my bed, and started leafing through the book. To my delight, I found several colorful illustrations next to passages that were difficult to decipher. As I understood from the context, they showed the magical forests of Avalon crossed by numerous rivers and brooks. One picture showed mighty, broadly rooted trees whose branches filtered golden sunlight onto a sea of ferns and an abundance of flowers in all the colors of the rainbow. In another I discovered elfin creatures with pointed ears. They wore gossamer clothes, which flowed around their bodies, and let their hair blow in the wind. Those must be the nymphs Enid had spoken about—they were magnificently beautiful. I couldn't look away from the enchanting creatures for some time. Only when curiosity for what else waited to be discovered in this book overcame me did I continue leafing through it. Suddenly I froze. The next image showed a blue-green shimmering jewel I would have recognized among a million: my amulet! Or better put: *Nimue's amulet*. I stared as if a spell had been cast on me. I adored the finely worked chain links and the so-familiar triangular crystal into which two superimposed waves had been cut. Immediately underneath, a verse was written in an elaborate old English script that reminded me of a sonnet by Shakespeare I had to learn by heart in school.

> Hidden from misfortune's watchful glance,
> this jewel shall guard my heart, for it is yours.

Were these Merlin's words? It was possible, since he'd made the amulet for Nimue, after all, to protect her, as Jared had said. But what misfortune was meant here? Morgana? I snorted bitterly. After everything I'd heard about this witch, it was better not to cross her path. I tried to imagine what she might look like. Wild red hair, a wart-covered, crooked nose, a pointy black hat, and a broom? But perhaps that was just a cliché like the ancient, white-bearded Merlin with his half-moon spectacles, who in reality couldn't have been much older than twenty-five—at least, if Ruth's assumption was correct.

I continued to look through the book excitedly, when suddenly my eyes caught a single word: *Prophecy*. I immediately felt hot. Jared had spoken of a *Prophecy of the Nymphs of Avalon*! Back in the woods. His words still resonated clearly in my thoughts. I stared for a moment at the book's open pages without seeing anything. Then my eye caught a verse in the middle of the page that was a bit offset from the rest of the text. Was this really *the* Prophecy? If so, then the words I was about to read were the reason why Karen Mayflower wanted Jared to keep away from me. Not just that, but the reason she was convinced I was a danger to him. I closed my eyes for a moment, breathed in deeply, opened my eyes, and started to read.

> The blind heart tormented by longing
> Readily walks into darkness so far.
> Deprived of its light, deprived of its might,
> Only Death watches over the wight.

Even in my thoughts, these words sounded so calm and yet so urgent that they gave me goose bumps. I was unable to move for several seconds. Then I swallowed with difficulty.

What is that supposed to mean? I tried to breathe evenly while thoughts flew through my head. What was meant by *darkness?* The cave in which Merlin supposedly died? Or death? Why would Jared, if this prophecy really related to him, *readily* go into this darkness?

I read the verse again.

Deprived of its light . . . Jared's magic was light! In my mind I saw the golden light in his hands. *Deprived of its light* must mean someone would steal his magic. But who? Morgana?

Deprived of its might . . . Magic was might—I had never before seen anything mightier. Or was it something else I knew nothing about?

Only Death watches over the wight . . . You didn't have to be a Rhodes scholar to know what that meant.

I tried to concentrate. Did this mean he'd die for love? For the love of . . . *me?*

That was impossible! I'd never expose Jared to such danger! As I shook my head to regain my composure, the shrill ring of my phone made me flinch. Frightened and yet curious, I answered.

I said, "Hi," sounding like a lovesick teenager despite the queasy feeling the lines I'd just read caused me. Since I didn't have the faintest clue of how Jared would react if I brought up the Prophecy, or even if he found out I knew about it, I decided to keep it to myself for the time being.

"Hi, babe, where are you?" Jared asked with a happy tone.

"At home."

"I'm done here. Do you still feel like doing something?"

"Sure," I said, a little too excited. Could he hear in my voice I was trying to hide something?

Jared chuckled. "Colin asked if we'd go with him and Sally for some drinks. What do you think?"

I was torn. I'd actually hoped Jared would visit me here and we'd have a little time to ourselves. But I'd hardly seen Sally in the last few days and missed her. Also, I . . . Well, to be honest, I was terribly afraid of doing something wrong if . . . we became more intimate. Even though the thought put a smile on my face and released a wave of warmth inside me, I wasn't sure I was ready for it.

"Of course. When?" I said.

"I'll pick you up in fifteen, if that's all right?"

"Certainly." I was already rummaging through the contents of my closet in my mind.

"I can't wait to be with you," Jared said gently. "See ya soon."

I reached the bathroom in three long strides and a few seconds later was already brushing my teeth. As much as I would have liked to go through the book some more, I had to put it off for another time.

Fifteen minutes later, I was walking down the stairs to open the door for Jared. My knees wobbled when he stood before me with ruffled hair and a breathtaking smile.

"Hi," I barely got out and grinned back. But rather than returning a formulaic greeting, he came directly toward me, pulled me into his arms, and kissed me.

"I missed you," he said.

"Oh, I missed you, too," I said and tried to control my heartbeat—to the extent this was possible in Jared's presence. "So, where are we going?"

"To Berry's, I think," he said and waited to see if I had any objections. When I nodded, he took a strand of my hair that hung over my shoulder and gently twirled it between his fingers. "I love it when you leave your hair down," he said, kissing me again. "It's also more convenient," he added, lifting a black motorcycle helmet from the stairs.

"Oh," I said, surprised when I noticed the matte black machine at the curb. "I've never ridden on a motorcycle."

"No big deal. Just hold on to me tightly and lean into the curves when I do. That's all there is to it."

"That thing looks like Batman hunts criminals on it at night," I said, frowning as he handed me the helmet.

Jared laughed. "The Ducati?"

"Oh, you've even named it?" I said, trying to keep a serious look on my face.

I awkwardly put the helmet on my head, noticing its rather pleasant scent. It must be new. Did he buy it just for me? After Jared had put on his helmet—it was also all black—he swung his right leg over the motorcycle before helping me on and putting my hands around his waist.

"Hold on tight," he said with a grin, started the engine, and got the motorcycle going slowly so I'd adjust to its motion. Only after he'd driven to the end of the street did he signal me with a nod to hold on tighter, and then he stepped on the gas. Really stepped on it! We ran down the street at breakneck speed while I wrapped my arms tightly around his waist.

It was simply wonderful! Like riding on a roller coaster—and almost as good as swimming. *Would he let me ride the Ducati alone some time?*

Jared stopped right before the entrance to Berry's, flipped the kickstand down with a practiced motion, and let the motorcycle settle. Then he slid from the saddle before helping me down.

"Your eyes are really shining," he said when I'd taken off the helmet.

"That was fabulous," I said enthusiastically, causing Jared to smile from ear to ear.

"What silly grins you two have!" It could only be Sally. She stood outside the entrance, holding Colin's arm and laughing.

I rolled my eyes and bumped playfully into Sally and walked inside.

The pub had its usual cloud of typical bar odors—beer, sweat, and stuffy furnishings.

"There's an empty table back there," Sally yelled above the loud music, pointing to a table with four empty chairs. She really had a talent for quickly scanning a room for empty tables. We hurried behind her across the pub to grab the seats.

Sally cast a dreamy look at the pool tables.

"When we were here the last time, I fell in love with you," Sally told Colin with a smile.

"Same," Colin said and placed his hand behind her neck, pulled her onto his lap, and kissed her. Jared gave me an amused look and held my hand on the table. I thought back to that evening when Sally, Colin, Felix, and I had played pool and suddenly remembered something.

"Hey, were you here that evening? I thought I saw you next to Colin at the pool table, then suddenly the light went out, and you were gone."

Jared nodded hesitantly, bent toward me, and whispered into my ear, "Meeting you in those weeks when I was trying to avoid you required certain . . . preparations. I had to adjust to seeing you—physically and mentally." He paused briefly. "But when I discovered you inside completely unexpectedly, there were only two options: get away or . . ." Instead of finishing the sentence, he bent forward a little more, took my face in his hands, and kissed me with such passion that I forgot everything around me. I immediately turned hot and my breathing involuntarily quickened, which Jared acknowledged with a glowing look. He squeezed my hand a bit firmer and buried his face in my hair. I bit on my lower lip.

"Four Guinnesses," I heard Colin suddenly say and looked up. A waitress had come to our table. I wasn't particularly fond of beer, but since Colin had ordered for all of us . . .

"And a ginger ale," Jared said just as the waitress turned to leave. Only then did I notice she had bright red cheeks. I could only guess which of the two guys at our table had caused her to blush. Both were exceedingly good-looking, though Colin was a bit too muscular for my taste. Jared, however, had a perfect athletic body, not to mention a flawless face and extraordinary dark-blue eyes.

I smiled at him tenderly. "Thank you," I said. "I'm not that fond of Guinness."

"I noticed," Jared said with a twinkle in his eyes.

"So, what shall we toast?" Sally asked after the waitress had returned and set the glasses on the table.

"To physical love," Colin said with a festively raised glass and a grin in Sally's direction.

"To *true* love," Sally said, giving Colin a bemused, warning look.

"To a love that outlasts death," Jared said quietly, looking deep into my eyes.

"To Manchester United!" a drunk guy yelled at us from the table beside ours, sending the four of us into gales of laughter.

After he'd driven me home, I handed Jared the motorcycle helmet and ran my hands through his disheveled hair.

"Good night," he gently said, took my face into his hands, and pressed his lips against mine. "Sleep well," he added, brushing my hair before putting on his helmet again. He looked one last time at me through the opened visor with his twinkling eyes. Then he flipped it down, started the motor, popped a wheelie, and raced away, nearly vertical.

I fell asleep with a wonderful feeling. When the alarm clock finally pulled me from my vague dreams of woods, lakes, and golden light, I actually felt reasonably rested.

In the hope that Jared might be waiting for me outside, as on the previous day, I quickly got dressed, rushed down the stairs, threw open the door, and looked with a pounding heart at Jared's wonderful face. Would it ever end? The gasping breath, the racing heart, the fluttering in the pit of my stomach?

"Good morning," he said with a smile and enclosed me in his arms. My hands moved to the back of his neck and my mouth pressed longingly against his.

"Good morning," I whispered, my knees wobbly, while his tender lips moved along my neck, breathing kisses against it at regular intervals.

"God, how wonderful you smell," he said and deeply inhaled so I felt his breath on my skin, which immediately formed sensitive goose bumps under his touch. An indefinable sound escaped me at his next kiss. As if in a trance, I pulled him closer, breathing heavily. Jared paused, then kissed me passionately until he abruptly stopped. "Damn it, what are you doing to me?" he asked as if he were frightened of himself and stepped back. "Seriously, Evelyn, you've got to be careful with me," he said, still wrestling for air. "I lose control when I'm near you, and if we don't want lightning to strike us or something strange to happen, we need to be more careful."

"Oh . . . okay." I nodded numbly while still trying to slow my heartbeat to its normal speed.

Jared scratched the back of his head, embarrassed. "It's all very new to me, you know? I've never . . . met someone like you. You're so . . ." He seemed to lack words and looked at me, shaking his head. "You're driving me crazy," he said, when I pressed back into his arms. "What are you doing to me?" he repeated gently into my ear, while swaying with me side to side.

"I thought the question was what are you doing to me? Because you're driving me crazy, too."

Jared held his breath for a moment, then continued. "Maybe we should leave now before I'm unable to let you go," he said, his voice trembling.

As soon as we got to the College, we had to separate. I'd only see Jared again during lunch. However, at least Colin would keep me company through my first lecture, with the bitter knowledge that Aiden, too, would be there. Colin sat down beside me with a stunning smile. If I hadn't already been in love with Jared with every fiber of my being, I might have swooned at his sight. It made perfect sense why Sally was crazy about him.

"Well, everything in order with you?" he asked with a grin.

"More than that," I said, beaming.

"And, that . . . I mean, are you fine with . . . ," he fumbled. There were far too many eavesdroppers in the lecture hall to discuss myth, magic, and bloodlines.

"Being such a good swimmer?" He nodded gratefully. "I don't quite know," I said after briefly thinking about it, "but so far nothing has changed for me because of it, and I don't think it will. It's not a big deal. It does feel a little strange, but as long as I'm myself . . . ," I said and shrugged.

"That's the way I see it," Colin said. "It's pretty much the same with me."

A moment later our conversation was suddenly interrupted when Aiden dropped into the chair next to Colin and looked me over with disdain. When Colin noticed the look, he elbowed Aiden so hard in the ribs that he made a wheezing noise. I turned away with a malicious grin—but it quickly went away.

I couldn't believe my eyes. I'd almost forgotten him, but there he stood in front of me in the flesh—Felix.

"Hi, Evelyn," he said with lowered eyes, "I just wanted to tell you how sorry I am. It . . . was all a terrible misunderstanding. I never wanted to . . ."

"That's enough. Beat it," Colin said. "And you'd better stick to our agreement, is that understood?"

"Yes," Felix said, daring to look at me for the first time. He seemed in bad shape. Really bad shape. His nose was hidden behind a splint, dark-red bruises surrounded his eyes, and it appeared as if he was missing an incisor.

"I just want you to know how sorry I am," he repeated with moist eyes and turned to find a seat at the furthest corner of the lecture hall.

"Everything okay?" I heard Colin ask a moment later.

"Yes . . . I think so." I shook my head in shock. "That was a real surprise. I didn't expect to see him—to be honest, I'd almost forgotten him." I looked at Felix. He sat in his seat like a little lump of misery and stared at the top of the desk in front of him. I almost caught myself feeling something like pity in my heart. But a second later, I remembered how he threw himself on me, thought of the fear, panic, desperation, and helplessness, saw Sally lie in her bed close to death . . . No! I would not pity him. Never! The only thing left was to decide whether to go to the police or not. He'd lose his scholarship, be expelled from the College, and probably wind up in jail. The important question was: Had he already suffered enough? Right now it looked that way.

"What kind of agreement is Felix supposed to stick to?" I asked Colin.

He breathed in deeply. "I'd prefer to spare you the details, but should he ever again get too close to you, Sally, or any other girl . . ." Colin shrugged and left the rest to my imagination.

I shuddered. "How would you keep track of that?"

"He's under constant observation," Colin said, and our conversation was over for the moment as the lecture started. So I attempted to focus on nothing but Psychology of Memory for the next hour.

I forgot all about Felix when I saw Jared waiting outside the hall after my last lecture in the afternoon.

"Would you like to go out?" Jared asked after giving me a tender kiss.

"Actually, I wanted to write my assignment for Professor Bronsen today," I said. "I have to hand it in early next week and don't think he'll give me an extension." I'd delayed this assignment too long. If I didn't deal with it in a hurry, I'd never get it done on time. However, next to the idea of spending the evening with Jared, the idea of spending the next few hours in drudgery, writing about female narcissism, made me feel downright depressed. How would Bronsen react if I begged him for an extension? I snorted internally. That guy probably wouldn't think twice about failing me. Especially since I'd drawn unfavorable attention to myself in the lecture hall on the first day.

"Oh," Jared said, disappointed, which made my resolve waver even more. "Of course, that comes first," he said a moment later with the disappointment in his voice giving way to his usual coolness. "First work, then pleasure."

I nodded, smiling. Of course, I couldn't imagine anything more wonderful than spending an evening with Jared, but what good would that be if I flunked the first trimester and wasn't allowed to continue going to school?

"How about tomorrow?" Jared suggested after correctly interpreting my mood.

"Oh, that'd be wonderful," I said, delighted. The prospect immediately improved my mood. The thought alone was enough to make me euphoric. If I could have it my way, I'd be with Jared 24/7. It still hurt each time I let him go. It almost felt like the dream I had the night Jared confided his secret to me. Pain shot through me when I remembered how Jared smiled, turned, and disappeared among the trees, leaving me alone in the lake in the woods. I swallowed with difficulty when it became clear that I probably wouldn't survive should he ever leave me. My heart would probably stop beating. But . . . no—he would never leave me. After all, there was this bond between us Enid had spoken of in the woods. That ancient, magical bond, which had spanned entire generations. I frowned. The thought should have consoled me a little, but suddenly a nagging thought forced itself upon me again: Could it be that Jared only loved me because of it? Would he still want to be with me if this bond didn't exist?

"What's the matter?" Jared asked—he didn't miss a thing. "What are you thinking about?" he asked just as we arrived at my dorm.

"I . . . ," I started, not knowing what to say.

Jared looked at me, concerned. "Something's making you sad, I can feel it." He took my hand and kissed my fingers. "Please tell me what's weighing on you."

"I'm worried you'll suddenly disappear again," I said without daring to look at him.

Jared placed his finger under my chin to lift my face. He smiled. "To keep away from you would kill me," he said as if it were an inviolable fact.

I gasped.

"It almost drove me crazy during the weeks I tried to keep away from you. What makes you think I could just disappear?" Jared asked while kissing the back of my hand again.

"Well, it's . . . I asked myself . . . if there really is this ancient magical bond between us . . ."

"Yes?"

I took a deep breath. "I'm asking myself if you . . . are in love with me because of me or if this bond is . . . well . . . forcing you to feel that way, and you can't help it?"

There, now it's out in the open!

Jared raised his eyebrows. "I could ask you the same," he said. "I mean, if this bond were *forcing* me to fall in love with you, surely it'd work the other way around, too."

I frowned. I hadn't looked at it that way.

"For my part, I'm pretty sure I'd have fallen in love with you even entirely without magic," he continued. "I mean, look at you!" he said, taking me into his arms. "In the end, it doesn't matter to me." He stroked my cheek with his fingers. "Whether this bond contributed a part or not, I thank providence for leading you to me." He gently placed his lips on mine. I couldn't help but return his passionate kiss.

He's probably right. Even if we found each other through magic, it didn't make a difference—what was important was *that* we'd found each other, and our love was real.

Again the images of my dream shot through my head. How much I'd wished Jared would come to me in the water, how happy it would have made me . . . "I dreamt of you," I said, embarrassed.

Jared laughed, gently took my chin between his thumb and index finger, then looked into my eyes. "I dream of you every night."

CHAPTER 16

Jared and I spent a wonderful evening downtown. First, he invited me for dinner—when I wanted to pay, he brushed it off with a smile—then we went for a walk by the Thames. While we walked hand in hand on the way back to my dorm, incessantly talking about everything under the sun, I watched Jared. I still couldn't believe it. Everything about him seemed perfect. I crinkled my nose. How did we look together as a couple?

Okay, I knew I wasn't exactly ugly—in school there had been a few guys who would have liked to have gone out with me. Probably because of my long blonde hair—apparently most guys like long hair—but next to Jared . . . I cast another longing glance at him with a sigh . . . Next to Jared I just looked like a little gray mouse. I was too thin, too pale, and I walked around with such dark rings under my eyes most of the time that people either thought I was ill or hadn't slept for several nights, which, if I thought about it, really did happen sometimes. And since nobody had ever been interested in me like this before Jared, I didn't have any experience to draw on in matters of relationships or even sexuality. Nil, nothing, nada! I was totally green at nineteen years old. And the way girls adored Jared openly and even tried to stake a claim on him, as Madison did every time we met, I was certain he wasn't a blank page. Though I found this thought a little painful, I tried to get used to it. After all, he was twenty-one, and it was perfectly normal to have had some experience. If anything, I was the abnormal one. To describe me as a late bloomer would be the understatement of the year!

Suddenly, Jared took my arm, stopped in his tracks, and turned to me. "If you don't tell me this instant what you're thinking about, I'll go crazy!"

There was no point in lying to him; he'd sense it if I didn't tell the truth. Still, it was terribly embarrassing to talk about. After all, we were only getting to know each other, and if I told him right away I was still a—I barely even managed to think the word—virgin, he'd maybe . . . He'd probably just think I was strange.

"Yes?" Jared said, bent forward, and waited for my answer.

"I . . . I . . . Oh, I don't know."

"What's it about?" His tone was sensitive, and he moved my hair out of my face. I stared embarrassed at my hands as he gave me a moment to think.

"Is there a reason why Madison is a total bitch to every girl who comes close to you?" Or, rather, had been before she disappeared without a trace—with my amulet.

Jared stiffened, then sighed. "She thinks she's in love with me. And . . . I'm not totally innocent in this."

I looked at him questioningly. *What was that supposed to mean?* A dark premonition made me shudder. My chest felt constricted. *Oh no! Not her! Please not her!*

"I slept with her—once," he said sheepishly and exhaled.

I started to feel sick. As lovely as the evening had been, with this confession he'd destroyed it all.

"She'd been after me forever and one evening, after a really shitty day, she caught me off guard . . . I'd had a little to drink and . . . It was a mistake."

I tasted bile. The idea of Madison . . . in bed with . . . *him*. I suddenly felt like crying. Jared tried to hug me, but I didn't want him to touch me.

"Evelyn . . . please don't," he said with a burdened voice as I struggled free of his embrace. A sad expression entered his dark-blue eyes. The thought of how close Jared and Madison had been caused me to grimace with disgust. "Evelyn, please," he said more emphatically and attempted to hold my hand, which I instantly pulled away. "It didn't mean anything, I . . ."

I snorted. "Maybe not to you! But some things have become clear to me now," I said as I recalled my encounters with Madison. I would have liked to run away to cry my eyes out somewhere in a quiet place, but since we were putting our cards on the table, I might as well ask the next question. Then I'd be done with it. "Madison wasn't the only one, was she?"

Jared's eyes widened, and he swallowed and shook his head.

"How many were there?" My attempt to sound casual failed miserably.

"I'm not sure," Jared said, scratching the back of his head. "God, it's not like I'm keeping track." He appeared uncomfortable as he rubbed his chin in embarrassment.

Tough luck—you wanted to know the score! I thought cynically, leaving him to stew.

"Don't make such a big deal out of it, Evelyn. I'm twenty-one. Anyway, that's all in the past—I admit I'd like to undo some of it, but I can't." He raised his hand to stroke my cheek. "Please don't be upset with me about it. I didn't know you then, and after all, you also had a life before you got to know me."

I raised my eyebrows. When I saw he'd understood, I averted my eyes, embarrassed. This was so humiliating!

He gasped. "You're still a . . . ?"

"Yes!" I said, louder than intended.

His eyes widened. "I . . . had no idea. Sorry." Disbelief resonated in his words, but there was something else there. You'd think part of him liked what he heard.

"How could you?" I said, irritated, stomping angrily up the stone stairs to the entrance of my dorm. "Good night, Jared!" I said when I'd opened the door and got ready to slam it in his face.

"Evelyn, please." He held me back and put his foot in the door. How did he get up the stairs so quickly? When I turned, I was surprised to see that he was having difficulties suppressing a grin.

"Oh, you think this is funny?" I asked, outraged.

Suddenly, he pulled me by my jacket, firmly wrapped his arms around me, and kissed me intensely. I stiffened for a moment, surprised, but when he wouldn't let go and kept kissing me, I caved. We stood intertwined for minutes.

"I love you," I suddenly heard him whisper into my ear, and I opened my eyes. "Oh God, I love you so much!" He held my hips and kissed me, moaning lightly. I believed I'd melt when his hands slipped under my coat and along my body. They were everywhere.

"I love you, too!" I managed to say between panting breaths, feeling my eyes fill with hot tears. When they silently ran down my cheeks, Jared stopped. The next moment he was kissing my face, gently, until the tears had ceased. Then he firmly held me while I rested my head against his chest.

"Please stop worrying about my past," he said in a quiet voice. "It should be as insignificant to you as it is to me." He gently kissed my forehead. "Ever since I first saw you, nothing but you has mattered to me. Everything I am is yours!"

I had no words for what was happening inside me at that moment. Even before I'd understood what my body was getting ready and longing for, my mouth started to speak as if on its own. "Do you want to come upstairs?" I said as if in a trance, narrowing my eyes as soon as the words had left my lips. I would have preferred to take it back. I felt Jared's mouth turn into a smile in my hair.

"Not tonight, my darling," he said, striking a heavy blow to my self-confidence. "Not after this talk. I don't want old burdens running around in your head." Again he pressed his lips tenderly against my forehead. "I want it to be something very special," he whispered into my ear, adding, with a deep, trembling voice, "There's nothing I want more than to be together with you—in every conceivable way." Even before the last word, he had pressed his abdomen firmly against me. *Oh!* When I felt how much he wanted to be with me, I didn't know whether to blush or immediately pull him upstairs. "You have no idea how much self-control it's taking for me to leave now!" His words caused a tremendous explosion in the pit of my stomach and . . . further down. "I have to leave." He let me go with a strange, abrupt motion.

We looked at one another with glowing eyes. Although he was completely right, I could not bring myself to let him go. He seemed to feel the same way, for suddenly he bent forward in a graceful movement, took my face into his hands and kissed me again—full of longing.

"Good night!" he said, pulling himself away once and for all, and bounded down the steps to put distance between us as fast as possible.

"Good night," I said when I was able to think clearly again, then rapidly disappeared inside before I begged him to sleep with me.

While climbing the stairs to my room, I brushed my fingertips over my lips. I could still feel his kiss. The thought of how his mouth fit against mine, how he embraced me and pulled me against his chest, how overwhelming it was to be so close to him . . . It almost made my legs give way. I breathed heavily. My whole body appeared to vibrate. Every single fiber of my being longed for Jared—I was completely and totally given to him.

Still caught in my sensual dreamworld, I unlocked my door and went into my room. Since the sun had set, it was dark inside except for the faint shine of the hallway light. I took my purse from my shoulder and placed it in the corner. Then, my thoughts still with Jared, I took off my coat and threw it over the back of the chair.

Bending down to take off my shoes, I suddenly froze. What was that strange feeling? My stomach contracted and the hairs on my arms rose in warning. Something was wrong . . .

Even before I understood why, my body was on full alert. My muscles stiffened, and an ice-cold shudder ran down my back, giving me goose bumps. My pupils dilated, the sensitive hairs in my ears rose to receive the faintest peep, and my nostrils flared.

Then I smelled it: the repulsive odor of rotting flesh almost made me gag. What the hell was that? In a flash I became aware I was not alone—someone was here!

I turned and rose as slowly as possible. Every single muscle was tensed to the point of bursting. From the corner of my eye I saw something moving on my bed. My eyes opened wide as I noticed another motion, this time closer. Whatever it was that produced this awful stench was coming toward me. Pure adrenaline shot through my body, sharpening my senses. I leapt toward the door to get out and save myself, sound the alarm, cry for help, do something—*anything*. I just needed to get as far away from this foul-smelling thing as possible. My fingertips brushed the door handle as something violently gripped my ankle and pulled me back. I fell to the floor with a loud thud, bumping my head harshly when I landed. I saw through blurred vision how the creature bent over me. The penetrating stench of pus and rotting flesh seared my nostrils. I wanted to scream but was rendered incapacitated. My throat was completely dry.

"You're staying here!" the creature said in a raspy voice. When my vision cleared and my eyes had become accustomed to the dark, I saw what was bent over me. I sucked in my breath and shrank back in a panic. The creature was wrapped in a long, black cloak and had an outline reminiscent of a person, but there was nothing remotely human about this thing. First, I thought of a burn victim, but then I saw the face was covered in countless scars, sores, and weeping boils. I barely kept myself from vomiting.

"You made me wait a long time," the monster said as an evil grin spread over its misbegotten face. The acrid stench of its breath burned inside my nose. I flailed about and kicked at anything within reach. The creature retreated, howling, when my heel hit it in the stomach full force. I clambered to my feet, but the monster was faster. Before I could reach the door, it grabbed my waist and hurled me back to the floor. A second later, it was on top of me, bearing down on me with its full weight and grabbing my wrists. I squirmed with all my strength. Suddenly, I felt a lack of pressure on my legs. *Now or never!* I raised my knee as hard as I could, hitting the creature in the most sensitive spot. It let go with a pain-filled howl.

Again I hurled myself toward the door, but it grabbed me by the hair and jerked my head back so violently it almost broke my neck.

"That's enough!" Scarface hissed, his black beetle eyes angrily looking at me. Everything around me blurred. What was happening? Was I fainting? The creature, still holding my hair in a rough grasp, began to look around, alarmed. It had also felt it. I was not fainting—the room really *was* quaking. A touch of hope arose inside me. Before I'd understood what was happening, the door exploded open. An enraged Jared stood in the doorway and hurled himself on the monster, who let my hair go.

"Evelyn! Into the hallway!" he commanded.

I obeyed without hesitation and scrambled into the hallway and cowered in a corner. *What the hell had attacked me?* I numbly noticed white, yellow, and blue sparks fly around me and disappear into my room. Suddenly, a bright, glowing light emanated from the room, followed by a deafening bang. Trembling, I buried my head between my knees, pinched my eyes shut, wrapped my arms around myself, and started to rock back and forth.

What the hell had attacked me? I rocked more intensely and sank my head deeper—I didn't want to see, hear, or feel anything.

Damn it, what had attacked me?

Suddenly, I felt a burning pain in my throat. I lifted my head and opened my eyes. Thick smoke billowed out of my room and snaked along the hallway. The burning became stronger, entered my wind-pipe, and made its way down to my lungs. Only when the pain had become unbearable and my eyes teared up, did it dawn on me I was inhaling pure smoke. My body was shaken by a violent coughing fit. I gagged, coughed, and wrestled helplessly for air, when something sud-denly lifted me by my shoulders. The dorm's sprinkler system triggered, and students poured out of their rooms, some only in their underwear or pajamas, to see what was going on. Then I felt the air clear and become cleaner. How could that be? I seemed to move forward without using my legs—as if I were floating. Only then could I see through my tear-filled eyes that Jared was carrying me outside. I wrapped my arms around his neck when another coughing fit shook me. I trembled with fear and cold. I held on tighter, trying to breathe regularly. But I couldn't subdue the rising panic. I started to hyperventilate and reached for my throat. I sucked in air as hard as I could but not a bit of oxygen seemed to reach my lungs—I was suffocating!

Panicking, I twisted in Jared's arms. Air! I needed air! I stared at him, my eyes wide with horror, a silent cry for help on my lips as Jared started to mumble something and slid his hand over my eyes. Then a wave of comforting, golden warmth flowed through my body.

"Sleep now, my darling," was the last thing I heard before my eye-lids became heavy and I went into a deep, warm dream.

CHAPTER 17

A strange tingling started from my fingertips, spread over my arms and chest, extended to my abdomen, and wandered along my legs to the tips of my toes until my body was filled with an unfamiliar, wholesome feeling. I opened my eyes and blinked. I didn't know where I was or whether it was day or night. I looked around disoriented and found to my astonishment that I was in a strange bed. Except for my boots, which stood by the door, I was fully clothed under a down comforter. It was morning and gradually turning light outside. What had happened? How did I get here? I had no memories of the previous night. Someone must have brought me here, taken my boots off, and covered me up. I sat up and rubbed my temples.

I strained to remember what had happened. Suddenly memories flooded in and hit me with the force of a wrecking ball. *The monster!* I gasped. It had lain in wait in my room and attacked me. The monster's awful grimacing face, I thought, repulsed. Full of scars, blisters, and sores. And the stench . . . that hideous stench.

I instantly felt sick—saliva collected in mouth, and my stomach contracted. I ran to the bathroom as fast as I could and, bent over the toilet, puked while one cold shudder after another ran down my spine.

When it was over, I used my last bit of energy to drag myself under the shower and turn the water on. Water—that was the only thing that would help me now. I sat there for a long time and let the water splash down on me. Then I heard the unmistakable sound of a door handle being turned somewhere in the distance.

"Evelyn!" someone called, almost in a panic. A heartbeat later the door was pushed open and Jared stood before me, gasping for breath. When he saw me sitting fully dressed in the shower, he instantly bent down and embraced me. He didn't seem to care that he would be soaked.

"I thought for a moment . . . Oh God, for a moment I thought . . . Are you all right? Is everything okay?"

"Jared," I said, relieved. He was here! "Jared, what happened? What . . . attacked me? What was that? Where am I?"

"Calm down," he said, gently brushing his fingers over my cheek. "You're safe."

"But what . . . ? The monster!" I said in a mixture of panic, confusion, and relief.

"You're in the Order's headquarters," Jared explained, looking at me. "You had a panic attack," he added, sounding almost apologetic.

Suddenly, an image from the previous night was clearly before my eyes: the hideous monster bent over me and blowing its stinking breath into my face. "What was that thing in my room? What attacked me? What did it want from me?" I tried to swallow.

Jared paused. "That was a damnatus, one of Morgana's repulsive creatures . . . Enid will convene a Council meeting today—she'll explain everything to you there."

I breathed in deeply. I could be patient till then, but the sooner I found out what I was dealing with, the better. Then I remembered something. "What did you do to me? The last thing I remember is that I wasn't getting air anymore and became terribly drowsy—and then I woke up here."

"I let you sleep," Jared said shyly. "You weren't able to calm down, and I feared you might suffocate if you didn't relax, so I let you sleep." He avoided my look.

I frowned. "Do you think I'm mad at you for that?"

"Well, it's probably not pleasant. To be put to sleep that way."

"Jared," I said, taking his face into my hands and forcing him to look at me. Could this be true? He'd saved my life but was apologizing for it? I pulled him to me with resolve, kissing him. "Thank you," I said a moment later. "Thank you for saving me—again."

"Oh God, I'm so glad you're okay," he said with a trembling voice and kissed me. Then he sank down into the shower with me and pulled me onto his lap. Suddenly, the fear, sadness, and desperation inside me were gone and replaced by a new feeling. A feeling coming from my innermost self that spread in warm waves from my center and migrated outward till it arrived at my fingertips—my love for Jared. I kissed him unbridled, letting my hands glide over his chest. The soaked fabric of his white T-shirt clung to his skin, highlighting every muscle and curve of his perfect torso. My fingers pushed under the material to touch his skin while Jared's hands wandered down my back to my behind. I couldn't help but run my hands over his stomach, chest, shoulders . . . Then I grabbed the T-shirt, impatiently pulling it over his head. He willingly raised his arms to let me proceed. I stared at Jared's naked torso until he held my chin and forced me to look into his eyes. His look seemed to penetrate me as we both breathed in and out in quick bursts. A moment later I felt his hand on the back of my neck. He pulled me closer with a firm tug, pushed his lips against mine, and thrust his tongue between my waiting, open lips. Without knowing what I was doing, I pulled at the top of his jeans, tearing open the top two buttons. Jared sucked in air between clenched teeth, let his long, slender fingers wander over my soaking sweater and pulled it with a practiced motion over my head. I was riding on his lap, only dressed in my pants and bra while the warm water rained down on us. Jared took in my belly and breasts with wide eyes. He gasped, then held my waist and began covering my body in kisses. Trembling, I threw my head back, while an unknown sound escaped my throat.

"I love you," I heard myself say, and a golden light enveloped his hands.

"Evelyn," he whispered before the light moved from his hands and up his arms until finally his chest, face, and whole body were surrounded by this wonderful golden glow.

"Evelyn?" A woman's voice caused me to open my eyes with fright. "Evelyn?" the voice called again.

"Err . . . yes?" I answered. "I'm in the bathroom—one moment please." I looked at Jared, pleading for help, but he appeared as alarmed as I was and merely stared at me with wide eyes. I knew I could not ignore whoever it was and risk them coming in. So I climbed out of the shower, took off my soaking pants and socks and wrapped a large towel around my body. Then, I brushed my bra straps from my shoulders and stepped out. It looked as if I had just showered.

Enid Speakerman stood in the middle of the room, looking at me. "Oh, there you are," she said with a friendly smile. "I'm terribly sorry to burst in here like this, but I wanted to see how you were."

"Hello, Mrs. Speakerman . . . Thank you. How are you?"

"Enid," she corrected me, and her smile broadened. "Has Jared been here to see you?"

"Yes," I said, straining not to let anything show. The idea that he was sitting half-naked in the shower, trying to be dead silent, made me grin.

"Good, then you know you're in the Order's headquarters. When Jared brought you here last night, you were unconscious, so I didn't want you to wake up completely disoriented in a strange bed—that's why I've come."

I smiled, uncertain. What would Karen have to say?

"The High Council would like to talk to you. I'll leave you alone now so you can get dressed in peace. The session starts in an hour. Jared will pick you up."

"Okay."

"Till later." Enid opened the door and turned to me. "Good to see you're well," she added in a soft voice, disappearing before I could answer.

"She likes you." Jared suddenly stood behind me and put his arms around my waist.

"What happened to my dorm room?" I asked as images of last night flashed through my head. I turned to him. "People are going to see there was a fire there, aren't they?"

"The Circle's already seen to it. They've made it look like a gas explosion caused by a leak in the heating system."

"They did that?"

Jared shrugged. "It's the usual procedure for this sort of . . . mishap," he said with a smile. "Fortunately, the sprinkler system came on, so the fire didn't spread to other rooms."

"What happened to my things?"

"They were brought here," he said. "At least, whatever wasn't burned in the flames. There." He pointed to a voluminous closet beside the bed.

I went over and opened the door. Indeed! My clothes lay nicely folded on the shelves. I marveled at how they didn't smell of smoke. Had they been washed while I slept?

"And in here," Jared said while opening the uppermost drawer of one of two identical dressers, "are your other things. Laptop, books, phone charger, and so on."

I went over to look at the dresser. "Everything's here," I said in astonishment. "Well, almost." The green book Ruth had lent me was nowhere to be seen. How was I going to explain that to her?

While Jared led me through the corridors of the huge headquarters, mostly built of massive stone blocks, I tried to memorize the route. He hadn't exaggerated when he said it was easy to get lost there. The count-less hallways and doors—all of them enormous and covered in ancient carvings—made me feel as if I were in a stone labyrinth. Only burning torches on the walls were needed to complete the appearance of a medi-eval castle. Despite the white-plastered walls and other modern touches, such as electric lights and insulating windows, this place seemed fitting for a secret society from the fifth century. I still couldn't believe I was here. That Jared had brought me. Suddenly, I remembered I didn't have the slightest clue where the headquarters actually were.

"Where exactly are we here?" I asked.

"About seven miles northwest of Oxford—in the middle of the woods."

"Does Karen know I'm here?"

"Yes, of course," he said.

"And she doesn't mind?"

Jared hesitated.

"She doesn't trust me," I said.

Jared breathed in deeply. "I'm really starting to believe she's paranoid."

I thought it better not to respond, though I would have preferred to congratulate Jared on this insight.

A few moments later, we arrived at the Council chamber and stood outside a mighty double door decorated with fine carvings. Jared lifted his hand to open it.

"What's waiting for me in there?" I asked, holding his arm.

"Six people who want to talk to you about what happened in your room yesterday."

I stared at the door with wide eyes.

"Don't worry. Enid will be there. Irvin and Colin, too, of course. They all like you. Nothing's going to happen to you. And I won't leave your side," he added with a gentle smile. Then he raised his eyebrows. "Ready?"

I breathed in and nodded resolutely, and Jared pushed open the heavy door.

A reception committee was waiting for us in the spacious, light-flooded room. I first noticed Colin, who stood in the middle of the room in front of a massive wooden table that could have comfortably seated fifteen people. He gave me a broad grin. Beside him was Enid leaning on the table, and she was also smiling at me. I was able to make out Professor Martin a little farther away. When Jared and I entered, he interrupted his conversation with an ancient-looking man in a dark-blue patterned kilt and knee-high socks. Then there was an older woman, who appeared completely disinterested. She was seated and looked at me with an indifferent expression. Finally, my gaze fell on Karen Mayflower. She stood with her back to me, looking out of one of the high windows.

"Welcome." It was Enid's friendly voice. I stopped looking at Karen and turned toward Enid, who waved me over.

"Evelyn," Jared started in a calm tone, "this is the High Council of Legatum Merlini. You already know Colin, Enid, Irvin, and Karen," then he gestured toward the bored-looking, older woman and the geriatric in the kilt. "This is Judith McHallern and Montgomery Grey."

"Good day," I said in greeting, whereupon Mr. Grey came over to shake my hand firmly.

"A pleasure to meet you, my dear," he said, then sat down beside the older woman.

"The pleasure's mine," I said and took my seat opposite Colin. Apparently, there was a firmly established seating order here, which Jared, going by the faces of the others, was disregarding when he sat down beside me.

Finally, Karen also came over and sat down at the middle of the large table—her back to the windows. "Well," she began, obviously struggling not to show how distasteful she found this. "I think I speak for all present by welcoming Evelyn to the Order's headquarters. We're all delighted you've come through last night's ordeal without any harm." She looked as if she was on the verge of choking on her own words.

"Thank you," I said, causing Karen's mouth to distort in a strange smile.

Since nobody was speaking, I took the opportunity to ask the question that had occupied me since I awoke in the strange room this morning. "What was that creature that attacked me last night? This . . . this . . ." I tried to remember what Jared had called that thing.

"Damnatus," Jared said.

Karen sat upright in her chair and pursed her lips. "I think it's best if you don't know everything—for your protection, of course."

"For my protection? How could I be protected, when I don't even know what attacked me or, more importantly, why?"

"We don't exactly know why," Professor Martin said. "But what we agree on"—he shot a look to Karen—"is that you"—he looked at me again—"have a right to know what you're dealing with."

Karen almost bit her lower lip off.

"What is a damnatus?" I pleaded with him for an explanation without concerning myself with Karen's displeasure.

"A damned one," Professor Martin said, slowly shaking his head. "Damnati are evil, soulless creatures that have lost their place in the world."

"What exactly does that mean?"

Heavy snorting made the rounds. Apparently, this was not a favorite subject among the Order. Before answering me, the professor's face looked tense, and he stared deeply into my eyes. "Whenever a life comes to a violent end—a woman is raped or a child is abused, whenever someone violates the natural order—the perpetrator pays with the loss of a part of his soul. In a manner of speaking, something is *split off*. That is the tribute demanded by nature," Professor Martin explained, taking a moment. "Only one thing awaits such persons—*damnation*. They're plunged into the eternal darkness that we know as Hell from the Bible.

Sometimes Morgana succeeds in tracking down these murderers, rapists, and child molesters at the very moment that they stand at the abyss of Hell, and then . . . Well, she offers them a deal: their crippled souls are spared a life in Hell in exchange for eternal bondage in her service."

I swallowed hard. That's what was waiting for me in my room? "So, these damnati are something like Morgana's followers?"

Colin, Enid, and Professor Martin nodded from the other side of the table.

"More like bondsmen," Enid said.

I swallowed again. There she was again. Morgana. The one—I didn't even know what to call her: *Creature? Monster? Witch? Woman?*—who was supposedly responsible for my family's death. It all felt like a twisted dream. My family, murdered by an evil witch? My boyfriend, the last descendant of the mightiest magician of all time? Myself, the last of Nimue's bloodline?

"A pact with the devil," mumbled the old gentleman in the kilt, thus releasing me from my thoughts. No. I was actually sitting here. All this *was happening.*

"Damnati are nothing but sick, soulless creatures who, to evade their just punishment, have bound themselves to Morgana, bending to her will," Enid added.

"Monstrous creatures, their *mere existence* violates all laws of nature!" said Professor Martin, disgusted.

I turned to Jared. "Then Morgana is behind all this?"

He nodded, but when Professor Martin opened his mouth to give another explanation, Karen suddenly slammed her palm on the table. Her face had taken on a dark shade of red.

"That's enough," she said, looking at Martin with grave doubt.

"Karen!" Jared yelled, casting her a warning glance.

There was silence in the room for several seconds, then Enid addressed me in a gentle voice. "Evelyn, maybe it's best if you simply tell us what happened in your room."

I took a moment to focus, then I told them a detailed version of what had happened the evening before. When I finally arrived at the point when Jared had placed his hand over my eyes and I'd suddenly become sleepy, he grasped my hand under the table and pleaded for forgiveness with his eyes.

"So the damnatus was waiting for you in your room?" Professor Martin asked when I'd finished.

I nodded.

"But that would mean it was waiting specifically for you and not for Jared, as I had assumed," he said.

"What does Morgana want from Evelyn?" Colin gave me a questioning look.

"I'd love to know," Jared said in a hard tone, breathing deeply. "Well, in any case, you're safe here," he said, looking at Karen.

"Yes, she seems to be," Karen said with a curled lip.

"Good, then we've clarified things for now," Enid said. "How about some breakfast? You must be hungry, Evelyn."

When my stomach growled, everyone laughed . . . except Karen.

Apparently, the Council session was over, and everyone rose. Jared was the first to the door but abruptly stopped when he opened it. I could clearly make out a head of red hair over his shoulder and took a step to the side to better see who was blocking our way. Claire McAdams stood right outside the door, giving Jared a frightened look. She was eavesdropping—that much was obvious. Visibly embarrassed at having been caught, she looked away and tried to appear aloof. But when she saw me half-behind, half-beside Jared, she glared and clenched her fists. Tears of rage welled up in her eyes as her lips narrowed to a thin line.

"Is there a problem?" I heard Enid ask. She gently nudged me aside and positioned herself beside Jared.

"No," Claire said, looked at me through narrowed eyes one last time, then turned and walked away. I was sure she was cursing me in her mind.

After watching Claire walk away, Jared whispered to me, "Everything okay?" He clearly felt her hatred and anger toward me. I could tell from his face that it was an effort to hold himself back.

"Don't worry," I said but couldn't help wonder why these people hated me so much.

Together with Jared, Enid, Colin, and Professor Martin I went down an arched marble stairway to the dining hall, which—apart from its size—resembled the dining hall of Christ Church College. The appearance of the dark wooden tables, which extended in two rows along almost the entire length of the room, felt familiar in the midst of this new and strange environment. I carefully looked over the men and women, who were already seated and helping themselves to tea, toast, oatmeal, eggs, baked beans, potato wedges, and bacon. As expected, everyone turned toward me and looked me over from top to bottom. At least they had enough manners to turn back to the food on their plates after a detailed examination. None of them looked familiar until I spotted a woman with short gray hair. No doubt about it—that was the librarian who wouldn't let me borrow the Calmburry book. Now I knew why it wasn't in its place the next day and then saw it weeks later in Karen's office. Next, I recognized another person and held my breath. There he sat—the man I'd noticed at Zara's funeral, the man who'd stalked me again and again and followed me to Oxford. Suddenly, it became obvious. He hadn't followed me here from Fleetwood—he'd been sent to Fleetwood because of me! Or rather, because of Zara. After all, no one knew of my existence until I showed up in Oxford. At least, that's what Enid told me. But how could that be? This man had followed me day and night. It was impossible that he hadn't known who I was. And why didn't he inform the Order about me? Or warn me, instead? Before I was able to think this through, Jared took my hand and led me across the room. Then, at the farthest end, he quickly took a seat, and I sat down beside him. Enid, Colin, and Professor Martin joined us.

Only when Jared motioned me to help myself to the abundance of food spread out generously in bowls and on trays at the center of the table did I notice a blonde head of hair sticking out from underneath Enid's arm. It was a girl with baby blue eyes, and she stared at me from across the table.

"Jessie, don't be like that," Enid said, and when the little girl sat up, I noticed she was remarkably beautiful and probably about nine years old.

"Evelyn, this is Jessica, my daughter. She's been all excited since she found out you were here," she said with a laugh, which caused her shy daughter embarrassment.

"Hi, Jessica," I greeted the little one and extended my hand to her across the table. "Pleased to meet you."

"Hi," the girl said with a faint voice, but then a beaming smile spread across her face.

"Help yourself," Enid said, motioning toward the bountifully set table. I didn't particularly feel like eating but took a piece of toast, spread butter and marmalade on it, and took a bite. It was delicious. I eagerly ate the toast and prepared another piece while Professor Martin poured me a cup of tea and pushed it over with a smile.

"Thank you . . . Professor."

"Just Irvin," he said.

Jared took my hand again under the table as if to say, "See, they like you."

But I had my doubts. I looked around the room at the faces, finding some gave me friendly looks but others seemed distrustful or even hostile. One might think I would have become used to being watched by now, but it still left me feeling uncomfortable. I'd never been someone who liked being the center of attention. I counted eighteen people plus the four sitting at the table with me. Then there was still Karen, Claire, and the two oldest members of the High Council, whose names I'd forgotten. And not to forget Madison, who had disappeared without a trace with my amulet. That made twenty-seven adults—I thought Jared had said the Circle consisted of twenty-seven people. That meant everyone was here. Except for Madison.

"Jared," I said.

"Yes?" he said, before placing a strip of bacon in his mouth.

"The Circle of the Order . . . Do they all live here? I mean, do you all live together?"

Jared laughed. "No, not normally. Every member has a job, and most have families. We gather here only on special occasions or under exceptional circumstances."

"Are you saying *I'm* an exceptional circumstance?" I asked, which caused loud laughter at the table.

"No, my darling," Jared said, still grinning, and kissed the back of my hand. "*You're* clearly a special occasion." Suddenly his expression hardened. "However, what happened in your room belongs to exceptional circumstances. That's the real reason the members of the Circle are here today."

"Though, in all honesty, they were all eager to finally see you in person," Enid added with a smile. "The last survivor of Nimue's bloodline, the Lady of the Lake." Was there a hint of awe in her voice?

After breakfast Jared told me he'd give me a tour and show me everything.

"What shall we start with?" he asked.

"I don't know what all there is to see here, but maybe we could start with your room," I suggested.

"Okay," he said, smiling, and led me to the south wing of the huge building.

"It's nothing special," he said as he opened the door. "The bedrooms actually all look the same." It was true: his room was no different from the one I woke up in. Only a few personal items suggested who lived here. I noticed a framed photograph of four people sitting on a dresser.

I stepped closer to gently brush my finger over the face of a wonderfully beautiful boy with bright blue eyes.

"That's you, isn't it?"

"Yes."

"Then those are your parents and your sister," I said while looking over the man and woman standing right behind little Jared and the girl, who couldn't be much older than him. Except for the blonde woman, they all had the same dark-blue eyes. All four were exceptionally beautiful. Jared's mother reminded me of a young Grace Kelly, his father looked like an athletic version of Professor Irvin Martin, and Laura, Jared's older sister, who must have been about thirteen or fourteen in the picture, could have competed with any top model. The more I looked at the picture, the more I felt—rather, knew for certain—that I would have loved these people. I would have loved Jared's parents and Laura as if they were my own family. Suddenly, I felt infinitely sad that I would never meet them. Was this feeling grounded in the magical link between our families?

"As I said, nothing special," Jared repeated, which I interpreted as an attempt to distract me from the photo. Only then did I realize I had tears in my eyes, so I turned away and went to a shelf crammed full of CDs. I looked them over. Chopin, Debussy, Yiruma, Einaudi, Florence and the Machine, Coldplay, Ryan Sheridan, Travis, Kings of Leon, Metallica, Linkin Park, TOS—an eclectic mix.

"You have a pretty broad taste in music," I said and smiled as Jared stepped behind me, put his arms around me, and kissed the side of my neck. He turned me around and pulled me close. I put my arms around his neck, pulling him even closer as our lips opened and I inhaled his breath. Then he gently pushed me toward the bed, and we let ourselves drop on it. My hands ran through Jared's hair, clawed into it, and then moved back to his neck. He moved over me the next moment, raised his head, tenderly stroked my cheek, and looked into my eyes.

"I love you." His words penetrated my entire being, shaking every fiber of my body. It felt as if I were about to burst into flames when he found my mouth again, rolled to his back, and pulled me on top of him. Now I was looking down on him as he brushed my hair away and firmly held me against him. The tips of his fingers began to glow in their unique golden way, and he held my face to look at it.

"I love you," he repeated, breathing heavily as the glow began to spread, first moving up his arms, then reaching his chest, and finally enveloping his entire face.

"I love you, too," I said with a wavering voice. Completely out of breath, I sat up and pulled his shirt over his head. I stared at his flawless, glowing upper body, then kissed his chest all the way down to his stomach. His muscles protruded under the touch of my lips and relaxed again when I moved to another spot. Then he firmly took me into his arms and rolled us over so he was on top of me again. He breathed in heavy bursts and looked at my face.

"Do you even know how beautiful you are?" He kissed me so intensely I thought I'd lose my mind. He glowed brighter, more radiantly, as he carefully unbuttoned my blouse, pulled it over my shoulders and freed my arms from it. He pulled me up, kissed my neck down to my collar bones, let his hands run down my side, over my belly, my breasts, my hips. Breathing heavily, I settled back on the mattress, crossed my arms behind my head, extended my neck, and threw my head back. I felt on the verge of bursting when Jared bent over me to cover my body in kisses. Arriving at my navel, he gently brushed along my body with his fingers until he reached the top of my pants. Jared's skin glowed so bright and radiant I was almost blinded. He slowly opened the button at the top of my jeans and pulled the zipper down—tooth by tooth. My body vibrated as he pulled the pants over my legs. Where his golden fingertips touched my skin, electrical impulses appeared to flow through my legs. In a single motion, he stripped off my tight jeans.

My hands went to the top of his pants once he was over me again. Compared with his gentle, practiced touch, my wild tugging and pulling on Jared's pants seemed pathetic. But I couldn't have cared less. Nothing other than *him* mattered at that moment. Finally, I managed to open all the buttons and pulled his pants down to his knees. Jared lifted an arm and quickly reached back without taking his eyes off me. Only a second later, he had rid himself of his pants and socks. Down to his skin-tight jockeys, Jared sat up, pulled me into a riding position on top of him, moved his hands along my back, and popped open the clasp on my bra. Now I was only wearing my panties while Jared held me firmly against him. My bare breasts touched his skin while he whispered my name with a pulsating voice. Without knowing what I was doing, I let myself fall back on the bed, pulling him down by the neck. I was ready. There was nothing I longed for more dearly.

Suddenly, there was a dull thud, followed by a deafening bang.

"What was that?" I sat up startled only to discover dense, white smoke streaming out of Jared's sound system.

"Shit," he said, jumped up, and tried to put out the flames leaping from the stereo system. Jared pulled the entire system from the shelf, carried it to the window, which I immediately opened when I realized what he was up to, and hurled the burning stereo out of the third-floor window into the inner courtyard of the headquarters.

We dropped back on the bed, panting, after the equipment had shattered on the pavement with a loud bang.

"I think I'll show you the rest of the building now," Jared said, and we were overcome for several minutes by a laugh attack.

"We have to seriously think of something if we don't want to have everything blow up each time we kiss," I said when we were getting dressed.

"We should," Jared said with a forced smile.

The imposing library was probably the most impressive room Jared showed me during our tour. Maybe I'd find a few minutes to look around there sometime. After he'd guided me through the underground garage, similar to a small municipal parking garage, we stepped outside through the heavy, wooden entrance door, perhaps more aptly described as a gate. The first thing I noticed were the four mighty stone pillars, two to the right and two to the left of the door, which reminded me of the pillars of the Acropolis. After I'd gone down the stone stairs, I looked over the large lawn that extended before me. I walked a few steps and looked around. Only from there did I recognize that the area was surrounded by dense woods.

"We really are in the middle of a forest," I said, walking on the lawn. When we arrived at the edge of the woods, where our tour ended, I turned one more time to look at the imposing sandstone building from a distance. "You once told me that the headquarters are a safe house," I said, letting my gaze glide over the structure again. Except for the impressive size, I noticed nothing to set it apart from other houses of the same kind. There was no evidence that it was particularly *safe*. When Jared told me of it, I imagined security guards, alarm systems, unscalable walls, barbed wire—but from here, I saw nothing but a huge stone building in the woods. "How is it possible not to be found in this house?" I asked, turning to Jared, who—to my surprise—broadly grinned.

"What did you expect? Machine gun nests and land mines?"

I laughed. "Not exactly, but I figured at least video surveillance or something."

"The headquarters aren't protected that way," Jared explained as we walked back. "A protective spell was cast."

"How does it work?"

"That's not so easy to explain. It's hard to understand if you haven't seen the before and after effect."

I frowned and raised my eyebrows.

Jared grinned. "You can only see all this because I brought you here. Anyone who isn't welcome in this place can't find it. All a stranger would find here is an ordinary clearing in the woods."

"Is that supposed to mean that if I'd come a few days ago, I wouldn't have been able to see all this?" I asked, making a hand gesture toward the building.

"Nothing but trees and meadows," Jared said.

"Oh." I was stunned. Of course, I'd had to deal with the strangest things and . . . creatures in recent days and weeks, but the idea that magic could simply make an entire house, not to mention one of this size, disappear almost floored me. I wondered what might happen if a stranger—or, as Jared had put it, anyone who wasn't welcome—found the clearing by chance. Would he simply trip over the stairs and bump into the massive walls?

"What if someone comes by here?" I asked, trying to imagine it. "You can't just walk through the building . . . can you?"

Jared laughed. "No, of course not. You're deflected. The protective spell makes the entire property invisible and anyone who comes here will feel a strong urge to walk away from the building."

"Ah." I nodded, still looking skeptical.

"Jared, may I talk to you for a moment?" Enid's voice, which came across the lawn from the building's entrance, interrupted us. She stood on the stairs. Jared breathed in deeply. He probably already knew what it was about and didn't feel like talking about it—at least, that's what it looked like. "Sorry for interrupting your tour," Enid added when we had reached her.

"It's all right, we were just about done, anyway," I said.

"It won't take long," Jared said, kissing my hands. "Shall I walk you to your room?"

"No, I'll stay outside for a little longer." This garden seemed like a good place to reflect, and I had some catching up to do.

"Are you sure?" Jared looked at me, concerned. He seemed to feel bad about leaving me alone in a strange environment.

I raised my eyebrows. "You yourself said nothing would happen to me here."

Jared sized me up. It almost looked as if he were playing through all sorts of horrific scenarios of what could happen to me in the next twenty minutes.

"Okay, then we'll see each other later," he finally said, gave me a quick kiss, and disappeared into the headquarters with Enid, who gave me an apologetic smile.

"I won't play this game for much longer," I heard Jared say in a threatening tone as the two vanished into the labyrinth of corridors.

I sat comfortably on the sandstone stairs, pursuing my thoughts. Jared and Enid were only gone for a few minutes when I suddenly noticed someone standing behind me.

"Lovely weather today, isn't it?" I heard a male voice ask. I turned and suddenly froze. There he was—the man who had followed me everywhere for weeks. I would have preferred to run away when I saw him but suppressed the urge. Jared had assured me nothing would happen to me. I was safe in this place. So I forced myself to remain seated.

"Yes," I said, sounding surprised.

"Please forgive me, but I haven't been able to introduce myself yet," he said with a smile, extending his hand. "My name's Gareth."

I accepted and shook his hand. "I take it you know who I am," I said. It was more than strange to shake the hand of the man who'd followed and watched me for so long.

Gareth smiled apologetically. "I hope I didn't frighten you. That was never my intention."

"Well, somewhat," I said. "A person isn't often stalked like that."

"I wouldn't think so," he said and sat down beside me on the steps.

"Is that your job? Tailing people?"

"You could say that. I'm a retired police officer, and, well, some old habits are tough to shake, you know."

"My sister was a police officer," I said without knowing why I told him that.

He nodded thoughtfully. "I know."

Of course he knew. Why had I even mentioned it?

"I'm really sorry about what happened to her."

"Yes," was all I could say. We sat thinking. Then I said, "May I ask you something?"

"Certainly."

"Why didn't you tell Karen about me? I mean, you must have already found out in Fleetwood who I was."

Gareth thought for a moment. Deep folds formed on his forehead. "My duty is to the Order, not to Karen Mayflower."

"But she was the one who assigned you to me or, rather, to my sister, right?"

"Which doesn't mean I approve of her methods. I still decide what I consider right or wrong. And that's how I act."

"Is that why you warned me? Back in the alley."

Gareth looked at me for a moment. His eyebrows, pinched together above his amber-colored eyes, were almost completely gray. But his look was clear and unclouded. "Yes," he said. Although I felt there was so much more behind this plain *Yes*, I didn't have the courage to ask.

Back in my room—I probably wouldn't have found the way there without Jared's help—my phone rang.

"Evelyn, finally! Where the heck are you? I've been insanely worried!" Sally said. She was completely beside herself.

"Everything's all right, I'm with Jared."

"There was a fire in your dorm. Haven't you heard?"

"Yes, I know," I said, still trying to be as calm as possible. "That's why I'm with Jared. There was a gas explosion in my room—a leak in the heating system or something," I fibbed. Good thing she couldn't see over the telephone that I was blushing from embarrassment because of the lie.

"In *your* room?" She was starting to sound panicked.

"Calm down, Sally. I'm fine. I wasn't even there when it happened."

"Are you living with Jared now?" she asked, finally seeming calmer after a short pause.

"For the time being. Until I've found something else."

"Hmm," Sally said distrustfully.

"What are you up to these days?" I asked, to change the subject.

"I have to turn in my assignment to Bronsen, and I've only got four pages so far."

"Oh, that'll keep you busy this weekend," I said.

"Thank you for reminding me," Sally said, irritated, though I heard a giggle.

"Well, till Monday, then."

"Yes, till then," she said and hung up.

When Jared and I entered the dining hall for supper, all the members of the Circle were already sitting at the long tables, helping themselves to steaks, salads, sauce, and something in cast-iron pots that looked like bubble and squeak. You had to grant Legatum Merlini one thing: no one was going to starve here. Only when we were seated did I notice that, unlike at breakfast, Karen, Claire, and the two elderly Council members—I remembered their names were Judith and Montgomery—sat at our table. However, it seemed they were not in a mood for conversation and ate in silence. Only old Montgomery Grey, who had traded in his kilt for corduroy pants, grinned at me.

"Hi, Evelyn," Jessica greeted me shyly as soon as I sat down.

"Hi, Jessie," I said, smiling.

"Would you like something to drink?" she asked, pointing at my empty glass and the pitcher with apple juice that stood next to it.

"Why, yes, I would," I said, and she filled my glass and slid it over to me.

"Thank you," I said, taking a sip.

"One might think you're in love with Evelyn," Colin mumbled with a full mouth, whereupon Jessica made a face at him. I smiled. It really wasn't so bad here.

CHAPTER 18

Blinking the sleep out of my eyes, I tried to orient myself and needed a few seconds to realize where I was. Suddenly something moved beside me. Jared lay on his back, in a deep sound sleep. The way he was lying there with ruffled hair, an almost childlike, satisfied expression on his face, and his lips slightly open—he looked like an angel. I could have watched him for an eternity, but a second later he opened his eyes.

"Good morning," he mumbled.

"Good morning." I smiled wide.

"I could get used to this," he said, leaning on his elbow and brushing my hair out of my face.

"To what?"

"Waking up beside you." He tenderly kissed my mouth. "Every morning, for the rest of my life." We looked at each other for a while in silence. "Are you hungry?" Jared finally asked.

"Yes, a little," I said.

We got up, dressed, and headed out to the dining hall. I wouldn't have believed it possible, but the tables were set even more opulently than the morning before. This was probably a brunch rather than just a breakfast. That's the way it probably was here on Sundays, I figured.

If this was going to continue, I'd have to buy new clothes because I wouldn't fit into my old ones.

Colin was already at the table, heaping large amounts of bacon, fried eggs, home fries, and baked beans onto his plate.

"Are you going to eat all that?" I asked.

"Well, what do you think?" he said. "Not all of us can live on three puny beans a day."

"Ha. I'm sure I've already gained two pounds since I came here."

"Three more wouldn't hurt you," Jared said, dumping a large pile of home fries onto my plate. "Eat up!" he said.

"Are you meeting Sally today?" I asked Colin, struggling with my mountain of home fries.

"No, she has to write a paper," Colin said while chewing.

"Oh, right. She told me yesterday," I said, feeling a little sad about missing her.

"Will you ever tell Sally about all this?" I asked.

Colin stared pensively into space. "That's not such a good idea right now," he said.

"But I thought you were so happy with each other and—"

"That's not what it's about," he said with an unfathomable expression.

I frowned in surprise. "What, then?" I asked when he'd been silent for a while.

Colin breathed heavily. "I don't want to put Sally at risk," he said quietly. "I'd never forgive myself if something happened to her."

I swallowed hard as I understood what he was getting at. The thought of one of those stinking, scar-faced monsters attacking Sally caused my stomach to turn.

"It's just too dangerous right now. I want to keep her as uninvolved as possible."

"Yes, of course," I said. After reflecting for a moment, I said, "Then it's probably best if I don't spend as much time with Sally, either. If

Morgana really is after me and tries to get to me through Sally . . ." I didn't dare complete my sentence.

"We'll all have to avoid Sally for a little while," Jared said while Colin turned away, nodding. It hit Colin far harder than he'd admit. Jared put a comforting hand on his shoulder. "We'll work it out," he said to us as encouragement, but neither of us answered.

"You were really lucky Jared was nearby when the damnatus attacked you," Colin said after a short while, observing me lost in thought.

"I know," I said, trembling inside at the thought of what might have happened otherwise.

Suddenly, a determined expression returned to Colin's face. "You need to learn to defend yourself," he said.

Jared uneasily looked back and forth between Colin and me.

Colin grinned. "Don't worry, I won't be too hard on her." Colin seemed to be his old self again. Jared didn't say anything, but I didn't miss the *watch yourself* look he gave Colin.

"What does that mean?" I asked. "Are you going to teach me how to fight?"

"How to defend yourself," Colin corrected.

"I hope you know what'll happen if you injure her," Jared said.

"That I'm not going to train Evelyn the same way I train you should be obvious, shouldn't it?" Colin said, irritated.

"I just wanted to be certain," Jared said, a bit more relaxed, and pushed his plate away.

"Good," I said. "When do we start?"

"Right now if you want. Why don't you put on something comfortable, and we'll meet in fifteen minutes at the gym."

Jared accompanied me to my room, where I changed into jogging pants, a sports top, and my worn Chucks.

"Done?" he asked, amused, giving me a smile.

I looked myself over. "I think so—what do you think, will this do?"

"I liked it better when you had less on." He came toward me, placed both hands on my hips and pushed his fingers under my top. My skin began to tingle the moment he touched me, and my breathing quickened. He bent forward with a deep sigh and pressed his lips against mine. Jared's hands slowly pushed under my top, moved along my back, over my hips, to my belly . . .

Suddenly there was a knock at the door.

"Remind me later where we left off," he said, his glowing look nearly making me swoon. "Yes?" he called out toward the door.

Jessica, Enid's nine-year-old daughter, entered hesitantly. With a shy smile, the pretty blonde girl with blue doll's eyes walked past Jared and gave me a roll of athletic tape. I took the narrow roll from her hand.

"What's that for?" I asked.

"Colin said I'm supposed to give this to you," Jessica said, somewhat embarrassed. Apparently she didn't know what it was for, either.

"Let me handle that," Jared said and unrolled a few lengths of tape.

"What's it for?" I asked while Jessica and I watched Jared wrap the bandage tightly around my right wrist. Then he switched to my left.

"For stabilization, to keep you from straining your wrists."

Jessica followed each of Jared's movements as if she were trying to remember everything precisely.

"Okay, let's go," he said, and I skeptically looked over my bandaged wrists.

The *gym* was more like a splendid ballroom than what I'd expected. In addition to huge windows framed by golden curtains, this oversized room was furnished with several paintings and wall mirrors that made it look larger than it was. To top it all off, a monstrous chandelier the size of a small car dangled from the stucco ceiling. Only the padded mats scattered around on the polished wood floor told me we hadn't stepped through the wrong door. Nevertheless, I felt out of place in this beautiful hall with my worn gym clothes.

"You aren't going to stay here, are you?" I heard Colin ask from the other corner of the hall while he casually walked toward us. "Because in that case we might as well stop right now." I realized his words were directed at Jared and not at me.

"I only thought . . . ," Jared started, but Colin gave him an unyielding look. Jared sighed. "I'll pick you up in an hour."

"Okay," I said and nodded before Jared reluctantly left.

"I promised Jessica she could watch," Colin said. "She'll start her training next year and wants to have a little preview, if that's okay with you."

"Sure," I said without knowing what I'd gotten myself into.

Jessica smiled gratefully and went to find a suitable observation post in the huge room.

"Okay," Colin said, looking me over from top to bottom. "Do you have enough room to move in those pants?"

What kind of question was that? "I think so," I said and kneeled to check.

"Good, then let's start. For somebody like you, a combination of Krav Maga and Wing Chun is probably the most sensible. These martial arts are very effective because they're based on the principle of using your opponent's weight and strength against him."

"What's that supposed to mean, 'for somebody like me'?" I asked, inadvertently sounding a little huffy. I was sure he didn't mean to be rude, but I somehow felt like a limp rag.

"Well, you've got passable muscles from swimming, but you clearly lack the strength and mass to be a serious opponent for somebody like, well, me."

I raised my eyebrows. Maybe I should seriously kick him in the shin. Then we'd see if he'd take me seriously as an opponent . . .

Colin looked at me apologetically. "Nothing personal, Evelyn, but we have to be realistic." His detached, professorial tone startled me. I wasn't used to it. But he was probably right, and I should trust him. "Okay." He rubbed his hands together, stood upright, and said, "Hit me!"

"Pardon?"

"Well, hit me!" Colin said again.

"You can't be serious."

"I'm totally serious," Colin said with a laugh. "So. Punch me in the face."

I looked around for help. But there was only little Jessica, whose big eyes were directed at me and nobody else.

"Evelyn, we don't have all day," Colin said impatiently, but then his expression changed. "Don't tell me you're afraid you might hurt me, little water sprite," he said with a provocative, crooked grin.

Water sprite? Something tightened inside me. Felix had also called me something like that! Suddenly, anger rose inside me, which Colin acknowledged with a challenging smile.

Well, as you wish. Faster than I even intended, I clenched my right hand into a fist and punched as hard as I could at Colin. Everything went terribly fast. Just a fraction of an inch away from his face, he grabbed my arm with a lightning-fast movement and twisted it with a firm jerk to my back. When I cried out in pain, Jessica put both hands in front of her mouth, and her eyes went wide. After seeing her disturbed little face, I clenched my teeth and silently bore my pain, though Colin immediately let go of me. If I hadn't known for sure that he'd just twist my arm again, I would have given him a ringing slap in the face that would have left him with a bright red cheek for the rest of the day.

"I'll teach you that now," he said.

I figured out the move after only a few tries, and to my satisfaction Colin rubbed his hurt shoulder after I'd twisted his arm several times.

"Well done," he finally said, wincing in pain. "Next I'll show you how to choke someone without using much strength or expending much energy."

I shuddered at the thought that he'd demonstrate that on me first.

"If you manage to escape from your opponent's grip, step behind him, put an arm around his neck, grip your elbow with your free hand, and pull up—that's all."

I frowned as I tried to remember his words. "Arms around the neck, hand to the elbow, pull up," I repeated.

"I'll show you," Colin said, and I shrank back from him. He smiled. "I won't hurt you, promise. I only want to show you the effect."

"Okay," I hesitantly consented, casting a look at Jessica, whose blue doll eyes were still rigidly fixed on me. She was more afraid than I was.

Colin stepped behind me, put his arms around my neck, and gently pulled up. Although he only made a tiny motion, the pressure it exerted on my throat triggered an intense coughing fit that almost drove me to tears.

"I thought you weren't going to hurt me!" I said between gasps for air.

"Sorry, I didn't know you were so sensitive," he said.

"It's my turn," I said resolutely and stepped behind him.

"Gentle, Evelyn. This grip is very effective," he warned, his hands raised.

"You don't say," I said, put an arm around his neck, grabbed my elbow, and pulled up, to which Colin immediately responded with a gargling noise. I immediately let him go. He bent forward, wrestling for air and rubbing his throat. I turned to Jessica and winked, which she answered with a conspiratorial grin.

"Okay, we don't have to practice this one anymore, I think," Colin said and coughed as he straightened up again. "I'd better show you how to get behind your opponent." He needed a moment to catch his breath. "If an attacker approaches you—it doesn't matter if it's from the front or the side—you can simply steer him with a well-aimed kick in another direction and use his momentum to your advantage." As soon as Colin was finished explaining, he demonstrated a series of kicks and punches that didn't look particularly complicated. "Ready?" he asked, and again I nodded hesitantly.

I attacked Colin as he instructed me, whereupon his hand quickly thrust forward to strike me on the cheek, completely unprepared because I hadn't anticipated it. Although he hadn't even caught me properly, it felt as if I'd been kicked by a horse.

"Damn it, Colin, are you nuts?" Jared shouted and several lightbulbs in the huge chandelier popped. Where had he come from so suddenly? Had he been watching without my noticing? A second later he pulled me to his side, glowering at Colin.

"Sorry," Colin said with an embarrassed look. "I didn't mean to hurt you, it was an accident," he said and extended his hand to my cheek, but Jared roughly pushed it away.

"Oh, it's all right," I said, trying to calm Jared. "It barely hurts, and it was my fault, anyway. I focused on his legs and—"

"Your fault? If it weren't for me, you wouldn't have to learn how to defend yourself at all! If anything, it's my fault!"

"Jared, stop it now!" I said, winding myself out of his grip. "If it wasn't for you, I'd probably be dead!" I looked at him with glowing eyes. "You saved me from Felix and that damnatus, remember?"

"If Madison hadn't stolen your amulet for my sake, all that wouldn't have happened!"

"Are you yelling at me?" I yelled back, toying for a second with the thought of twisting his arm behind his back as Colin had just shown me. I was enraged by Jared blaming himself for everything. "Stop talking such garbage! You're the best thing that ever happened to me, damn it!"

Jared suddenly froze. "What?" he quietly asked.

"You heard me," I said, crossing my arms in front of my chest.

His expression softened. He took a step toward me, put his arms around me, and tried to kiss me. But I was still mad at him.

Colin laughed.

"Oh shut up," Jared said to him. "You've already lost your bonus for the day."

"Colin showed me some really neat moves," I said, trying to defend him, but Jared gave both of us a warning glance.

"Sorry," Colin said, giving me an apologetic look.

"It's all right, but thank you. It's good for today. I'll head for the showers and recharge my batteries," I said with a grin, which caused both Jared's and Colin's expression to brighten. Even Jessica, who'd hidden in the farthest corner of the room, was smiling again.

Dressed and with my hair dried, I left my room to look for Jared and ran into Jessica. Apparently, she'd stood outside my door the whole time. The poor girl was so frightened it looked like she'd tear up at any moment.

"Jessica," I said, surprised, "what are you doing here? Can I help you with anything?"

"I'm . . . sorry . . . I," she stammered, ashamed.

"Jessie, please leave Evelyn alone." Enid came along the corridor. "Sorry, Evelyn—but it seems you've acquired a fan." Enid smiled while putting an arm around her daughter.

"It's all right," I said and brushed my hand over the girl's hair. She was really sweet. "Do you know where Jared is?" I asked Enid.

"In Karen's office. She wanted to talk to him."

"Ah." Surely this was about me again, or rather, about how Jared was not supposed to be with me. Because of this dubious old prophecy from a millennium and a half ago.

"Shall we take you there?" Enid asked.

"Oh, please."

"How do you like it here?" Enid asked as we walked along.

"Good. It's just . . ."

Enid turned to me. "What?"

I exhaled. "Enid, can I ask you something?"

"But of course."

"You appear to like me . . ."

"Yes, I do like you."

I smiled. "Well, most people here don't seem to have a problem with me, but some others . . ." What was their attitude toward me? Distrust? Hatred? Jealousy? I didn't have a clue. "Some people don't seem to be particularly fond of me. I'm wondering why."

Enid looked at me with empathy, then turned with a smile to her daughter. "Jessie, why don't you see if you can help Hilda in the kitchen? I'm sure she's already preparing supper."

"Oh, Mom," Jessica said unenthusiastically. "She's gonna make me peel potatoes again."

"Be a dear," Enid said, sending Jessica grumbling on her way to the kitchen.

"See you at supper," I called after her, whereupon she turned one last time and smiled.

"*She* likes you for sure," Enid said as we continued walking through the long corridors.

Then Enid looked pensive. "The reason why some members of the Circle aren't particularly friendly toward you is that they believe you constitute a danger to Jared."

"Because of the Prophecy," I said. "The Prophecy that supposedly foretells that I'll do something to Jared, right?"

"Yes," Enid said and breathed deeply. "It's an odd thing about the Prophecy." She paused. "It doesn't outright say that Jared will be killed by his lover. It's about life and death and how they relate to each other. The meaning of any prophecy is a matter of interpretation. Some understand it this way, others that way."

"So Karen, Claire, and some others believe I'll do something to Jared, but you, Irvin, and Colin don't?"

Enid nodded. "I believe you're as innocent as Jared. In my opinion, there's only one enemy."

"Morgana," I mumbled, and Enid nodded again.

"I've read the Prophecy," I said a moment later.

She looked at me, astonished. "Where?"

"In a book a friend lent me. Unfortunately, it was destroyed during the fire in my dorm room."

Enid was silent for a second, then looked at me. When she spoke, her voice had taken on a meaningful, almost grave, tone:

> The blind heart tormented by longing,
> Readily walks into darkness so far.
> Deprived of its light, deprived of its might,
> Only Death watches over the wight.

I nodded with difficulty. Enid, too, required a moment before she could continue.

"There are many ways of interpreting this verse," she finally said.

"I would never harm Jared," I said a moment later with a heavy heart.

"I know."

CHAPTER 19

The next few days passed in the same way: I got up in the mornings, drove to the College with Jared and Colin, and tried to lead the life of a perfectly normal student—at least, to the extent this was possible in the company of Gareth, with whom I'd become friends in the meantime, and Ian, another member of the Circle. Both followed our every step. During the break, Jared and I ate lunch with Colin and Sally. However, these shared lunches and the lectures Sally and I attended together were the only things that continued to connect us. In the afternoon, Jared and I always drove back to the headquarters, where Colin trained me and Jared watched. Jared insisted on being there since Colin had accidentally hit me the first time. Initially, this bothered Colin because Jared intervened every time the training got a little rough. Nevertheless, I made good progress, and my trainer was quite satisfied with me despite Jared's presence.

Things were good except for the fact that I missed Sally and always had sore muscles from the training. Actually, you could even say I was . . . *happy*. Jared and I spent almost the entire day together and slept in the same bed every night. But sleeping in the same bed was the only thing we did. After the incident with the sound system, we decided to take things slow—at least, until he could find a way to control his magic.

One afternoon after a particularly hard training session, I flopped down on the bed.

"I want to show you something," Jared said, glowing, as he took me by the wrists and pulled me up.

"What?" I asked as he gently pushed me out the door.

"A room I haven't shown you yet," he said as he led me along a narrow corridor. It was in a part of the huge building that I'd never been in before. Just as I was about to ask how far it was, Jared stopped in front of an unassuming door. Unlike most other doors here, it was not decorated with elaborate carvings, and it appeared rather plain and modern. Apparently, it had been retrofitted. Only when looking more closely did I notice that it wasn't secured with just one but three different locks at different levels. Jared pulled a key ring from his pocket and opened the locks in sequence, each lock with a different key. When he was done, he turned to me, beaming with joy.

"I've wanted to show you this for a while," he said. "It took me a lot of persuading to get the keys."

I could barely contain my curiosity. If you needed to lock something behind three locks in a *safe house*, whatever was in the room had to be something very special.

Jared finally pushed the door open. "This is the relic room."

I stepped in full of anticipation, not knowing where to start looking. I was in the middle of a medieval museum. I first noticed the mighty bookshelves that immediately reminded me of the part of the College library where I'd found the Calmburry chronicle. Then my eye caught the large glass cases. Some were mounted on the wall, some were freestanding, and they all held pure treasure. Golden chalices, sparkling rings, necklaces and armbands, shining daggers . . .

"Wow," I said when I had surveyed the room and finally stopped in front of the largest case. This massive glass case contained a huge sword, whose brilliant blade and jewel-encrusted handle shone in the brightest colors.

"Is that . . . ," I said, not daring to trust my eyes. "Is that . . . what I think it is?"

"Excalibur himself," Jared said proudly, pulled the key ring out of his pocket again, and opened the glass door.

Suddenly I needed to sit down. By now, I really should have been able to handle these situations better, but each new confrontation with Jared's world of magic and legends threw me completely off balance.

"It belongs to Colin," he said, moving his fingertips in awe over the brilliant blade.

I have no idea how long I stood there observing the legendary sword. Only when Jared locked the case again and led me to another corner of the room was I able to turn away from it.

"Look," Jared said, pointing at a thick book lying open on an ancient, one-legged table made of polished mahogany. "You once asked me about the members of the Order." He pulled me over to the book to carefully look through it. "They're all listed in chronological order here. From its foundation in the fifth century to the present."

I stood beside him with anticipation.

"Have a look," he said, smiling. I looked in wonder at the book. The binding and the faded pages reminded me of the Calmburry chronicle, which immediately aroused my interest.

"Look here," Jared said, as he opened to a page in the last third of the book, and pointed at a name written in elaborately arched letters.

"Jean-Jacques Rousseau?" Jared nodded. I impatiently moved my index finger along the list of names until three more caught my eye. "Queen Victoria? Charles Dickens? Albert Einstein?" My voice sounded shrill. "This is wild!" Again, my finger moved over the pages. "Pierre and Marie Curie . . . Oh my God!"

"Impressive, isn't it?" Jared said, smiling. "When I was little, I spent entire evenings leafing through this book."

"I can see that," I said and suddenly had an idea. Didn't Jared say that I'd be surprised who the members of the Order were these days? I hastily turned the pages to the back, which held the latest entries. I almost became dizzy glancing over the pages. Interspersed between names I'd never heard before were a British bestselling author, a musician, two actors, a top athlete, a few company executives, and even a head of state.

"Wait a second!" Jared said and stopped. He pressed his finger on the page I was about to turn. Suddenly, he stiffened and stared with wide eyes at the open book. I couldn't tell which name had rattled him so much.

"What's the matter?" I asked.

"I . . ." He wrestled with his words, and I could tell his brain was running at full speed. "I have to talk to Karen," he finally said with difficulty, swallowing hard. "Do you feel like taking a bath or something?" he asked, unable to hide the nervous undertone in his voice.

"Jared, what's the matter?" I asked after he'd shut the book and gently guided me toward the door.

"We'll talk about it later," he said, once again sounding like his usual controlled and convincing self. He kissed me on the tip of my nose as he led me out into the hallway.

"Okay," I said skeptically. "I'll be in my room if you need me."

"Good. Till later, babe," Jared said before he disappeared down the hallway. I was almost certain he'd run once he was out of sight. I looked after him, shaking my head. What had he discovered in that book that caused him to take off? He'd been so completely distracted that he'd forgotten to lock the door again. I knew I shouldn't be doing this, but right then there was only one way to find out!

As quietly as possible, I went back to the relic room and closed the door behind me. I stepped up to the book and opened it where I believed Jared had read the name. Just to be sure, I flipped five pages back and went through the register line by line. I was able to remember a few of the names, so I knew I hadn't passed the page I was looking for.

"Roberta Flackman, Ray Jackson, Selma Forbes . . . ," I mumbled to myself without noticing anything out of the ordinary. I probably wouldn't recognize the name Jared had reacted to so strangely. Maybe it had something to do with his family.

"Lewis Haller, Grace Middton, Gerald Barner, Frank Tempton . . ."

I felt a shock and suddenly froze. I stared at the letters I'd read last as if struck by lightning. *Frank Tempton?* I wrestled for air. *That* Frank Tempton? The man who was sentenced to prison for life for the murder of my sister? Stunned, I stared at the book as a sudden intense dizziness overcame me. I numbly went over to the leather couch on the other side of the room and sat down.

Frank Tempton was a member of Legatum Merlini? What did that mean? Quickly, I jumped up and ran from the room. A few seconds later, I arrived at Karen Mayflower's office and stopped in front of her door. It was still shaking on its hinges. Jared must have slammed the door shut—he couldn't have been there for long. I had just reached out for the door handle when I heard Jared's voice inside. I withdrew my hand and placed my ear against the door.

"Colin was right, wasn't he?" Jared's words were loud and clear. "He was right all along!" It was impossible to miss the rage in his voice.

"Jared, please," Karen said, attempting to calm him down, but he wouldn't let her have a word.

"You've told me this lie since I was a boy!" *Lie?* I moved closer to the door.

"Evelyn never was a danger to me, just as Nimue never was a danger to Merlin—she loved him! She could never have harmed him!" Jared took in a big breath. "There never were two enemies. There was always only Morgana. Just her!"

"Jared, I—"

"You invented this crap to keep me away from Evelyn, didn't you?" he asked, his voice sounding dangerously calm.

I looked down the corridor to ensure I was alone and again pressed my ear against the dark wooden door and listened, spellbound.

"Jared, that—"

"Does the name Frank Tempton mean anything to you?" he asked with a threatening undertone in his voice. My eyes widened.

"Jared, you don't understand," Karen said.

"What have you done? How could you do this?" he said in a sad, almost desperate voice.

"I had to do everything within my power to protect you. Everything!" she said. Then her voice turned hard. "It's my duty, and you know it!" I heard her take a few steps. "I couldn't take any chances after the plane crash." Her words were marked by anger and sadness. "*You*, Jared, are the only one left. You survived that terrible accident because you're the strongest of them all. Your magic let you walk away unscathed from the fire and the carnage. *You are* Merlin's very last descendant." She raised her voice and spoke full of fervor. "*It is you* to whom his power has passed. Only you are left, Jared. You are the *only one*. The only one who bears Merlin's magic within him. *You* are the heir of Myrddin Calmburry, the greatest magician to have ever lived." Karen breathed heavily. "No!" she said resolutely. "I *had* to have her killed. I just had to do it. To protect Merlin's magic. His legacy. To protect *you*, my dear boy."

Silence.

Then, suddenly, something strange happened. A great unwholesome energy spread through the air. I felt the threatening, crackling electricity surrounding me. You could almost touch it. The hair on my arms stood, while white, yellow, and blue sparks flew from the electrical outlets in the hallway. A deep, dark rumbling sounded. A terrible, hateful rumbling generated from Jared's body.

"You made Evelyn an orphan and then took her sister from her! Zara was everything to her!"

What? It took a moment for it to sink in. Then the insight struck me like a blow to the face. I collapsed into myself, sinking to my knees, my right cheek still pressed against the door. I gasped. My parents and Zara had been murdered—by *her?*

There was a roaring in my ears. Karen Mayflower had my entire family killed? Breathing became more difficult with each inhalation.

I heard Karen's pleading. "Jared, don't . . ." Her voice trembled. Then I heard hasty steps. "Jared, please understand. I did it all for you!"

"Don't you dare involve me in this! Murderer!" he yelled.

"But Jared, if this girl were gone, you'd have nothing to fear. Morgana cannot find you as long as you're under the Order's protection. That girl is your doom. Morgana will find you because your love for the girl will dissolve the link to the Order and with it the protective spell. Then she will kill you." Her voice broke. "You can only bind yourself to one of the two. The Order or the girl. Morgana has already found *her,* so it's only a matter of time before she finds *you.* We can still protect you." She took a second to catch her breath. "But not much longer. The link between you and the girl will sever the bond. I can feel it. Then we won't be able to do anything for you. Please understand, Jared. Act before it's too late, my boy!"

I heard Jared's steps and then Karen's frightened voice. "If you choose her, you'll die. And the magic will die with you."

Again the rumbling. "Should anything happen to Evelyn, the Order will no longer have anything to protect," Jared said, full of anger.

"Jared, my boy," Karen said.

"No one touches her!"

"I know you love her, but that's your curse. Your love for her will cost you your life."

That was more than I could bear. My breath was slow and dragging, my lids became heavy, and the noise was unbearably loud. Then it went black around me. I fell. I fell into a deep, black hole and welcomed the darkness with open arms. The only thing I wanted was to give myself to nothing. See nothing, hear nothing, feel nothing. But a slowly rising thought held me from it and kept me conscious.

I've got to get away from here!

The thought became clearer. Stronger. I could almost grasp the bold letters of that thought before my inner eye.

I've got to get away from here!

These people murdered my family.

I've got to get away from here!

From one second to the next, adrenaline raced through me. I could feel my pupils widen and my heart pump hot blood into my arms and legs. My muscles tensed. I leapt to my feet, looked around, and ran.

I've got to get away from here!

That was all I could think at that moment: the firm resolution to flee and never again return to this horrible place. A few moments later, I'd crossed the large entrance hall, run out underneath the stone archway and past the mighty columns, made it into the open, and left the huge headquarters behind. I ran on. I practically flew over the acres of meadow outside the building, finally reached the edge of the forest, and fought my way in through the thick bushes, whose sharp branches scratched my arms and face. Stumbling, I evaded the mighty tree trunks, often only at the last second. I ran farther and farther and farther. As far as my legs could carry me.

CHAPTER 20

It was dark and cold. Dreadfully cold. I had no idea how far I'd run and knew even less about where I was. All I could make out in the dark forest was the faint light of the moon high above the treetops. I'd have to admit it sooner or later: I was lost. There was no point in going on. I'd probably only get lost deeper in the forest. The best thing I could do in this situation was find shelter and wait for sunrise.

While I collected fir branches to make a shelter under two trees, I shrank in fright from every sound the nocturnal forest and its inhabitants made. For someone as afraid of darkness as I was, this was the worst conceivable spot for spending the night—even the snapping of twigs under my own steps caused me tremendous fright. When I'd finally finished building my emergency shelter, I sat under the provisional moss roof, pulled my knees to my body, and tried to block out the recurring thoughts of the past day. In vain. Tears ran down my cheeks and dripped onto my pants and the damp forest floor.

I must have fallen asleep somehow, for when I opened my eyes, I'd rolled over on my side. I couldn't have slept for long, at most an hour or two, because it was still pitch-black and bitterly cold—so cold I shivered all over, and my teeth were chattering.

"I can smell her."

I startled. Who the hell had said that? I clasped my hands over my mouth to suppress a cry. I hastily looked around, but my eyes were still heavy with sleep and hadn't become accustomed to the dark yet, so I couldn't see anything through the branches of my shelter.

"The slut can't be far," another croaking voice said from the same direction, but this time I was able to identify the sound: *damnati*. I tried to breathe as silently as possible. The horrible memory of the scarfaced monster that had lain in wait for me in my room flared up in my thoughts. There was no doubt—they were after me! How many were there? Just these two? Or more? *What should I do?* Panic and desperation overcame me as I feverishly thought of how I might escape the clutches of these hideous creatures. My muscles tensed, ready to flee . . . or fight—depending on what happened. I slowly raised myself and, like a sprinter before the starting gun, squatted on my haunches when a thin twig broke with a crack under my left foot. I held my breath.

"Did you hear that?" one of the scarfaces said.

"What?"

"There was a noise, a cracking—from there," said the first.

"Have you found anything?" another, deeper croak asked.

Shit! There were three of them—at least!

"I heard something," the first said, somewhat subdued.

"Well, then go take a look and see what it is, you idiot," the third one said. "Or do you want to try Her patience any longer?"

"No, of course not," the first said.

"If we don't find the brat soon, she'll pluck our eyes out."

Suddenly, I heard steps coming straight for me. I was running out of time. What should I do? *Flee or fight, flee or fight, flee or . . .* flee!

With one bound I was up. I pushed aside the branches I'd so painstakingly piled and ran for it.

"There!" cried the first one. "There she is!"

"Grab her, you numbskulls!" yelled the third croaking voice.

I ran as fast as I could in a blind panic. My lungs ached from the cold air as I drove my legs relentlessly forward. My steps were uncoordinated, and I could only guess where I was going in the darkness. I dove under a low branch at the very last second—otherwise it probably would have knocked me out—and stumbled when a wide tree trunk appeared before me. My lungs burned with every breath; it felt like a thousand pinpricks. I angled away fast—a desperate attempt to shake my pursuers—but tripped on a protruding root and fell down. *Shit!*

As fast as I could, I rose and continued to run, but two of the hooded ones had almost caught up with me. Where was the third? I could almost feel their acrid breath on the back of my neck. They were right on my heels, panting and gasping. It wouldn't be long before they'd catch me. I clenched my teeth and ran as fast as I could, forcing myself not to look back. Then I perceived another shadow approaching, this time from the side. I saw from the corner of my eye how he got ready to jump. I tried to change direction but the figure in the fluttering cloak had already taken off and thrown himself on me. I immediately went down under his weight. I rolled on my back underneath him, kicked with all my strength into his stomach and drilled my thumb deep into his gooey eye socket, just as Colin had taught me. There was a howl. The scarface attempted to grab my arms, but I rolled to the side and rammed my knee with full force into his groin, causing him to double over. A second later, I'd torn away and scrambled to get to my feet, but the others had already reached me. They were so close it would've been futile to run. So I gritted my teeth to suppress my flight reflex and focused on what Colin had taught me. One damnatus charged me from the front—and I knew just how to counter it. When he was only a few feet away, he widened his eyes in fright because I stood rooted. I took him down with a well-aimed kick and brought the tip of my boot down on his head and face. There was no time to completely neutralize him because the other one had reached me and grabbed me by the hair. I rammed my elbow into his stomach as hard as I could. He immediately doubled over with a retching sound.

I thought I had overcome all my assailants but suddenly bumped into another one and heard ringing laughter. I turned around, frightened. I was surrounded. At least thirty of the cloak-wearers had appeared and formed a circle around me. I shrank back, stumbling with fear, noticing only too late that one of the ones I'd taken down had risen to his feet again. I saw him move in my direction from the corner of my eye, then something cracked against my temple, and I collapsed.

"That bitch was hard to catch." The voice echoed dully as I came to. At first, I felt as if I was anesthetized—but then came the pain in my head.

"Where did she learn to fight like that?" croaked another voice.

As I slowly came to my senses, I noticed my body was tilting back and forth in an odd way. I opened my eyes—just the tiniest bit so the monsters wouldn't know I was awake—and found one of the hideous creatures had slung me over his shoulder, my wrists and ankles tied up.

"For your sake, I hope she didn't suffer any brain damage from that blow. Our orders are to bring the girl unharmed to Her," the one carrying me said. The stench emanating from him was unbearable.

"What should I have done? I couldn't know she was going to fight like that," the other damnatus said. That must have been the one who'd knocked me out.

"But did you have to hit her over the head with a rock?"

"Oh calm down. You can hardly see it now that I've washed the blood off," he said, pulling on my hair to lift my head and look at my face. I closed my eyes and feigned unconsciousness.

The creature carrying me shrugged his shoulders. "I couldn't give a damn," he said. "I just don't want to be the one who delivers this one to Her all bloodied."

"Do you think I'm eager?" the first asked. "Remember Billy? She ripped his left arm off because of old Mary Hayman."

"Mary Hayman?" the one carrying me asked. "Wasn't that the old woman who was snooping around everywhere?"

"Yeah, Billy was supposed to grab her, but the Order got to her first." He made an indefinable sound, a kind of gurgling grunt. "They shut up the old snoop before she was able to unpack. And *She* was less than thrilled about it."

"We're almost there," a third, somewhat deeper, voice said, cutting off the conversation. "Untie her hands and feet and see to it that she wakes up."

They're going to untie me? This was my chance! I raised my head—just barely—to look around and let it drop immediately. *Damn!* There were too many! At first glance in the light of the dawning day, I counted about ten damnati walking behind me and heard at least as many walking ahead. But I had no choice, I had to try. This could be my last chance to get out of here alive.

"Be careful with that knife!" warned the one carrying me. "You'll pay dearly for the slightest scratch."

"You think I don't know that?" the other said, irritated.

A second later, a scar-covered hand grabbed my tied wrist, then I felt the cold steel on my palms as he effortlessly cut me loose. My feet were next. A hand held my ankle, used the knife to cut the rope, and I was free. Adrenaline shot through me, and I kicked the creature in the chin. I slid off the creature's shoulder and landed on my feet. But before I could run, the others encircled me.

"Where do you think you're going?" the one with the deep voice said. "We're almost there, and you want to leave before the party's even started?"

I looked around in a panic and saw that we were at the edge of a huge clearing in the forest. As far as I could see, there was nothing but scarfaces in black cloaks. There must have been hundreds, if not thousands.

Then I saw *her*.

Morgana! I blinked several times to be sure my wits hadn't left me and what I was seeing was true. No. She had to be real—even in my wildest dreams I couldn't have imagined such an unbelievably beautiful woman. Wait! That wasn't quite true . . . I had seen such a beautiful woman once before in my dreams. Eowyn. Myrddin's mother. That was on the night after I'd seen the Calmburry book for the first time.

Out of a curiosity to see how much resemblance there was between the Eowyn of my dreams and the woman standing in front of me, I raised my eyes and looked closer at Morgana. Everything about her seemed perfect. Big, dark, almost-black eyes framed by long, full eyelashes gave me a penetrating look. Perfectly arched eyebrows, high cheekbones, full, pale-red lips, and a flawless, light skin tone. A face that looked sculpted, surrounded by waist-long, shining, raven-black hair and a body even the gods would envy. I swallowed hard as I attempted to process the flood of impressions. In the presence of this perfect being, any other creature—man, woman, splendid songbird, or majestic flower—must feel ashamed. At least, that's how I felt.

She slowly stepped toward me with the dignity and glory of a Roman empress as the eyes of hundreds of scarfaced cloak-wearers followed her. The train of her hooked-lace, black-as-the-night gown trailed on the damp forest floor. A gentle smile spread across her face. When she began to speak, I caught a glimpse of her immaculate white teeth, though they seemed too pointed to be human.

"Welcome, my child," she began in a clear, singing tone, came directly toward me, and spread her arms in invitation. "We have eagerly awaited your arrival."

The dangerous undertone in her voice caused me to shrink back from her embrace. A murmur went through the ranks of the surrounding cloak-wearers when I evaded Morgana's touch. But when I looked into her face again, she smiled leniently.

"Please, no false modesty, my little one," she said in a soft voice.

"What do you want from me?" I asked.

"Oh," Morgana answered surprised. "It would appear you're not shy, after all, by the way you address me." She began to stroll back and forth in the clearing. "I merely want to ask a small favor of you," she said while looking at me kindly. "Just a little help with a ritual. No more." She waved her hand in the air as if her "favor" was hardly worth mentioning. "But first things first. I want to show you something, my love." As she smiled, her long, slender fingers slid into the right pocket of her gown and pulled out a thin, silver-and-green piece of jewelry.

"Do you know what this is?" Morgana asked, sweet as sugar, looking at me expectantly.

I looked closely at the shining object in her hand. Is that . . . ? I gasped. Where did she . . . ? "My amulet!" I shouted, my eyes wide.

Morgana smiled, satisfied. Obviously, I had reacted as she had hoped. "Not quite, my little one." She stopped for a moment to enjoy the sight. "This really is Nimue's amulet," she said, tenderly stroking the jewel with her fingers as if trying to put it to sleep. "It had been lost for so many years I believed it had disappeared in the eddies of time," she continued, deep in thought. Then she looked into my eyes. "Where did you get it?" she asked.

I wasn't sure how to answer, so I said, "My mother gave it to me."

She looked at me skeptically. "You don't know what kind of amulet this is, do you?" Morgana asked smugly. "This isn't just an ordinary necklace, my dear. This"—again she tenderly stroked the crystal—"is a magical jewel that was crafted with a special purpose. It conceals the wearer from all those who want to harm her." A gentle smile spread across her face. "Merlin made it for Nimue to protect her after she'd given up Avalon, her magic, and, therefore, her immortality. For his sake. To be together with him as a human." Morgana looked up at the sky. "That surely was one of his most outstanding achievements," she said and suddenly appeared lost in thought.

It will protect you, the voice of my mother echoed again in my mind. She was right. The amulet had protected me over the years. Until . . . Madison had ripped it from my neck.

The damnatus standing closest to Morgana loudly cleared his throat, bringing the witch back. It appeared she was frequently lost in her thoughts. She immediately trained her dark eyes on me and smiled.

"The amulet made you a *Concealed*, my dear. All those years . . . when I was first able to sense your mother and a few years later finally your sister, this miserable Order did all the dirty work for me." Again her look drifted away. "Hmm, I'd thought pretty little Zara was the last of Nimue's bloodline . . ."

I felt a stab in my chest when she spoke Zara's name, making it impossible for me to suppress a quiet whimper. Morgana gave me a pointed look. "The amulet hid you from all of us"—she glared, smiling, self-satisfied—"until your little friend arrived and begged me to get rid of you. In return for the amulet." Morgana nodded toward her subjects, whereupon one of the disfigured, scarfaced cloak-wearers disappeared into the dense woods and returned a little later carrying something heavy. As soon as the hideous monster was within sight again, I saw that he was roughly dragging a delicate, unconscious girl by her bright red hair.

"Madison!" I cried out, horrified, when I recognized her. "What have you done to her?"

The damnatus let the lifeless body drop in the dirt a few feet in front of Morgana. I ran over to the unconscious girl, bent over her, and frantically searched her neck for a pulse. On the third try, I felt a weak beat under her pale skin.

"Thank God!" I said, relieved. She was weak, but she was alive.

"You're happy she's alive?" Morgana asked, startled. "Didn't you listen to me? She came to me because she wanted me to kill you!" She was clearly incapable of understanding my reaction. "Actually, she was supposed to be a present for you," she said, slightly offended. "But if you don't want to kill the traitor yourself . . ." She took a step toward me and Madison, bent down to us, and pressed the tips of her long delicate fingers into the tender depression at the bottom of Madison's neck. "Then I'll do it for you."

At the moment Morgana's fingertips touched Madison's skin, Madison convulsed in a seizure, gasping for air, opened her bloodshot eyes wide, and looked at me in horror while the blood vessels in her neck bulged out and turned black. I was so frightened, I shrank back. I saw nothing but pure terror in Madison's eyes. Then, she exhaled with a rattle. When her body went completely limp, I knew she was dead.

At the sight of the dead girl, I could no longer keep my tears back. One after another, they ran down my cheeks. Although I didn't like Madison and she'd tried to make my life miserable at every opportunity during my brief stay in Oxford, I was still overcome with grief by her cruel and senseless murder. The grotesque manner in which her life had ended seemed to contravene all laws of nature. It was hideous. Everything here was simply hideous. This unreal place, these scar-covered monsters hidden under their long, black cloaks lurking in this clearing and at the edge of the forest behind the trees . . . Everything around me was unnatural. No, worse yet—it was *perverted*. But what was more perverted was the vicious, terrifyingly beautiful witch standing right in front of me, smiling at me with maternal warmth.

"Oh don't be sad, my little child. She was only a human. For her, death is only the logical outcome of life." She shrugged indifferently. "Whether she'd snuff it a few years sooner or later doesn't matter in the least."

I stared at Morgana through the murky veil of my tears, full of hate. This mad woman's complete disdain for human life drove an ice-cold shiver down my spine. She despised life and glorified death. Love and friendship meant nothing to her. Morgana only seemed to delight in the pain and suffering of others. And it would be my turn next.

How did I get here? Why had I run away? Away from . . . *Jared.* I could barely think his name. Maybe he would have come with me and started a new life with me somewhere, far away from all the misfortune the two of us had experienced in our lives.

I'm so sorry, Jared! I started to cry again. *I love you!* That was the only thought my brain was capable of. I loved Jared. I loved him more than anything else. I loved him with all my heart. From the very first moment I saw him. And now I'd have to console myself with his memory. There was no escape from this horror.

"Will you kill me now?" I said. Better to know what was coming than to be tormented by uncertainty.

"Why no, my dear! What are you thinking?" she said with feigned shock and then fixed her merciless eyes on me. "I have something special in mind for you," she added as her eyes darkened and an evil grin spread across her flawless face. She was finally letting the mask drop to reveal her true nature. Morgana was evil incarnate. In the shape of a gorgeous woman who could crush an empire with a single bat of her eye. "At first, I really did plan to kill you, but when your little friend here"—she kicked Madison's corpse—"told me that lovely Jared had fallen head over heels for you, my plans changed." She looked at me with contempt. "Just so we don't misunderstand each other: although you descend from the bloodline of the mighty Lady of the Lake, you are only a human and, therefore, not worth much more than this one." She again nudged Madison's corpse. "That dear Jared has totally fallen for you changes the situation significantly. You've become, shall we say, a precious little toy for me."

Toy? I felt the blood freeze in my veins, which she acknowledged with a satisfied smile.

"Well, my little toy . . . let's not waste any more time." She rolled up the sleeves of her tightly fitting cloak so far that her left arm was exposed to the elbow.

What happened next made my jaw drop. I watched in disbelief as Morgana took a small, black dagger from her pocket, grasped it in her right hand, turned the inside of her left arm up and, with an ecstatic smile, slit her lower arm open along its entire length. A burst of dark-red blood poured out of the gaping wound, ran along her downward-pointing fingers and dripped onto the ground. Morgana laughed when she noticed my horror at her self-mutilation.

"Now it's your turn, dear," she said. "Not to worry, the dagger isn't meant for you. I just want to . . . produce a small *work of art* for you." *Work of art?* Why didn't she just kill me so this cruel game would be over! "I need you to undress for that," she said as if she were about to perform a medical examination. Considering what stood before me, I was incapable of moving. Disappointed by my lack of cooperation, Morgana angrily pursed her lips before raising her eyebrows and casually nodding to one of her subjects.

"Undress, slut," the nearest cloak-wearer ordered and came at me and suddenly pushed me so hard that I fell to the ground. While looking down on me with his flashing black button eyes, he greedily licked his misshapen, sore-covered lips.

"Oh dear," Morgana said in a cheery voice. "We mustn't be impolite. After all, Evelyn is our guest." She gave me a friendly wink. "Now, please, would you take your clothes off, dear?" I was rigid with fear and even if I had known what to say, I wouldn't have been able to utter a single word. "You're not hard of hearing, are you?" Morgana asked when I didn't react, and she again nodded at the damnatus who'd pushed me into the dirt. The smug smile spreading over his ugly face made me gag. What would this disgusting creature do to me? Slowly and calmly, as if he enjoyed every moment of what was about to happen, he approached me. He bent over me, licking his repulsive lips once again, and reached out his sore-covered hands to pull the sweater over my head. I shrank back.

"So you want to play a little, do you?" he said with a dangerous undertone while moving toward me.

Play? This had gone beyond play long ago. This creature wanted to hurt me—hurt me badly. I knew that. I began to boil inside. No! I would not simply allow this hideous monster to touch me! It would have to kill me for that! I tensed my muscles, waited till the scarface had come close enough, angled my right leg, and kicked with full strength against his chest. He stumbled for a moment, couldn't maintain his balance, and fell to the ground, causing the attending cloak-wearers to break out in scornful laughter. Completely confused, he lay there on the muddy ground for a moment, then an enraged, hate-filled expression took over his disfigured face.

"You will regret that, you bitch!" he said through his half-rotten teeth while scrambling to his feet. It was clear this would end badly if I didn't find a way to render the monster harmless once and for all. I frantically looked around for something to use as a weapon. I noticed a broken branch a few steps away from me, a branch as long as my arm and about twice as thick. The horrible creature was getting close, and I dove with lightning speed for the branch, grabbed it firmly in both hands, and attempted to regain my balance. *Damn!* That thing was heavier than I expected. Surprised by my fast reaction, the damnatus also changed direction and charged me, burning with rage. Adrenaline pumped through me. I focused on my attacker, raised the branch as high as I could, waited for the right moment, and, when the scarface was close enough, hit him in the face. The hood of his soiled cloak slipped off his misshapen head to reveal countless scars, warts, and pustulant sores from which a repulsive odor of decay emanated. I gagged violently but forced myself not to vomit. When the creature landed on his hands and knees, he was again rewarded with ringing laughter from the bystanders. His eyes narrowed to thin slits as he angrily stared at me.

I had humiliated him—twice—and for that he'd kill me . . . or worse. I could see it in his black eyes. If I valued my life, I had to finish him off before he got on his feet again. A violent surge of resolve ricocheted through my body. I grasped the branch firmly, charged the kneeling figure, struck him with full force on his head, lifted the branch again, and struck even harder. And again. And again and again. Until his limbs stopped twitching.

Morgana's ringing laughter tore me from my blood frenzy. "It would appear we've caught a little tigress," she said, amused, and slowly approached me. Neither she nor the surrounding damnati seemed particularly bothered by the corpse with the bashed-in skull. Death and mutilation were obviously part of their daily fare. "But enough horseplay," Morgana said seriously. "We don't have forever. At least not all of us." There was a hint of a smile on her voluptuous lips. "Put that down," she said gently, pointing at the blood-stained branch I was still clutching as if my life depended on it. When I didn't react, she smiled, lifted a hand, and slowly started bringing it down. As she did so, I could feel the branch becoming heavier and heavier in my hands until, when Morgana had almost completely dropped her hand, I had to let it go. "Come to me," she said with an inviting gesture. This time she didn't even wait to see if I'd follow her command. Unable to resist, I was dragged across the ground by an invisible force that seemed to follow Morgana's hand motion until I was lying at her feet. "You're about to become a little tired," she said and pressed her index finger on my forehead. I was immediately overcome by an unstoppable exhaustion as Morgana's magic flowed relentlessly through my body. I fought it with all my strength, but it was hopeless.

A burning pain flashed through my body, bringing me back to consciousness. I opened my eyes and looked myself over. Morgana was bent over my naked body, intently drawing a five-pointed star on my abdomen. Where did she get the red color from? I drew in my breath as if suffering a seizure and watched how she squeezed the bleeding wound on her lower arm and used her pointy index finger to smear the warm blood onto my body. Panicked, I attempted to pull back to escape Morgana's diabolical ritual, tried to struggle with my arms and legs, to kick her, to keep her from me . . . but my body refused to obey my mind's commands. Morgana had paralyzed me with her cruel magic—I was at her mercy.

"*Muladhara*," she mumbled in a strange, dark sing-song, drawing another line. Was that a . . . *pentagram*? Something wasn't right about it. Was it . . . upside down? It was. While Morgana enclosed the strange symbol in a circle, I noticed that instead of one tip, two tips pointed upward. At that very moment, a sudden, brutal pain shot through me, almost causing me to lose my mind. I'd never felt anything like it before—it felt as if my insides were being torn to pieces and a part of them was violently pulled from my body. In my unbearable torment, a passionate, bright red suddenly flared before my inner eye, but when it extinguished a moment later, I knew that this red glow was a part of me that Morgana had taken for herself. As if to confirm my fears, the witch bent her head back and moaned lustfully. Then she moved her blood-soaked fingers a hand's width below my navel. Morgana began to draw another inverted pentagram after she had again pressed her index finger into the bleeding wound in her arm. I helplessly watched in panic as she enclosed the second pentagram in a circle. Again, I endured the ghastly torment of this unimaginable pain. I suffered pure agony.

"*Svadhisthana*," Morgana whispered as if in a trance, whereupon a lively orange appeared in my mind, only to die like the red before it. Now that Morgana had severed and torn out another part of my innate self, I became aware with infinite sadness that these pieces inside me that she tore to bits to incorporate into herself, these sacred shreds that she claimed by force, were parts of . . . my soul. While I felt as if I were standing in flames, she moaned again, ecstatic, and moved with her pitiless claws over my belly to the depression between my ribs—the solar plexus.

"*Manipura,*" she mumbled while I had to endure another part of my soul being transferred to her after a yellow light like sunshine was extinguished.

"*Anahata,*" Morgana relentlessly continued after she had drawn the fourth pentagram—right over my heart—and she made the resulting flare of saturated green, this part of my innate being, her own.

The bright sky blue she tore from my throat with a croaked "*Vishuddha*" caused me more torment than I would have imagined in my worst nightmares. I gasped.

"*Ajnya.*" The witch closed the circle around the sixth pentagram on my forehead and, as the remainder of my soul was rent asunder with the flaring up and extinction of a dark blue, I knew what dying felt like. No. Dying would have been a release. This was worse. Far worse. Morgana tore my innermost self, piece by piece, from my body and bound it to herself—for all eternity. I would be her slave until she tired of me. At the moment when she had completed her diabolical witchcraft, not even death would liberate me. I gasped with pain and exhaustion as she began to draw another pentagram on my limp body. The seventh— above my forehead. I was at the end of my strength, and I surrendered to my fate. The last part of my maimed soul was being detached from my mind and body. Darkness encroached a little more with every line of the seventh pentagram that she drew with her blood at the roots of my hair. An eternal darkness with none of the peace darkness brings when one closes one's eyes to sink into a deep sleep. No. This darkness was simply the absence of light—the certainty the sun would never shine again. A horrifying blackness from which there was no escape. I had nothing left to put forward against it.

Suddenly, I sensed a strange energy in a part of my foggy brain. A wild, unbridled force whose anger and hatred I felt down to the tips of my toes. The air began to crackle, and sparks flew about me and made my hair stand on end. I barely managed to open my eyes and look into Morgana's frightened face. She, too, must have felt this uncontrolled, raging power as it approached us like a destructive force of nature. A violent gust seized my body and pulled it from Morgana's grasp. I was thrown into the air and slammed against a tree, and again I lost consciousness.

When a bright, searing bolt of lightning struck the middle of the clearing, I came to. I managed to open my eyes with a tremendous effort. Despite my blurred vision, I was able to discern two shapes among the hideous creatures whose cloaks fluttered in the wind. One of the two struck in a blind rage with a mighty sword at the countless scarfaces who came charging. I saw heads severed and rolling like marbles on the muddy ground. I strained my eyes. *Colin!* I recognized his face. Another searing lightning bolt struck, though it did not appear to come from above, like normal lightning. Rather, it appeared as if the buzzing electrical sparks that were flying about all over were gathering around the second figure, next to Colin, among the hundreds of black cloaks. The sparks congealed into a bright golden lightning bolt on the chest of the second warrior before he threw back his head, spread his arms, and unleashed a wild energy that ripped apart at least fifty of the scarfaced cloak-wearers.

"There you are!" Morgana was suddenly over me, glaring at me with her hate-filled eyes. She grabbed me roughly by the hair, yanking my head down.

"No!" a desperate, pain-filled voice screamed. I recognized that voice instantly, despite the sadness and incomprehension distorting it. *Jared!* He was here.

"We're not done with each other yet," Morgana said with a dark smile, pressed her index finger into the bleeding wound in her lower arm, and hastily drew a circle to complete the seventh pentagram. *"Sahasrara,"* she said, almost crying out the strange word.

I gasped when a purple light became extinct with a final flicker and an unimaginable, consuming pain spread inside me. A pain that surpassed my powers of imagination and even my worst nightmares. It was as if I were freezing, burning, suffocating, and being ripped apart all at once.

Then there was complete silence as I sank into a deep, cruel darkness.

CHAPTER 21

"Very good, Jared. As I see, you've understood," Morgana said with a self-satisfied smile. "I'm very proud of you, my boy. You do honor to your ancestors."

"What's going on here?" I heard Karen Mayflower say.

"I think it would be best if Jared explained it to you," Morgana said.

"Jared?" Karen uttered, close to tears.

"Morgana has bound Evelyn's soul to herself," he said, full of pain. "I can't kill her without also killing Evelyn." The finality of this fact resonated in each of his words.

"You're such a clever boy, Jared," Morgana said. "So we have a classic stalemate, I would say," she said cheerily and clapped her hands.

"How is she?" Colin asked with a harsh voice.

"Oh, she can hear you," Morgana said, almost euphoric. "I'm keeping her just barely under the surface." She gently shook my shoulder as if waking a sleeping child. "Open your eyes, my love." I felt the darkness clear away and slowly found I was able to sense my body again. Bit by bit, I returned to the light, but I was painfully aware that Morgana could plunge me back into darkness at any time. I was nothing more than a puppet whose strings were held by *her* hands. I was lying in

Morgana's arms while she stroked my head with her long, slender fingers. My naked body was enshrouded in the stinking black cloak of some dead damnatus.

"Evelyn," Jared whispered, barely audibly. "I am so sorry." I thought I could hear his heart break in his words.

"What are you waiting for, Jared? Kill her," Mayflower said, staring at Morgana, full of hatred.

"If only it were that simple, my dear," Morgana said, clearly enjoying the turn of events. "Jared *loves* Evelyn. Can't you see that?" She looked at Karen with contempt. "It's just as it was with Merlin and Nimue. The two loved each other so much"—she breathed in dramatically and crossed her hands over her heart—"that I would have almost gone soft." Suddenly, the dark smile returned to her face. "But only *almost*." She gave me a warm look and again stroked my hair with her fingers. "You, my child, are almost like Nimue. Too bad you're just as stupid as she was." Morgana inhaled deeply. "She should have stayed in Avalon but instead decided to become a human to be with Merlin." Judging from the expression of her face, Morgana was completely disgusted. "The Lady of the Lake voluntarily trades immortality for a life as a housewife and mother." She snorted contemptuously. "I've never seen anything so pathetic." She looked at Jared. "My dear boy, did you know that it was the Order itself who blamed Nimue for Merlin's death?" she asked, smiling. "To keep Merlin's descendants away from Nimue's, they invented a story according to which Nimue lured Merlin into a cave and killed him there. Rather unimaginative, if you ask me." Jared closed his eyes, tormented at Morgana's words. Again the witch smiled triumphantly.

Karen Mayflower, who had been half hidden behind Jared and Colin, suddenly appeared to boil over with rage. Eyes wide, she clenched her teeth, drew a shimmering, dark-blue dagger and rushed Morgana. "Die, witch!" she angrily shrieked, aiming the dagger at Morgana's heart.

"No!" Jared cried, ran forward, and deflected the dagger at the last second, so it barely missed Morgana's heart but instead dug into her arm. The witch cried out in pain, pushed me away from her, and pulled the dagger out of her flesh. Then she directed her evil, dark eyes at Karen, lifted her other hand, and slowly clenched it into a fist. Karen opened her eyes in horror and clasped her throat with both hands. Aiden, who stood a bit farther back with other members of the Circle, kept in check by several damnati, managed to tear himself loose and rush to his mother's aid. But before he'd even come close, Morgana raised her free hand so her palm was facing Aiden, who, as if grabbed by an invisible force, was hurled through the air and smashed against a tree, where he lay motionless on the ground. Karen Mayflower's face had taken on a reddish-blue tinge in the meantime, and the tighter Morgana clenched her hand, the more Karen struggled. Then Morgana suddenly loosened her fist, and Karen collapsed, bent over forward, groaning, and took in several deep, strained breaths.

"No," Morgana said. "I will not kill you, High Priestess. I'll let you live so you can see everything firsthand."

"What do you want?" Jared shouted.

"No reason to get upset, my boy," Morgana, who had settled down beside me, said. "But the question is superfluous. I think you know very well what I'm after," she said with unholy laughter. Then she straightened herself and took on a businesslike tone. "I will grant you a chance to save the girl."

Jared was silent for a moment, then lowered his eyes. "What must I do?" he asked.

"No, Jared! Don't do it!" I cried out.

"Silence!" Morgana said, as night immediately engulfed me once again. I no longer felt my body, could not speak or move. She had not entirely taken my vision and hearing, so I was able to watch events unfold through a veil of threatening darkness. It was obvious Morgana *wanted* me to see what would happen next.

"I will release Evelyn's soul if in return you promise to give me something of yourself."

"That will kill him!" Colin cried, full of anger, and raised his sword, causing the damnati closest to him to retreat timidly.

"Well, there's always a catch with these things, isn't there?" Morgana said with a sarcastic smile.

Jared looked into my clouded eyes, while I pleaded with him not to accept Morgana's treacherous offer—but no words passed through my lips.

"All right," he finally consented without looking away from me.

No! No! No! No! Don't do it! Jared, please, don't do it!

"Excellent," Morgana said, clapping her hands. "But surely you understand that I won't rely on your word alone."

Jared's eyes filled with tears as he looked at me intently.

No, Jared, no! Please!

"We'll have to conclude a little covenant," she said. At these words, I was overcome with such hatred that I began to tremble inside. All my emotions—sadness, anger, desperation, and, above all, my limitless love for Jared—bundled into a ball at my center, thrust through the fog, and led me out of the darkness.

"No!" I cried, infinitely relieved to hear the word aloud. I tried to get up, but every movement felt as if I were struggling against an incredible wind.

All eyes turned to me. Morgana looked at me, startled, and even Karen, who was only now catching her breath, tried to raise her head. Jared rushed toward me, took me into his arms, and pressed his lips on mine.

"I told you to be silent!" Morgana said menacingly, and darkness again encroached on me. I strove against her, tried with all my strength to remain in the light, and clung with every ounce of my strength to Jared.

"No," I repeated again, tormented.

"Silence!" Morgana yelled, full of rage, clenching her fists and distorting her face to an angry scowl. Then darkness overcame me like a mighty avalanche, overpowered me, and pulled me deeper and deeper until it swallowed me up.

In this terrible place, neither time nor space existed. Nothing but darkness and silence, which pulled on me and drew me ever deeper into a whirlpool of night and emptiness. I was a prisoner. Imprisoned in cruel black nothingness that sucked every last remnant of happiness from me, leaving me an empty husk. I was a shadow of myself, lost in all eternity, buried by the blackness that mercilessly pressed upon me and destroyed everything that once was.

But . . . what was that strange feeling? A feeling . . . that something was returning to me . . . something that once belonged to me and had been taken from me . . . a faint shimmer in the darkness . . . a light . . . a . . . a . . . Just what was it?

Then it hit me. A purple light rushed in on me, penetrated my body with force, and filled me with an energetic feeling. Then the other colors returned. One after another they streamed into me: dark blue, sky blue, green, yellow, orange, and red. Each color flowed with unrestrained vigor into me, filled me with life, and warmed me from the ends of my hair to the tips of my toes. I sucked in air as if in a fit. It felt like the very first breath of my entire life.

"*Evelyn,*" Jared's voice broke through the darkness. First, hearing returned to me, then my vision, and then, one after another, my other senses.

"You have five minutes," Morgana said.

What? Five minutes for what? Suddenly, I grasped the terrible truth. *No! No! No!* That could not be. I opened my eyes and looked into Jared's angelic face.

"Oh Jared," I said, anguished. "What have you done?"

He enclosed me in his arms.

"No," I shook my head. "No, please don't go! Please!" I asked desperately.

Jared pressed firmly against me, then took my face into his hands and looked straight into my eyes. "I love you. With everything I am."

"No, no, please!" Tears flowed over my cheeks. I felt his mouth on mine. He kissed me, full of longing. Full of need. Full of love. Then he gently placed his hand over my eyes. "Sleep now, my darling," he whispered into my ear—loving and pain-filled at the same time—then I felt his magic flow through my arteries. A soothing warmth made my lids drop and led me into a deep, deep sleep.

CHAPTER 22

I dreamed of a beautiful place. A place full of love. A place full of magic. Although I knew it was only a dream, I wanted to stay: I was happy in this place. In vain, I tried to push back the light of the dawning day, which—muted to a red glow—penetrated my eyelids, but my dream inescapably neared its end. Struggling against it was futile. I began to feel my body bit by bit. It felt well. Everything was filled with a wonderful tingling, a beautiful, though unfamiliar, sensation. I'd only felt it once before—that morning when I woke from the magical sleep into which Jared . . .

I rose with a start and opened my eyes. *Jared!*

"She's awake," I heard someone say and looked around in a panic. I lay in my room in the Order's headquarters. Irvin Martin sat at the foot of the bed.

"Jared!" I cried as the memories flooded in on me, threatening to shatter me.

"Calm down, Evelyn," Irvin gently said. He took my shoulders and looked at me.

"Jared!" I cried again. "No! No! Jared!"

"Evelyn, look at me!" Irvin said, shaking me vigorously.

A cry escaped my lips, and tears shot from my eyes. I began to hyperventilate.

"Quick, get Enid!" Irvin said, then spoke to soothe me again, held me, and forced me to look into his eyes. A moment later the door was pushed open. Somebody rolled up my sleeve, and a second later, I felt a prick in my arm. A hypodermic?

"Calm down," Irvin repeated. "Calm down."

Gradually, I recovered my breath, but the tears wouldn't stop.

"Jared, no, please don't. Jared . . . ," I desperately mumbled to myself.

"Evelyn, look at me. Look at me," Irvin said again. He had also cried, as had Enid, who sat next to him on the bed. Colin, who stood at the foot of the bed, wiped the tears from his face. He looked at me for a moment, then turned away, walked to the window, and looked outside.

"Jared, no, no. Please don't . . . ," I cried, shaking my head back and forth. Finally, my eyes came to rest on Colin, whose heart must have been as broken as mine. He, too, had loved Jared—had loved him like a brother, like . . .

Suddenly, the expression in Colin's face changed, became angry. "Jared cannot be dead," he said with clenched teeth. "That's impossible. No, he simply cannot be dead," he repeated, slamming his fist on the windowsill.

There was a moment of silence in the room.

"Jared is not dead *yet*," Irvin said.

I listened closely. "What did you say?" I asked.

"Morgana won't simply kill him," Irvin said, hesitating for a moment. "She'll want to practice an elaborate ritual on him." He was barely able to pronounce the words. "And I'm sure she'll be better prepared this time than on her last two attempts."

"How much time do we have?" I asked. My voice sounded firm and full of resolve.

"Difficult to say."

"Take a guess," I impatiently urged him to answer my question.

"Two days, maybe three," he finally said.

"Three days," I repeated, already forging plans in my head. What if there was a way to save Jared? What if he wasn't lost yet? I'd do anything to get him back.

"Evelyn," Irvin said in a quiet but forceful tone. "It's hopeless. We don't have the slightest chance against Morgana—"

"So you just want to let him die?" Colin screamed.

"No, of course not, but—"

"We've got at least two days and you don't want to do anything?" Colin said. He had taken up position beside me so that we formed a front against Irvin and Enid.

"Colin, Evelyn . . . please understand," Irvin started. "Jared made a covenant with Morgana. A magical covenant, an oath—"

"We still have two days, damn it. I'm not just going to let Jared die!" Colin was almost boiling over with rage.

Suddenly I thought of something. Why hadn't it occurred to me sooner?

"I know someone who may be able to help us," I said excitedly. "Her name is Ruth. Ruth Hayman."

ACKNOWLEDGMENTS

Many thanks to my husband, Holger, for his unconditional love and support—no matter how addlebrained my plans are. I also thank Corina, Karina, Laura, and Jessi for their enthusiasm and criticism. As well as, of course, my editors, Elizabeth, Jonathan, and Ben; my translators, Michael Osmann and Audrey Deyman (AAD Abies), who brought out the best in the narrative; and Laura Klynstra for that beautiful cover. And not to forget Nina, AmazonCrossing, and my wonderful readers for making my dream come true.

Last but not least, a heartfelt thank-you to these wonderful musicians who are blessed with the gift of turning sounds into feelings: Coldplay, Silbermond, Yiruma, Anna Nalick, 2Cellos, Florence and the Machine, Lykke Li, TOS, Clueso, Einaudi, Philipp Poisel, and many more.

ABOUT THE AUTHOR

Photo © 2014 Fokus Fotographie

Sarah Kleck, born in 1984, studied education, psychology, and sociology at the University of Augsburg. Currently, she's working as a human resources officer and lives with her husband and a newborn in Germany, near Lake Constance. *The Concealed* is her first novel.

ABOUT THE TRANSLATORS

Left photo © 2012 Audrey Deyman, Right photo © 2013 Michael Osmann

Michael Osmann and Audrey Deyman are trained medievalists, linguists, former orchardists, and mythology enthusiasts. They live in Ontario's Beaver Valley near Georgian Bay, where they enjoy the company of their children, dogs, cats, poultry flock, and the local wildlife.

2015